THE ROBOT MAKERS BOOK 04

NEXT-LEVEL COMPETITION

Story by Podoal Friend
Art by Hong Jong-hyun

내일은 로봇왕 4- 대결! 코딩 요리
The Robot Makers- #4 Next-Level Competition
Copyright © 2018 by Podoal Friend and Hong Jong-hyun
English translation copyright © 2024 by Lerner Publishing Group, Inc.
English translation by Zab Translation Services.
The translation copyright is arranged with Mirae N co., Ltd. through KCC (Korea Copyright Center Inc.), Seoul and Chiara Tognetti Rights Agency, Milan.

Graphic Universe™ is a trademark of Lerner Publishing Group, Inc.

Graphic Universe™
An imprint of Lerner Publishing Group, Inc.
241 First Avenue North
Minneapolis, MN 55401 USA

For reading levels and more information, look up this title at www.lernerbooks.com.

Main body text set in CCDaveGibbonsLower.
Typeface provided by Comicraft.

Library of Congress Cataloging-in-Publication Data

Names: Friend, Podoal, author. I Jong-hyun, Hong, artist.
Title: Next-level competition / Podoal Friend, Jong-hyun Hong.
Description: Minneapolis : Graphic Universe , 2024. I Series: The robot makers ; book 04 I Audience: Ages 9–14 I Audience: Grades 4–6 I Summary: "At coding camp, La Ion's friends wake up to an usual lesson: how to make breakfast with robots! The group learns how robots prepare meals by algorithm. Then, camp heats up with a robot soccer match"– Provided by publisher.
Identifiers: LCCN 2023026130 (print) I LCCN 2023026131 (ebook) I ISBN 9781728492421 (library binding) I ISBN 9798765623459 (paperback) I ISBN 9781728495033 (epub)
Subjects: CYAC: Graphic novels. I Robots–Fiction. I Science clubs–Fiction. I Computer programming–Fiction. I Soccer–Fiction. I BISAC: JUVENILE FICTION / Comics & Graphic Novels / Manga
Classification: LCC PZ7.7.F7846 Ne 2024 (print) I LCC PZ7.7.F7846 (ebook) I DDC 741.5/973–dc23/eng/20230606

LC record available at https://lccn.loc.gov/2023026130
LC ebook record available at https://lccn.loc.gov/2023026131

Manufactured in the United States of America
1-53308-51218-6/27/2023

THE ROBOT MAKERS BOOK 04

NEXT-LEVEL COMPETITION

Podoal Friend ✦ Hong Jong-hyun

Graphic Universe™ • Minneapolis

Table of Contents

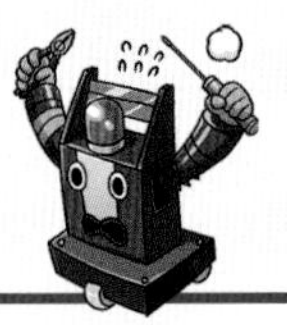

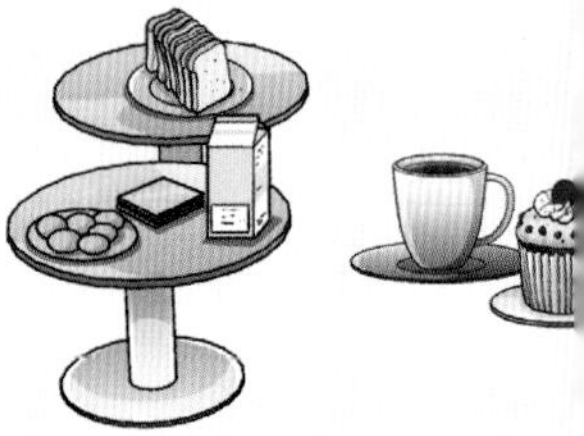

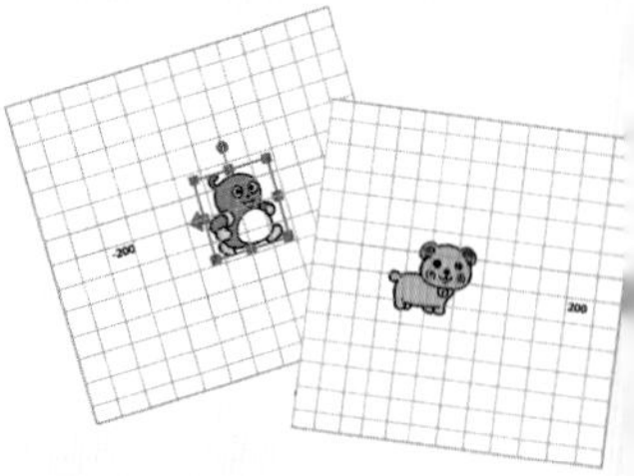

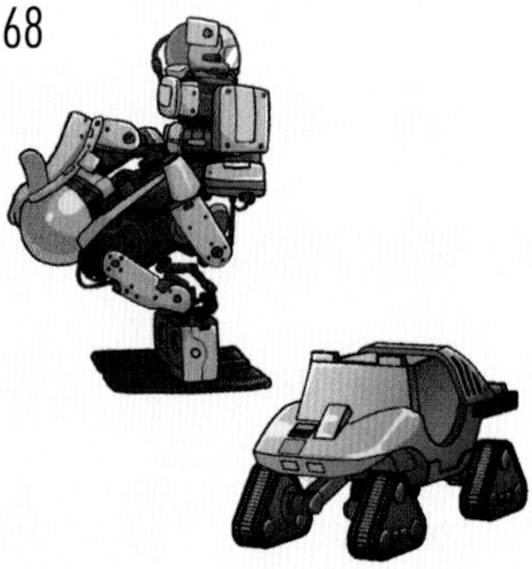

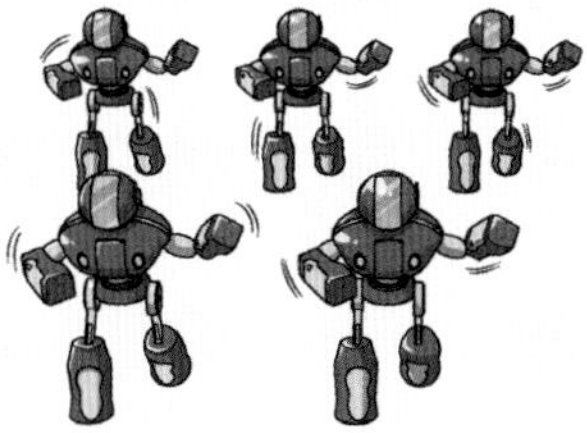

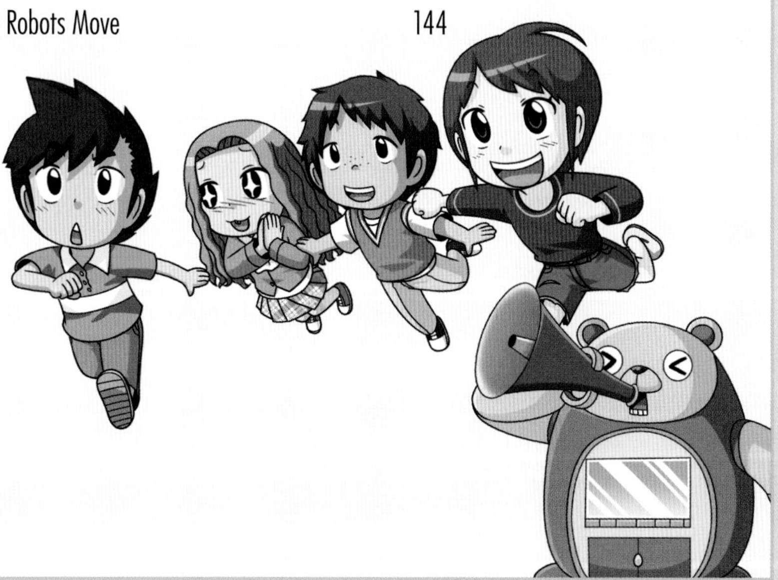

Character Guide

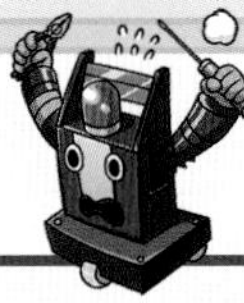

LA ION

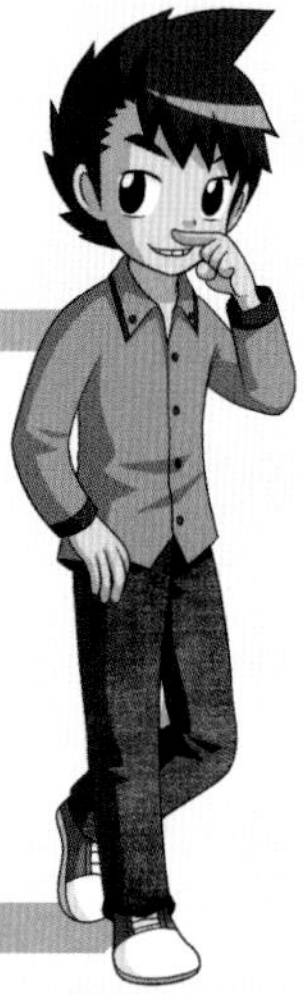

- Recently fascinated by the variety of robots and robot competitions
- Gaining an interest in robot manufacturing after watching robots being built

Special skill: Urge to gain more information as he begins to accumulate knowledge about robotics and coding

SORI OH

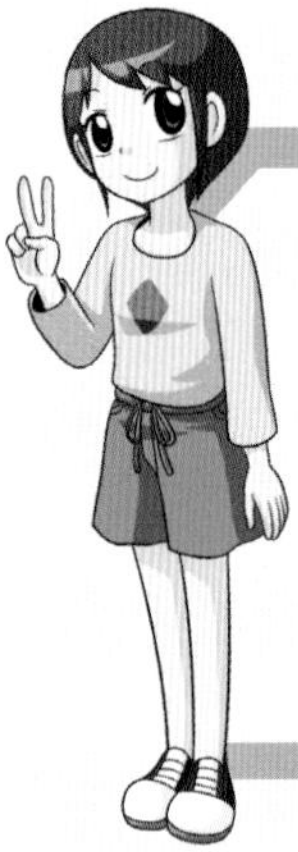

- Ready to show off her passion for robots at a national robotics competition
- Showing her skills to Dr. Cybo in hopes that her robot soccer club will become her school's one remaining robot team

Special skill: Knowing enough information to have an insider's perspective on any robotics competition

GEORU KANG

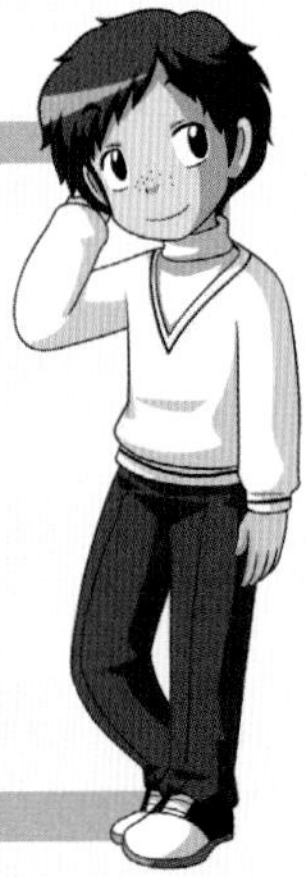

- Excited to see what sorts of matches a national robotics competition hosts
- Also overwhelmed by preparations for the national competition and wondering if he will need an expensive robot to take part in the dance challenge

Special skill: Being considerate and telling La Ion about unfamiliar games at the national competition in a way that's easy to understand

RUDA LEE

- Willing to watch matches at the national robotics competition but sore he won't be able to participate himself

- Agitated to see a team he beat easily in a robot soccer competition one year ago has improved its skills and joined the national competition

Special skill: Competitive spirit that will help him seek a way to win the upcoming coding cooking competition

EUNSE KOH

- Had hoped Dr. Cybo's coding camp would end quickly, and will get really annoyed after the start of a strange coding cooking competition

- Poised to regain his enthusiasm for engineering robots after visiting a national robotics competition

Special skill: Focus that allows him to watch a match all the way to the end once he starts, regardless of what is happening around him

OTHER CHARACTERS

1. Dr. Cybo, who wants to give kids from the two school robot teams a chance to compete on the next level

2. Ruby Lee, finds robotics boring but may change her mind after watching a robot dance competition

Chapter 1

Never-Ending Coding Camp

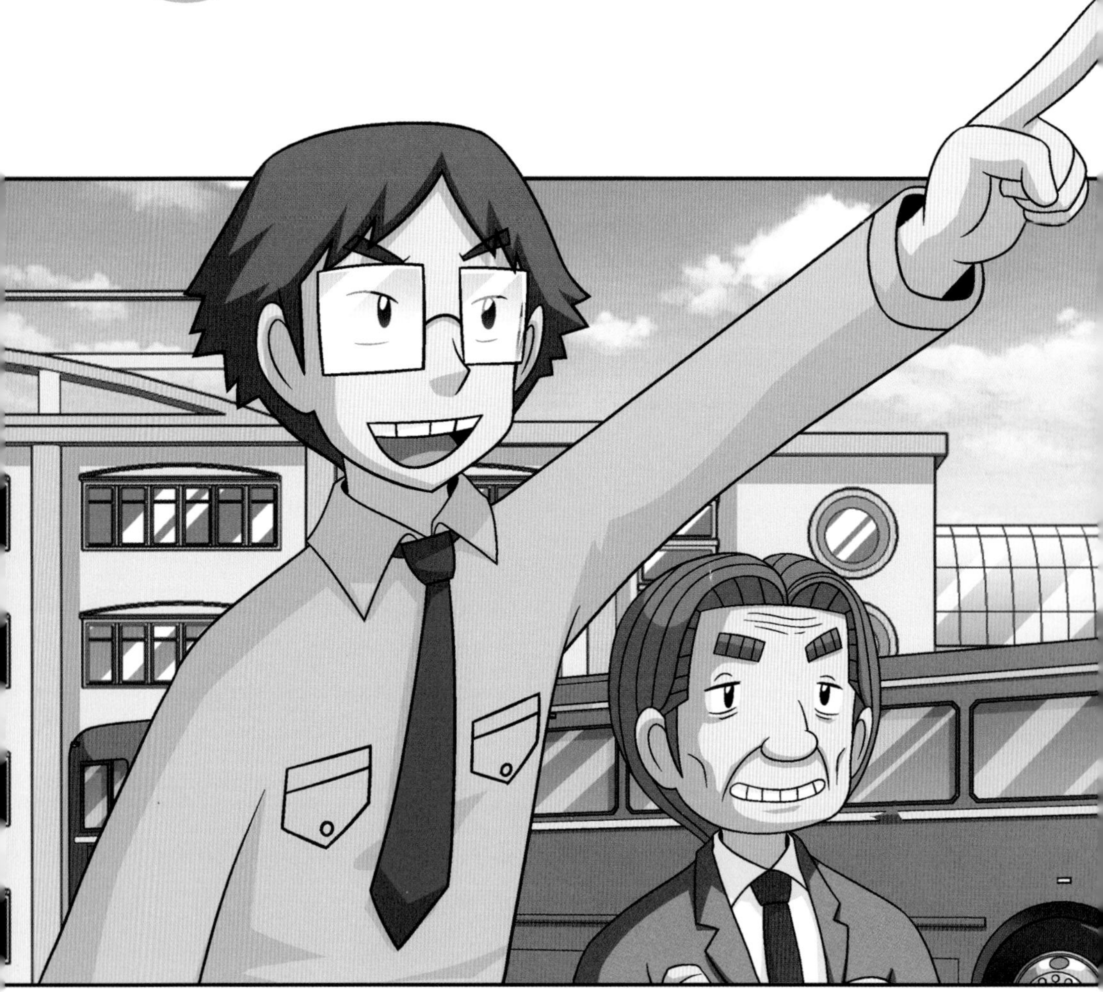

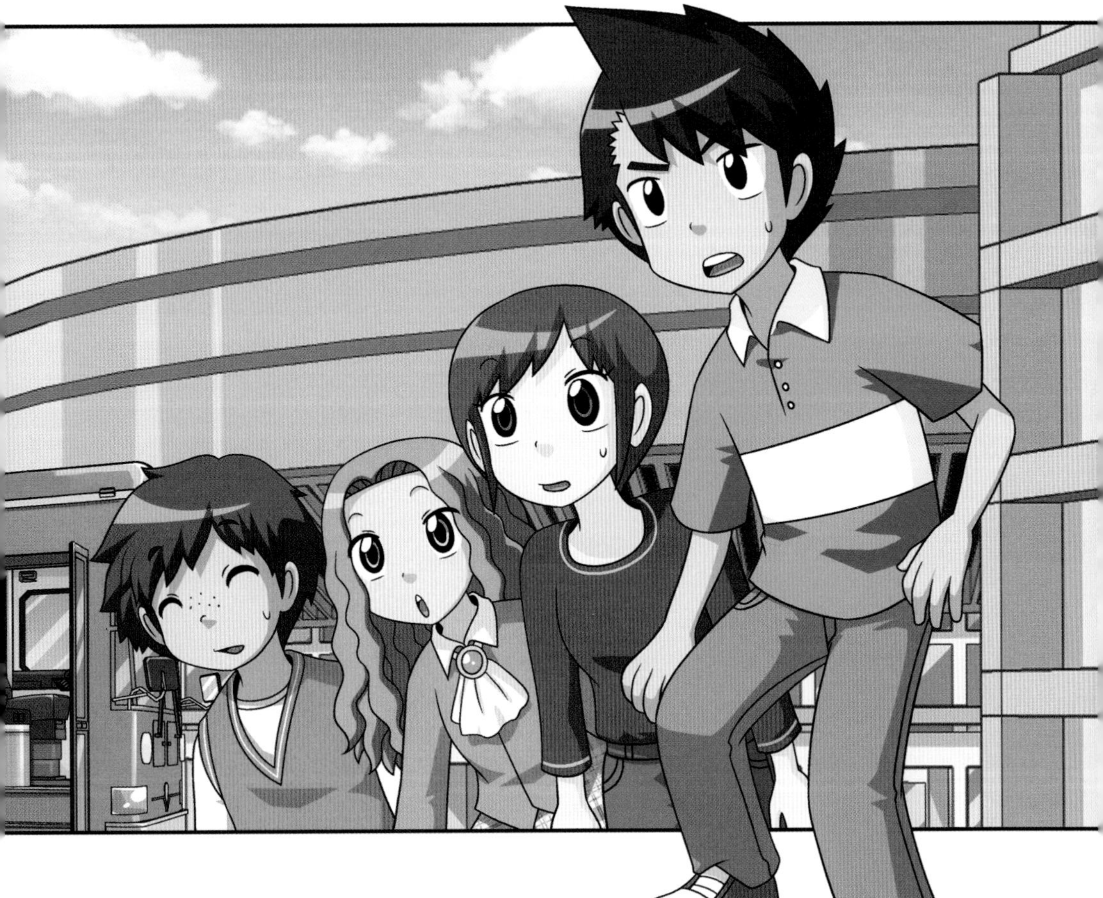

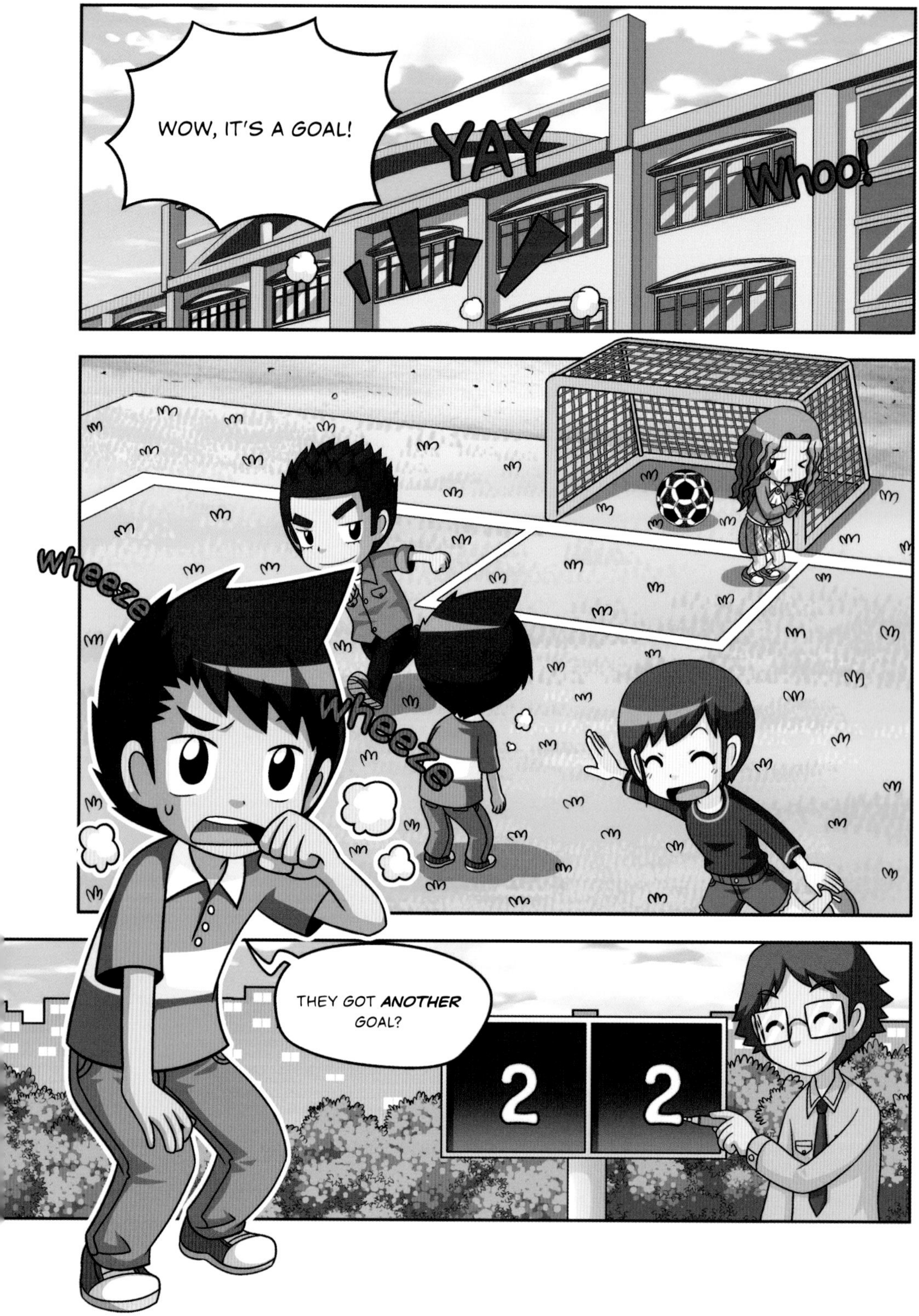

WOW, IT'S A GOAL!
YAY
Whoo!
wheeze
wheeze
THEY GOT ANOTHER GOAL?
2
2

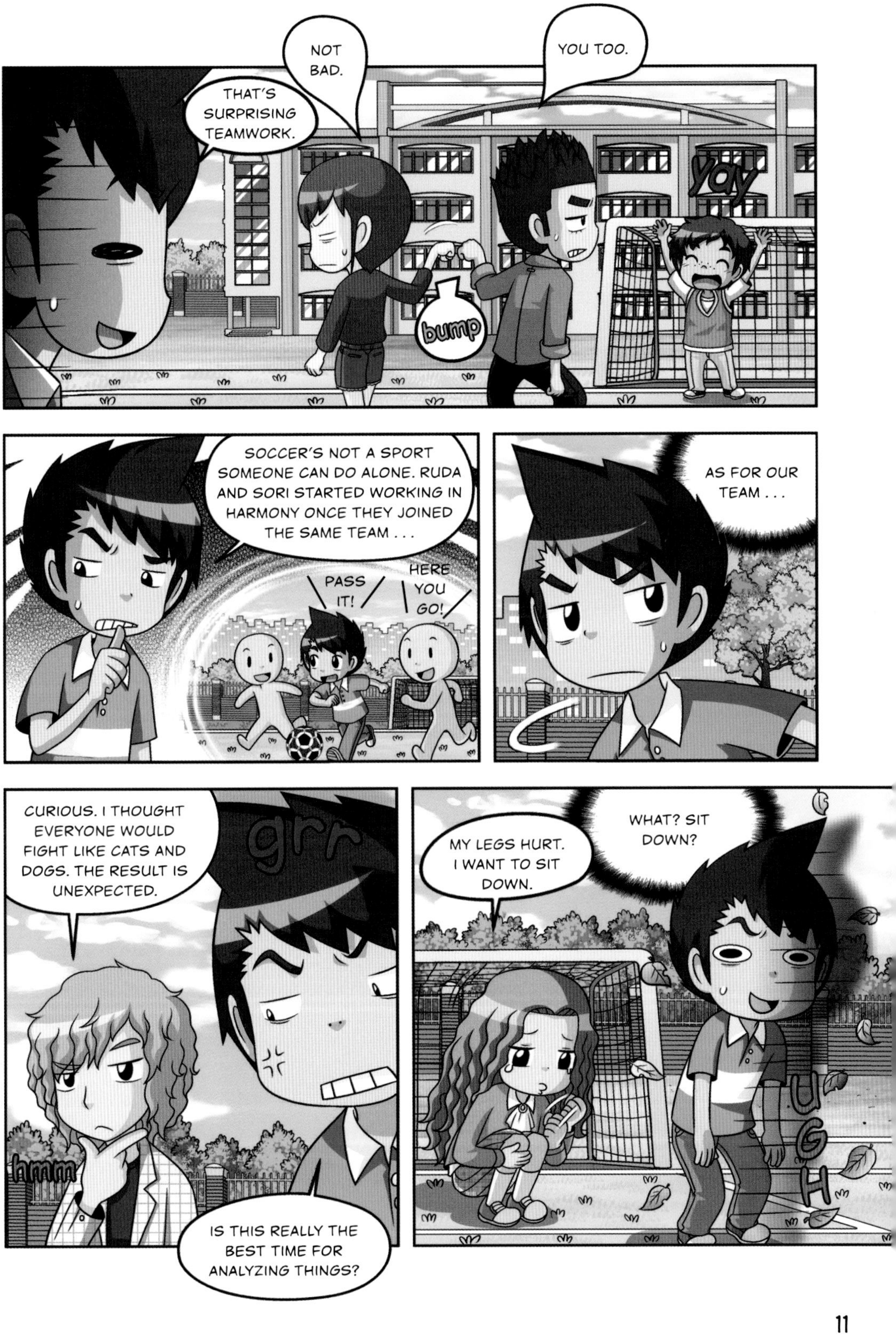
THAT'S SURPRISING TEAMWORK.
NOT BAD.
YOU TOO.
bump
yay
SOCCER'S NOT A SPORT SOMEONE CAN DO ALONE. RUDA AND SORI STARTED WORKING IN HARMONY ONCE THEY JOINED THE SAME TEAM . . .
PASS IT!
HERE YOU GO!
AS FOR OUR TEAM . . .
CURIOUS. I THOUGHT EVERYONE WOULD FIGHT LIKE CATS AND DOGS. THE RESULT IS UNEXPECTED.
grr
hmm
IS THIS REALLY THE BEST TIME FOR ANALYZING THINGS?
MY LEGS HURT. I WANT TO SIT DOWN.
WHAT? SIT DOWN?
UGH

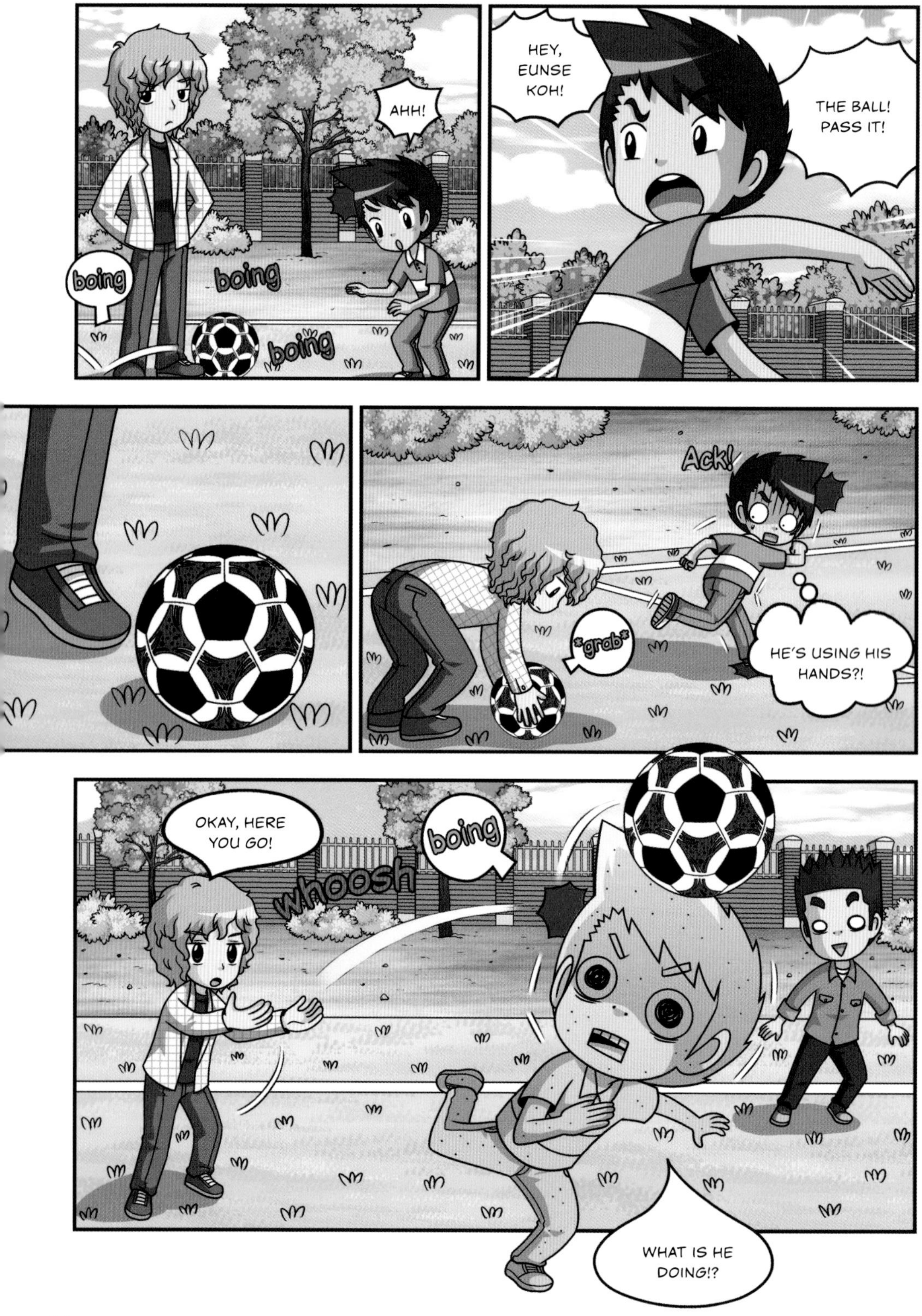

AHH!
boing
boing
boing
HEY, EUNSE KOH!
THE BALL! PASS IT!
Ack!
grab
HE'S USING HIS HANDS?!
OKAY, HERE YOU GO!
whoosh
boing
WHAT IS HE DOING!?

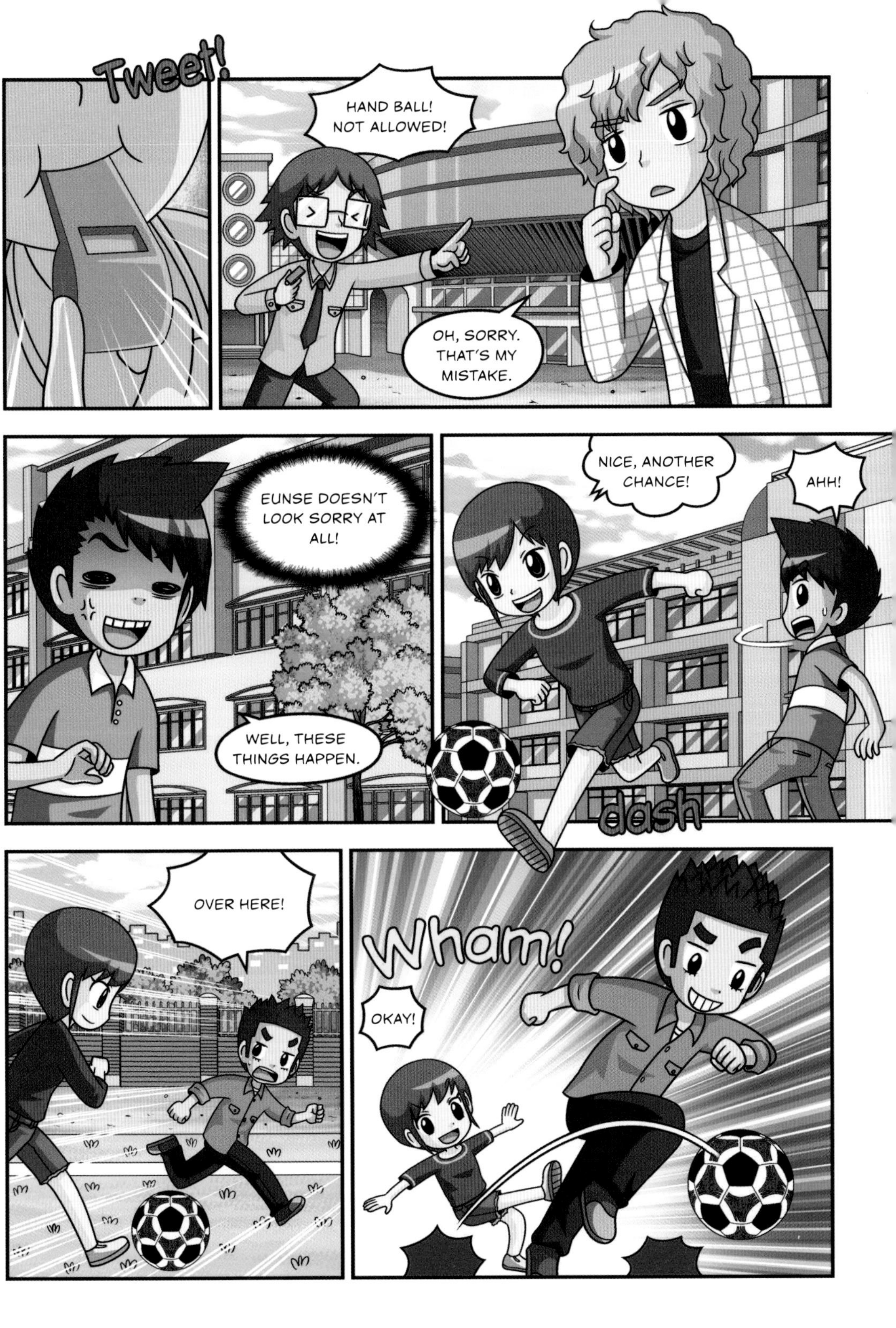
Tweet!
HAND BALL! NOT ALLOWED!
OH, SORRY. THAT'S MY MISTAKE.
EUNSE DOESN'T LOOK SORRY AT ALL!
WELL, THESE THINGS HAPPEN.
NICE, ANOTHER CHANCE!
AHH!
dash
OVER HERE!
Wham!
OKAY!

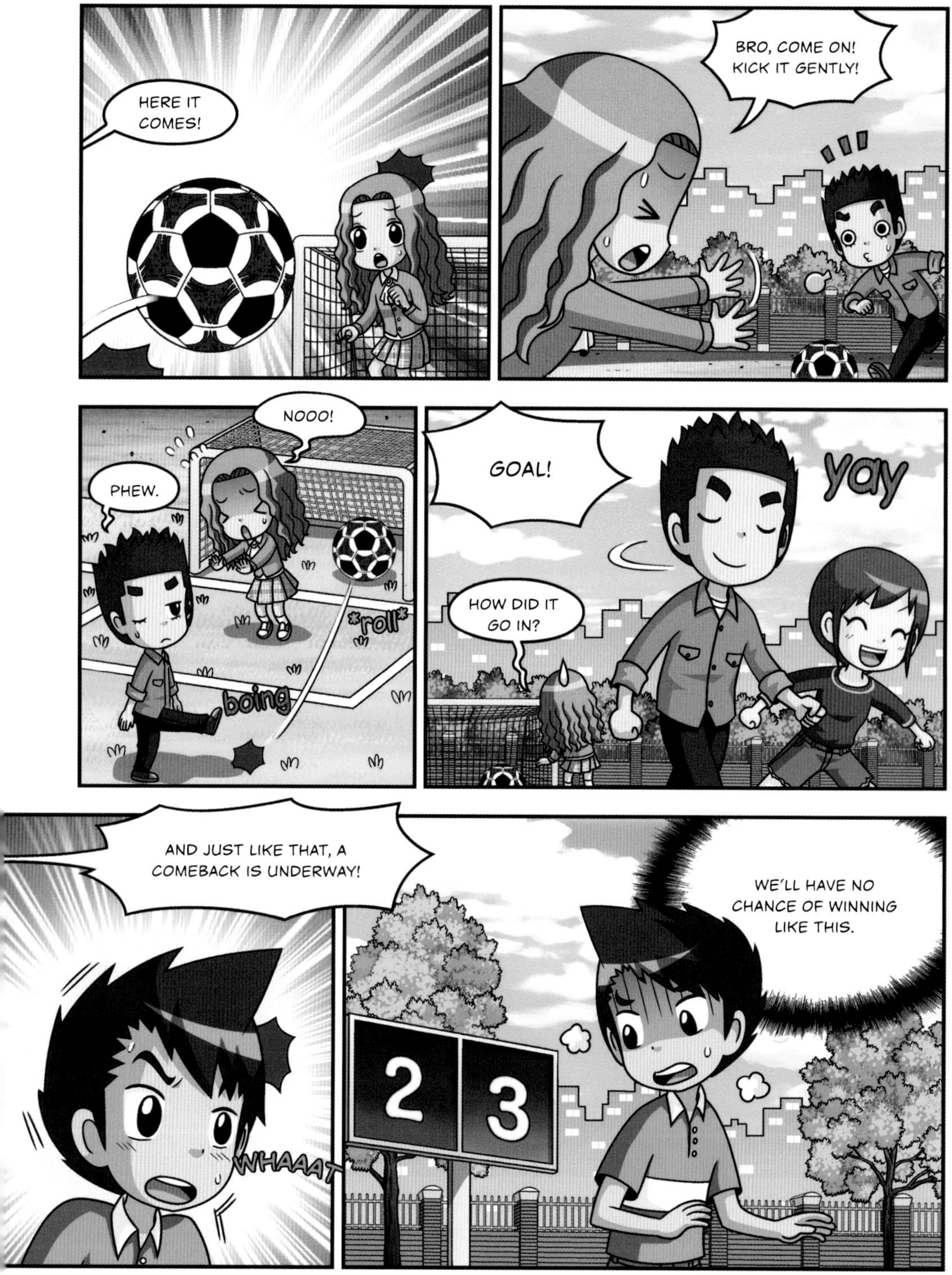
HERE IT COMES!
BRO, COME ON! KICK IT GENTLY!
PHEW.
NOOO!
roll
boing
GOAL!
yay
HOW DID IT GO IN?
AND JUST LIKE THAT, A COMEBACK IS UNDERWAY!
WHAAAT
2
3
WE'LL HAVE NO CHANCE OF WINNING LIKE THIS.

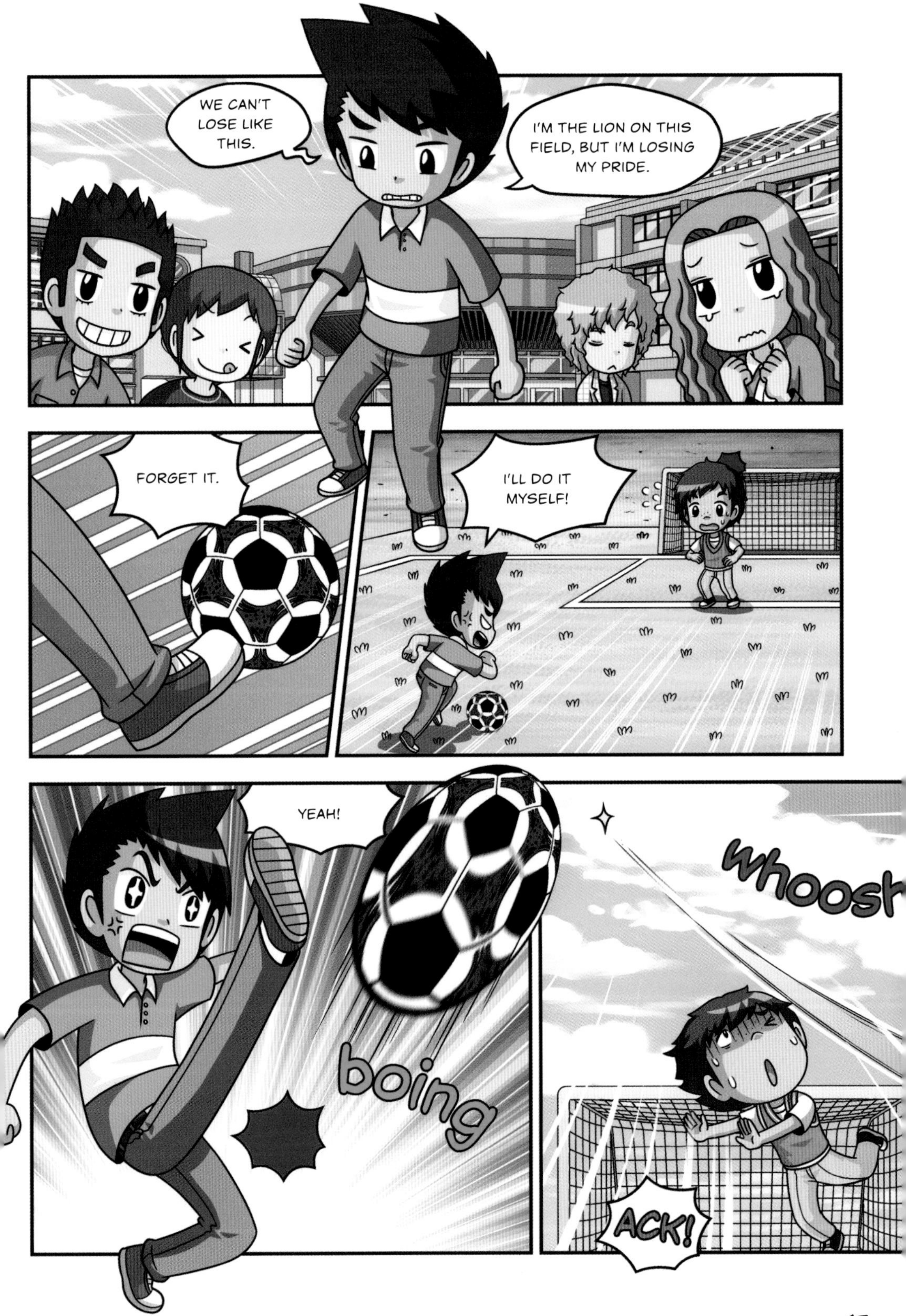
WE CAN'T LOSE LIKE THIS.
I'M THE LION ON THIS FIELD, BUT I'M LOSING MY PRIDE.
FORGET IT.
I'LL DO IT MYSELF!
YEAH!
boing
whoosh
ACK!

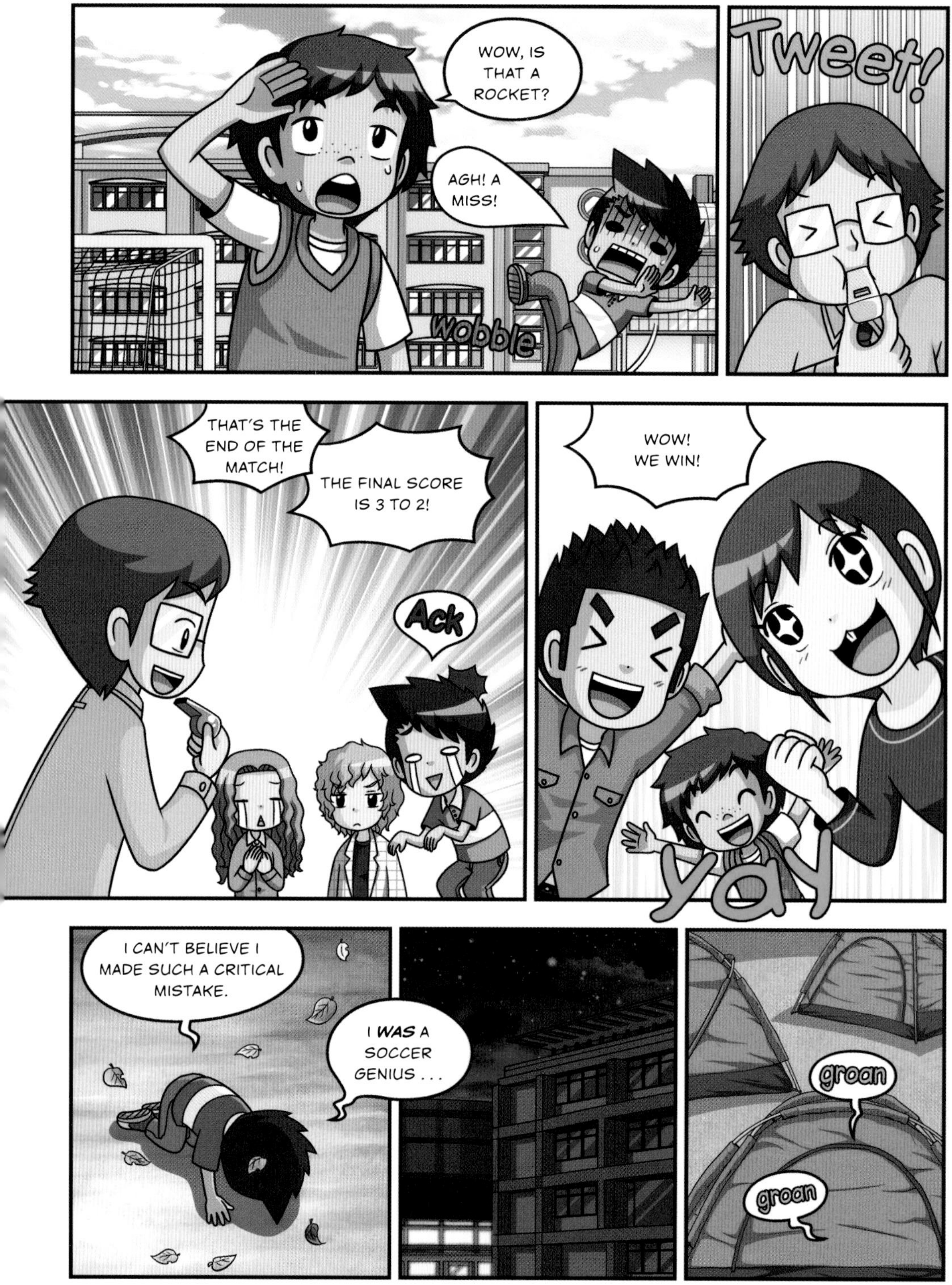

WOW, IS THAT A ROCKET?
AGH! A MISS!
wobble
Tweet!
THAT'S THE END OF THE MATCH!
THE FINAL SCORE IS 3 TO 2!
Ack
WOW! WE WIN!
yay
I CAN'T BELIEVE I MADE SUCH A CRITICAL MISTAKE.
I *WAS* A SOCCER GENIUS . . .
groan
groan

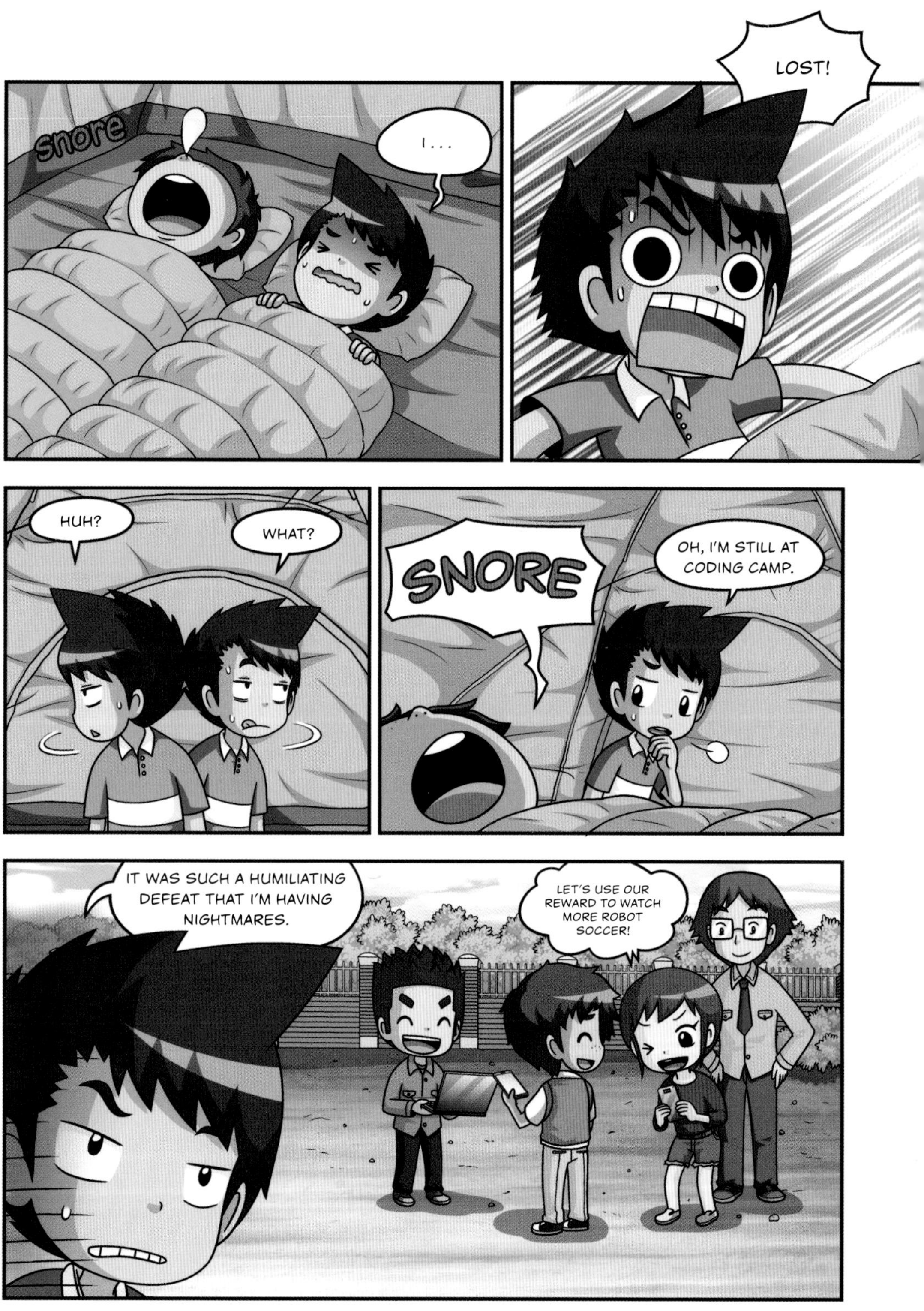
Snore
I...
LOST!
HUH?
WHAT?
SNORE
OH, I'M STILL AT CODING CAMP.
IT WAS SUCH A HUMILIATING DEFEAT THAT I'M HAVING NIGHTMARES.
LET'S USE OUR REWARD TO WATCH MORE ROBOT SOCCER!

WELL . . .

BOTH TEAMS WERE ABLE TO WATCH THE THINGS ONLINE THEY WANTED TO SEE.

SO IT'S NOT TOO BAD THAT WE DIDN'T WIN THE PRIZE.

YES, IT'S A GOAL!

THE DEFEAT WAS EMBARRASSING, BUT I STILL CAUGHT THE PRO MATCH I WAS HOPING FOR.

snore

AND WHILE I COULDN'T ESCAPE, AT LEAST I GET TO GO HOME TOMORROW.

I JUST WANT TO SLEEP.

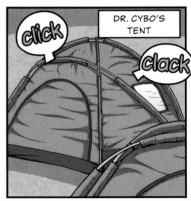

DR. CYBO'S TENT

click

clack

18

ALGORITHMS BEGIN WITH THE COLLECTION AND ANALYSIS OF DATA.

HMM . . .

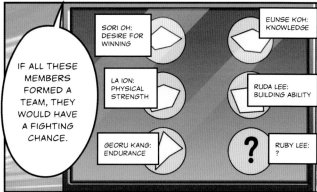

IF ALL THESE MEMBERS FORMED A TEAM, THEY WOULD HAVE A FIGHTING CHANCE.

SORI OH: DESIRE FOR WINNING

EUNSE KOH: KNOWLEDGE

LA ION: PHYSICAL STRENGTH

RUDA LEE: BUILDING ABILITY

GEORU KANG: ENDURANCE

RUBY LEE: ?

?

EACH OF THEM EXCELS IN THEIR OWN AREA . . .

HMM

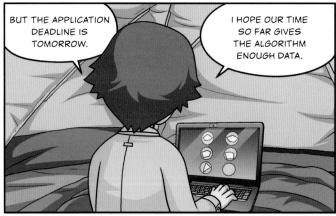

BUT THE APPLICATION DEADLINE IS TOMORROW.

I HOPE OUR TIME SO FAR GIVES THE ALGORITHM ENOUGH DATA.

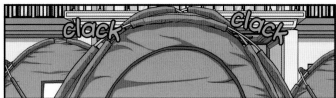

clack   clack

19

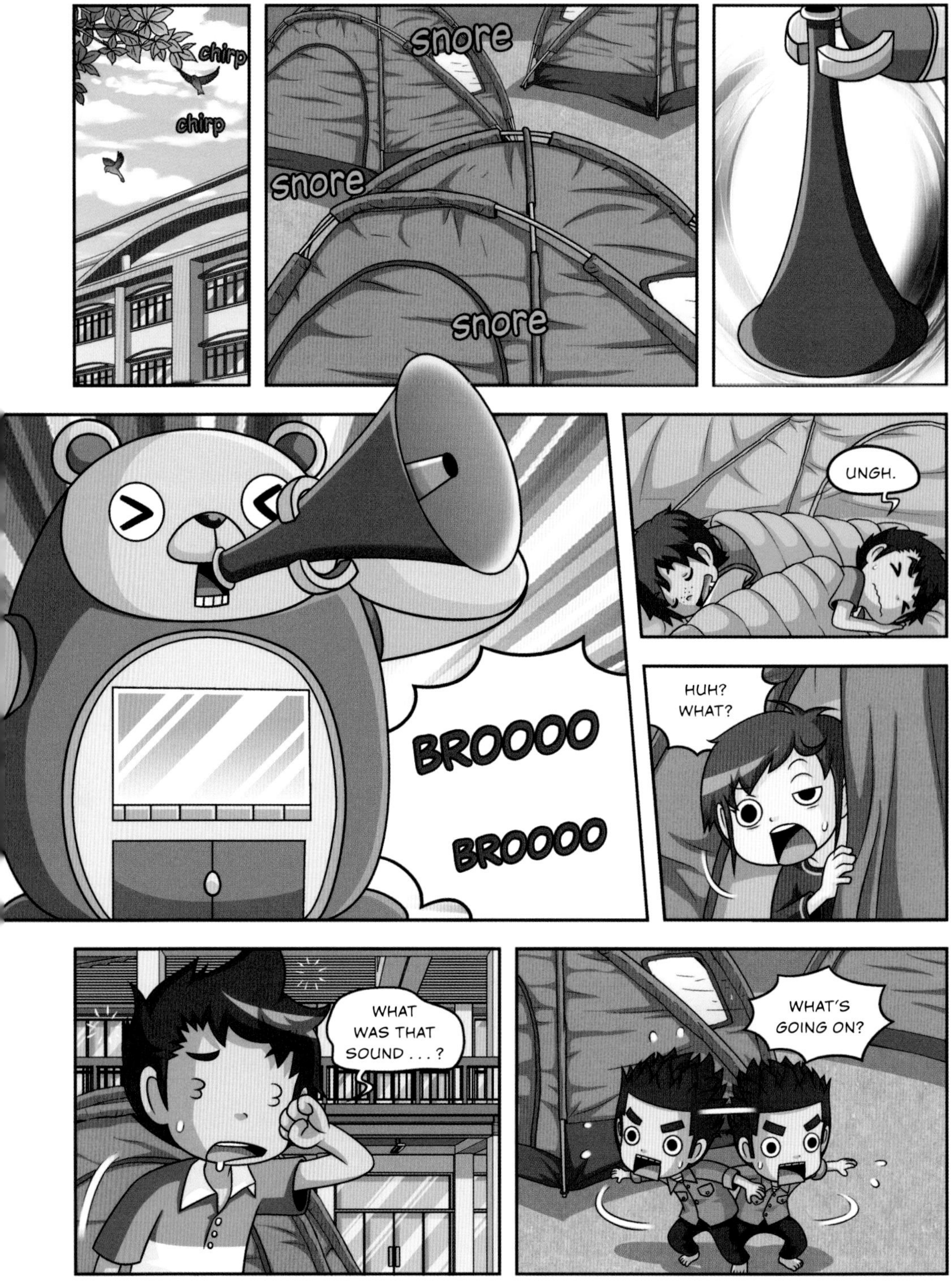
chirp
chirp
snore
snore
snore
BROOOO
BROOOO
UNGH.
HUH? WHAT?
WHAT WAS THAT SOUND . . . ?
WHAT'S GOING ON?

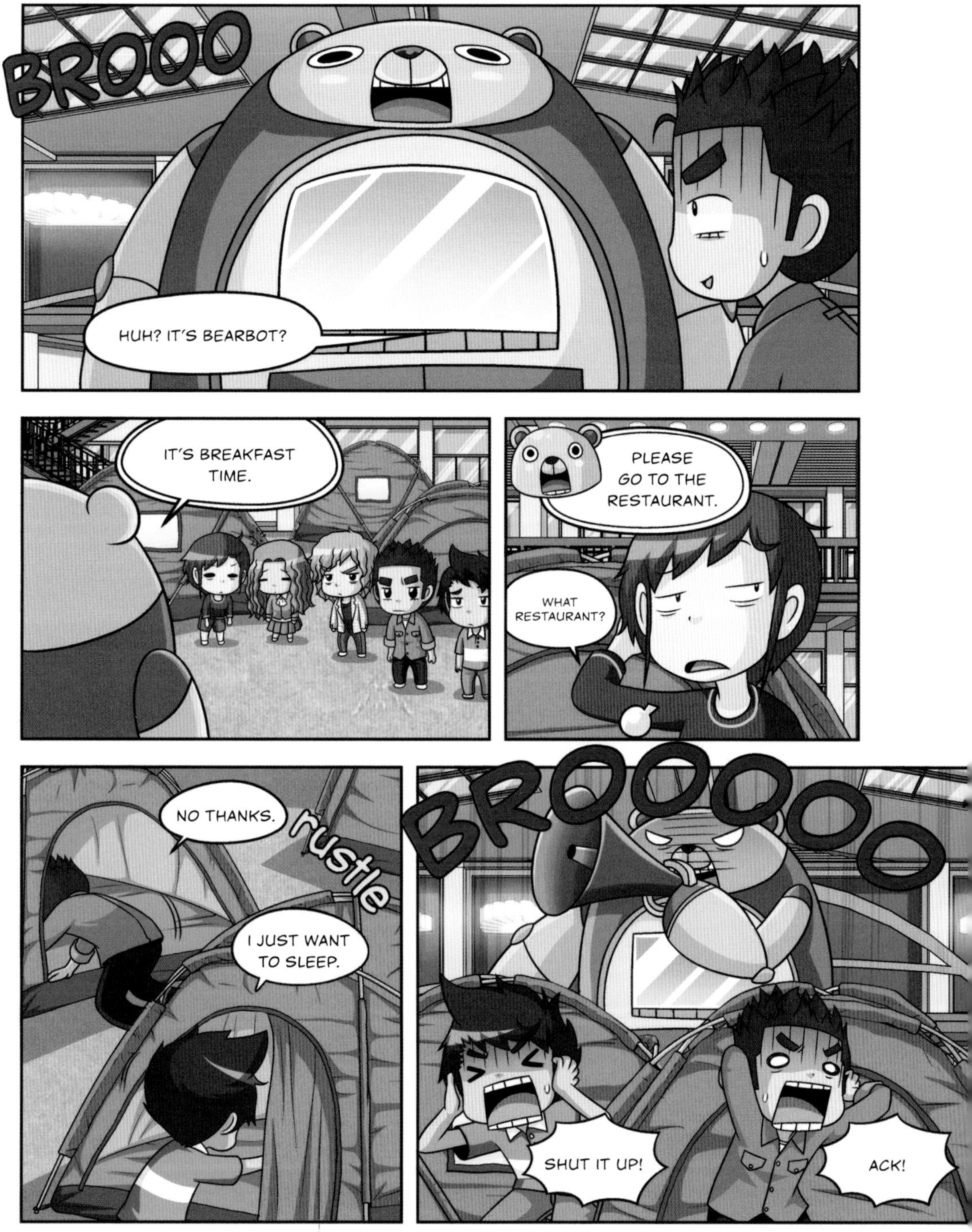
BROOO
HUH? IT'S BEARBOT?
IT'S BREAKFAST TIME.
PLEASE GO TO THE RESTAURANT.
WHAT RESTAURANT?
NO THANKS.
rustle
I JUST WANT TO SLEEP.
BROOOOOO
SHUT IT UP!
ACK!

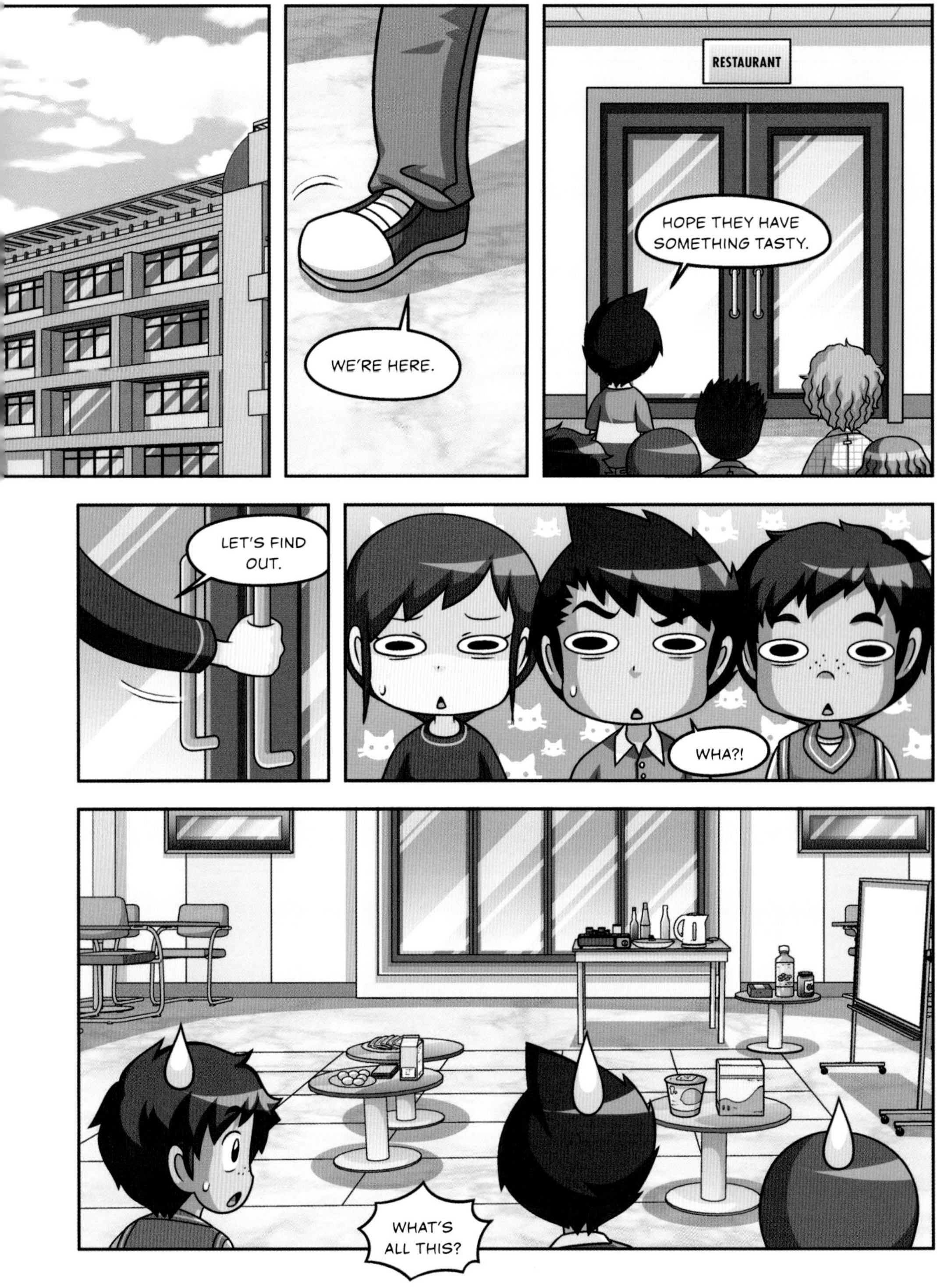
WE'RE HERE.
RESTAURANT
HOPE THEY HAVE SOMETHING TASTY.
LET'S FIND OUT.
WHA?!
WHAT'S ALL THIS?

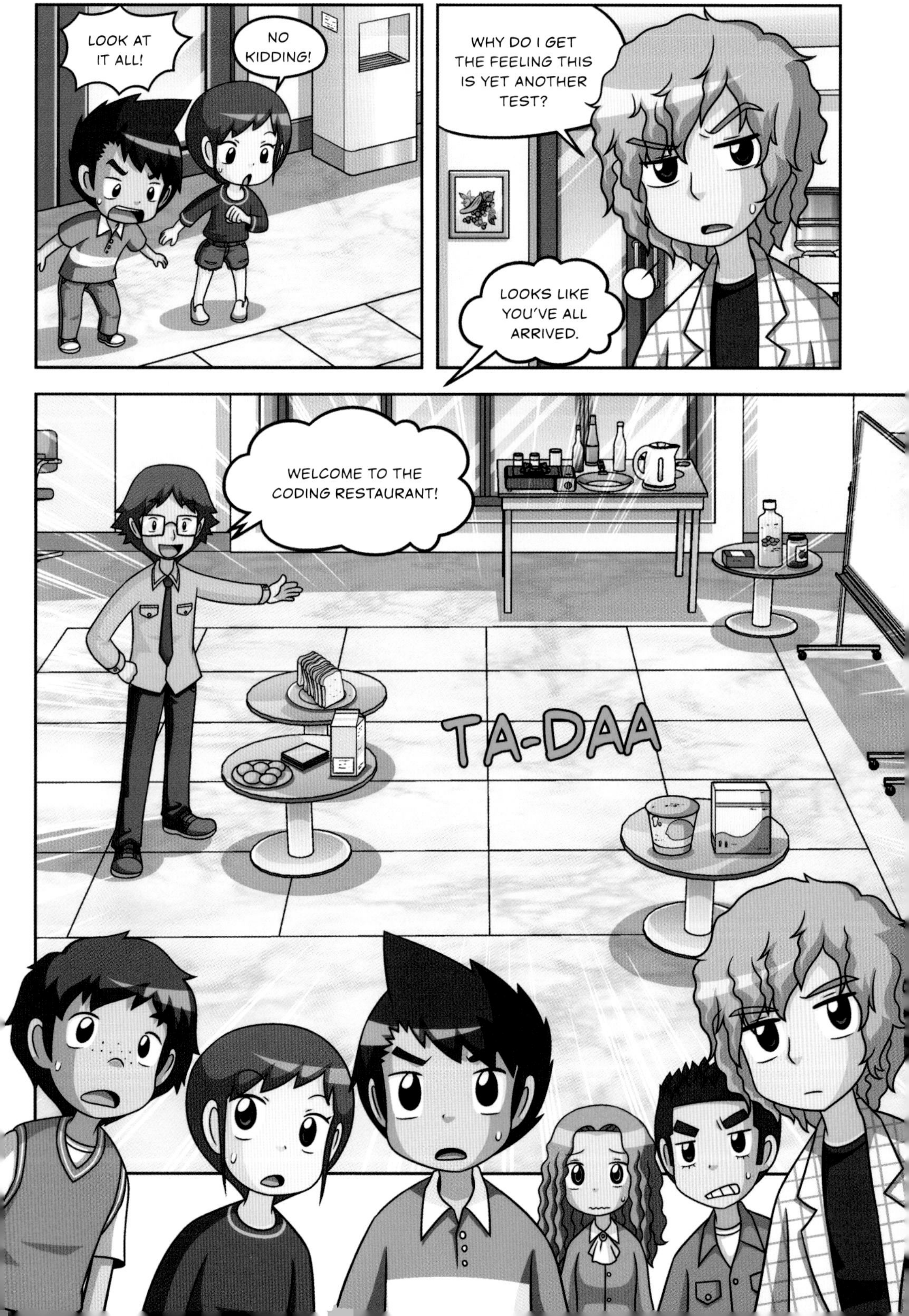

LOOK AT IT ALL!
NO KIDDING!
WHY DO I GET THE FEELING THIS IS YET ANOTHER TEST?
LOOKS LIKE YOU'VE ALL ARRIVED.
WELCOME TO THE CODING RESTAURANT!
TA-DAA

ABOUT SOFTWARE

Algorithms and Programming

An algorithm is a set of commands that must be followed to solve a problem. Programming involves giving commands based on the algorithm so that a computer or a robot can work according to each step. Let's find out the criteria for efficient programming.

Sequences

A computer works so fast that it may seem to be taking care of multiple tasks at the same time. However, while the machine is working quickly, it can only deal with one task at a time. It cannot provide an answer to the next command without solving the previous command. Because a computer or a robot doesn't think about the problem-solving process on its own, you need to give it a task in specific, sequential steps.

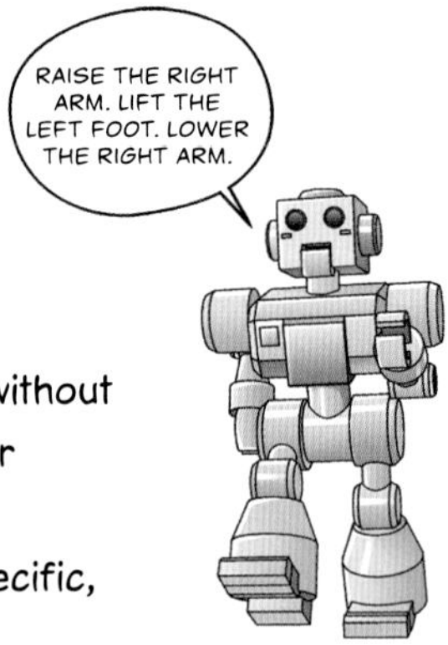
RAISE THE RIGHT ARM. LIFT THE LEFT FOOT. LOWER THE RIGHT ARM.

Repetition

Humans may get different results for the same task when doing it repeatedly due to changes in circumstances. However, robots can produce the same, accurate results when repeating a task over and over. This is why robots have replaced human workers in certain roles in fields such as manufacturing. Programming is also more efficient when it groups multiple repetitive commands into one algorithm.

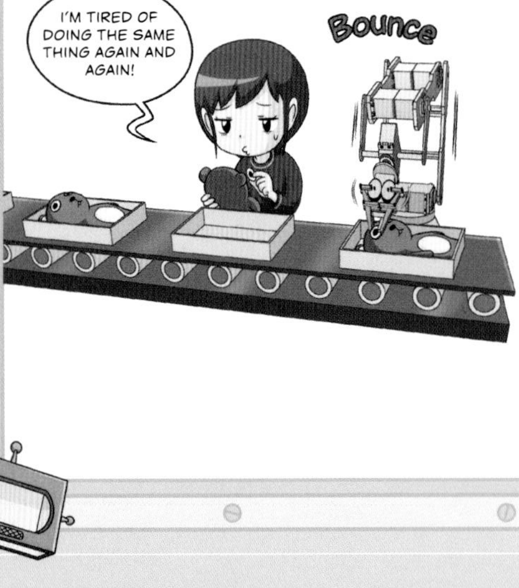
I'M TIRED OF DOING THE SAME THING AGAIN AND AGAIN!
Bounce

Select Commands

Since a computer or a robot cannot judge an outcome by itself, it must be programmed to react to every possible outcome for each task. For this, a select command with an "if-then" input is utilized.

AI Robot Sophia

HMM, THAT'S INTERESTING.

YOU ARE RIGHT. IT IS INTERESTING.

WHO ARE YOU?

SAY HI. THIS IS SOPHIA.

I AM SOPHIA, AN AI ROBOT.

WHOA, YOU REALLY LOOK LIKE A HUMAN!

I HEAR THAT A LOT.

SOPHIA WAS DEVELOPED IN HONG KONG. IN 2017, IN SAUDIA ARABIA, SHE BECAME THE FIRST ROBOT TO OBTAIN CITIZENSHIP.

WOW

WOW! NO WAY!

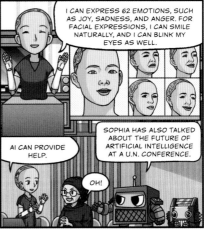

I CAN EXPRESS 62 EMOTIONS, SUCH AS JOY, SADNESS, AND ANGER. FOR FACIAL EXPRESSIONS, I CAN SMILE NATURALLY, AND I CAN BLINK MY EYES AS WELL.

SOPHIA HAS ALSO TALKED ABOUT THE FUTURE OF ARTIFICIAL INTELLIGENCE AT A U.N. CONFERENCE.

AI CAN PROVIDE HELP.

OH!

SOPHIA ALSO HAS DEEP LEARNING TECHNOLOGY. THE MORE CONVERSATIONS SHE HAS, THE MORE ANSWERS SHE WILL BE ABLE TO GIVE.

YOU WILL BECOME MORE HUMAN AS YOU HAVE MORE CONVERSATIONS. LET'S TALK A LOT.

YES, I WOULD LIKE TO HAVE LOTS OF CONVERSATIONS.

DR. CUBI IS A REAL NITPICKER.

NITPICKER. THAT'S A NEW WORD FOR ME.

I ALREADY KNEW THAT WORD!

whisper

Chapter 2

The Coding Cooking Disaster

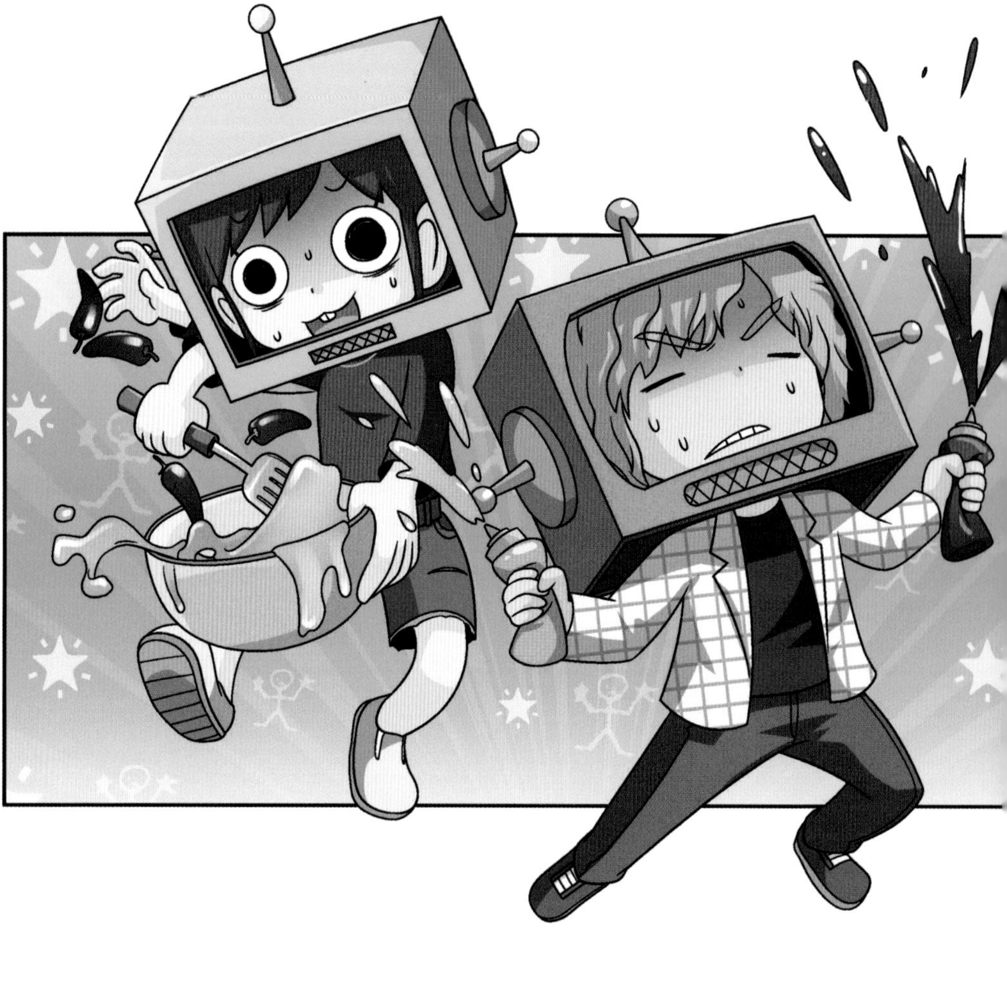

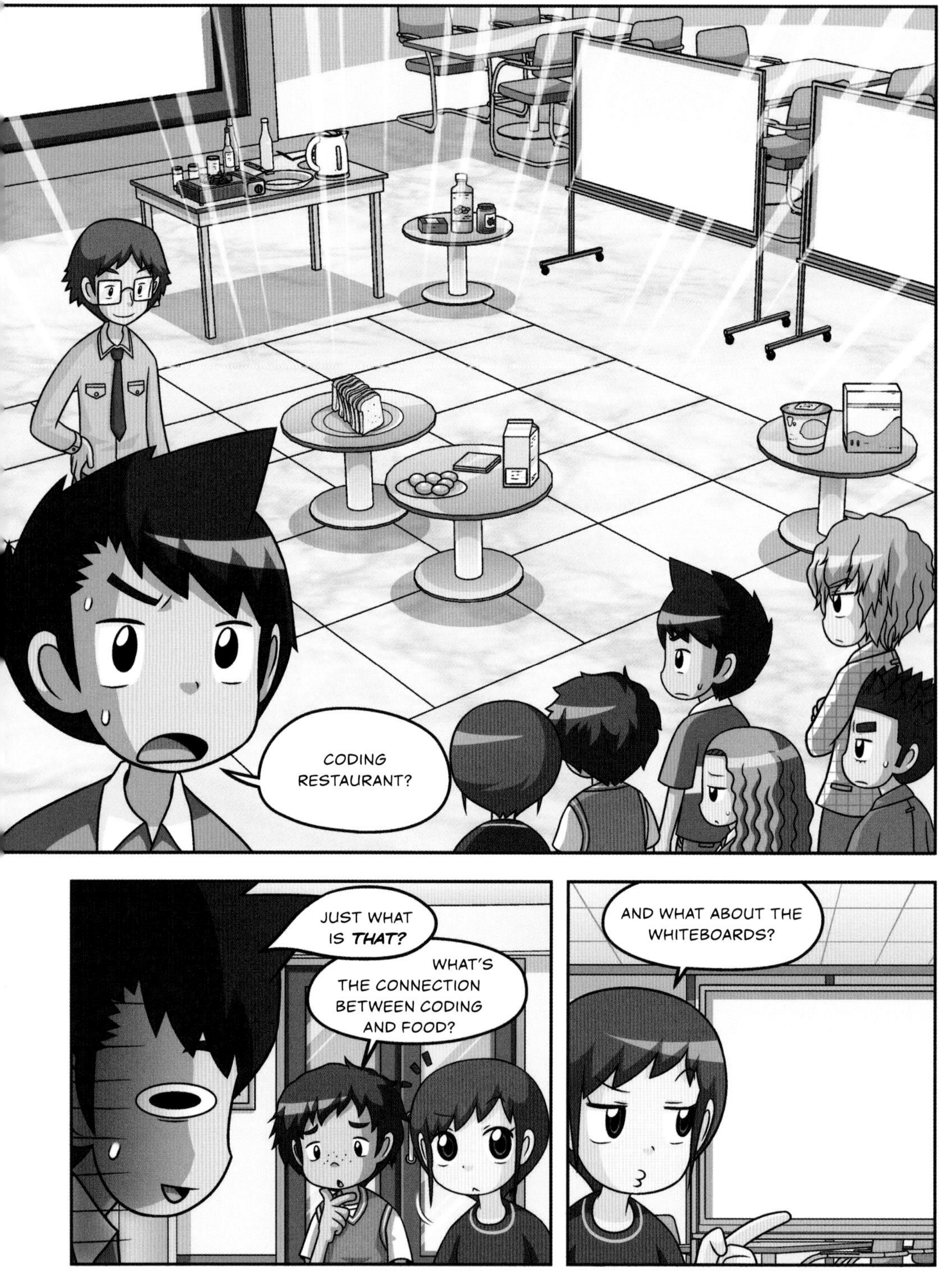
CODING RESTAURANT?
JUST WHAT IS ***THAT?***
WHAT'S THE CONNECTION BETWEEN CODING AND FOOD?
AND WHAT ABOUT THE WHITEBOARDS?

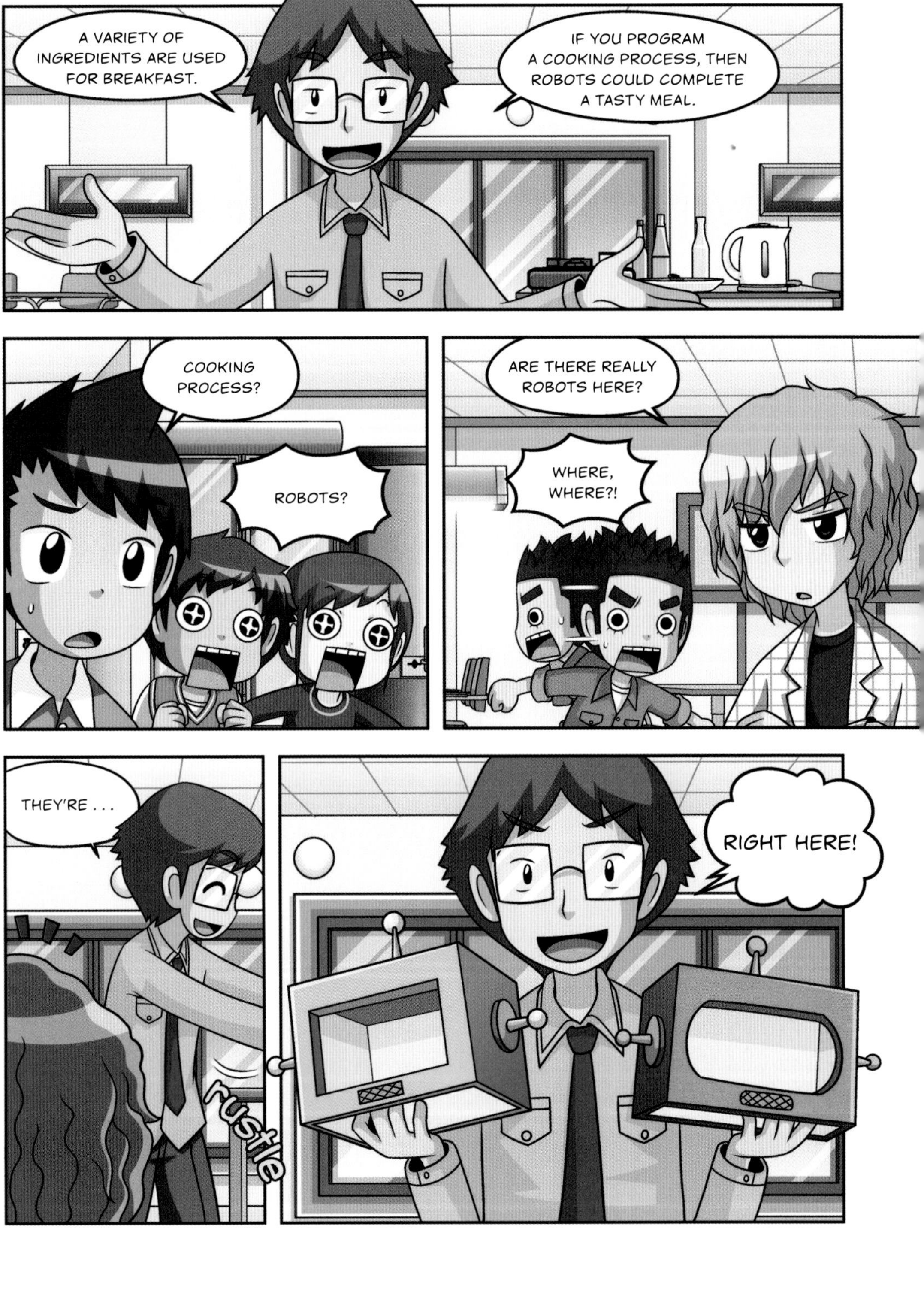
A VARIETY OF INGREDIENTS ARE USED FOR BREAKFAST.
IF YOU PROGRAM A COOKING PROCESS, THEN ROBOTS COULD COMPLETE A TASTY MEAL.
COOKING PROCESS?
ROBOTS?
ARE THERE REALLY ROBOTS HERE?
WHERE, WHERE?!
THEY'RE . . .
rustle
RIGHT HERE!

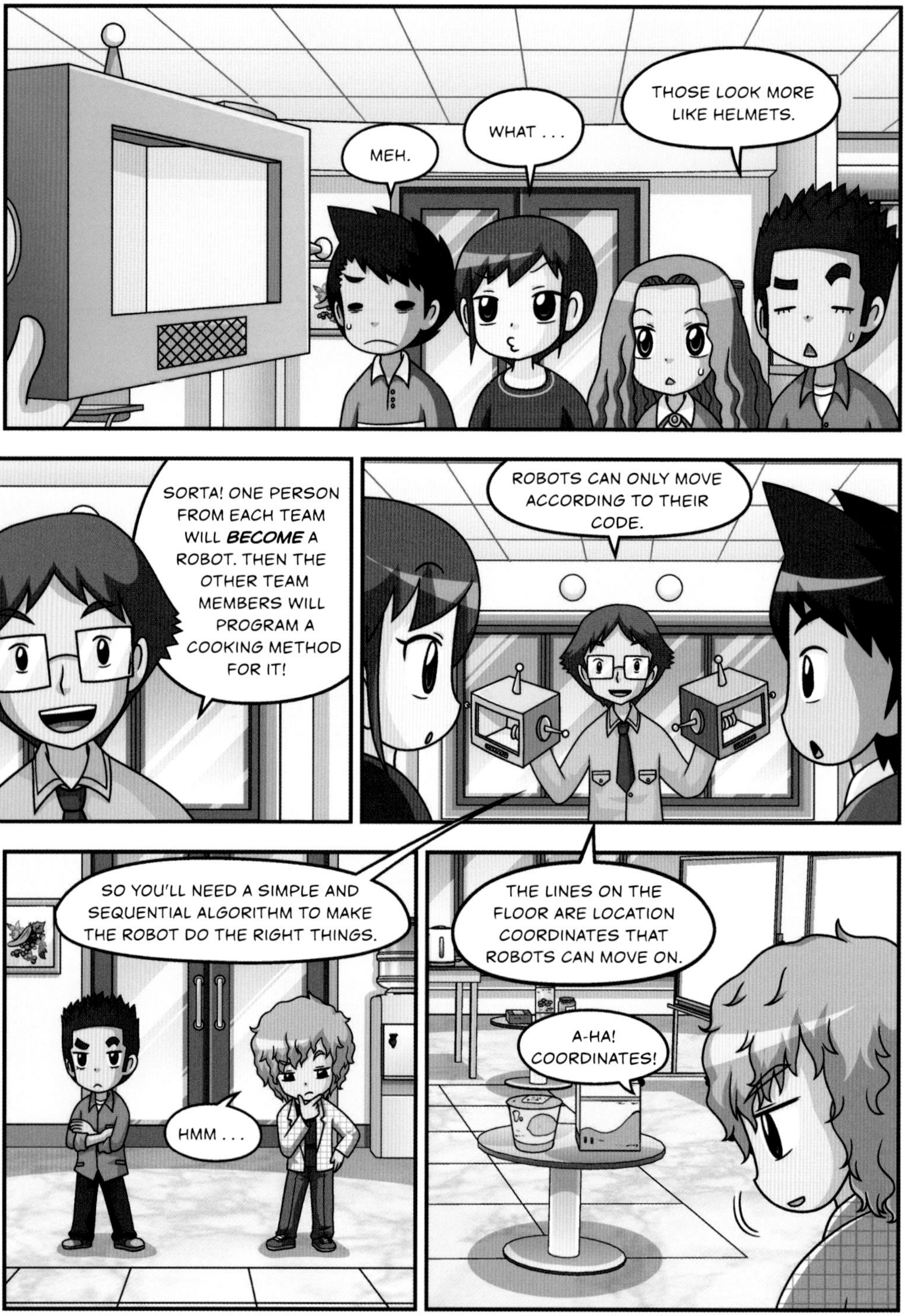
MEH.
WHAT . . .
THOSE LOOK MORE LIKE HELMETS.
SORTA! ONE PERSON FROM EACH TEAM WILL *BECOME* A ROBOT. THEN THE OTHER TEAM MEMBERS WILL PROGRAM A COOKING METHOD FOR IT!
ROBOTS CAN ONLY MOVE ACCORDING TO THEIR CODE.
SO YOU'LL NEED A SIMPLE AND SEQUENTIAL ALGORITHM TO MAKE THE ROBOT DO THE RIGHT THINGS.
HMM . . .
THE LINES ON THE FLOOR ARE LOCATION COORDINATES THAT ROBOTS CAN MOVE ON.
A-HA! COORDINATES!

WITH SOME CODING LANGUAGES, IT'S POSSIBLE TO MAKE A PROGRAM INVOLVING SET COORDINATES.

HUH?? COORDINATES?

nod

nod

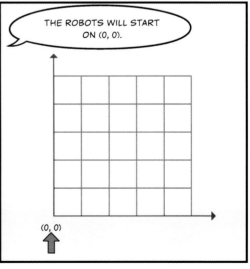

GREAT. ANOTHER THING ONLY I DON'T KNOW.

YAWWWN.

AS YOU CAN SEE, OUR COORDINATES ARE DRAWN ON THE FLOOR. COORDINATES ARE SET FROM (0, 0) TO (5, 5).

THE ROBOTS WILL START ON (0, 0).

(0, 0)

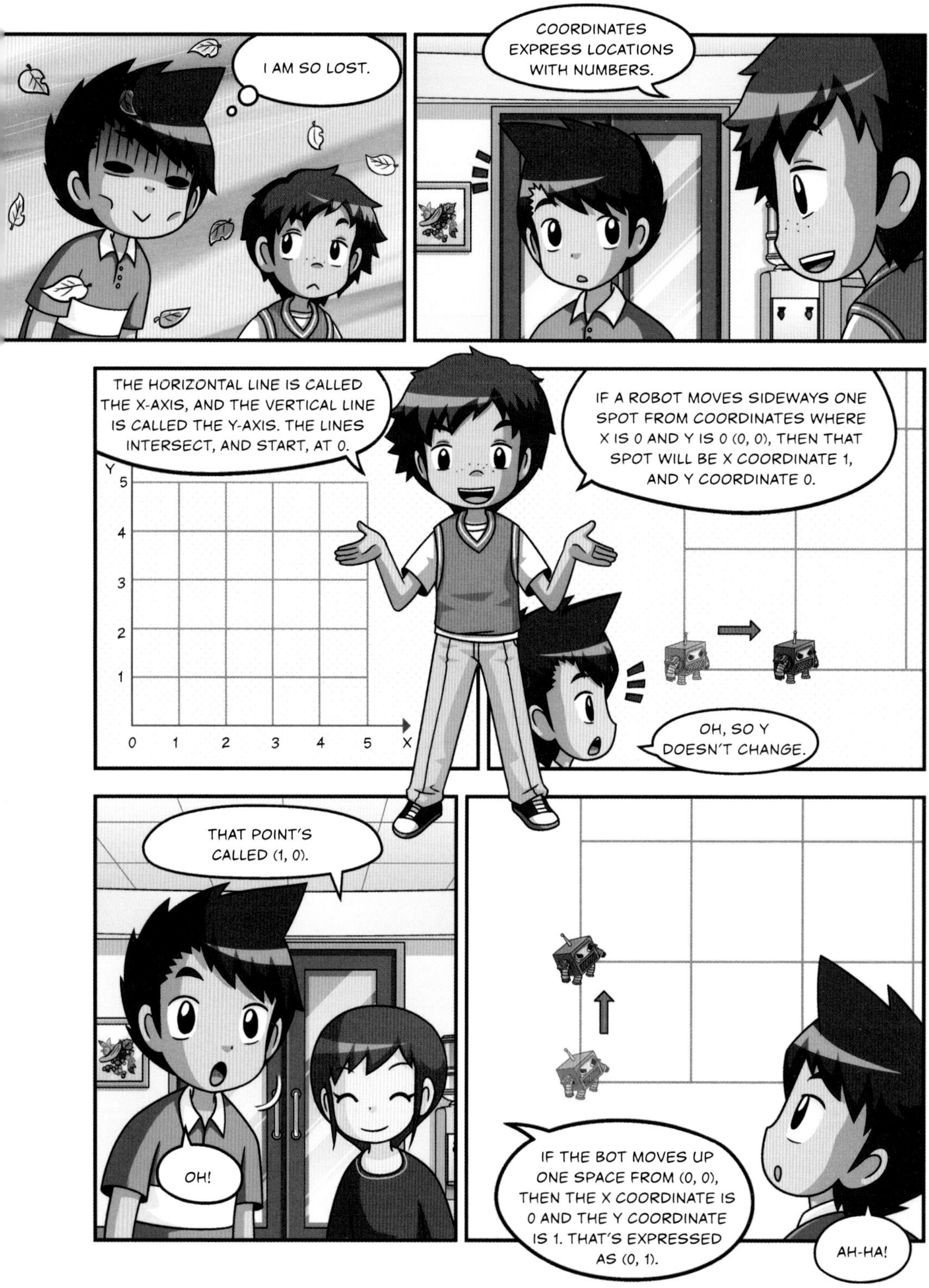
I AM SO LOST.
COORDINATES EXPRESS LOCATIONS WITH NUMBERS.
THE HORIZONTAL LINE IS CALLED THE X-AXIS, AND THE VERTICAL LINE IS CALLED THE Y-AXIS. THE LINES INTERSECT, AND START, AT 0.
Y
5
4
3
2
1
0 1 2 3 4 5 X
IF A ROBOT MOVES SIDEWAYS ONE SPOT FROM COORDINATES WHERE X IS 0 AND Y IS 0 (0, 0), THEN THAT SPOT WILL BE X COORDINATE 1, AND Y COORDINATE 0.
OH, SO Y DOESN'T CHANGE.
THAT POINT'S CALLED (1, 0).
OH!
IF THE BOT MOVES UP ONE SPACE FROM (0, 0), THEN THE X COORDINATE IS 0 AND THE Y COORDINATE IS 1. THAT'S EXPRESSED AS (0, 1).
AH-HA!

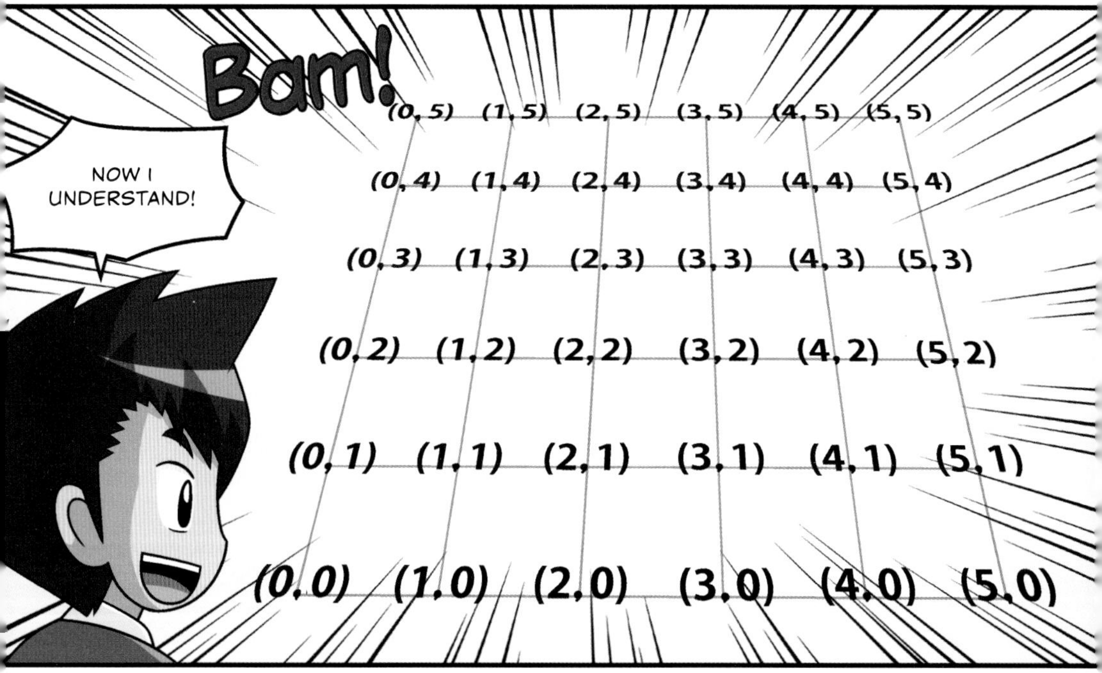
Bam!
NOW I UNDERSTAND!
(0, 5) (1, 5) (2, 5) (3, 5) (4, 5) (5, 5)
(0, 4) (1, 4) (2, 4) (3, 4) (4, 4) (5, 4)
(0, 3) (1, 3) (2, 3) (3, 3) (4, 3) (5, 3)
(0, 2) (1, 2) (2, 2) (3, 2) (4, 2) (5, 2)
(0, 1) (1, 1) (2, 1) (3, 1) (4, 1) (5, 1)
(0, 0) (1, 0) (2, 0) (3, 0) (4, 0) (5, 0)

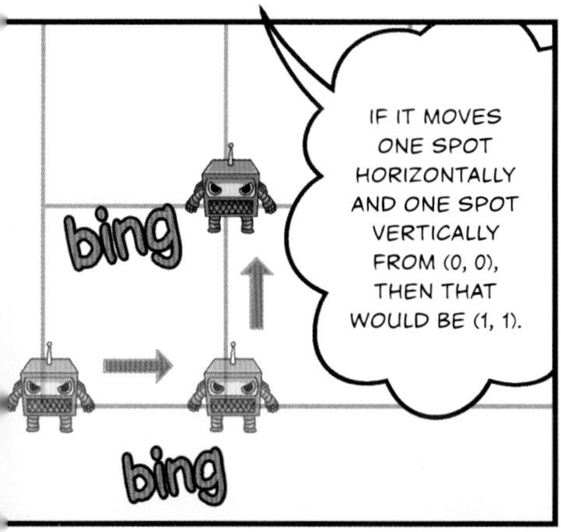
bing
IF IT MOVES ONE SPOT HORIZONTALLY AND ONE SPOT VERTICALLY FROM (0, 0), THEN THAT WOULD BE (1, 1).
bing

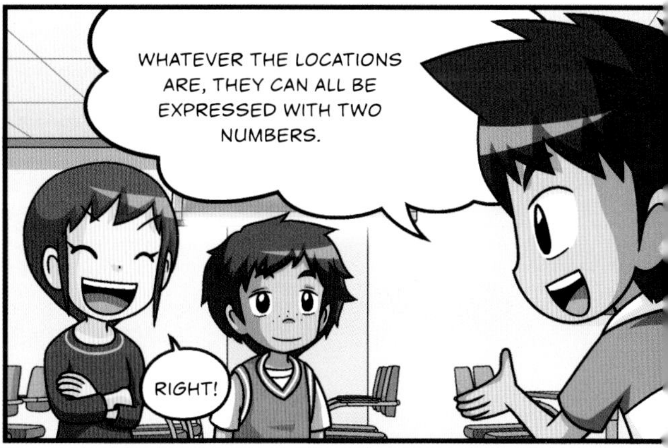
WHATEVER THE LOCATIONS ARE, THEY CAN ALL BE EXPRESSED WITH TWO NUMBERS.
RIGHT!

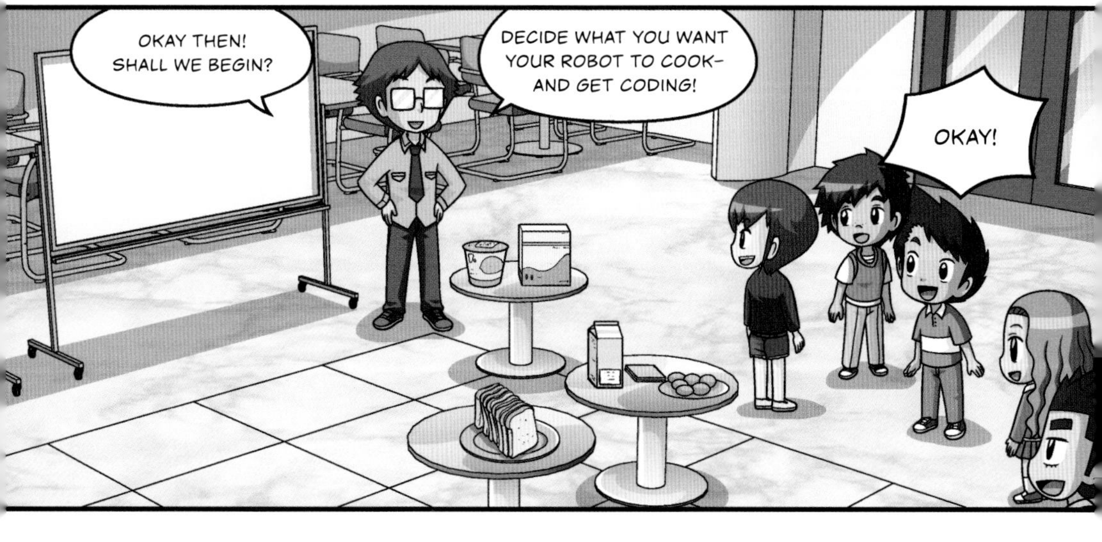
OKAY THEN! SHALL WE BEGIN?
DECIDE WHAT YOU WANT YOUR ROBOT TO COOK—AND GET CODING!
OKAY!

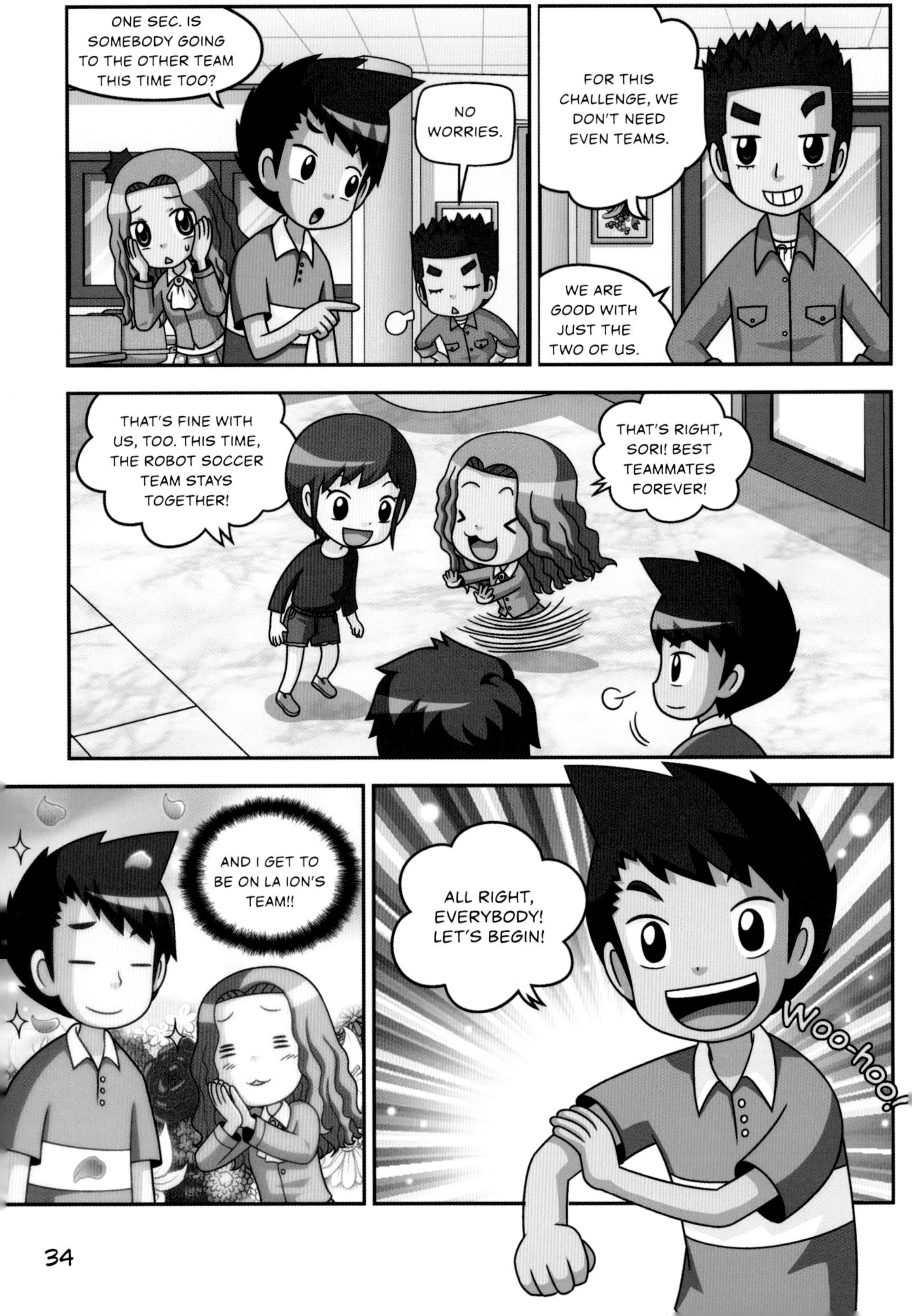
ONE SEC. IS SOMEBODY GOING TO THE OTHER TEAM THIS TIME TOO?
NO WORRIES.
FOR THIS CHALLENGE, WE DON'T NEED EVEN TEAMS.
WE ARE GOOD WITH JUST THE TWO OF US.
THAT'S FINE WITH US, TOO. THIS TIME, THE ROBOT SOCCER TEAM STAYS TOGETHER!
THAT'S RIGHT, SORI! BEST TEAMMATES FOREVER!
AND I GET TO BE ON LA ION'S TEAM!!
ALL RIGHT, EVERYBODY! LET'S BEGIN!
Woo-hoo!

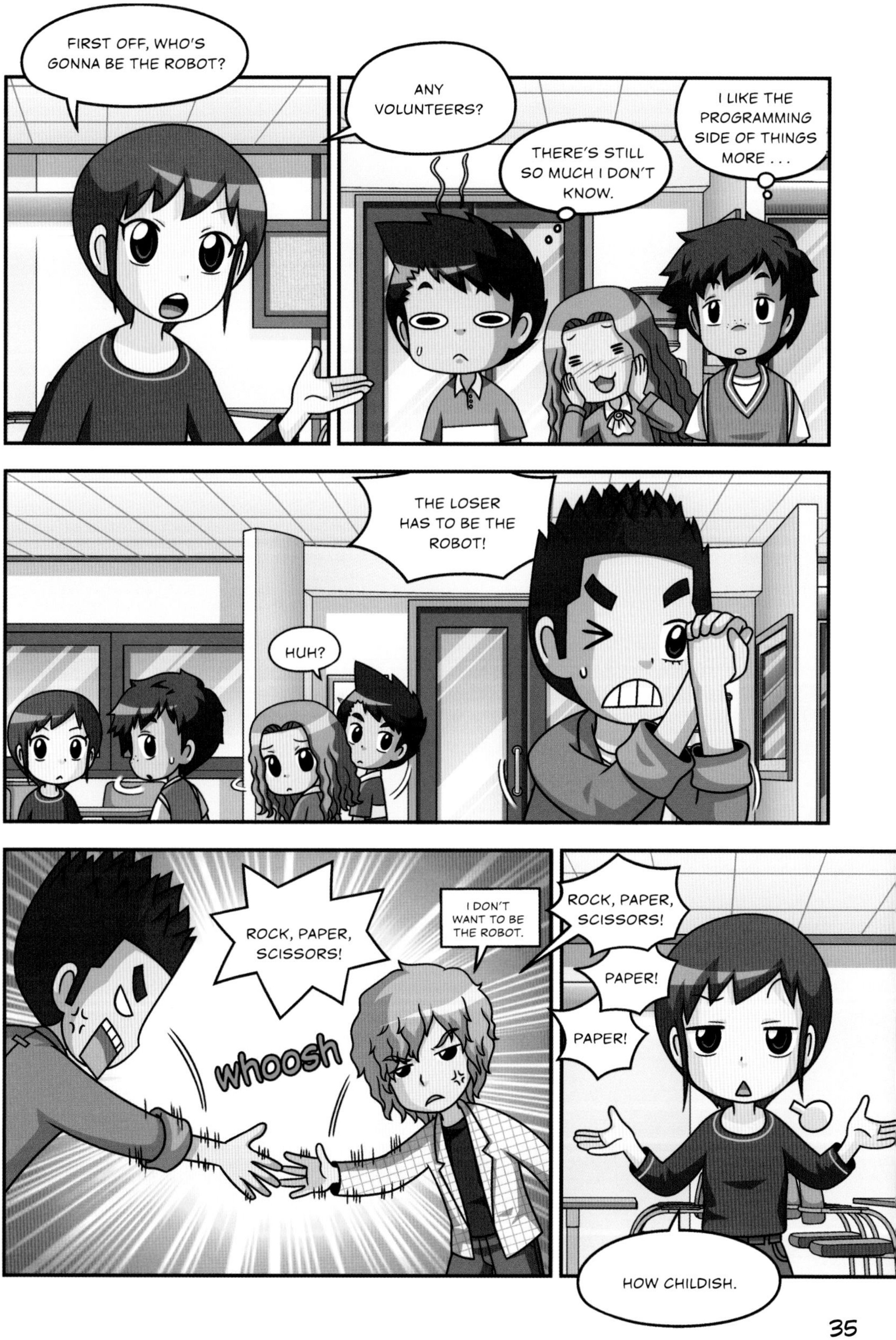

FIRST OFF, WHO'S GONNA BE THE ROBOT?
ANY VOLUNTEERS?
THERE'S STILL SO MUCH I DON'T KNOW.
I LIKE THE PROGRAMMING SIDE OF THINGS MORE . . .
THE LOSER HAS TO BE THE ROBOT!
HUH?
ROCK, PAPER, SCISSORS!
whoosh
I DON'T WANT TO BE THE ROBOT.
ROCK, PAPER, SCISSORS!
PAPER!
PAPER!
HOW CHILDISH.

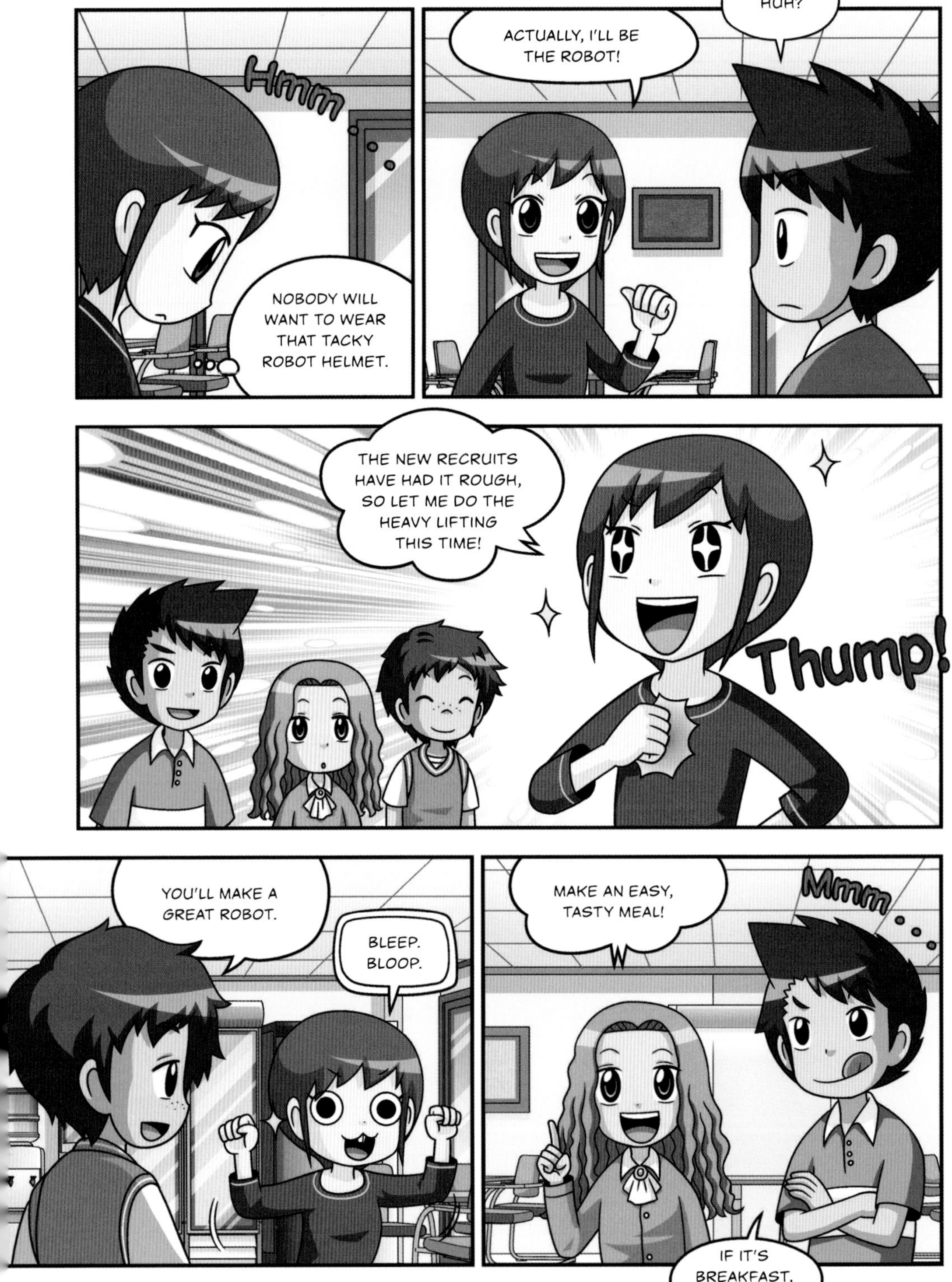
Hmmm
NOBODY WILL WANT TO WEAR THAT TACKY ROBOT HELMET.
ACTUALLY, I'LL BE THE ROBOT!
HUH?
THE NEW RECRUITS HAVE HAD IT ROUGH, SO LET ME DO THE HEAVY LIFTING THIS TIME!
Thump!
YOU'LL MAKE A GREAT ROBOT.
BLEEP. BLOOP.
MAKE AN EASY, TASTY MEAL!
Mmm
IF IT'S BREAKFAST, THEN . . .

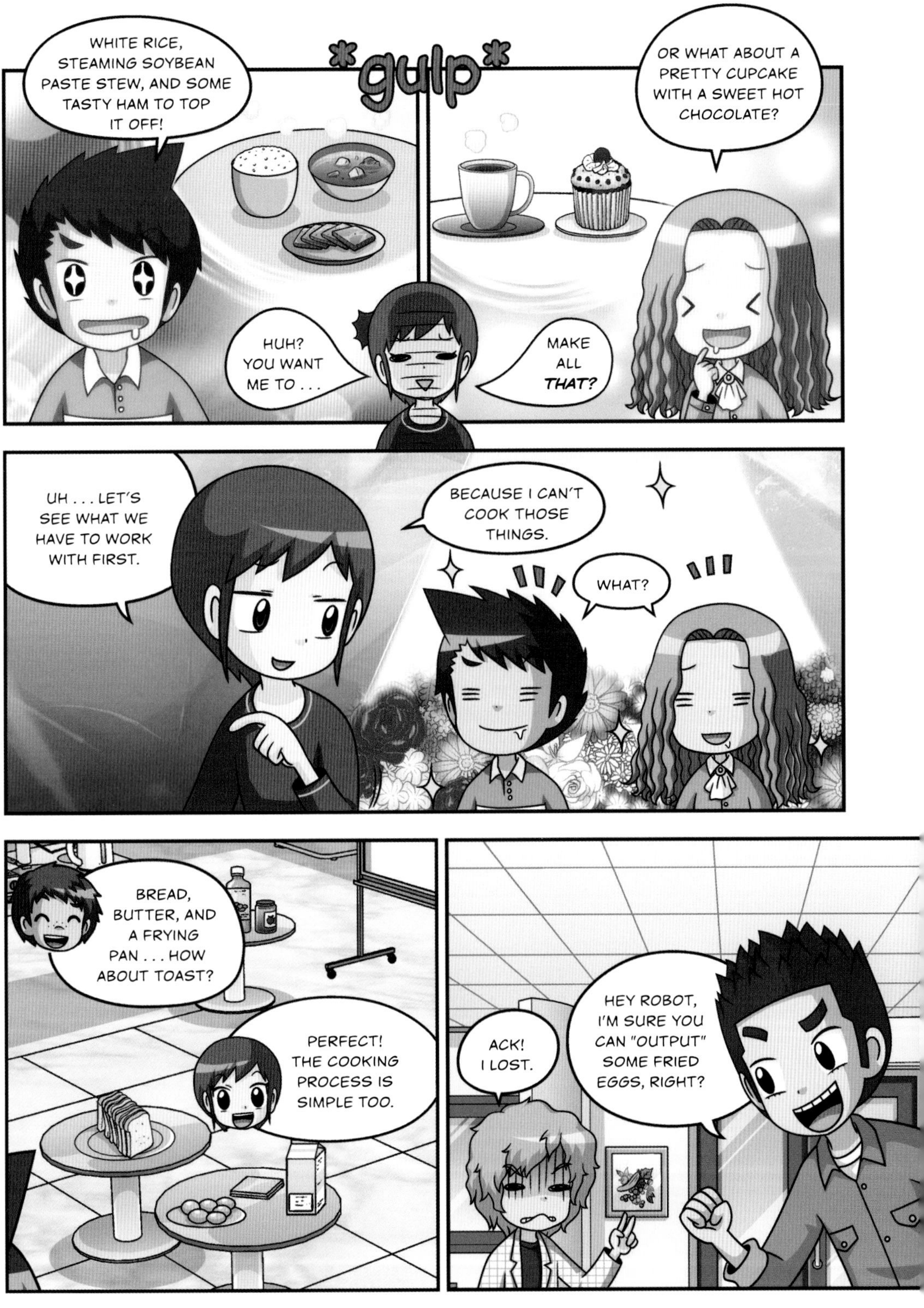
WHITE RICE, STEAMING SOYBEAN PASTE STEW, AND SOME TASTY HAM TO TOP IT OFF!
gulp
OR WHAT ABOUT A PRETTY CUPCAKE WITH A SWEET HOT CHOCOLATE?
HUH? YOU WANT ME TO . . .
MAKE ALL *THAT?*
UH . . . LET'S SEE WHAT WE HAVE TO WORK WITH FIRST.
BECAUSE I CAN'T COOK THOSE THINGS.
WHAT?
BREAD, BUTTER, AND A FRYING PAN . . . HOW ABOUT TOAST?
PERFECT! THE COOKING PROCESS IS SIMPLE TOO.
ACK! I LOST.
HEY ROBOT, I'M SURE YOU CAN "OUTPUT" SOME FRIED EGGS, RIGHT?

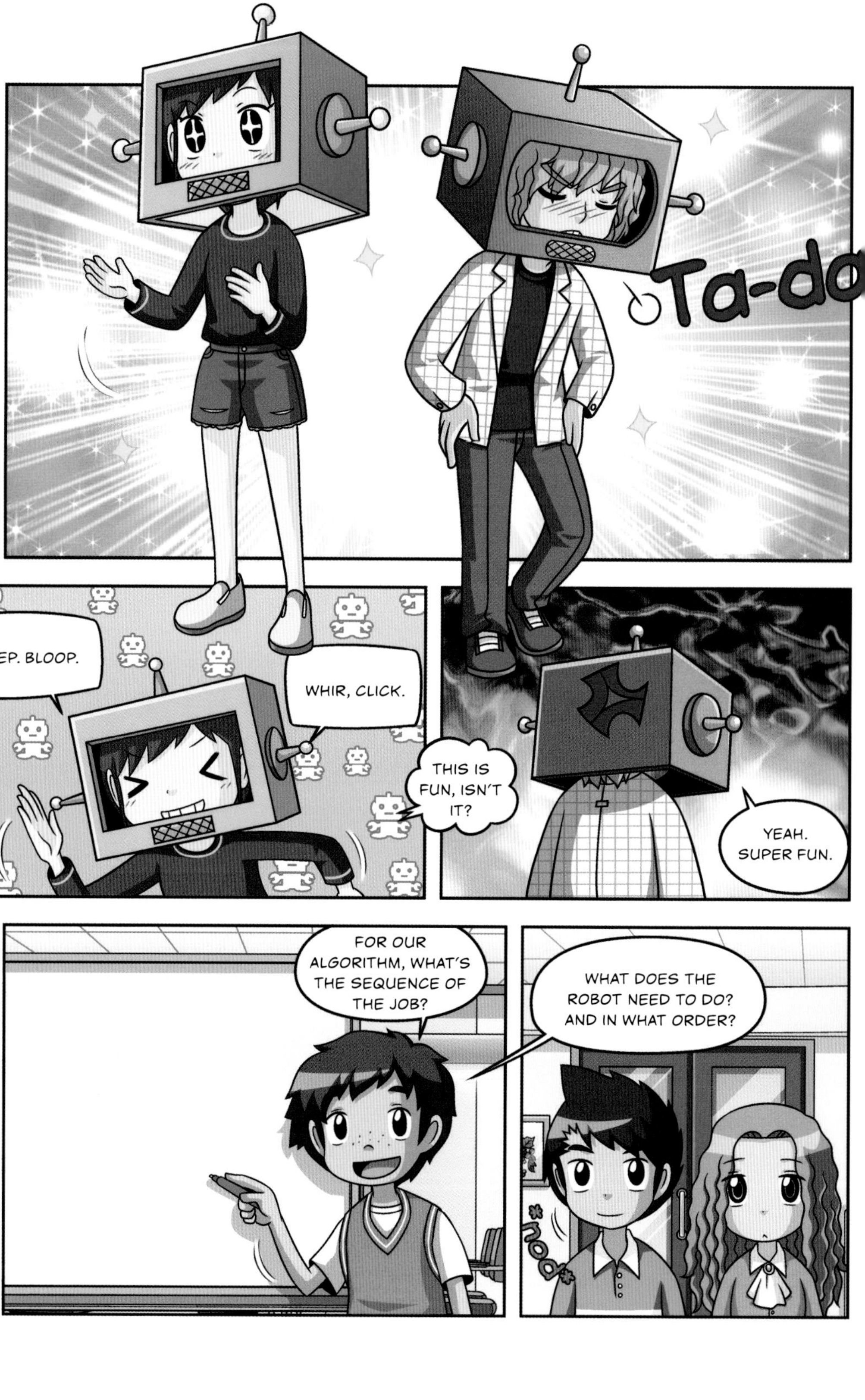
Ta-d
BLEEP. BLOOP.
WHIR, CLICK.
THIS IS FUN, ISN'T IT?
YEAH. SUPER FUN.
FOR OUR ALGORITHM, WHAT'S THE SEQUENCE OF THE JOB?
WHAT DOES THE ROBOT NEED TO DO? AND IN WHAT ORDER?
nod

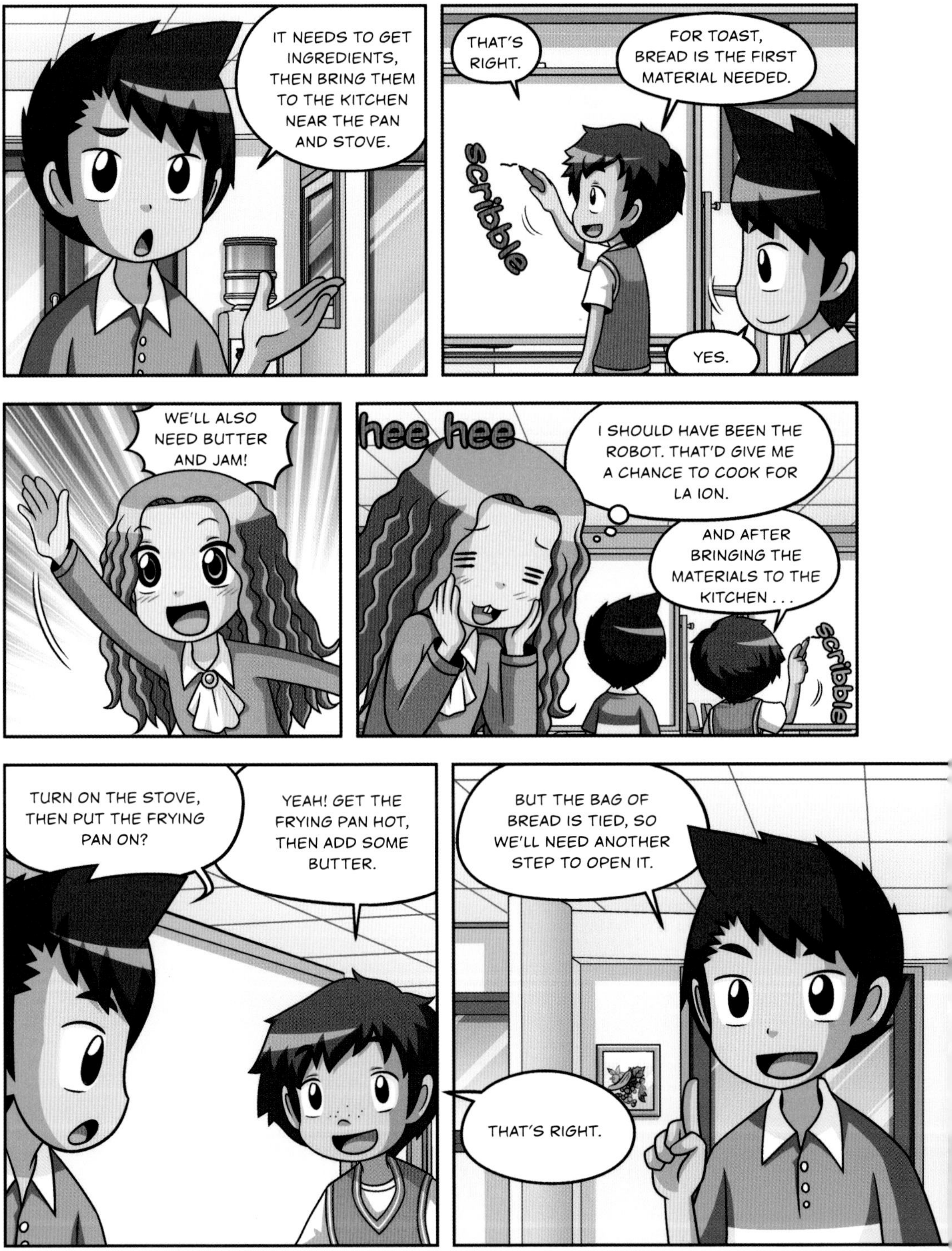
IT NEEDS TO GET INGREDIENTS, THEN BRING THEM TO THE KITCHEN NEAR THE PAN AND STOVE.
THAT'S RIGHT.
FOR TOAST, BREAD IS THE FIRST MATERIAL NEEDED.
scribble
YES.
WE'LL ALSO NEED BUTTER AND JAM!
hee hee
I SHOULD HAVE BEEN THE ROBOT. THAT'D GIVE ME A CHANCE TO COOK FOR LA ION.
AND AFTER BRINGING THE MATERIALS TO THE KITCHEN . . .
scribble
TURN ON THE STOVE, THEN PUT THE FRYING PAN ON?
YEAH! GET THE FRYING PAN HOT, THEN ADD SOME BUTTER.
BUT THE BAG OF BREAD IS TIED, SO WE'LL NEED ANOTHER STEP TO OPEN IT.
THAT'S RIGHT.

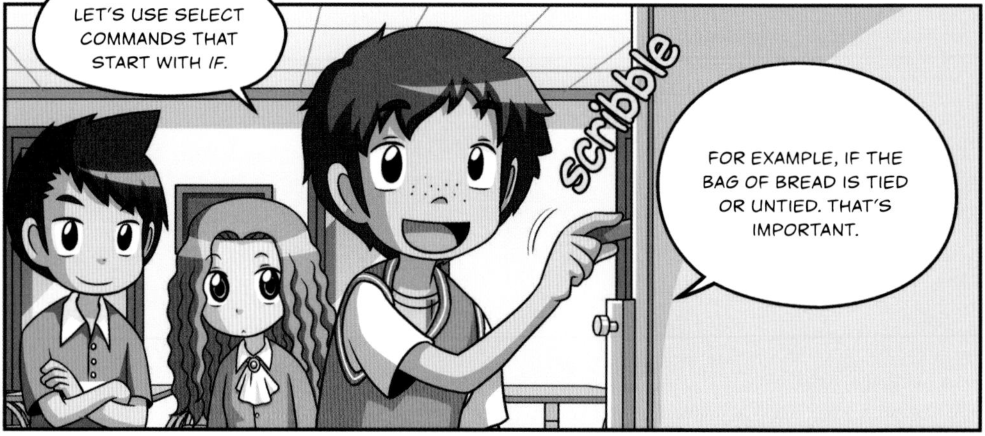
LET'S USE SELECT COMMANDS THAT START WITH *IF*.
scribble
FOR EXAMPLE, IF THE BAG OF BREAD IS TIED OR UNTIED. THAT'S IMPORTANT.

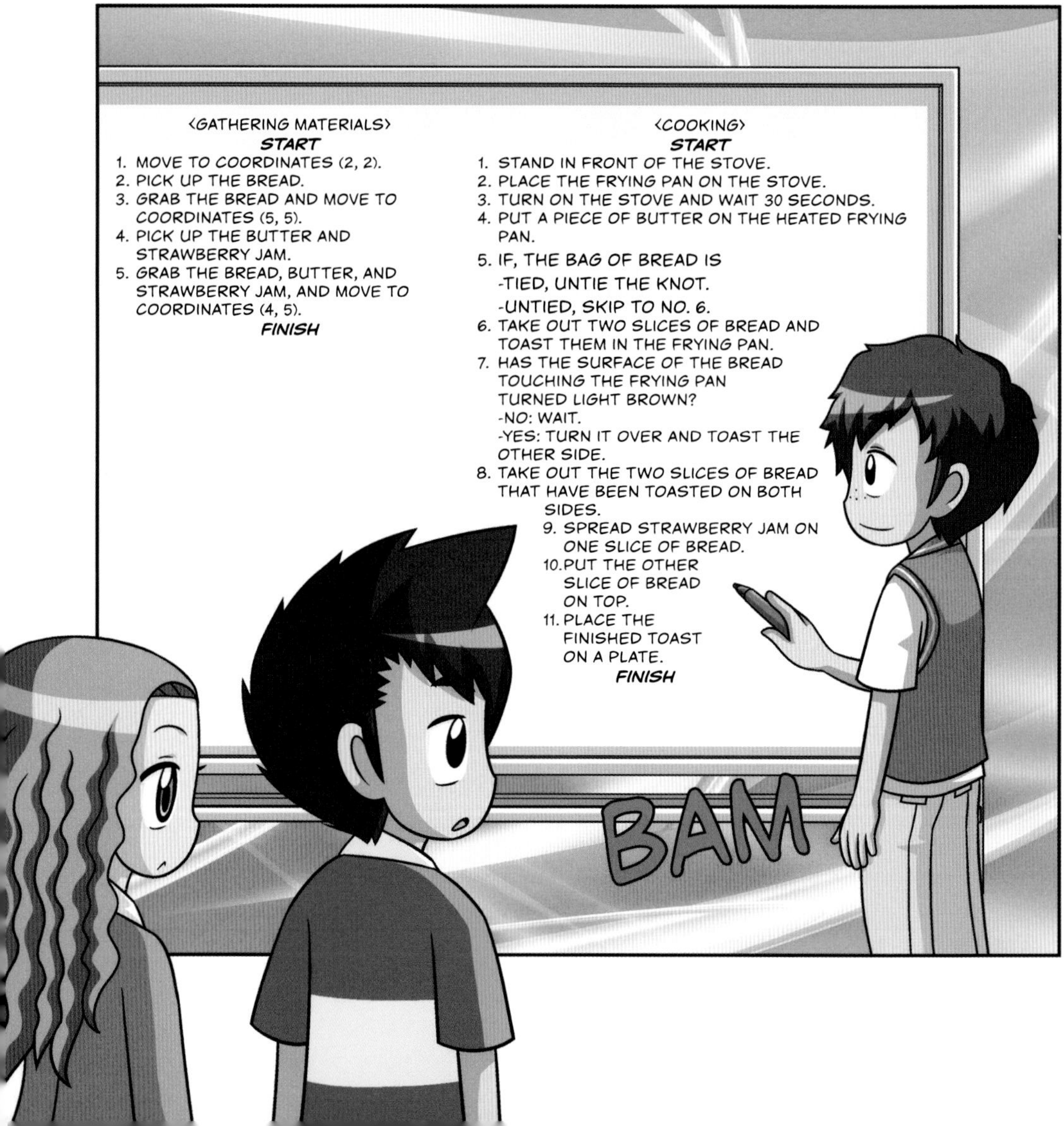
<GATHERING MATERIALS>
START
1. MOVE TO COORDINATES (2, 2).
2. PICK UP THE BREAD.
3. GRAB THE BREAD AND MOVE TO COORDINATES (5, 5).
4. PICK UP THE BUTTER AND STRAWBERRY JAM.
5. GRAB THE BREAD, BUTTER, AND STRAWBERRY JAM, AND MOVE TO COORDINATES (4, 5).
FINISH
<COOKING>
START
1. STAND IN FRONT OF THE STOVE.
2. PLACE THE FRYING PAN ON THE STOVE.
3. TURN ON THE STOVE AND WAIT 30 SECONDS.
4. PUT A PIECE OF BUTTER ON THE HEATED FRYING PAN.
5. IF, THE BAG OF BREAD IS
-TIED, UNTIE THE KNOT.
-UNTIED, SKIP TO NO. 6.
6. TAKE OUT TWO SLICES OF BREAD AND TOAST THEM IN THE FRYING PAN.
7. HAS THE SURFACE OF THE BREAD TOUCHING THE FRYING PAN TURNED LIGHT BROWN?
-NO: WAIT.
-YES: TURN IT OVER AND TOAST THE OTHER SIDE.
8. TAKE OUT THE TWO SLICES OF BREAD THAT HAVE BEEN TOASTED ON BOTH SIDES.
9. SPREAD STRAWBERRY JAM ON ONE SLICE OF BREAD.
10. PUT THE OTHER SLICE OF BREAD ON TOP.
11. PLACE THE FINISHED TOAST ON A PLATE.
FINISH
BAM

Heh heh heh

CODING COOKED MEALS IS A PIECE OF CAKE.

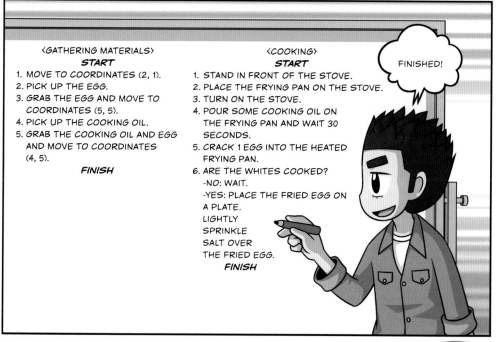

<GATHERING MATERIALS>
START
1. MOVE TO COORDINATES (2, 1).
2. PICK UP THE EGG.
3. GRAB THE EGG AND MOVE TO COORDINATES (5, 5).
4. PICK UP THE COOKING OIL.
5. GRAB THE COOKING OIL AND EGG AND MOVE TO COORDINATES (4, 5).

FINISH

<COOKING>
START
1. STAND IN FRONT OF THE STOVE.
2. PLACE THE FRYING PAN ON THE STOVE.
3. TURN ON THE STOVE.
4. POUR SOME COOKING OIL ON THE FRYING PAN AND WAIT 30 SECONDS.
5. CRACK 1 EGG INTO THE HEATED FRYING PAN.
6. ARE THE WHITES COOKED?
   -NO: WAIT.
   -YES: PLACE THE FRIED EGG ON A PLATE.
   LIGHTLY SPRINKLE SALT OVER THE FRIED EGG.

FINISH

FINISHED!

heh

WE'RE FINISHED TOO!

OH, I FORGOT SOMETHING.

41

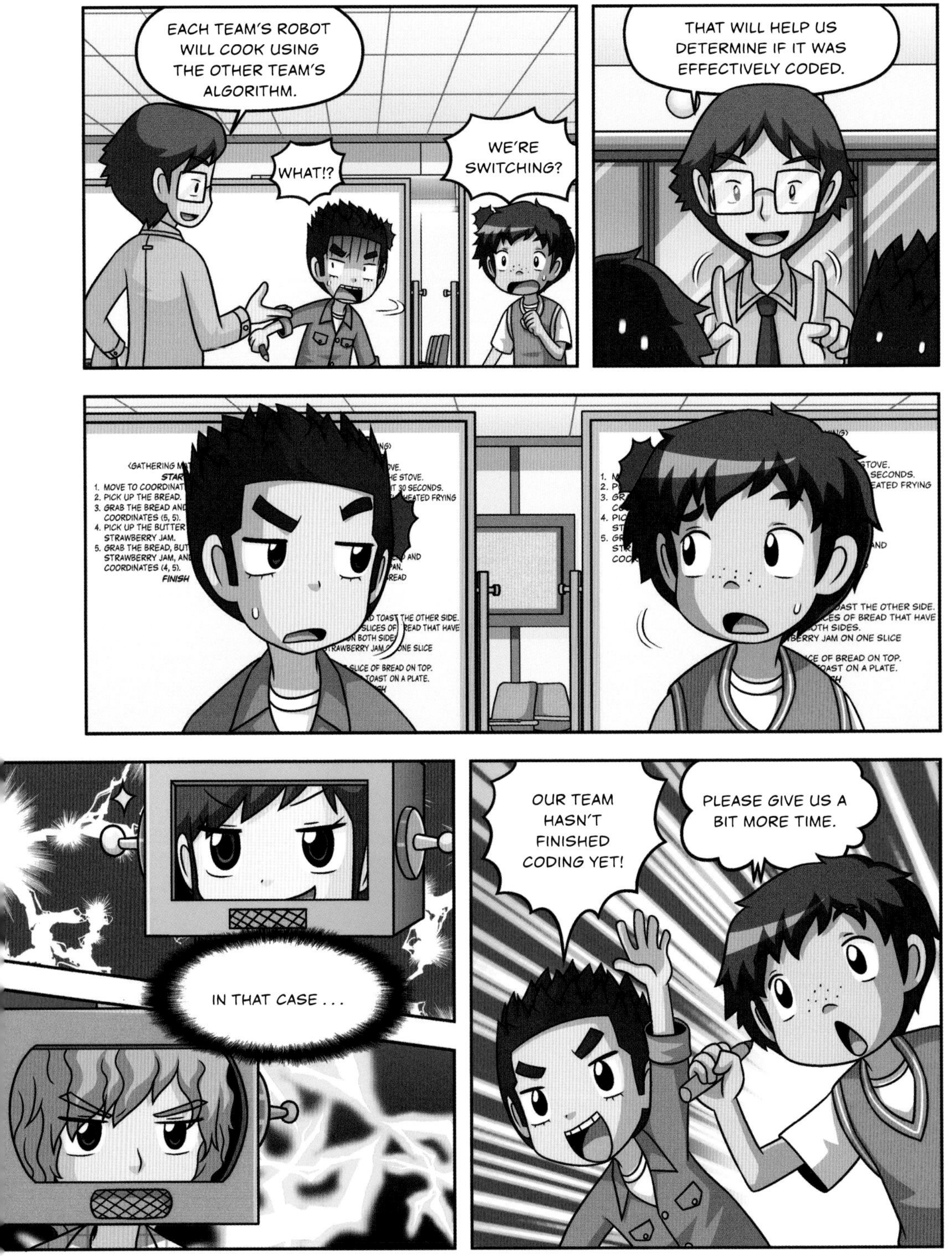
EACH TEAM'S ROBOT WILL COOK USING THE OTHER TEAM'S ALGORITHM.
WHAT!?
WE'RE SWITCHING?
THAT WILL HELP US DETERMINE IF IT WAS EFFECTIVELY CODED.
IN THAT CASE . . .
OUR TEAM HASN'T FINISHED CODING YET!
PLEASE GIVE US A BIT MORE TIME.

MAKE IT MORE COMPLICATED. MAKE THEIR ROBOT FLAIL WILDLY!

scribble

ONE LITTLE ADDITION HERE . . .

<COOKING>
START
1. STAND IN FRONT OF THE STOVE.
2. PLACE THE FRYING PAN ON THE STOVE.
3. TURN ON THE STOVE AND WAIT 30 SECONDS.
4. PUT A PIECE OF BUTTER ON THE HEATED FRYING PAN.
5. IF, THE BAG OF BREAD IS
   -TIED, UNTIE THE KNOT.
   -UNTIED, SKIP TO NO. 6.
6. TAKE OUT TWO SLICES OF BREAD AND TOAST THEM IN THE FRYING PAN.
7. HAS THE SURFACE OF THE BREAD TOUCHING THE FRYING PAN ... GHT BROWN?
8. ... URN IT OVER AND TOAST THE OTHER SIDE. ... T THE TWO SLICES OF BREAD THAT HAVE ... OASTED ON ...
9. ... RE ... AD STRAW ... SLICE
   ... TH ... BREAD ON TOP.
   ... E ... SHED TOAST ON A PLATE.
   FINISH

scribble

HEH, SORI IS GONNA COOK QUITE A FEAST!

INSTANT RAMEN

PUT INSTANT RAMEN NOODLES ON TOP OF AN EGG . . .

SHALL WE ADD SOME KETCHUP?

ha ha ha

scribble

scribble

scribble

OKAY, EVERYONE, WE'RE READY.

Hah . . .

OH, THOSE KIDS.

tremble

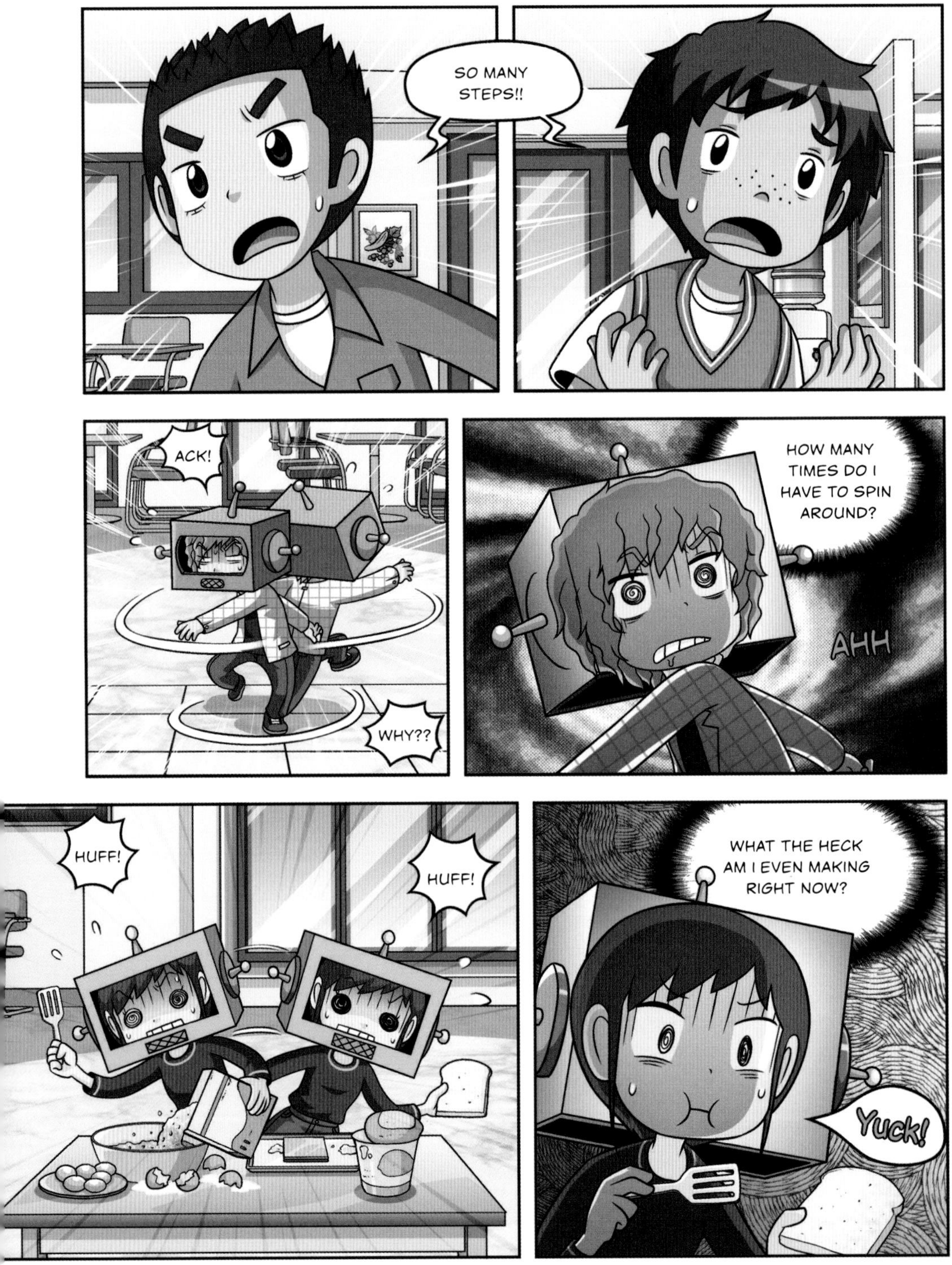
SO MANY STEPS!!
ACK!
WHY??
HOW MANY TIMES DO I HAVE TO SPIN AROUND?
AHH
HUFF!
HUFF!
WHAT THE HECK AM I EVEN MAKING RIGHT NOW?
Yuck!

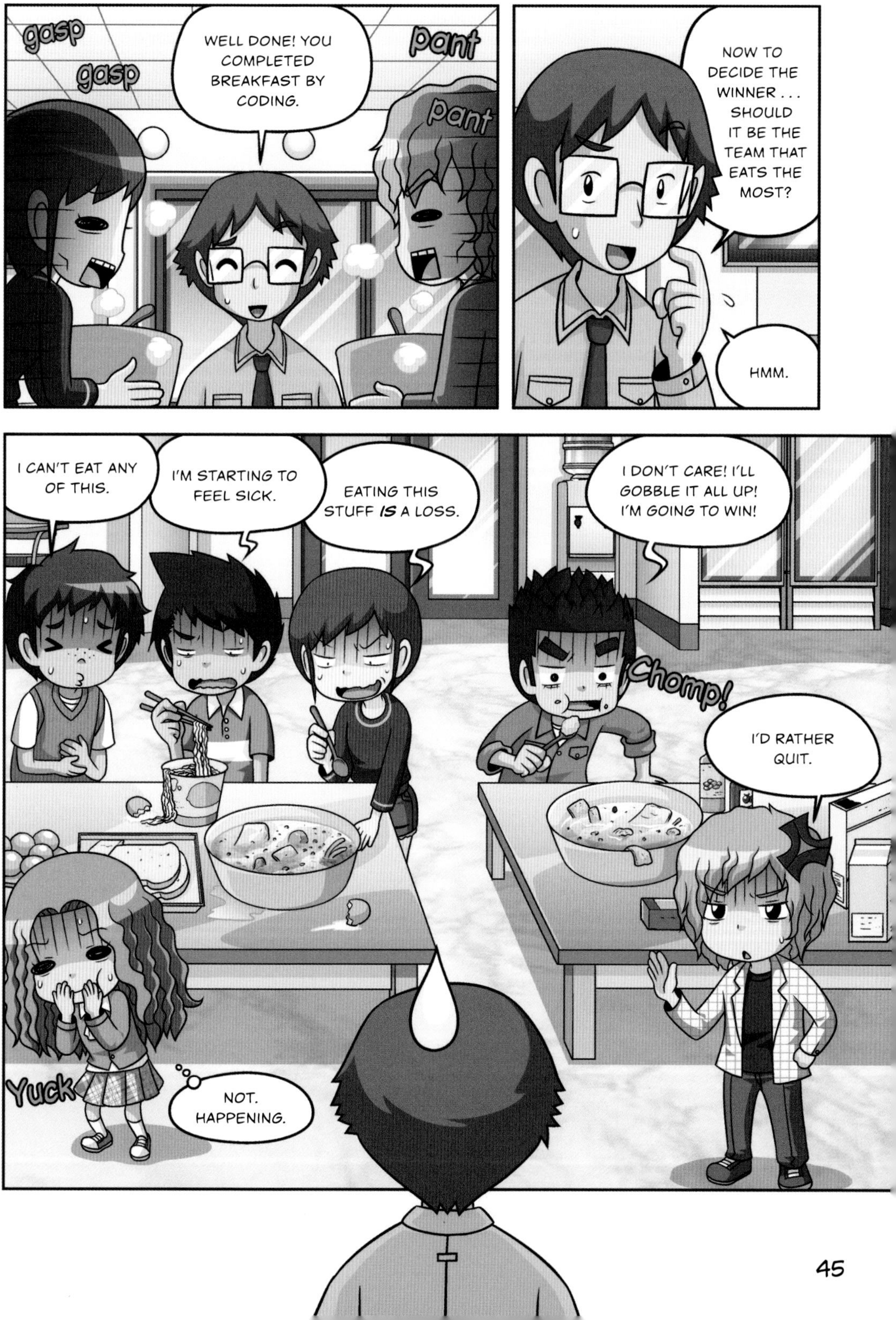
gasp
gasp
WELL DONE! YOU COMPLETED BREAKFAST BY CODING.
pant
pant
NOW TO DECIDE THE WINNER . . . SHOULD IT BE THE TEAM THAT EATS THE MOST?
HMM.
I CAN'T EAT ANY OF THIS.
I'M STARTING TO FEEL SICK.
EATING THIS STUFF *IS* A LOSS.
I DON'T CARE! I'LL GOBBLE IT ALL UP! I'M GOING TO WIN!
Chomp!
I'D RATHER QUIT.
Yuck
NOT. HAPPENING.

VALKYRIE: MARS EXPLORATION ROBOT

Wikipedia
NASA's bipedal Valkyrie robot

Valkyrie is a humanoid robot developed by the National Aeronautics and Space Administration in the United States. Its name is taken from Norse mythology. Valkyrie was originally built to compete in the 2013 DARPA Robotics Challenge (DRC) Trials. Since then, its abilities have been tested through NASA's Space Robotics Challenge. This competition simulates unexpected situations on Mars. Participants must develop a program for Valkyrie to deal with the situation and carry out its mission.

In 2017, 93 teams from all over the world participated in the challenge; 20 teams advanced to the finals. Coordinated Robotics took first place. Valkyrie was challenged by a simulated mission in which a sandstorm was approaching a space base on Mars. It had to adjust a communication antenna and open a solar panel. Another challenge involved going up a set of stairs, turning the valve on a door, then finding and fixing broken parts beyond the door.

Valkyrie is a bipedal robot, meaning it walks on two legs. It can move up and down stairs in addition to sets of precise movements with each body part, including its limbs and fingers. Because previous robots used to explore Mars were mainly on wheels or treads (tracks), researchers could not study the nooks and crannies as a human being would. Valkyrie has made it possible for humans to look around in more detail.

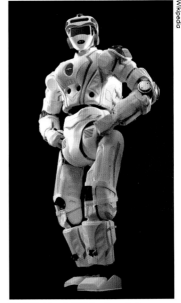

I'LL TAKE OVER THE MISSION ON MARS!
THANK YOU.
Valkyrie
Curiosity

Chef Robot Moley

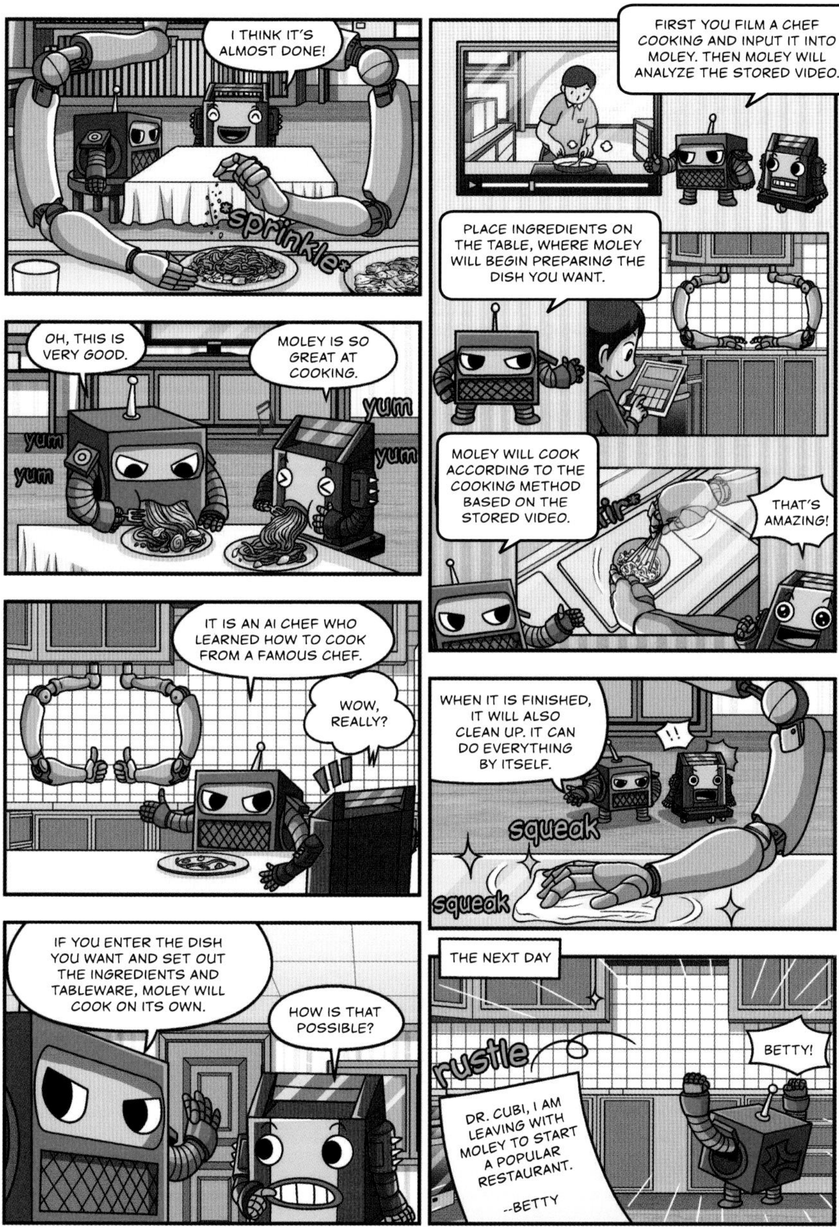
I THINK IT'S ALMOST DONE!
sprinkle
OH, THIS IS VERY GOOD.
MOLEY IS SO GREAT AT COOKING.
yum
yum
yum
yum
IT IS AN AI CHEF WHO LEARNED HOW TO COOK FROM A FAMOUS CHEF.
WOW, REALLY?
IF YOU ENTER THE DISH YOU WANT AND SET OUT THE INGREDIENTS AND TABLEWARE, MOLEY WILL COOK ON ITS OWN.
HOW IS THAT POSSIBLE?
FIRST YOU FILM A CHEF COOKING AND INPUT IT INTO MOLEY. THEN MOLEY WILL ANALYZE THE STORED VIDEO.
PLACE INGREDIENTS ON THE TABLE, WHERE MOLEY WILL BEGIN PREPARING THE DISH YOU WANT.
MOLEY WILL COOK ACCORDING TO THE COOKING METHOD BASED ON THE STORED VIDEO.
THAT'S AMAZING!
WHEN IT IS FINISHED, IT WILL ALSO CLEAN UP. IT CAN DO EVERYTHING BY ITSELF.
!!
squeak
squeak
THE NEXT DAY
rustle
BETTY!
DR. CUBI, I AM LEAVING WITH MOLEY TO START A POPULAR RESTAURANT.
--BETTY

Chapter
3

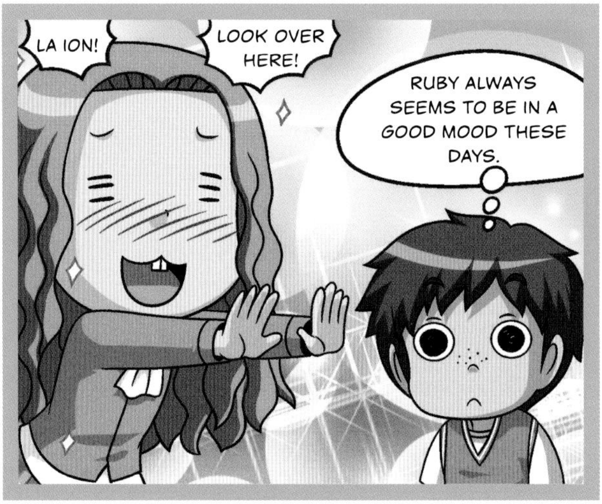
LA ION!
LOOK OVER HERE!
RUBY ALWAYS SEEMS TO BE IN A GOOD MOOD THESE DAYS.

The Last Level of Coding Camp

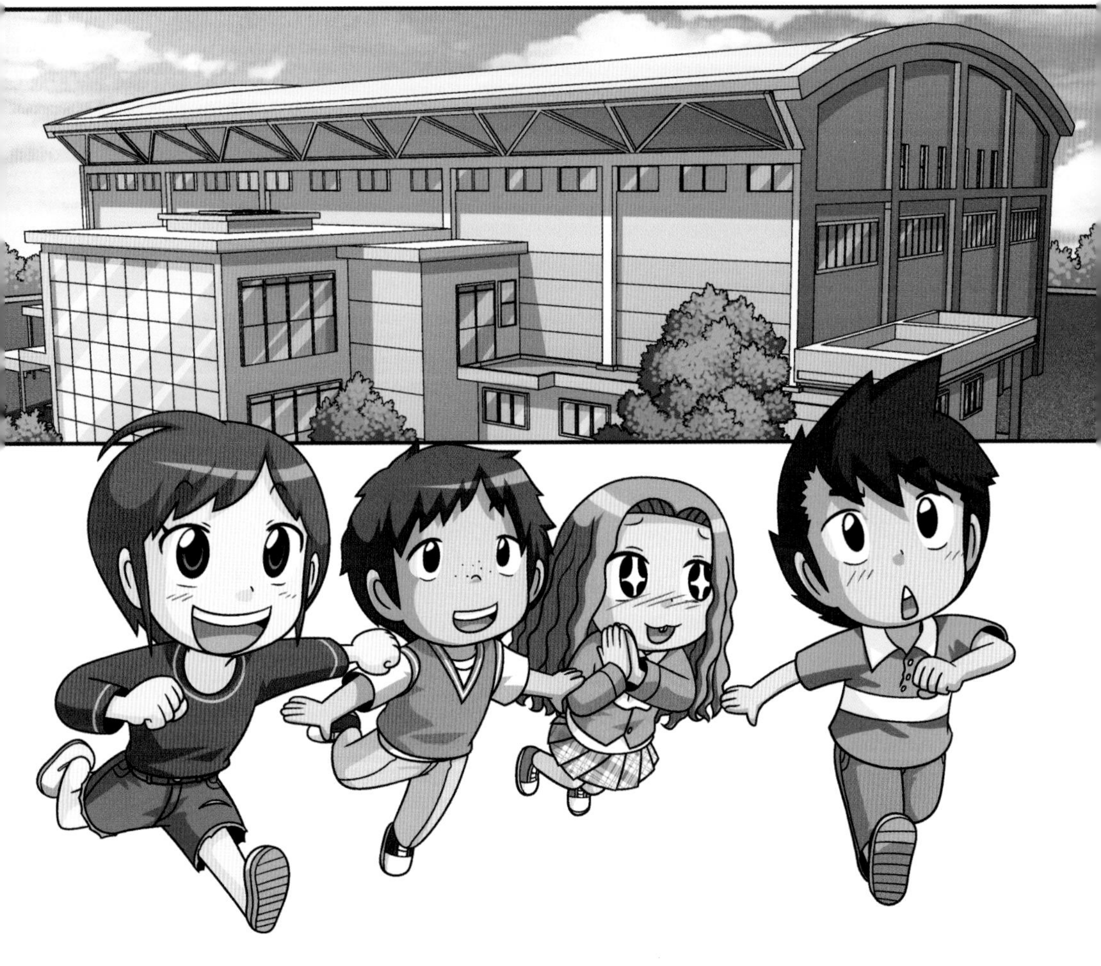

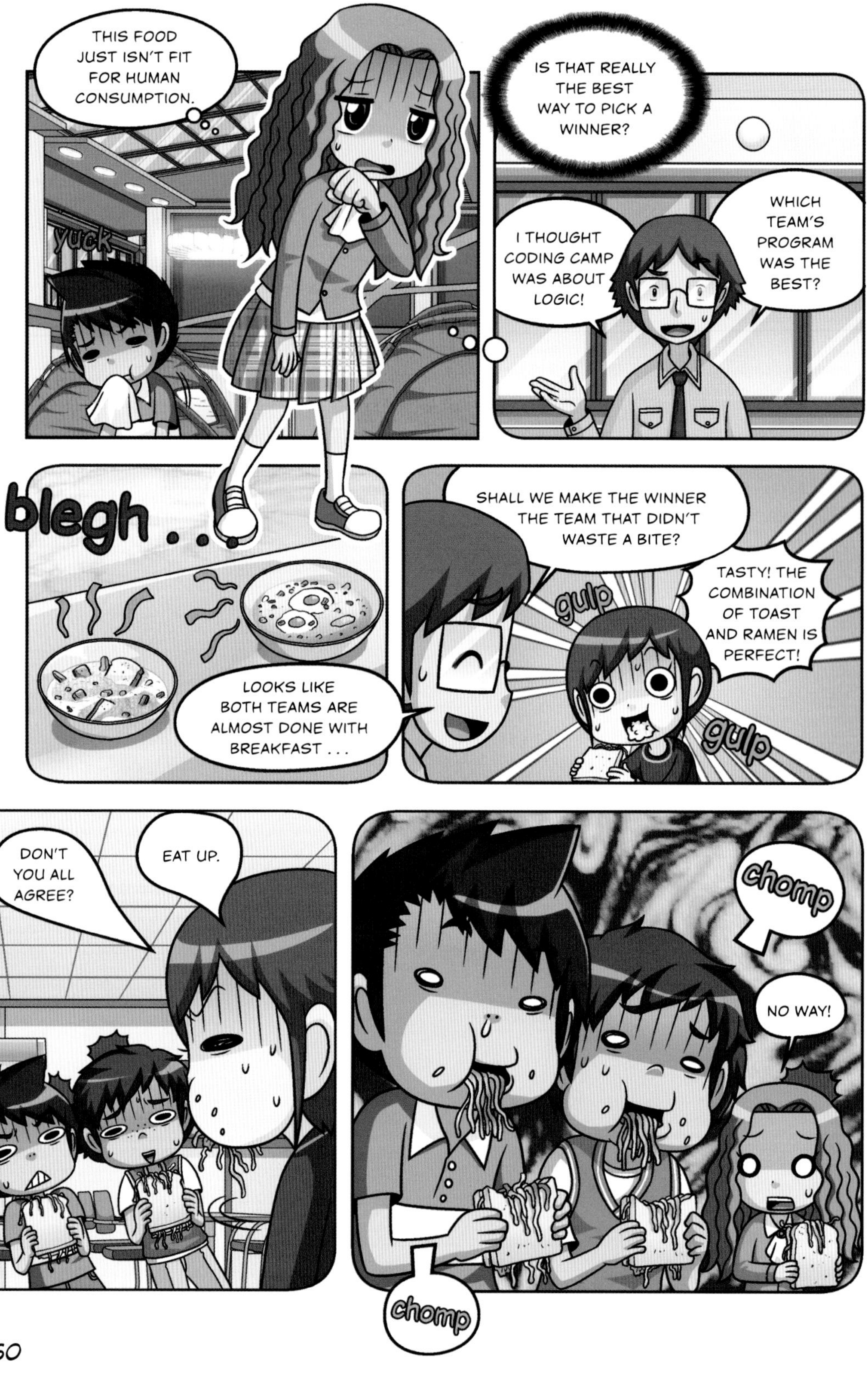
THIS FOOD JUST ISN'T FIT FOR HUMAN CONSUMPTION.
yuck
blegh . . .
IS THAT REALLY THE BEST WAY TO PICK A WINNER?
I THOUGHT CODING CAMP WAS ABOUT LOGIC!
WHICH TEAM'S PROGRAM WAS THE BEST?
LOOKS LIKE BOTH TEAMS ARE ALMOST DONE WITH BREAKFAST . . .
SHALL WE MAKE THE WINNER THE TEAM THAT DIDN'T WASTE A BITE?
gulp
TASTY! THE COMBINATION OF TOAST AND RAMEN IS PERFECT!
gulp
DON'T YOU ALL AGREE?
EAT UP.
chomp
NO WAY!
chomp

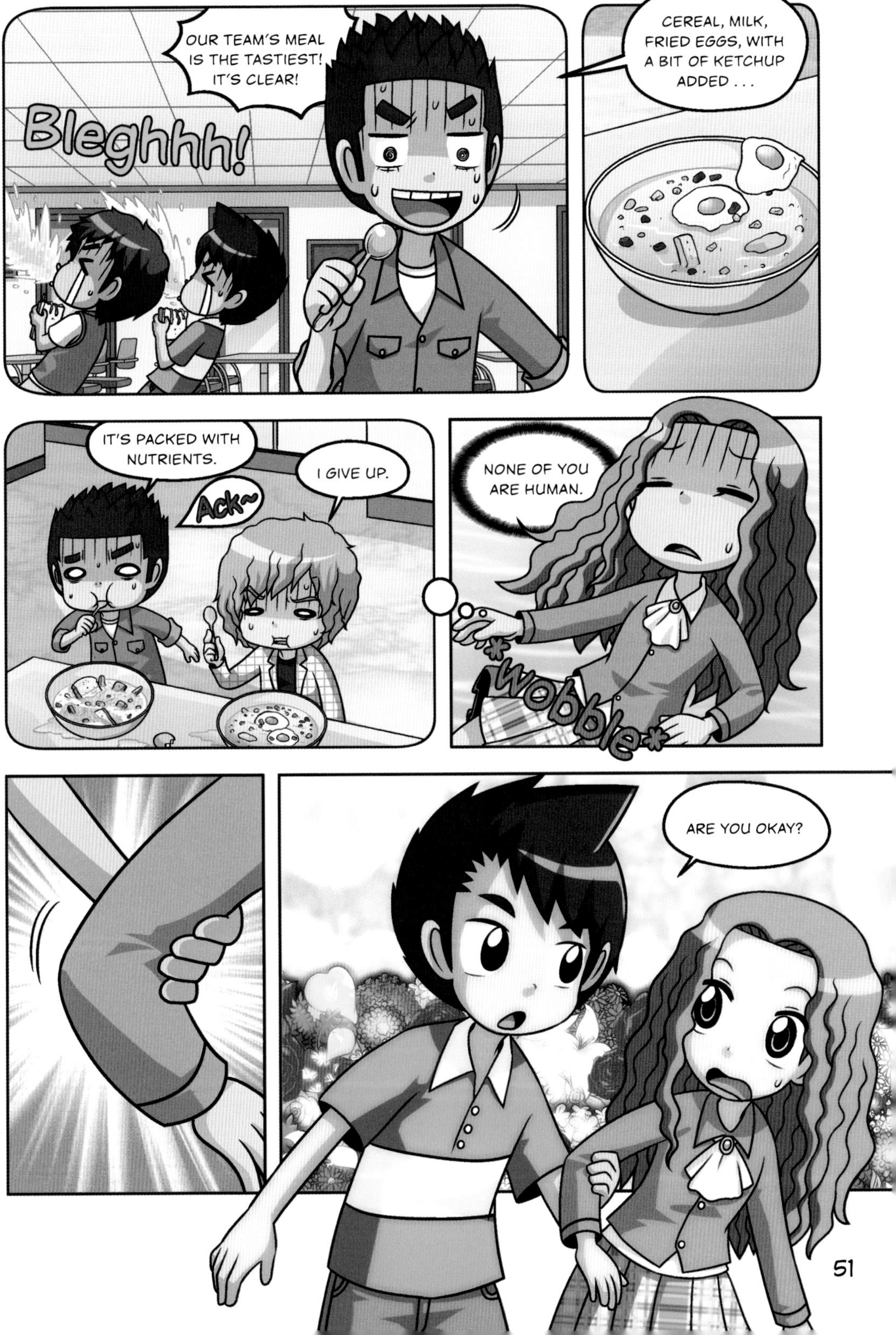
OUR TEAM'S MEAL IS THE TASTIEST! IT'S CLEAR!
Bleghhh!
CEREAL, MILK, FRIED EGGS, WITH A BIT OF KETCHUP ADDED . . .
IT'S PACKED WITH NUTRIENTS.
Ack~
I GIVE UP.
NONE OF YOU ARE HUMAN.
wobble
ARE YOU OKAY?

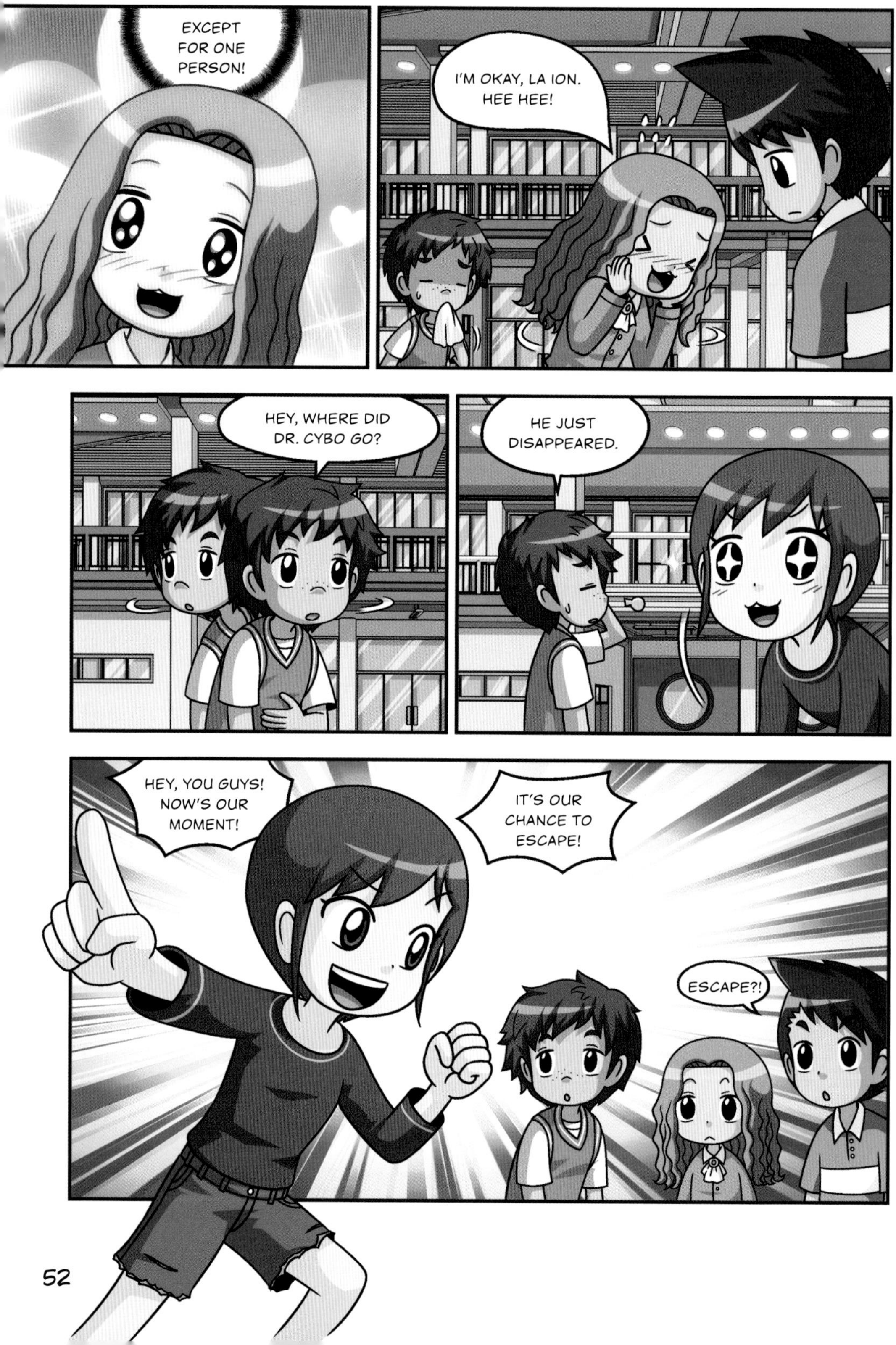
EXCEPT FOR ONE PERSON!
I'M OKAY, LA ION. HEE HEE!
HEY, WHERE DID DR. CYBO GO?
HE JUST DISAPPEARED.
HEY, YOU GUYS! NOW'S OUR MOMENT!
IT'S OUR CHANCE TO ESCAPE!
ESCAPE?!

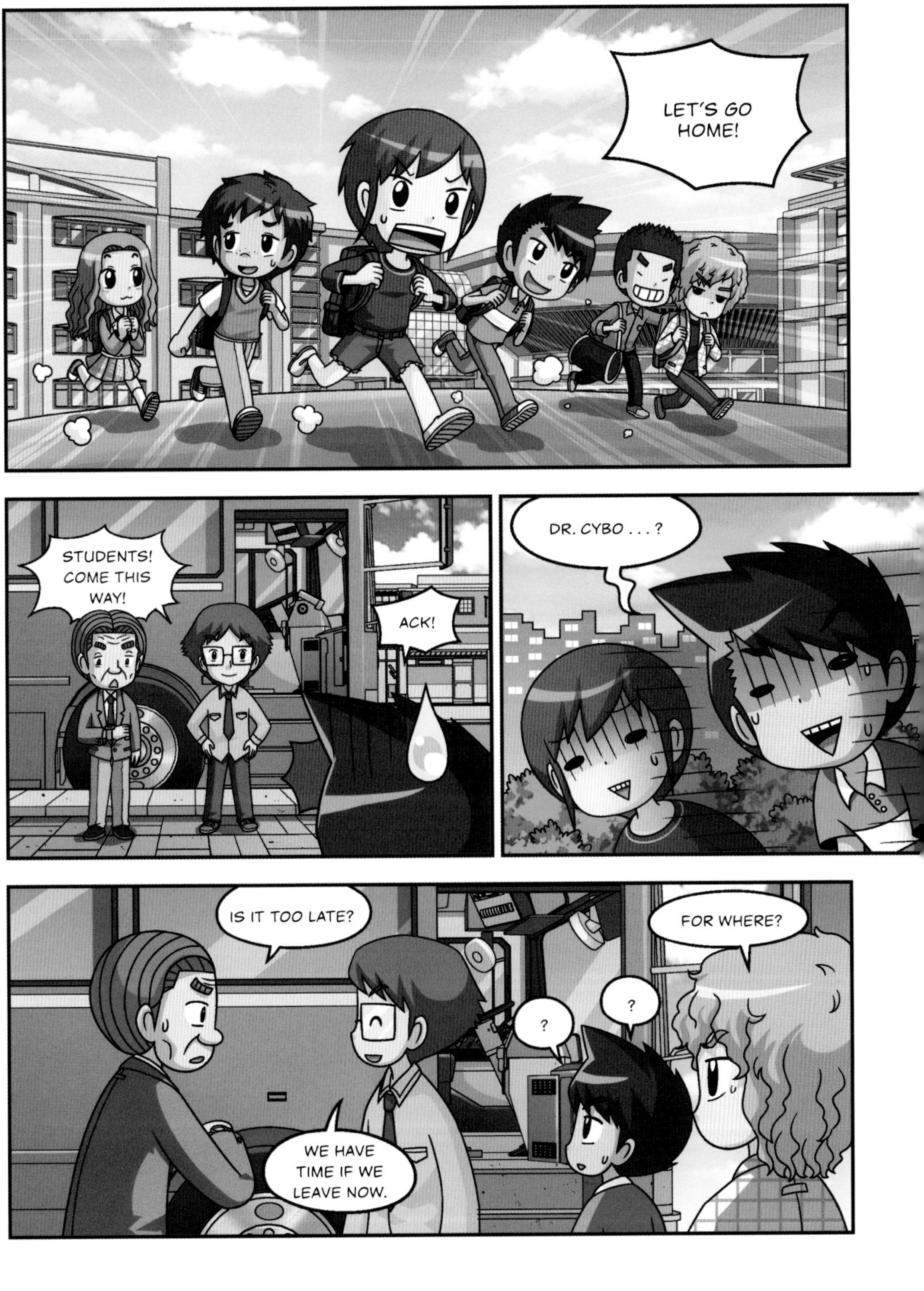
LET'S GO HOME!
STUDENTS! COME THIS WAY!
ACK!
DR. CYBO . . . ?
IS IT TOO LATE?
WE HAVE TIME IF WE LEAVE NOW.
?
?
FOR WHERE?

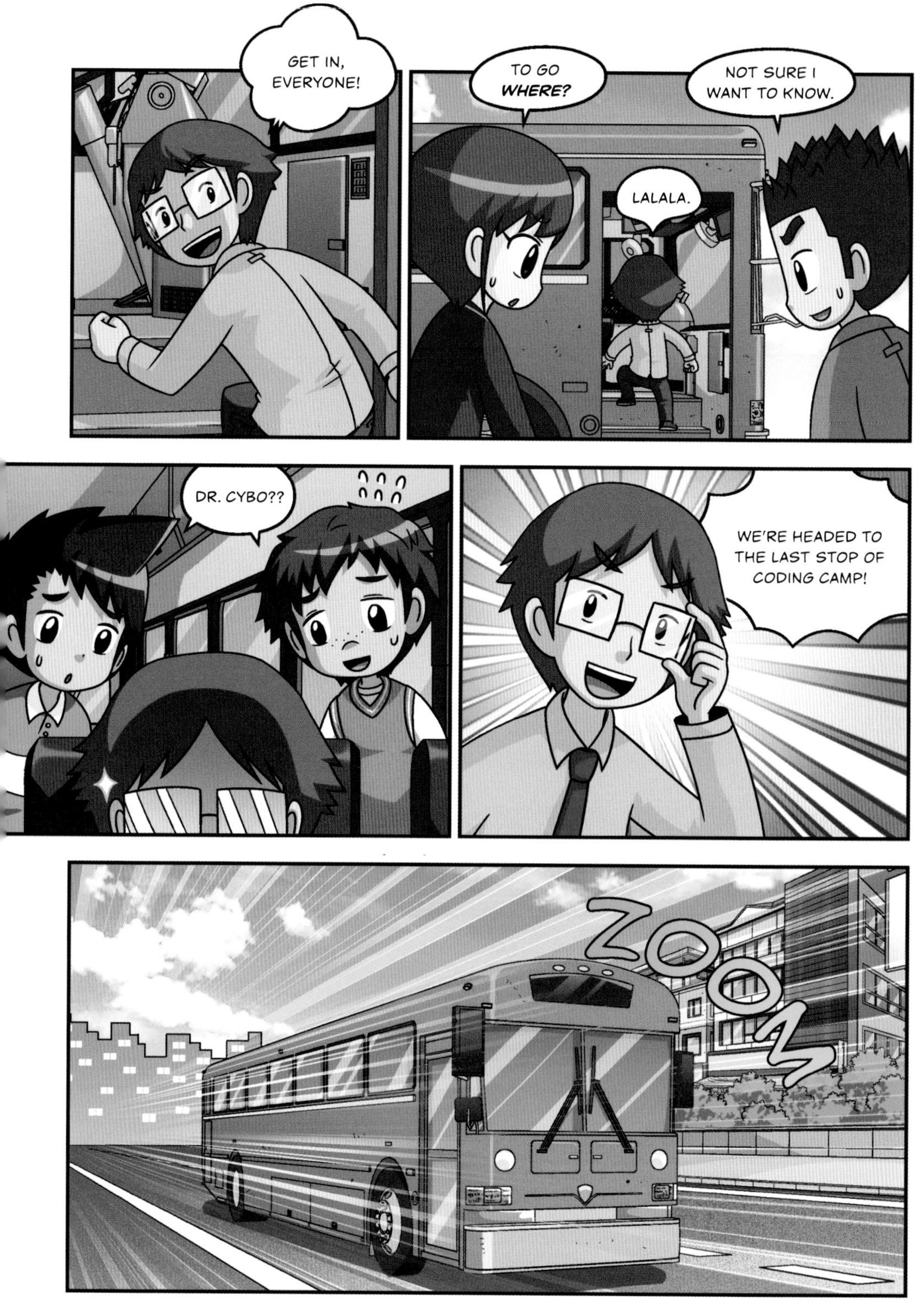
GET IN, EVERYONE!
TO GO WHERE?
LALALA.
NOT SURE I WANT TO KNOW.
DR. CYBO??
WE'RE HEADED TO THE LAST STOP OF CODING CAMP!
ZOOM

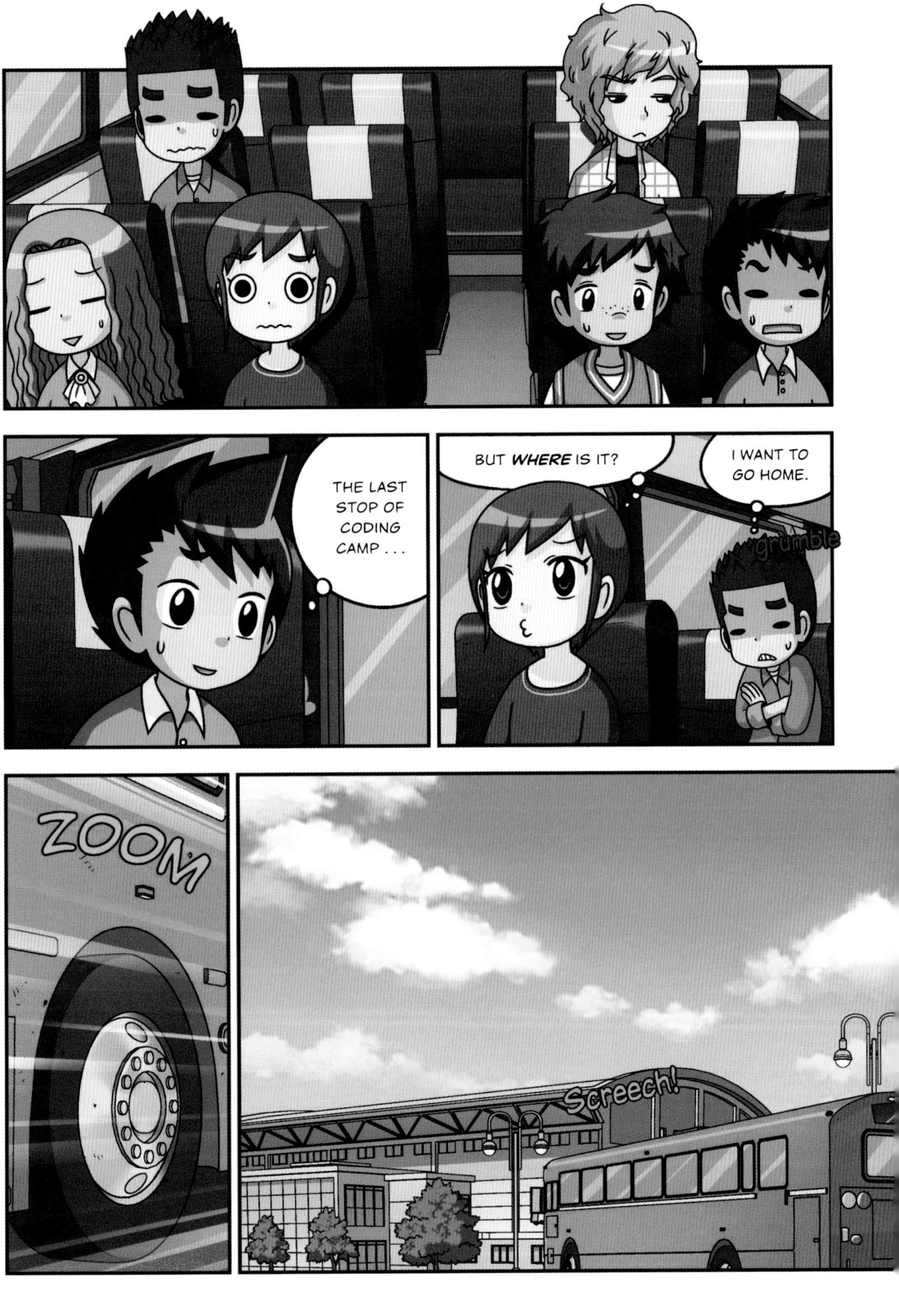
THE LAST STOP OF CODING CAMP . . .
BUT **WHERE** IS IT?
I WANT TO GO HOME.
grumble
ZOOM
Screech!

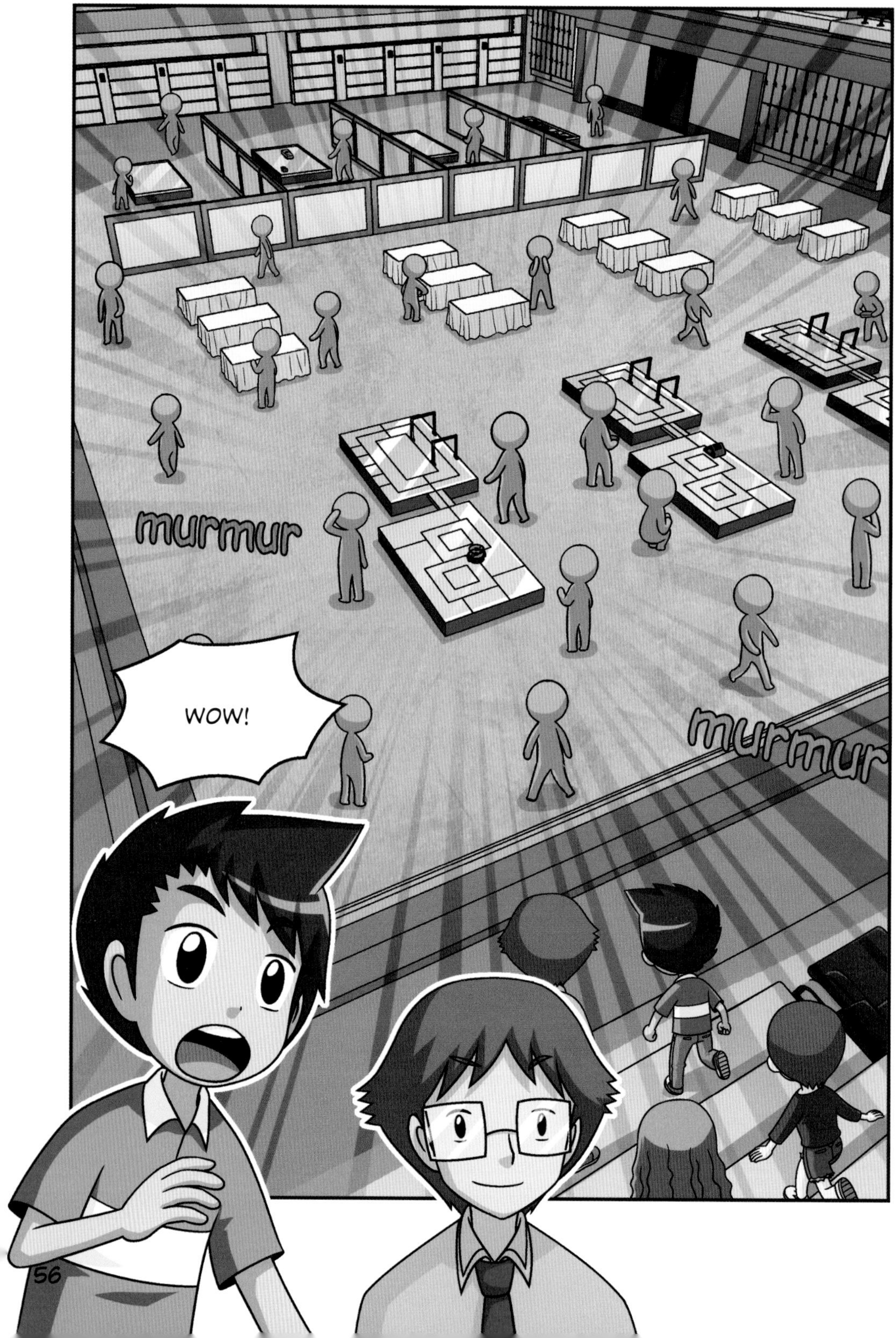
murmur
WOW!
murmur

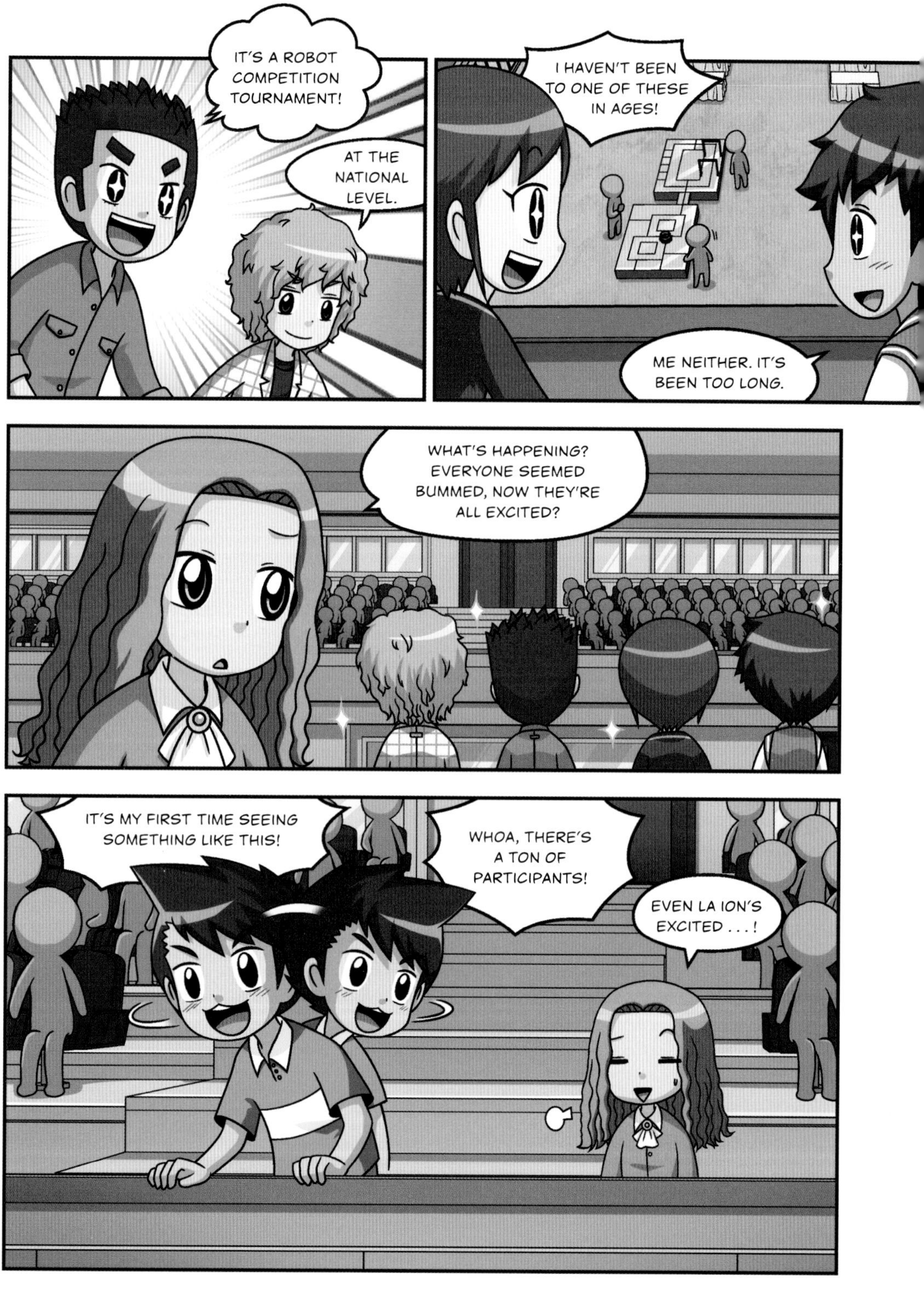
IT'S A ROBOT COMPETITION TOURNAMENT!
AT THE NATIONAL LEVEL.
I HAVEN'T BEEN TO ONE OF THESE IN AGES!
ME NEITHER. IT'S BEEN TOO LONG.
WHAT'S HAPPENING? EVERYONE SEEMED BUMMED, NOW THEY'RE ALL EXCITED?
IT'S MY FIRST TIME SEEING SOMETHING LIKE THIS!
WHOA, THERE'S A TON OF PARTICIPANTS!
EVEN LA ION'S EXCITED . . . !

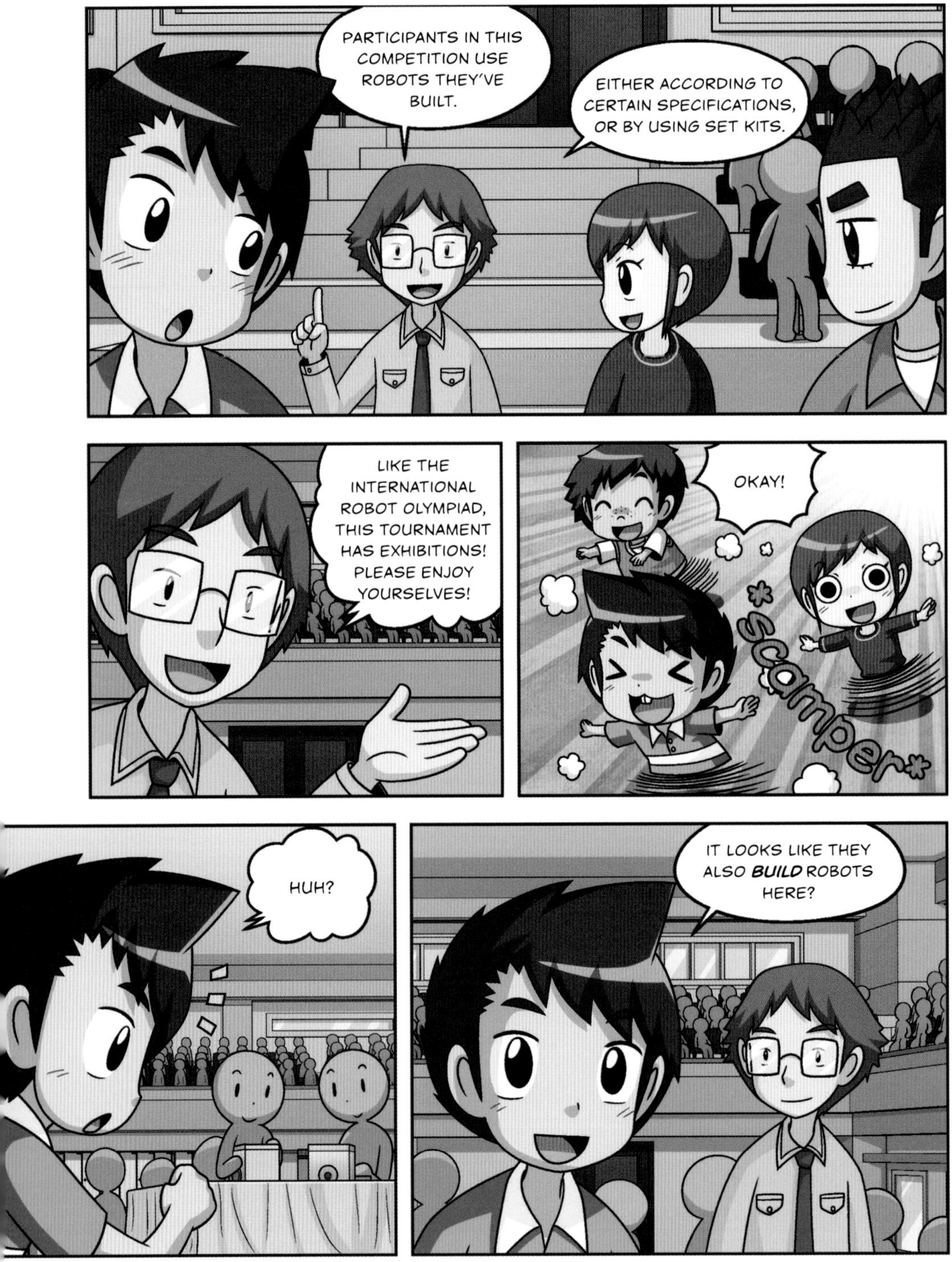
PARTICIPANTS IN THIS COMPETITION USE ROBOTS THEY'VE BUILT.
EITHER ACCORDING TO CERTAIN SPECIFICATIONS, OR BY USING SET KITS.
LIKE THE INTERNATIONAL ROBOT OLYMPIAD, THIS TOURNAMENT HAS EXHIBITIONS! PLEASE ENJOY YOURSELVES!
OKAY!
scamper
HUH?
IT LOOKS LIKE THEY ALSO **BUILD** ROBOTS HERE?

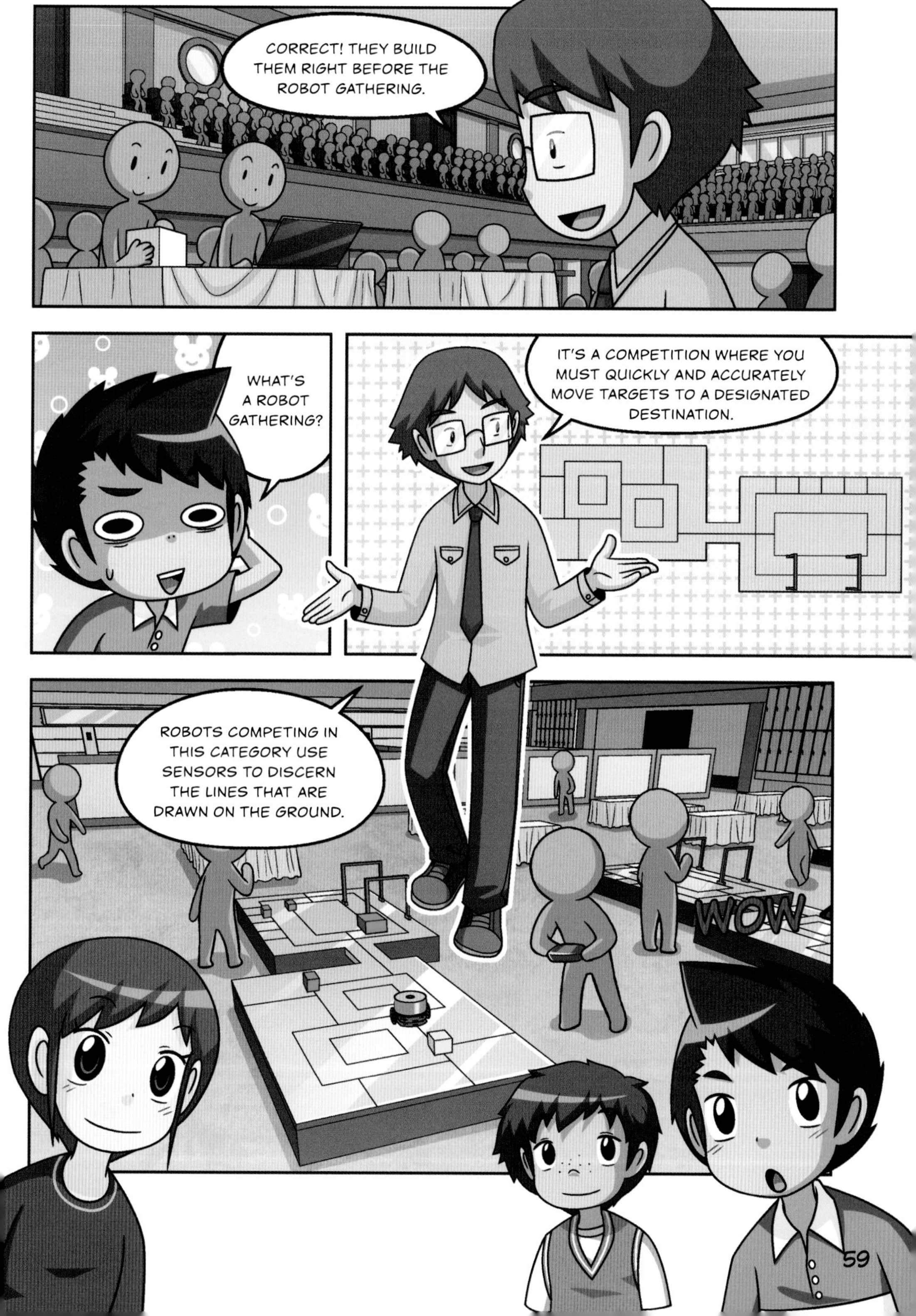
CORRECT! THEY BUILD THEM RIGHT BEFORE THE ROBOT GATHERING.
WHAT'S A ROBOT GATHERING?
IT'S A COMPETITION WHERE YOU MUST QUICKLY AND ACCURATELY MOVE TARGETS TO A DESIGNATED DESTINATION.
ROBOTS COMPETING IN THIS CATEGORY USE SENSORS TO DISCERN THE LINES THAT ARE DRAWN ON THE GROUND.
WOW

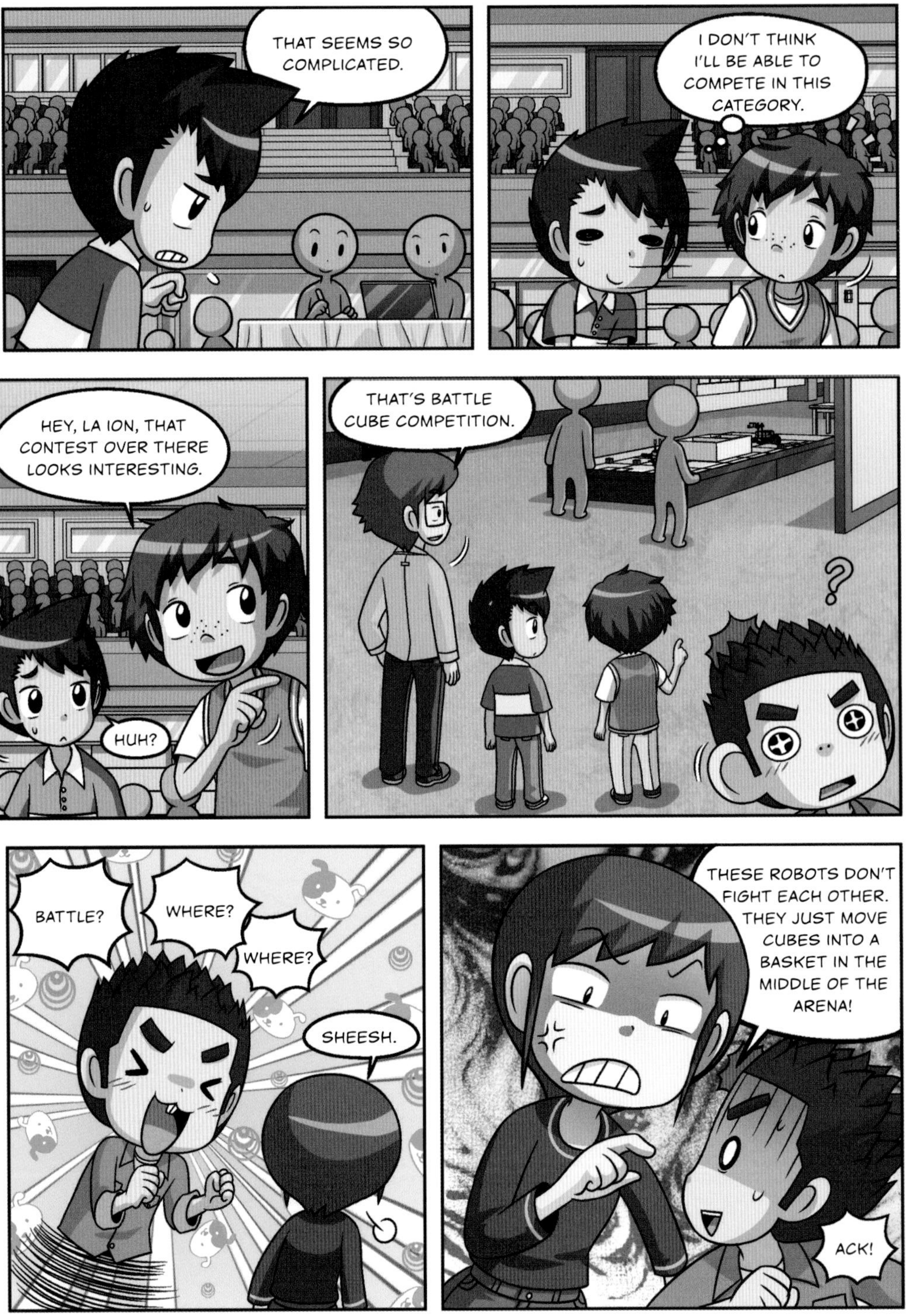
THAT SEEMS SO COMPLICATED.
I DON'T THINK I'LL BE ABLE TO COMPETE IN THIS CATEGORY.
HEY, LA ION, THAT CONTEST OVER THERE LOOKS INTERESTING.
HUH?
THAT'S BATTLE CUBE COMPETITION.
?
BATTLE?
WHERE?
WHERE?
SHEESH.
THESE ROBOTS DON'T FIGHT EACH OTHER. THEY JUST MOVE CUBES INTO A BASKET IN THE MIDDLE OF THE ARENA!
ACK!

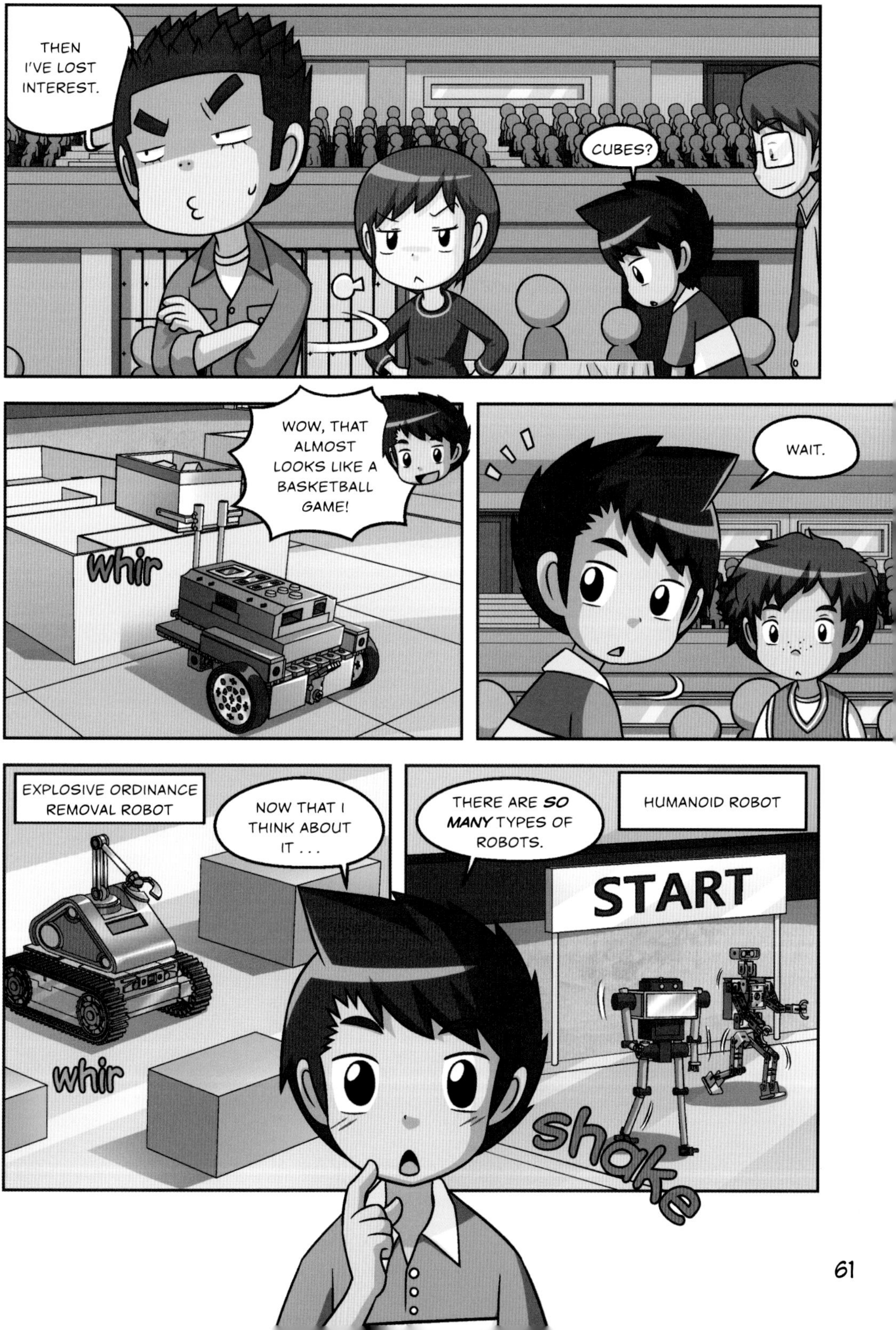
THEN I'VE LOST INTEREST.
CUBES?
whir
WOW, THAT ALMOST LOOKS LIKE A BASKETBALL GAME!
WAIT.
EXPLOSIVE ORDINANCE REMOVAL ROBOT
NOW THAT I THINK ABOUT IT . . .
whir
THERE ARE ***SO MANY*** TYPES OF ROBOTS.
HUMANOID ROBOT
START
shake

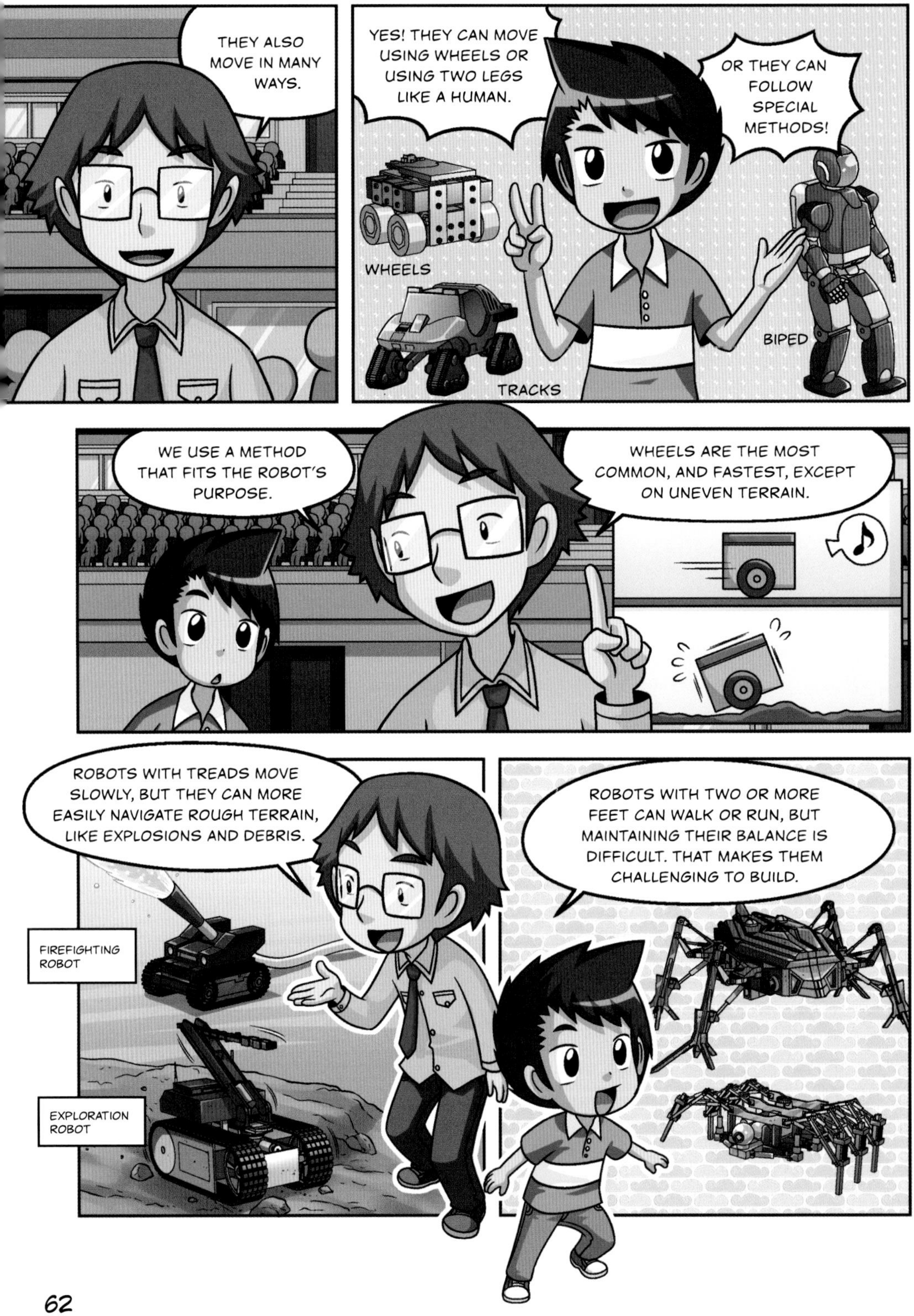
THEY ALSO MOVE IN MANY WAYS.
YES! THEY CAN MOVE USING WHEELS OR USING TWO LEGS LIKE A HUMAN.
OR THEY CAN FOLLOW SPECIAL METHODS!
WHEELS
TRACKS
BIPED
WE USE A METHOD THAT FITS THE ROBOT'S PURPOSE.
WHEELS ARE THE MOST COMMON, AND FASTEST, EXCEPT ON UNEVEN TERRAIN.
ROBOTS WITH TREADS MOVE SLOWLY, BUT THEY CAN MORE EASILY NAVIGATE ROUGH TERRAIN, LIKE EXPLOSIONS AND DEBRIS.
FIREFIGHTING ROBOT
EXPLORATION ROBOT
ROBOTS WITH TWO OR MORE FEET CAN WALK OR RUN, BUT MAINTAINING THEIR BALANCE IS DIFFICULT. THAT MAKES THEM CHALLENGING TO BUILD.

THAT ROBOT MAKES IT LOOK EASY.

shake

shake

WHAM

BALANCING ON TWO LEGS IS MORE DIFFICULT THAN YOU'D THINK.

OH, NO!

SO THEY OFTEN FALL OVER LIKE THAT.

HUMANS HAVE A CENTER OF GRAVITY AND AN INNATE SENSE OF BALANCE.

CENTER OF GRAVITY

WHEN STANDING

WHEN WALKING

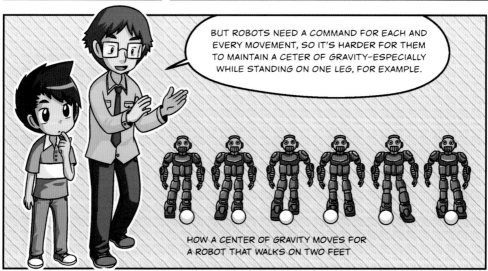

BUT ROBOTS NEED A COMMAND FOR EACH AND EVERY MOVEMENT, SO IT'S HARDER FOR THEM TO MAINTAIN A CETER OF GRAVITY–ESPECIALLY WHILE STANDING ON ONE LEG, FOR EXAMPLE.

HOW A CENTER OF GRAVITY MOVES FOR A ROBOT THAT WALKS ON TWO FEET

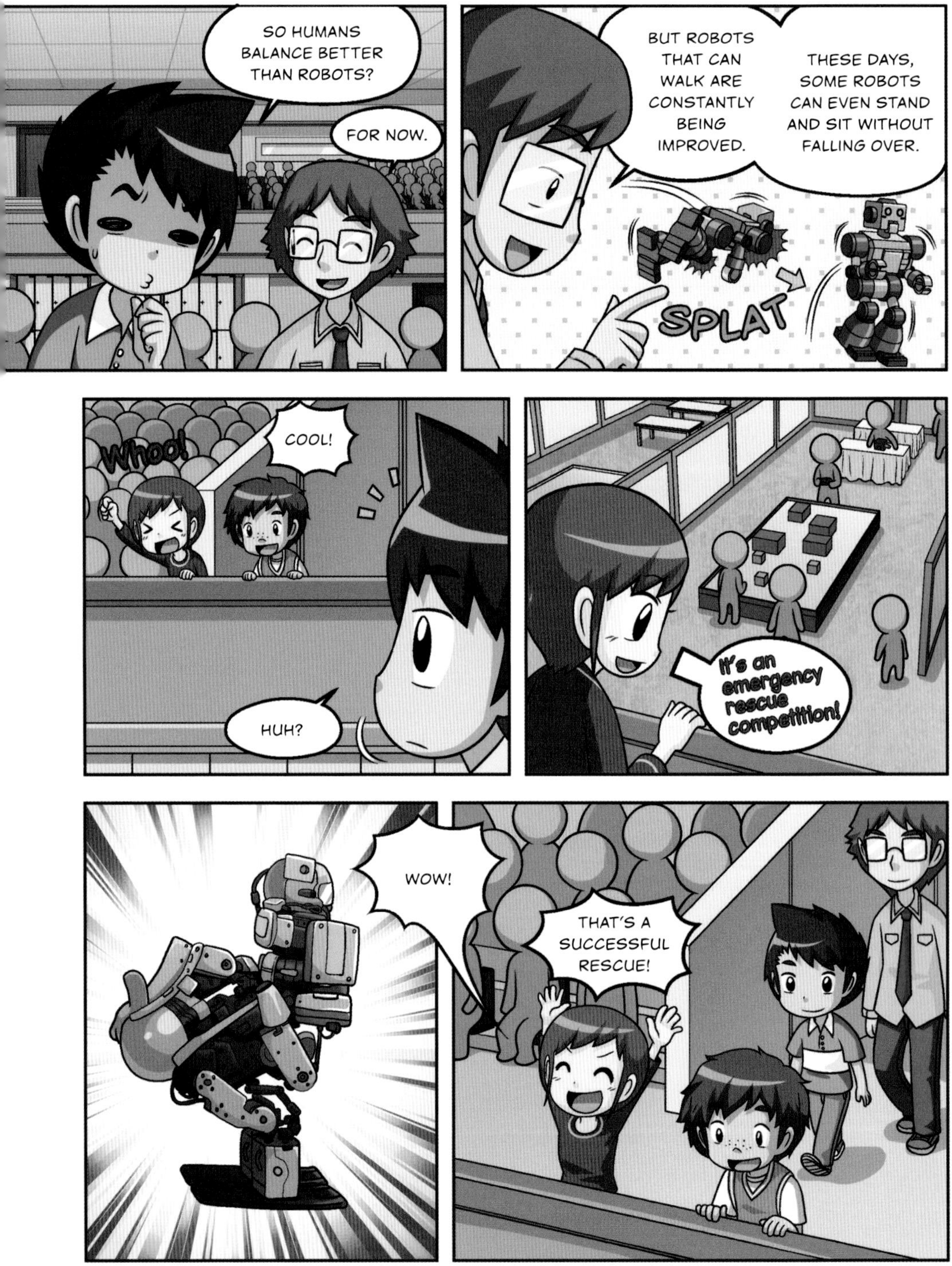

SO HUMANS BALANCE BETTER THAN ROBOTS?
FOR NOW.
BUT ROBOTS THAT CAN WALK ARE CONSTANTLY BEING IMPROVED.
THESE DAYS, SOME ROBOTS CAN EVEN STAND AND SIT WITHOUT FALLING OVER.
SPLAT
Whoo!
COOL!
HUH?
It's an emergency rescue competition!
WOW!
THAT'S A SUCCESSFUL RESCUE!

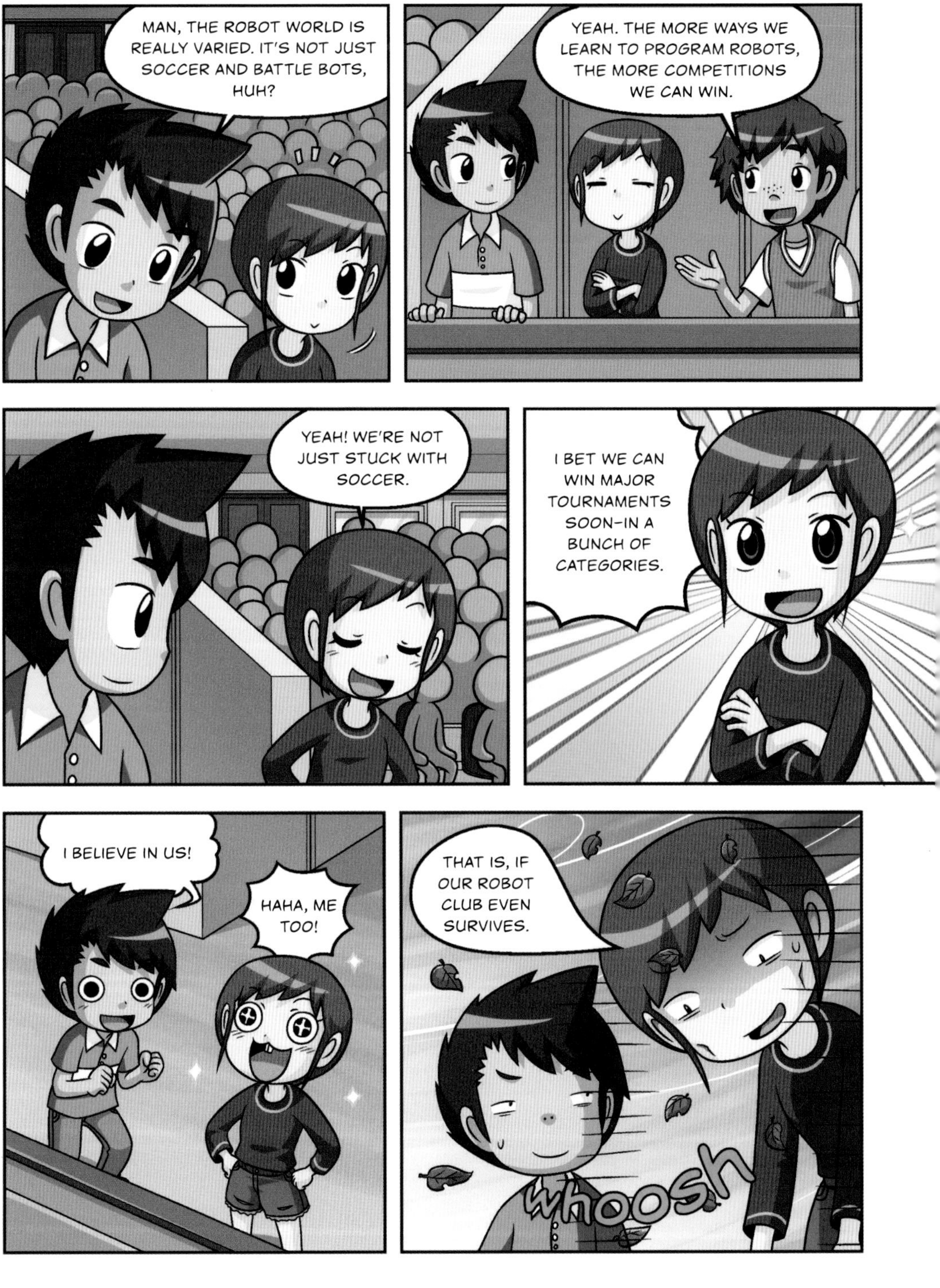

MAN, THE ROBOT WORLD IS REALLY VARIED. IT'S NOT JUST SOCCER AND BATTLE BOTS, HUH?
YEAH. THE MORE WAYS WE LEARN TO PROGRAM ROBOTS, THE MORE COMPETITIONS WE CAN WIN.
YEAH! WE'RE NOT JUST STUCK WITH SOCCER.
I BET WE CAN WIN MAJOR TOURNAMENTS SOON—IN A BUNCH OF CATEGORIES.
I BELIEVE IN US!
HAHA, ME TOO!
THAT IS, IF OUR ROBOT CLUB EVEN SURVIVES.
whoosh

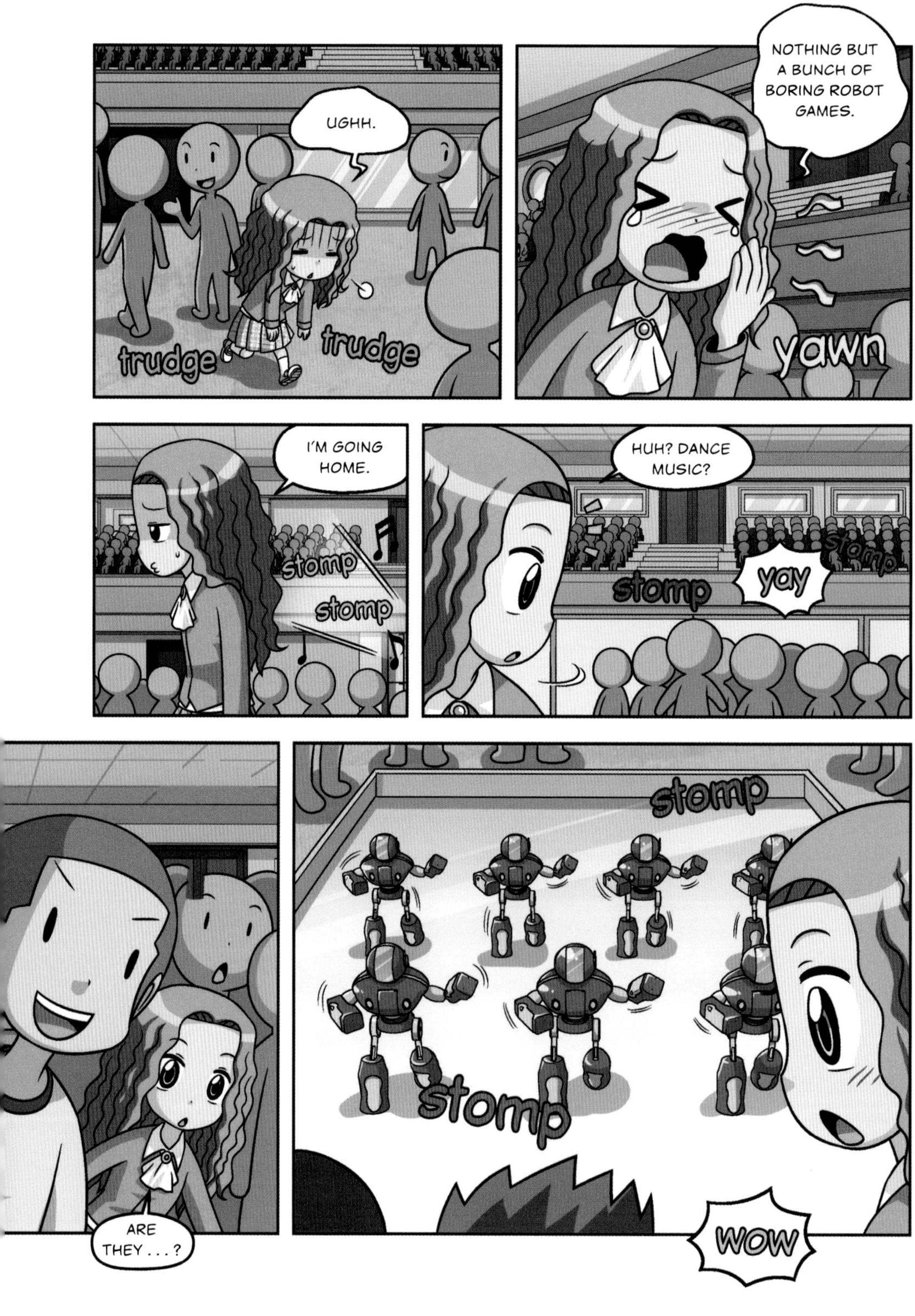
UGHH.
trudge
trudge
NOTHING BUT A BUNCH OF BORING ROBOT GAMES.
yawn
I'M GOING HOME.
stomp
stomp
HUH? DANCE MUSIC?
stomp
yay
stomp
ARE THEY . . . ?
stomp
stomp
WOW

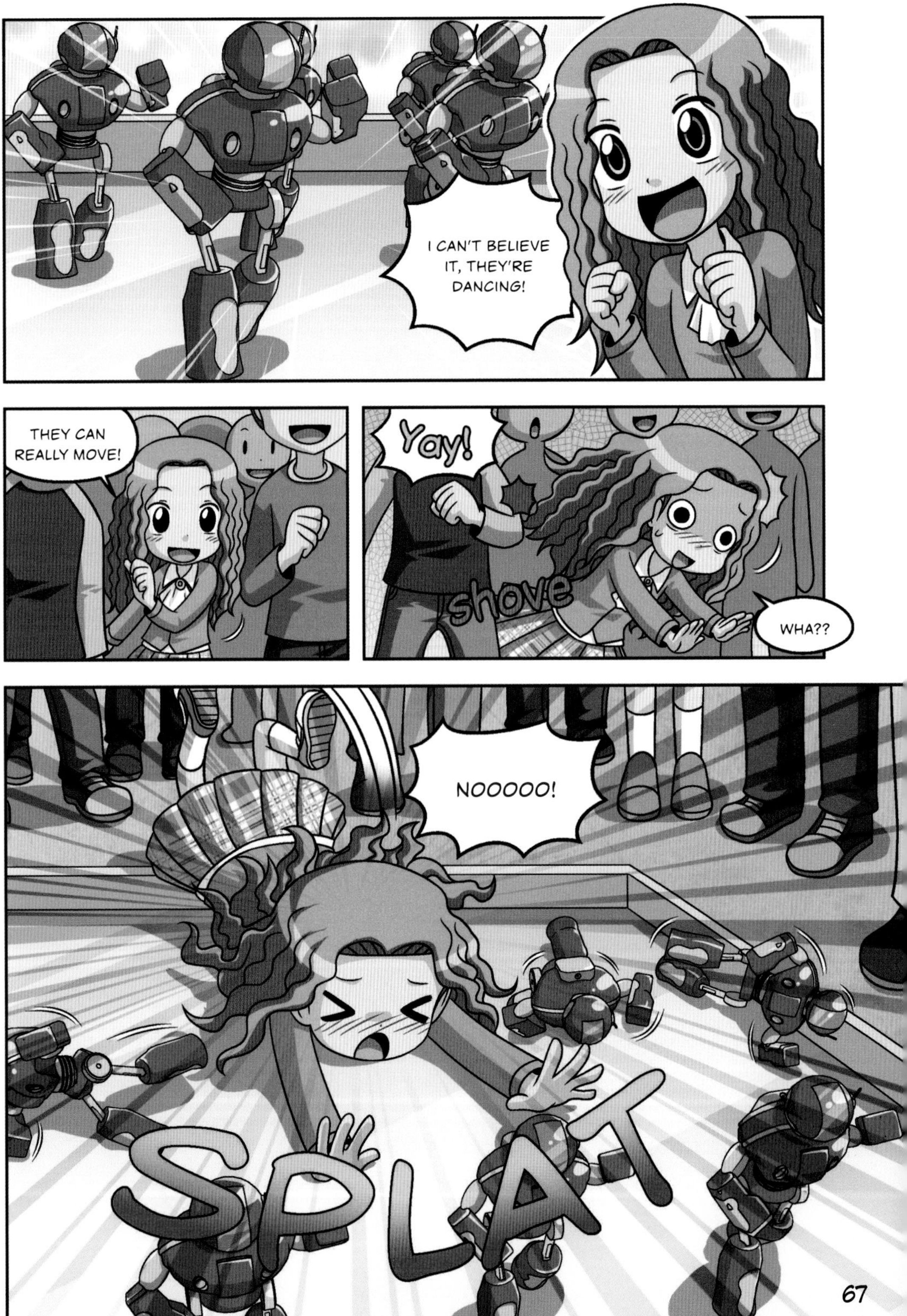
I CAN'T BELIEVE IT, THEY'RE DANCING!
THEY CAN REALLY MOVE!
Yay!
shove
WHA??
NOOOOO!
SPLAT

HUMANOID ROBOTS

A humanoid robot has a head, torso, arms, and legs, just like a human. And like a human, it often walks on two legs.

The First Humanoid Robot, WABOT

In 1973, Professor Ichiro Kato and his team at Tokyo's Waseda University completed work on WABOT-1. Many people consider this to be the first humanoid robot. It was able to walk on two legs, but only a few steps at a time at a very slow pace. The robot could also take part in simple, preprogrammed conversations in Japanese. In 1984, WABOT-2, an organ-playing robot, was invented. It was able to read musical scores and play the organ by hitting the instrument's pedals.

WABOT-1, the first humanoid robot

The Best Humanoid Robot?

In 2000, after years of development, the Honda company revealed the humanoid robot ASIMO (Advanced Step in Innovative Mobility). This robot was a breakthrough in the global humanoid robot industry. Since its initial development, engineers have continually upgraded ASIMO's appearance. The second model could not only walk but also run about 1.86 miles (3 km) per hour, making it the world's fastest humanoid robot. In 2011, a third model increased this speed to 5.6 mi (9 km) per hour. This third model

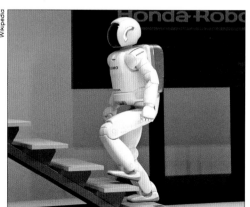

has been called the best yet for stable bipedal walking, running, and a natural movement of limbs. Honda retired ASIMO in 2022.

ASIMO 3 can walk up and down stairs.

Powered by Hydraulic Pump

In 2013, US robotics company Boston Dynamics announced the humanoid robot Atlas. Unlike robots that run on electric motors, this robot is powered by a hydraulic pump. That difference allows Atlas to produce explosive power in an instant. Atlas can walk and run on two feet as well as jump over obstacles and climb stairs. Thanks to its excellent control of its center of mass, it can land stably after doing a backflip, much like a gymnast. Atlas has been designed for recovery work in disaster zones.

flip

Atlas

PERFECT LANDING!

Hubo: Walking and Rolling

Developed by Professor Jun-Ho Oh and his team at the Korea Advanced Institute of Science and Technology (KAIST), Hubo is a humanoid disaster-response robot that can walk on two legs as well as move quickly on wheels built into its knees. In 2015, this humanoid robot won a worldwide disaster-robot competition. It was also selected as one of the relay runners for the PyeongChang 2018 Olympic Winter Games ceremonies, becoming the first robot bearer of the Olympic torch. The Hubo development team has continued research to make Hubo a multipurpose humanoid robot, rather than a single-purpose robot, to be utilized in many fields.

Wikipedia

Hubo participated in the torch relay ceremony at the PyeongChang 2018 Olympic Winter Games.

Chapter 4

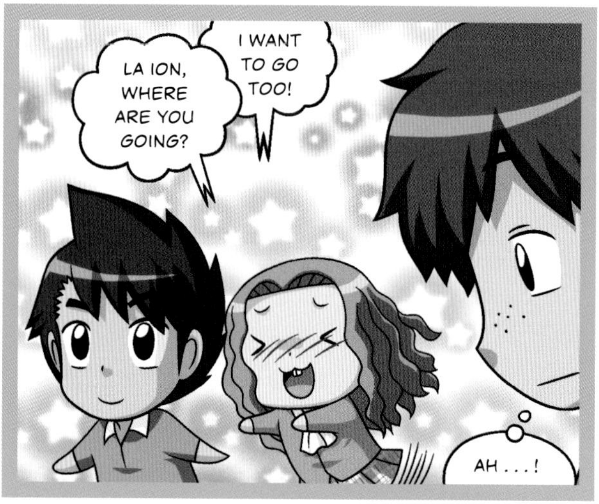
LA ION, WHERE ARE YOU GOING?
I WANT TO GO TOO!
AH . . . !

A Surprise Reunion

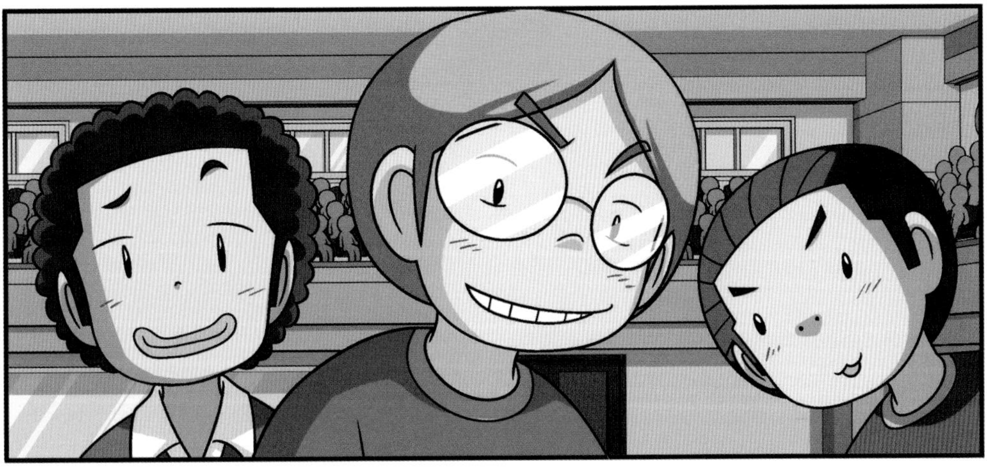

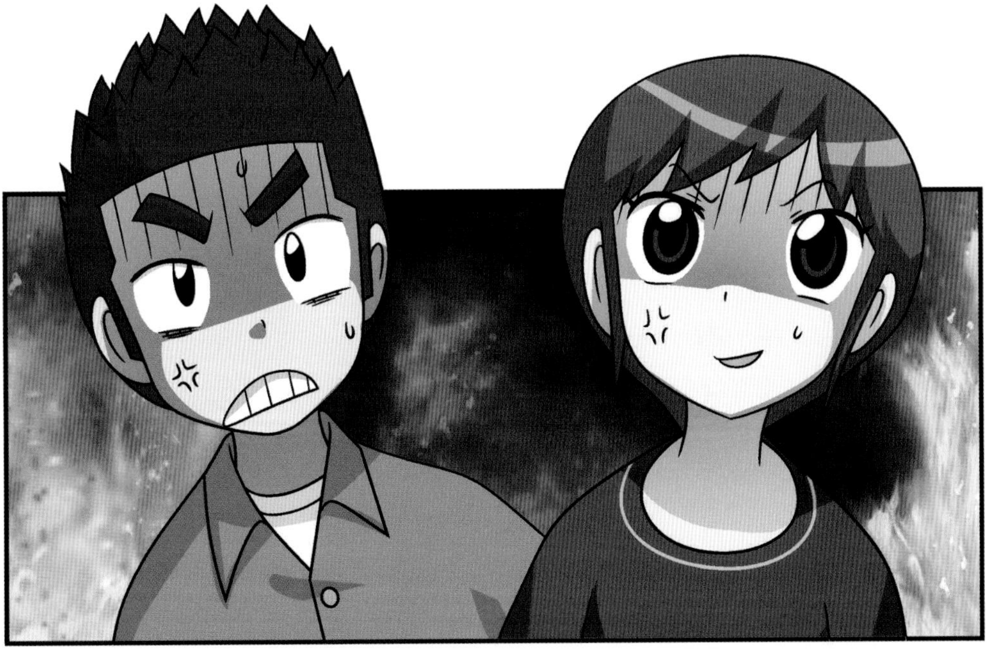

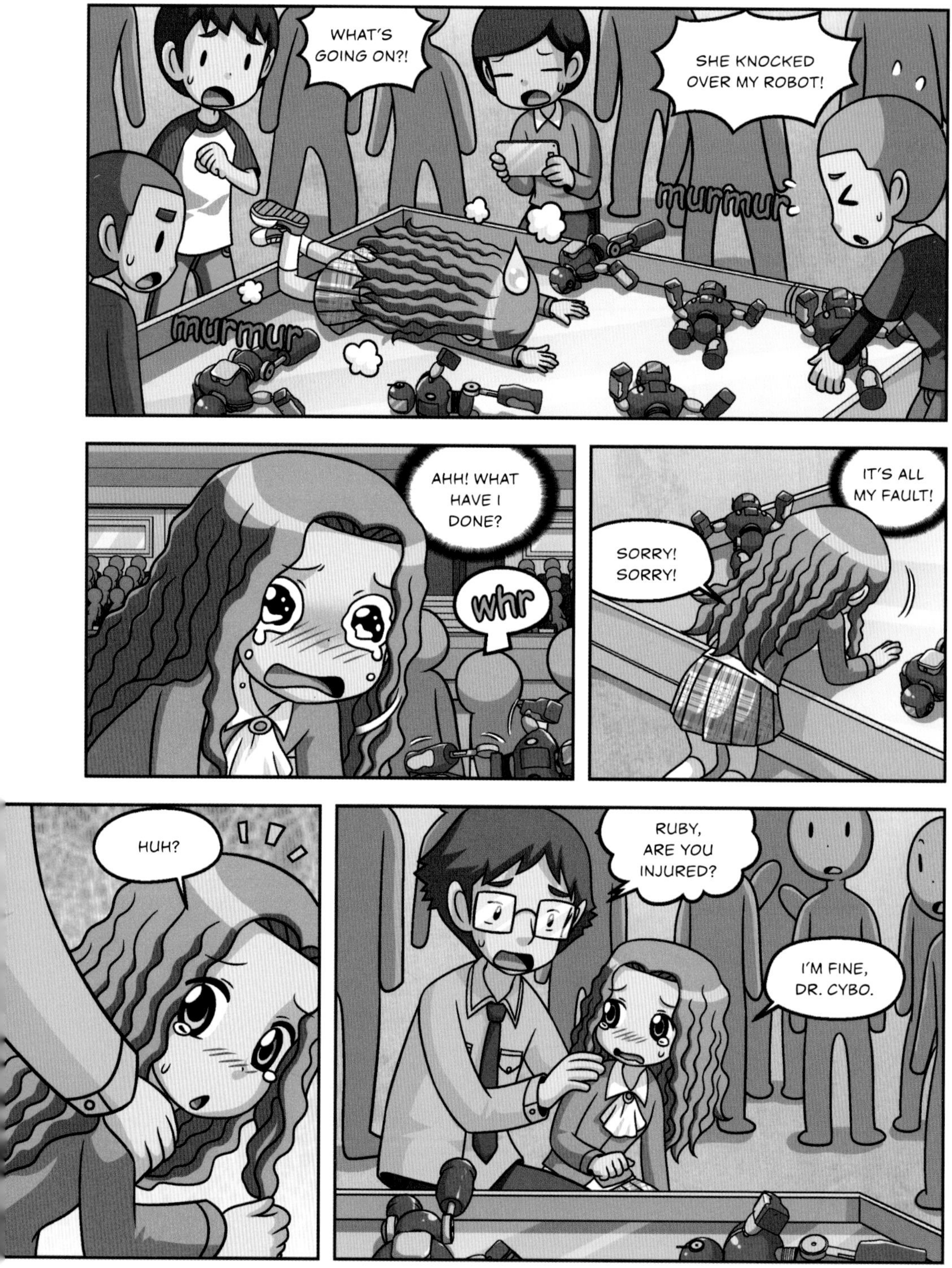
WHAT'S GOING ON?!
SHE KNOCKED OVER MY ROBOT!
murmur
murmur
AHH! WHAT HAVE I DONE?
whr
SORRY! SORRY!
IT'S ALL MY FAULT!
HUH?
RUBY, ARE YOU INJURED?
I'M FINE, DR. CYBO.

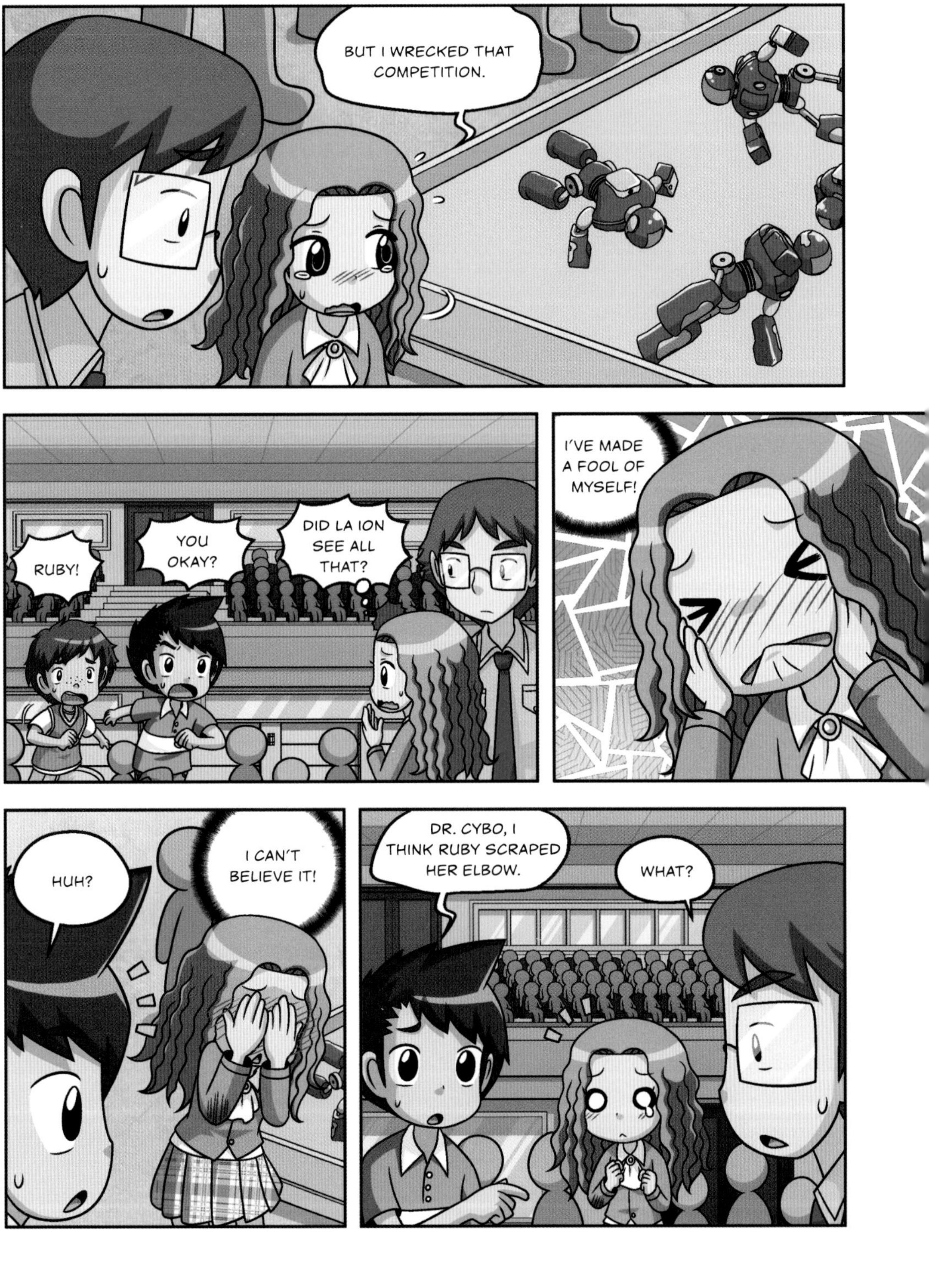
BUT I WRECKED THAT COMPETITION.
RUBY!
YOU OKAY?
DID LA ION SEE ALL THAT?
I'VE MADE A FOOL OF MYSELF!
HUH?
I CAN'T BELIEVE IT!
DR. CYBO, I THINK RUBY SCRAPED HER ELBOW.
WHAT?

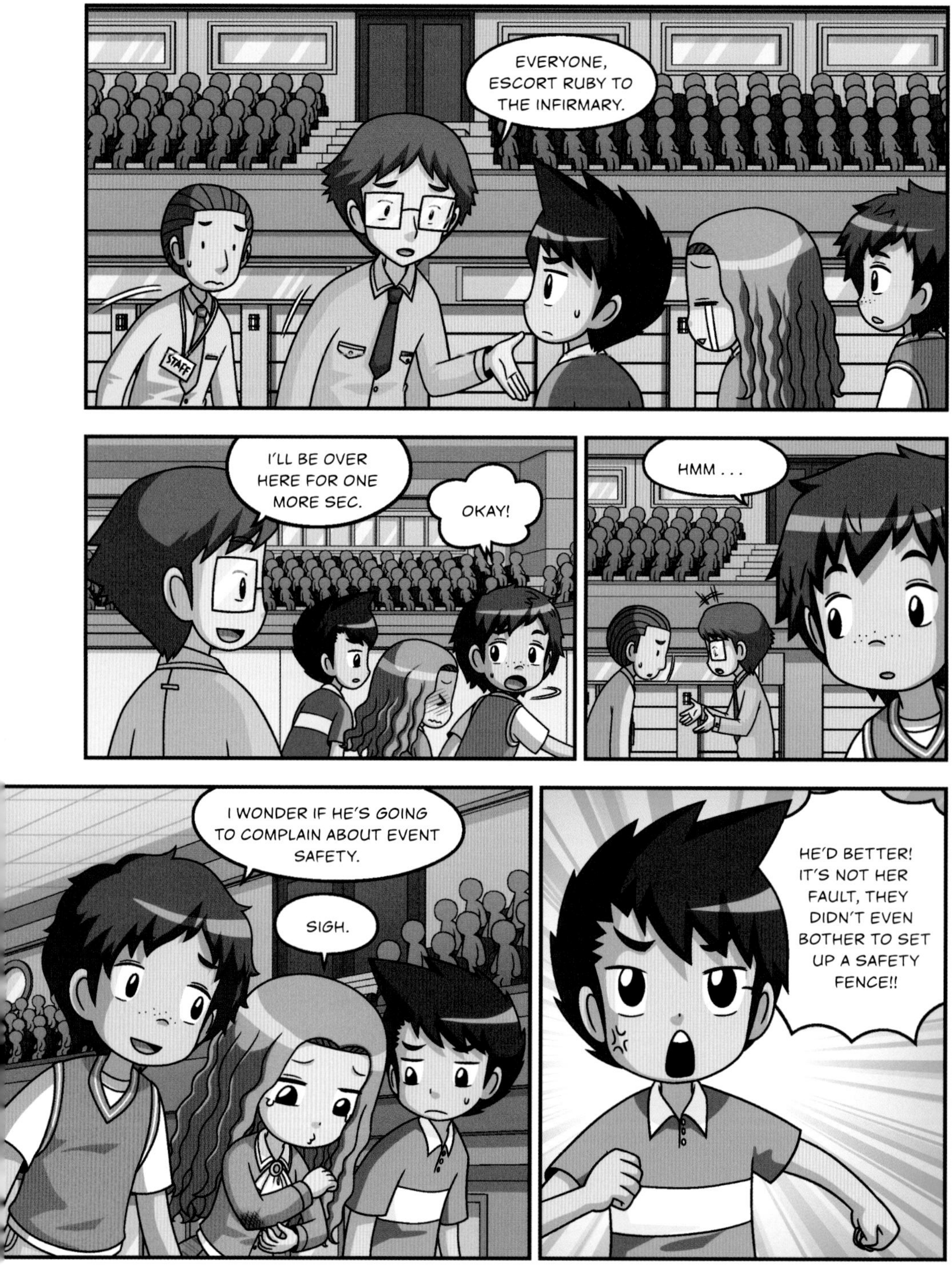
EVERYONE, ESCORT RUBY TO THE INFIRMARY.
STAFF
I'LL BE OVER HERE FOR ONE MORE SEC.
OKAY!
HMM . . .
I WONDER IF HE'S GOING TO COMPLAIN ABOUT EVENT SAFETY.
SIGH.
HE'D BETTER! IT'S NOT HER FAULT, THEY DIDN'T EVEN BOTHER TO SET UP A SAFETY FENCE!!

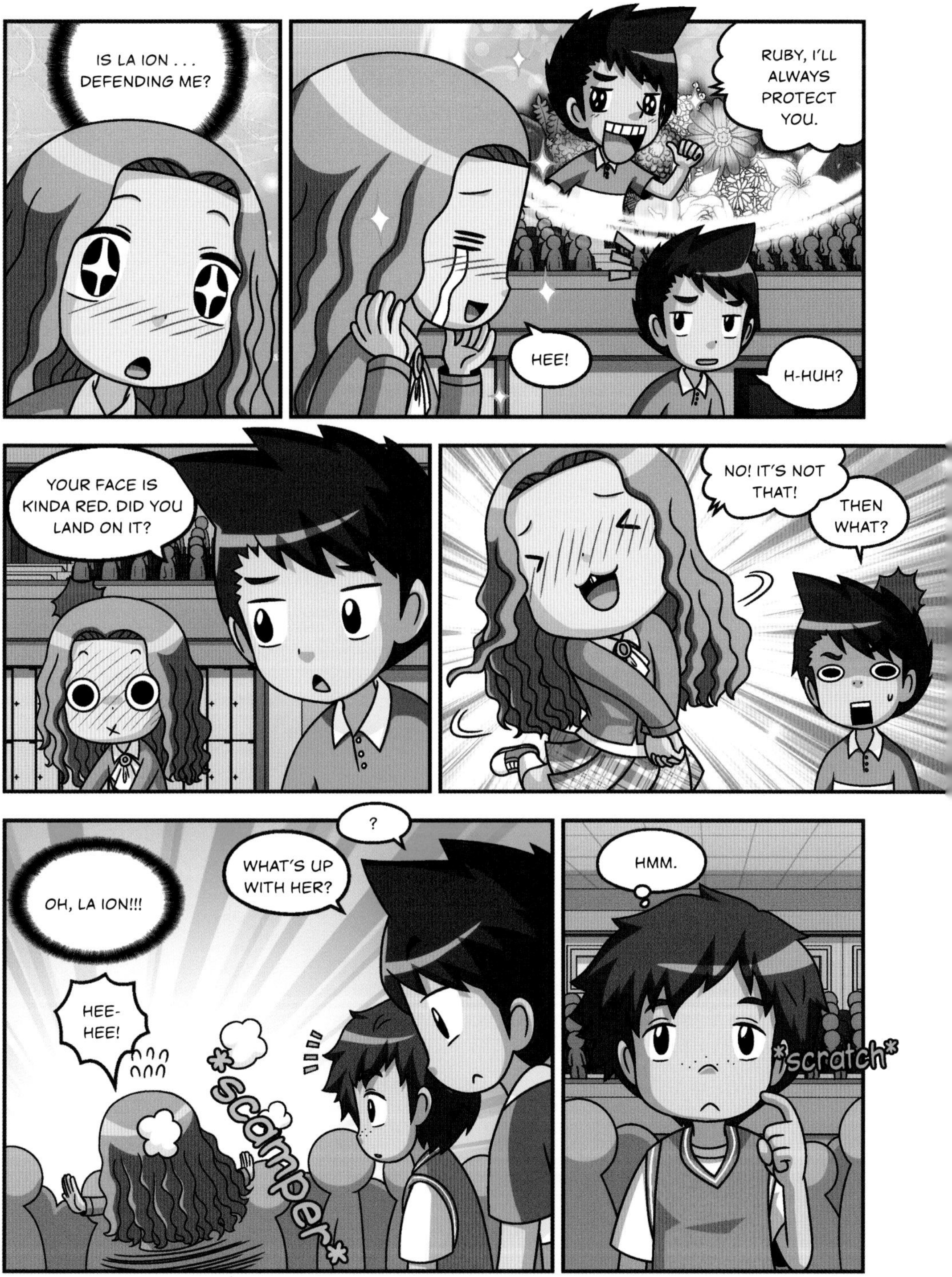
IS LA ION . . . DEFENDING ME?
RUBY, I'LL ALWAYS PROTECT YOU.
HEE!
H-HUH?
YOUR FACE IS KINDA RED. DID YOU LAND ON IT?
NO! IT'S NOT THAT!
THEN WHAT?
OH, LA ION!!!
HEE-HEE!
scamper
?
WHAT'S UP WITH HER?
HMM.
scratch

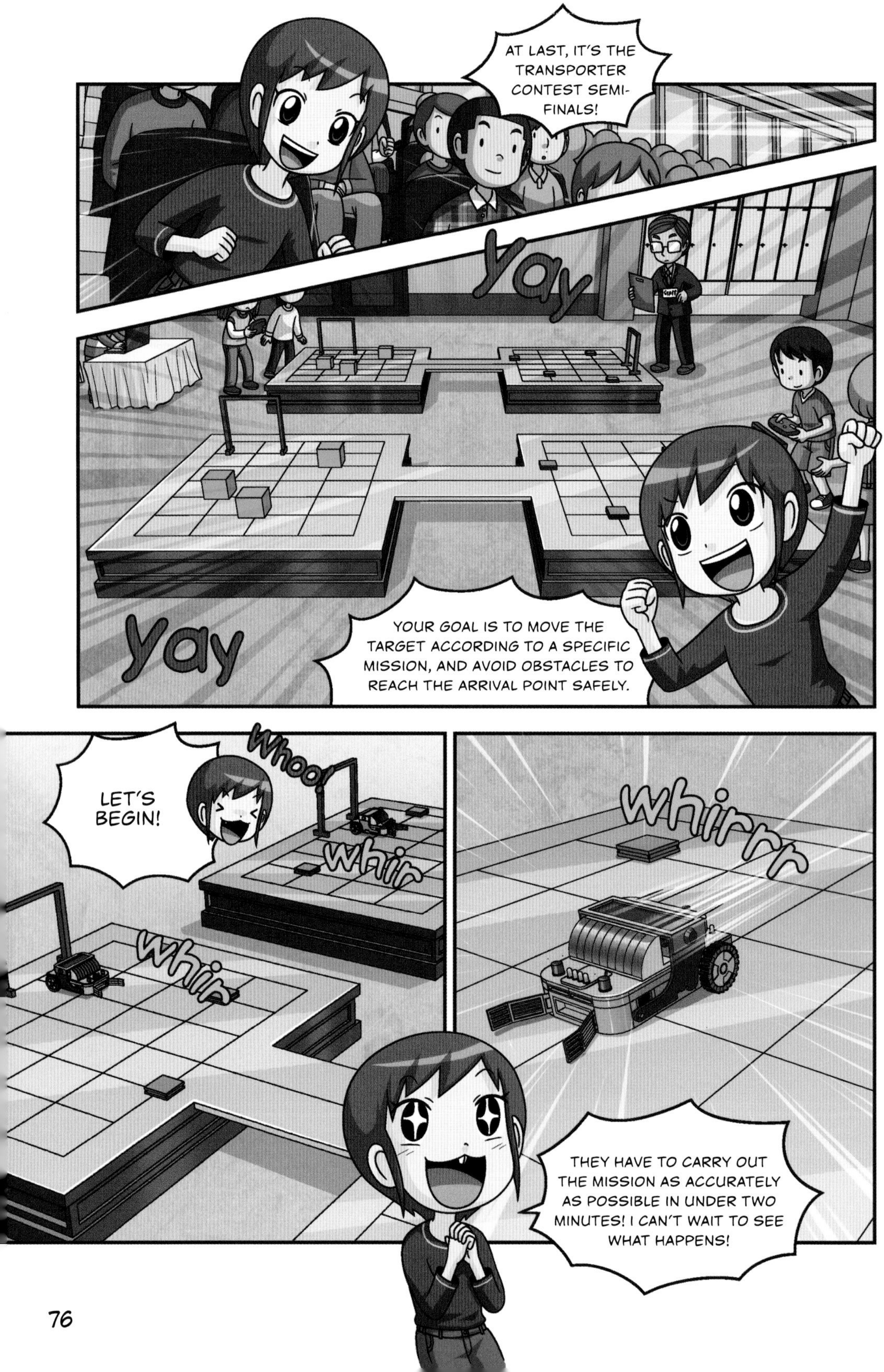

AT LAST, IT'S THE TRANSPORTER CONTEST SEMI-FINALS!
yay
yay
YOUR GOAL IS TO MOVE THE TARGET ACCORDING TO A SPECIFIC MISSION, AND AVOID OBSTACLES TO REACH THE ARRIVAL POINT SAFELY.
LET'S BEGIN!
Whoo!
whir
whir
whirrr
THEY HAVE TO CARRY OUT THE MISSION AS ACCURATELY AS POSSIBLE IN UNDER TWO MINUTES! I CAN'T WAIT TO SEE WHAT HAPPENS!

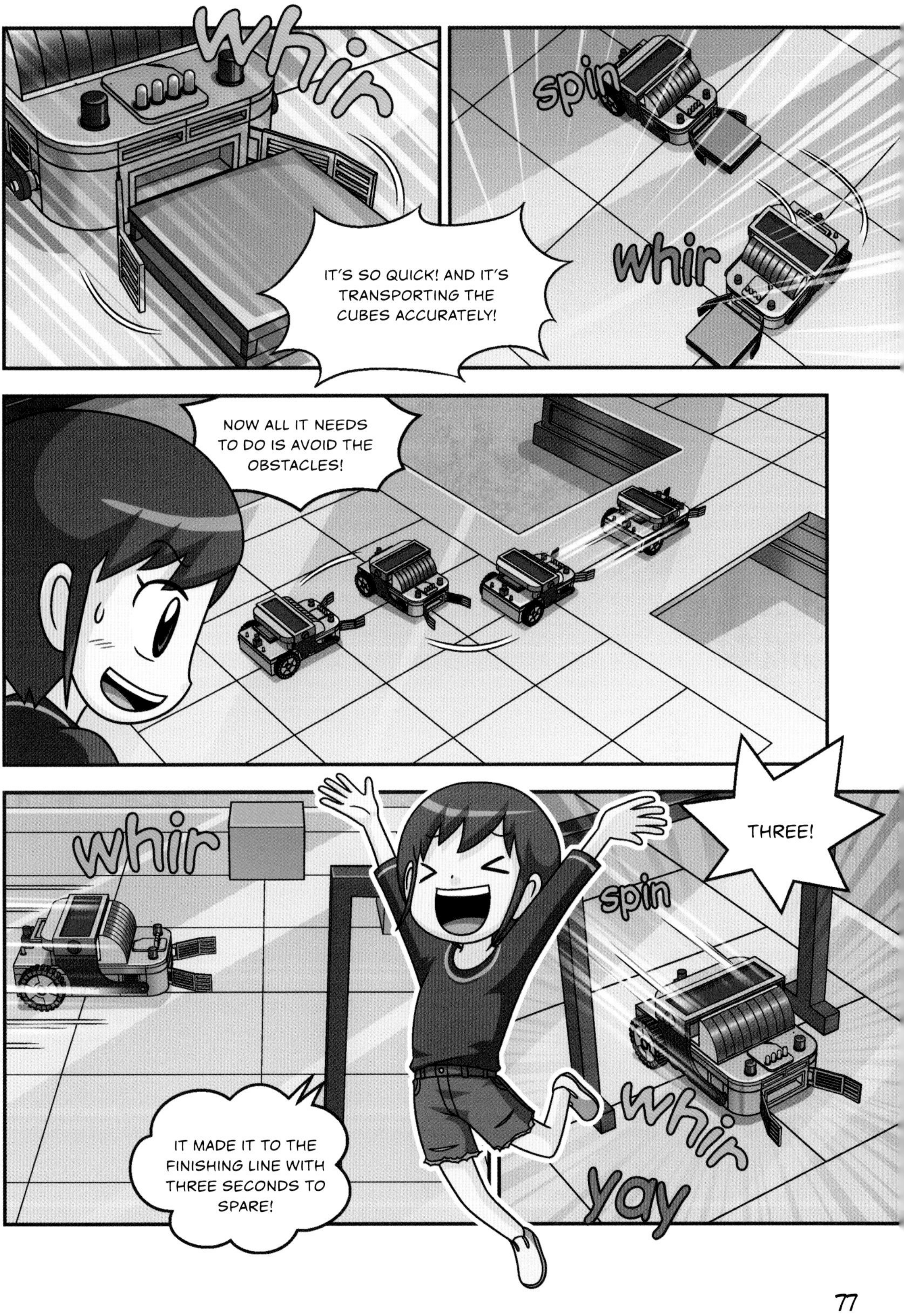
whir
spin
whir
IT'S SO QUICK! AND IT'S TRANSPORTING THE CUBES ACCURATELY!
NOW ALL IT NEEDS TO DO IS AVOID THE OBSTACLES!
whir
THREE!
spin
IT MADE IT TO THE FINISHING LINE WITH THREE SECONDS TO SPARE!
whir
yay

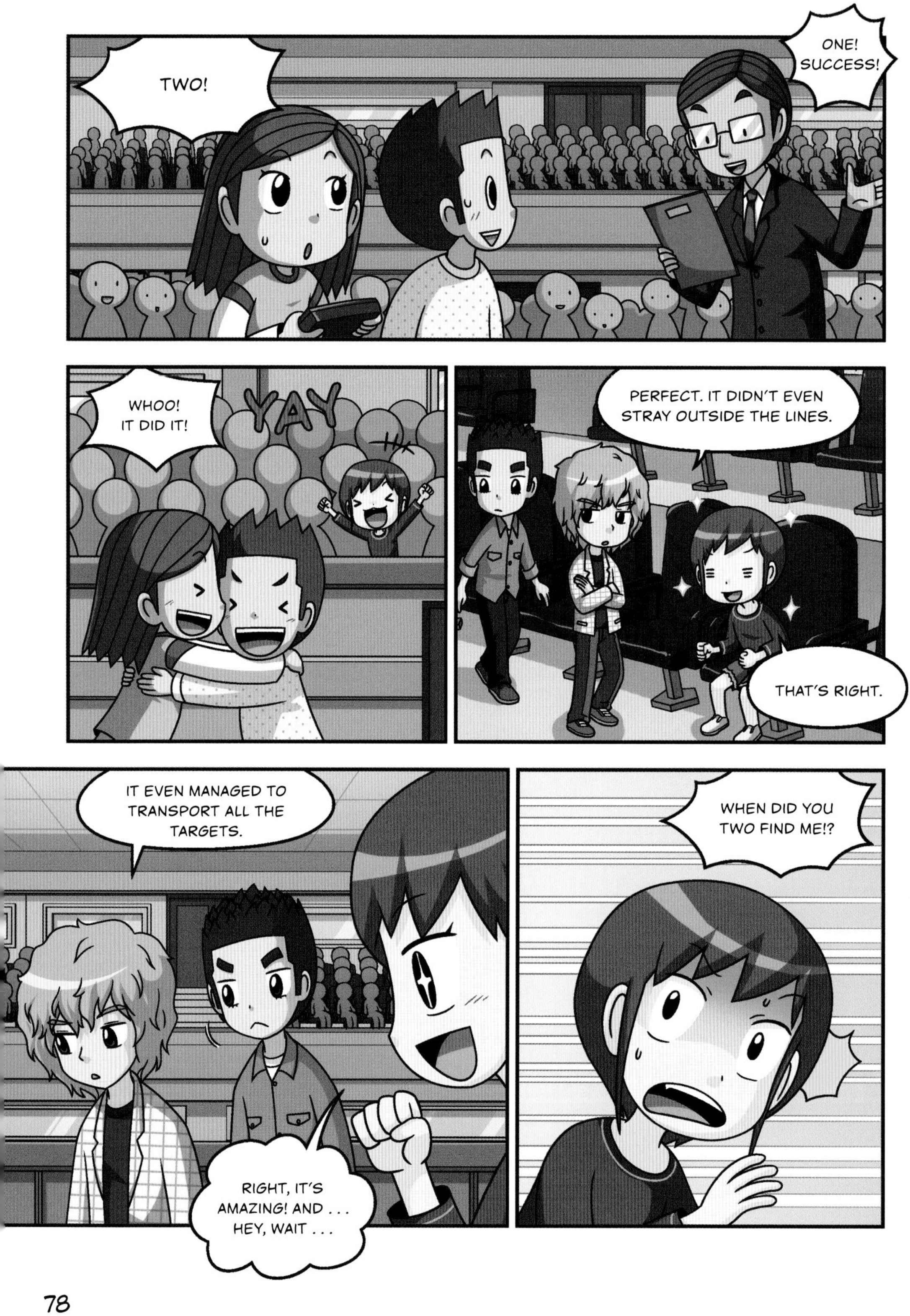
TWO!
ONE! SUCCESS!
WHOO! IT DID IT!
YAY
PERFECT. IT DIDN'T EVEN STRAY OUTSIDE THE LINES.
THAT'S RIGHT.
IT EVEN MANAGED TO TRANSPORT ALL THE TARGETS.
RIGHT, IT'S AMAZING! AND . . . HEY, WAIT . . .
WHEN DID YOU TWO FIND ME!?

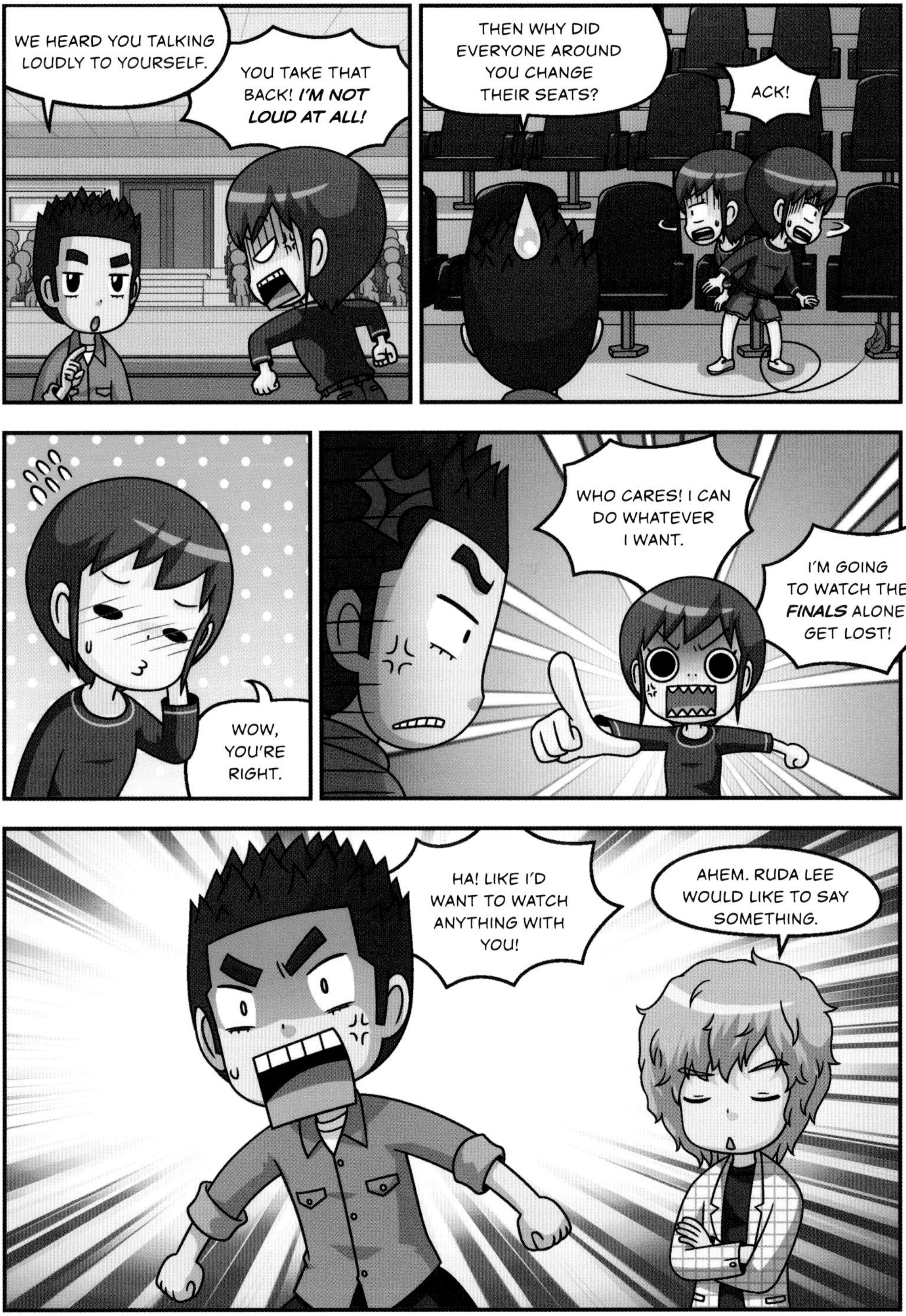
WE HEARD YOU TALKING LOUDLY TO YOURSELF.
YOU TAKE THAT BACK! I'M NOT LOUD AT ALL!
THEN WHY DID EVERYONE AROUND YOU CHANGE THEIR SEATS?
ACK!
WOW, YOU'RE RIGHT.
WHO CARES! I CAN DO WHATEVER I WANT.
I'M GOING TO WATCH THE FINALS ALONE! GET LOST!
HA! LIKE I'D WANT TO WATCH ANYTHING WITH YOU!
AHEM. RUDA LEE WOULD LIKE TO SAY SOMETHING.

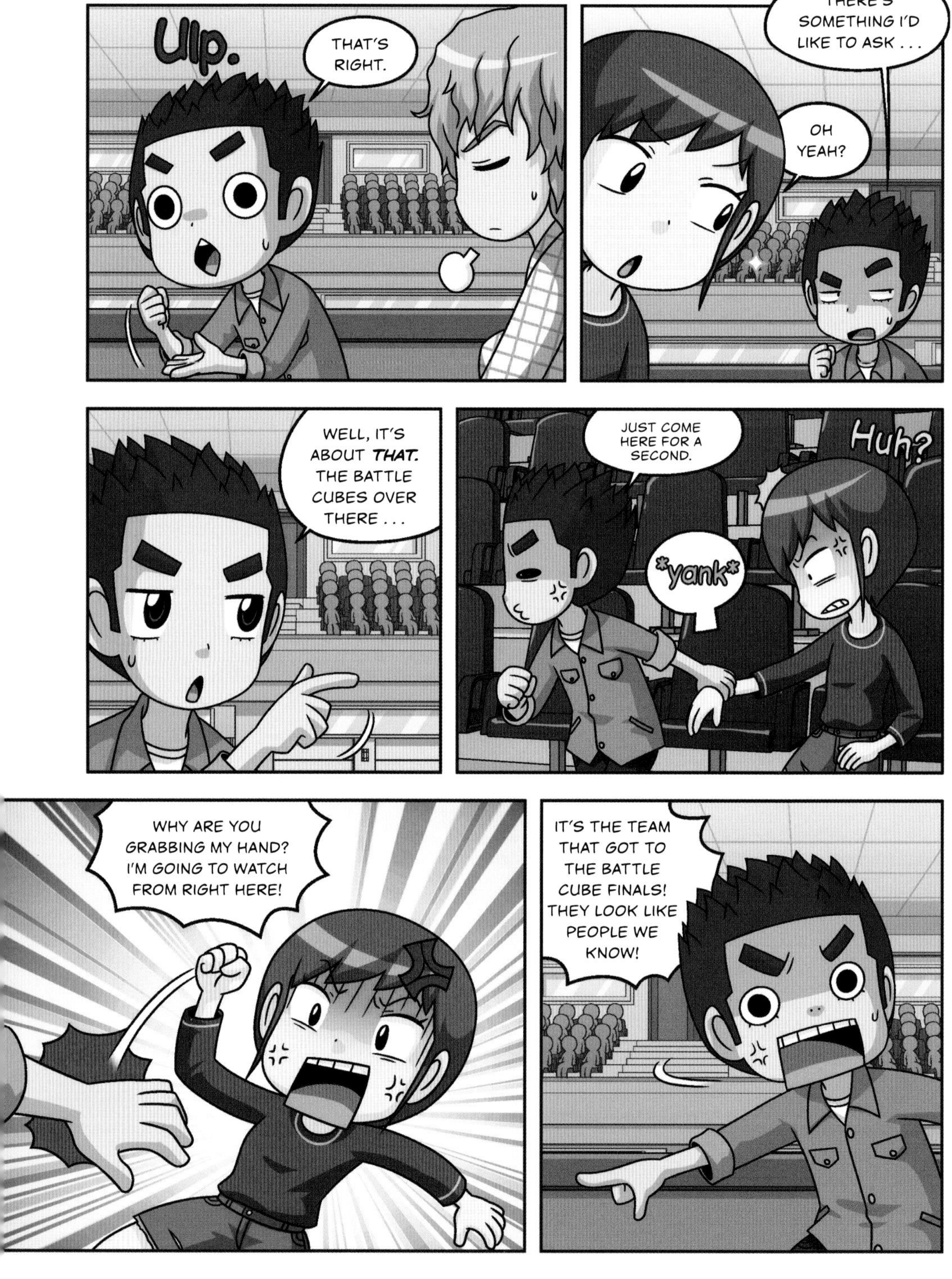
Ulp.
THAT'S RIGHT.
THERE'S SOMETHING I'D LIKE TO ASK . . .
OH YEAH?
WELL, IT'S ABOUT **THAT.** THE BATTLE CUBES OVER THERE . . .
JUST COME HERE FOR A SECOND.
Huh?
yank
WHY ARE YOU GRABBING MY HAND? I'M GOING TO WATCH FROM RIGHT HERE!
IT'S THE TEAM THAT GOT TO THE BATTLE CUBE FINALS! THEY LOOK LIKE PEOPLE WE KNOW!

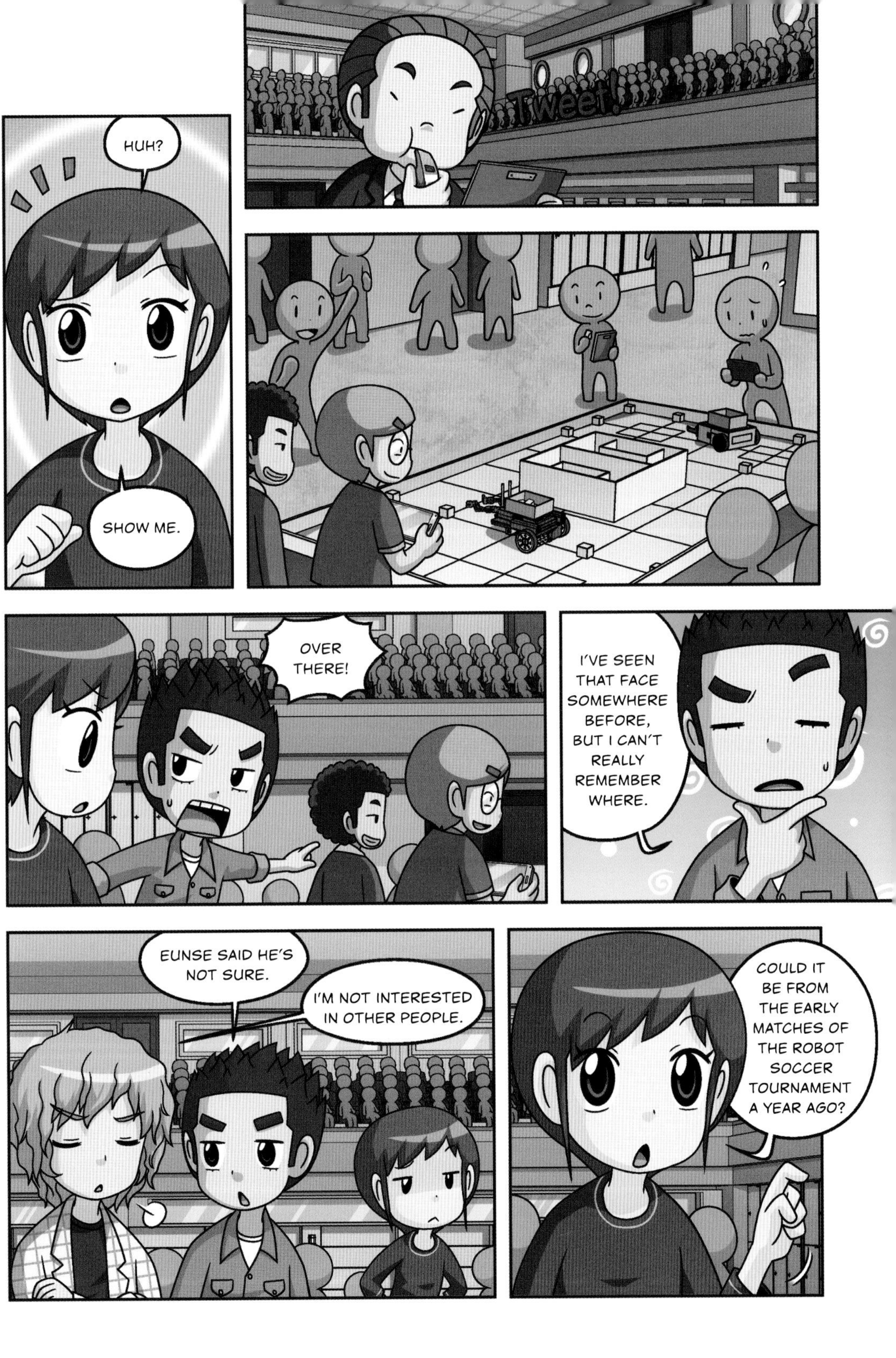
HUH?
SHOW ME.
Tweet!
OVER THERE!
I'VE SEEN THAT FACE SOMEWHERE BEFORE, BUT I CAN'T REALLY REMEMBER WHERE.
EUNSE SAID HE'S NOT SURE.
I'M NOT INTERESTED IN OTHER PEOPLE.
COULD IT BE FROM THE EARLY MATCHES OF THE ROBOT SOCCER TOURNAMENT A YEAR AGO?

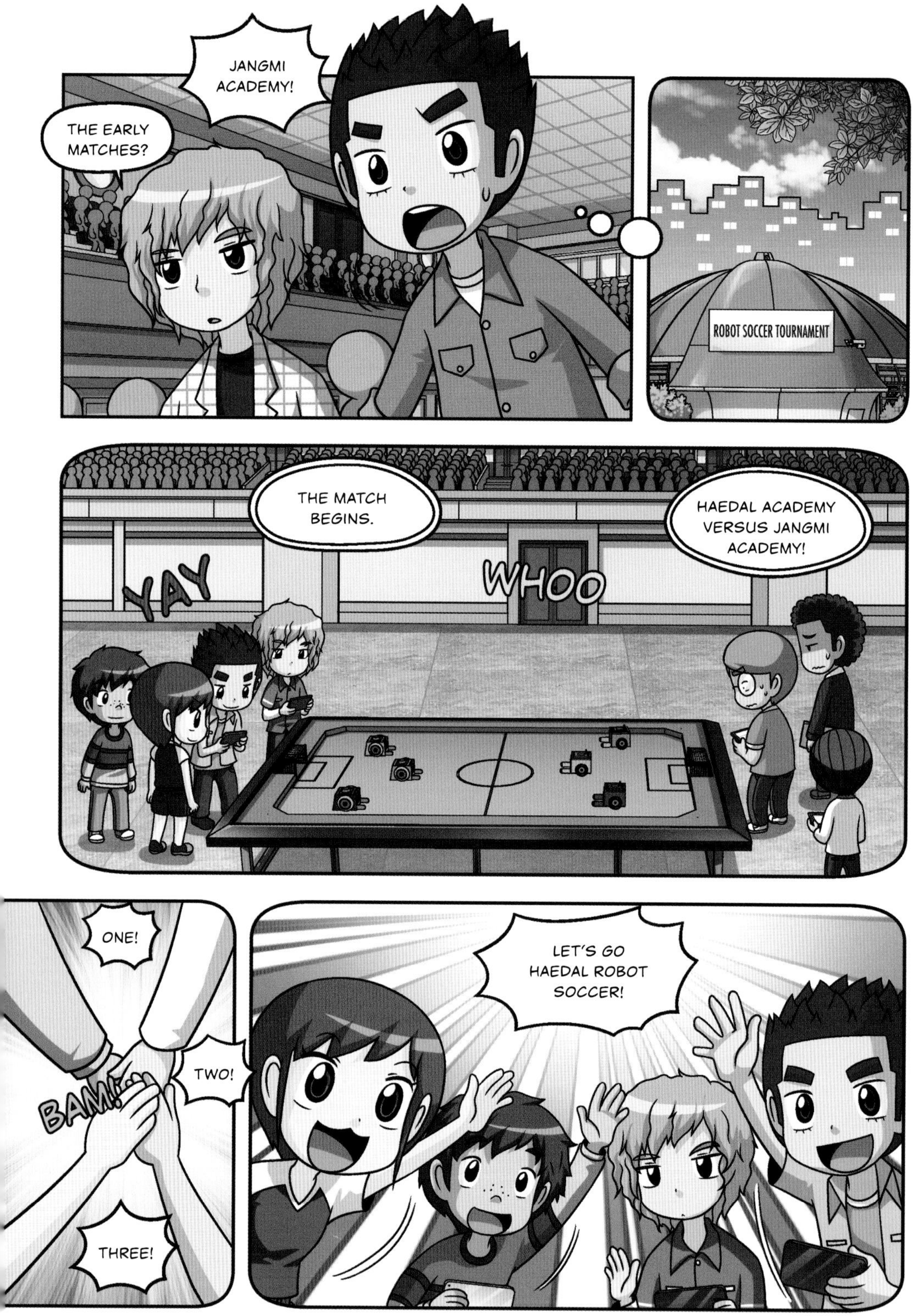
THE EARLY MATCHES?
JANGMI ACADEMY!
ROBOT SOCCER TOURNAMENT
THE MATCH BEGINS.
YAY
WHOO
HAEDAL ACADEMY VERSUS JANGMI ACADEMY!
ONE!
TWO!
BAM!
THREE!
LET'S GO HAEDAL ROBOT SOCCER!

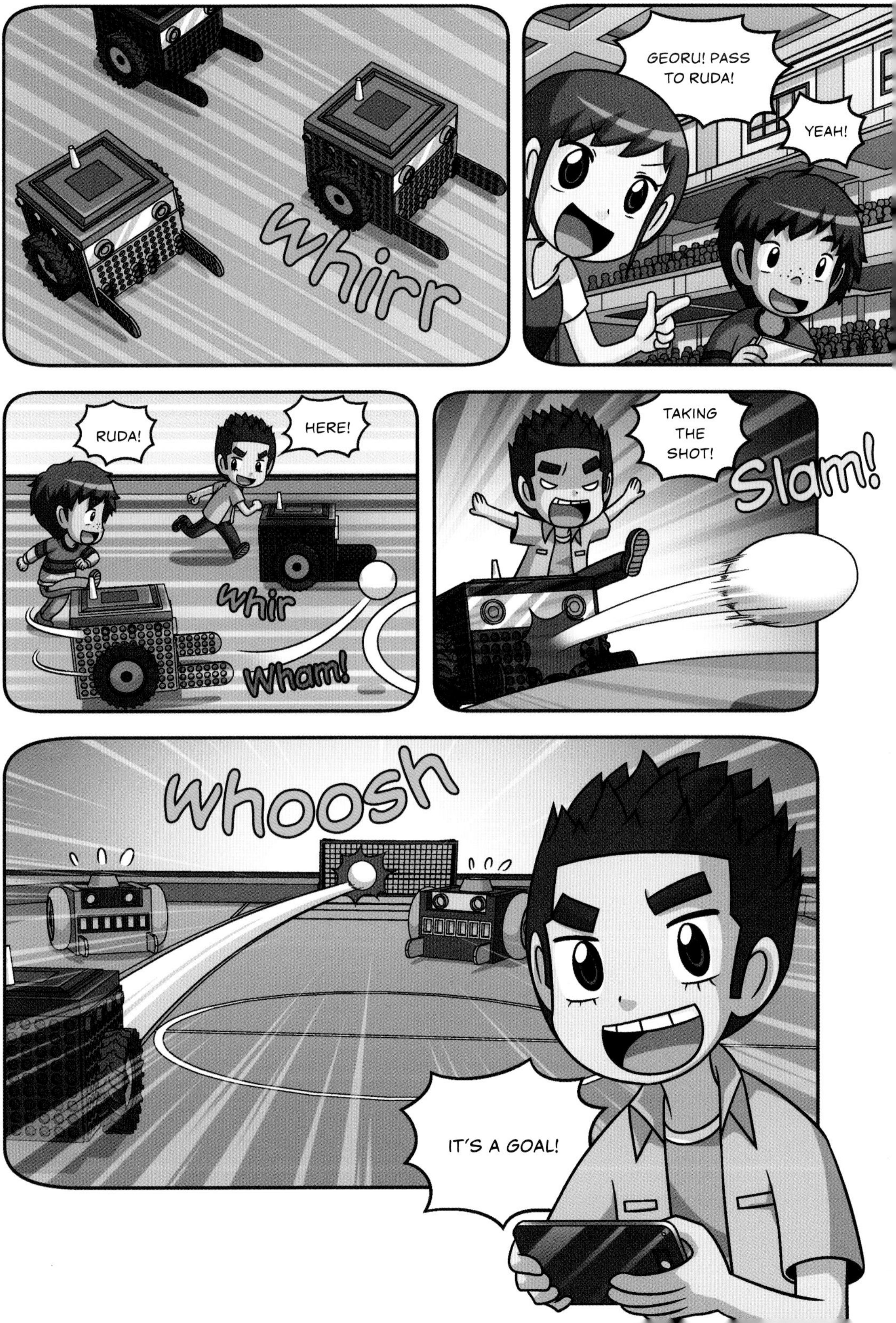
whirr
GEORU! PASS TO RUDA!
YEAH!
RUDA!
HERE!
whir
Wham!
TAKING THE SHOT!
Slam!
whoosh
IT'S A GOAL!

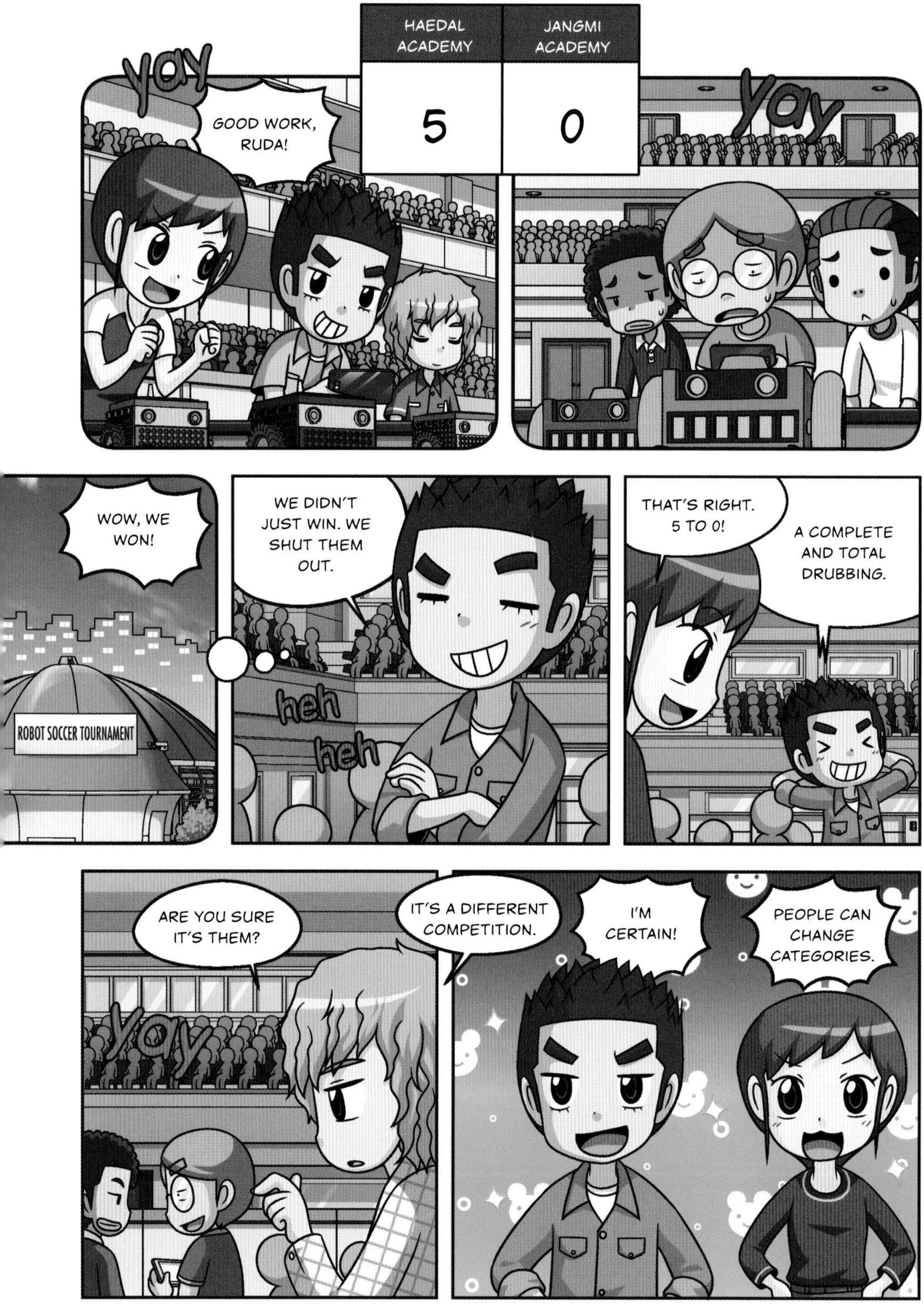
yay
GOOD WORK, RUDA!
HAEDAL ACADEMY
5
JANGMI ACADEMY
0
yay
WOW, WE WON!
ROBOT SOCCER TOURNAMENT
WE DIDN'T JUST WIN. WE SHUT THEM OUT.
heh heh
THAT'S RIGHT. 5 TO 0!
A COMPLETE AND TOTAL DRUBBING.
ARE YOU SURE IT'S THEM?
yay
IT'S A DIFFERENT COMPETITION.
I'M CERTAIN!
PEOPLE CAN CHANGE CATEGORIES.

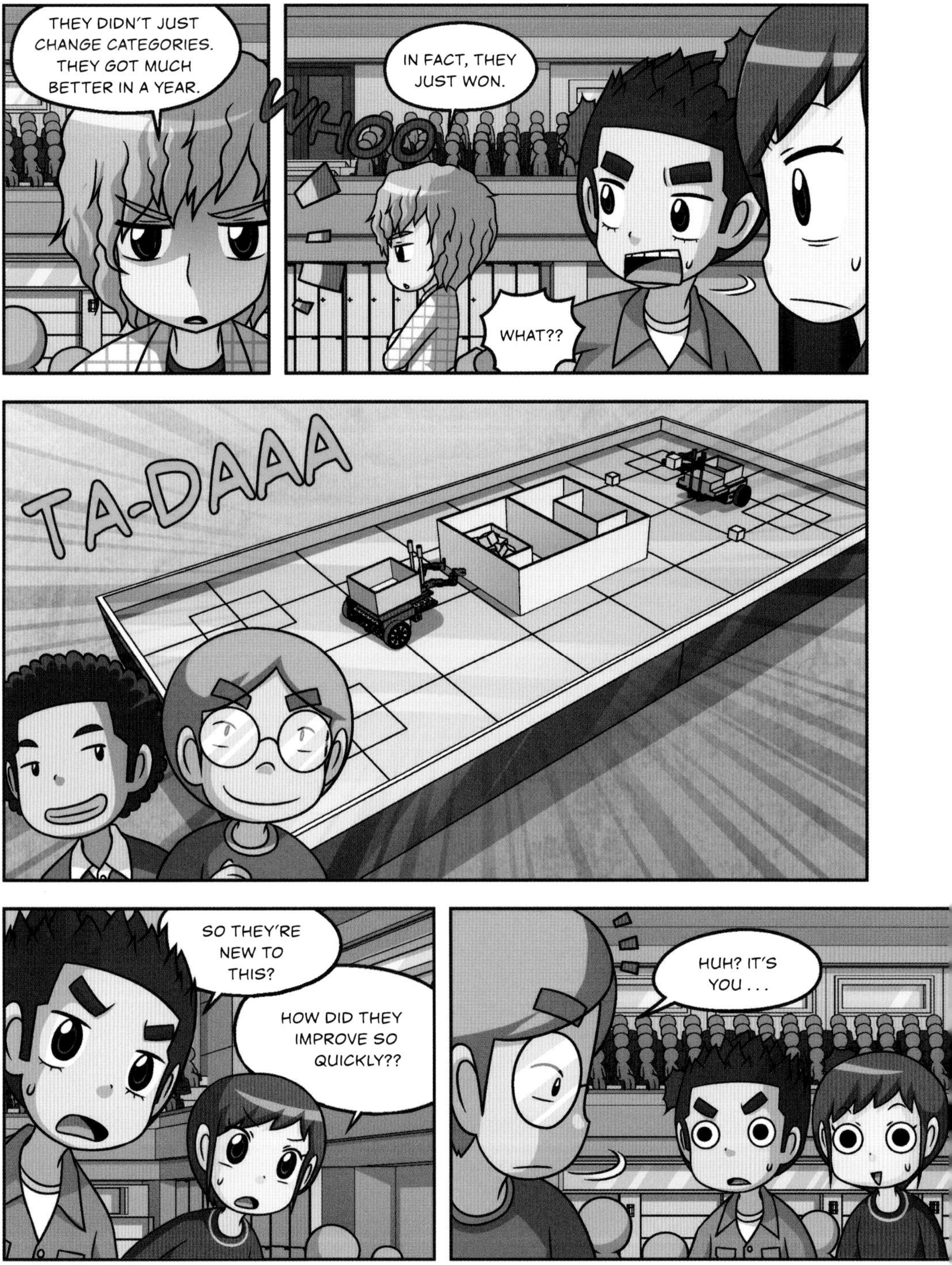
THEY DIDN'T JUST CHANGE CATEGORIES. THEY GOT MUCH BETTER IN A YEAR.
WHOO
IN FACT, THEY JUST WON.
WHAT??
TA-DAAA
SO THEY'RE NEW TO THIS?
HOW DID THEY IMPROVE SO QUICKLY??
HUH? IT'S YOU . . .

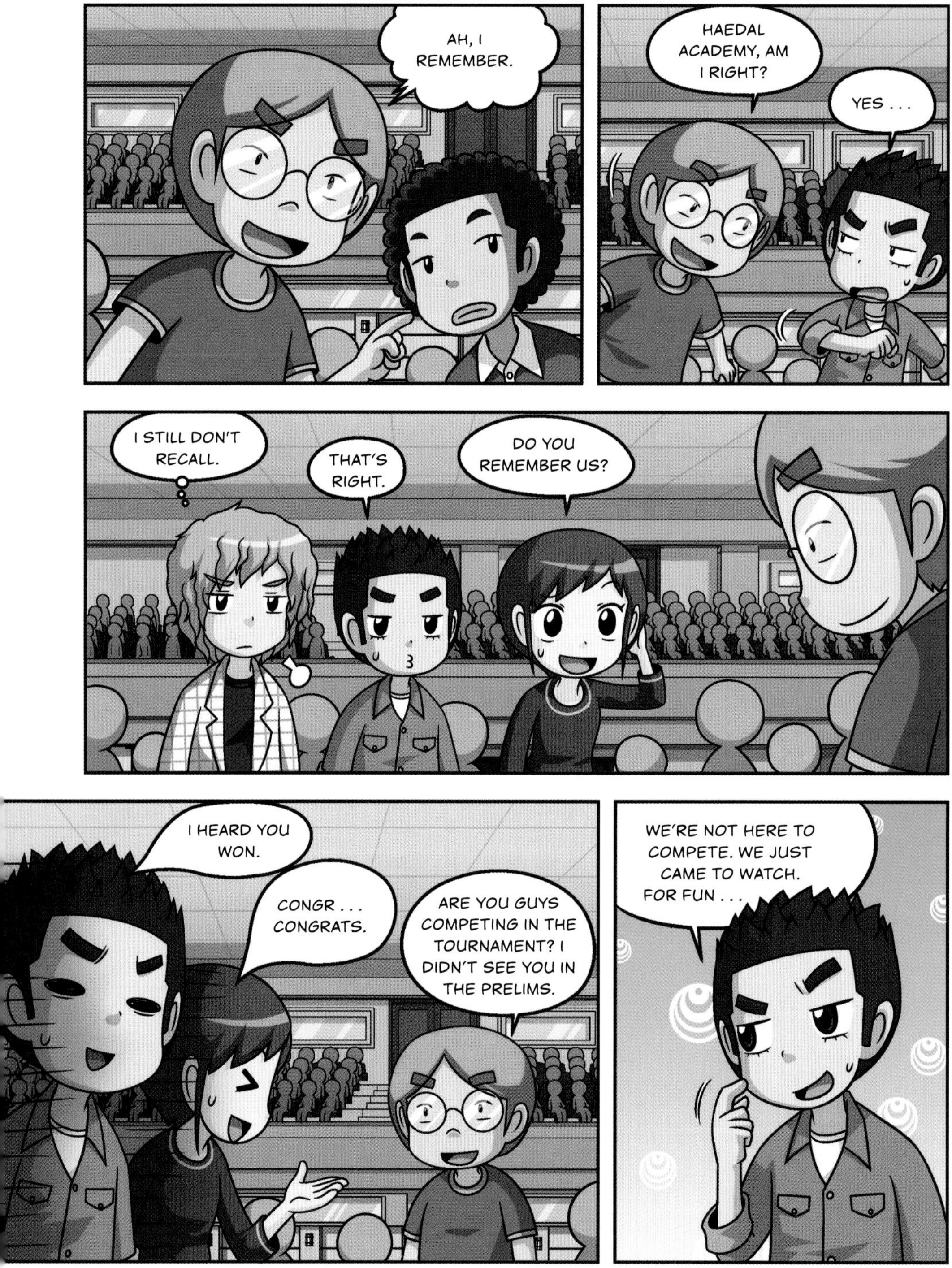
AH, I REMEMBER.
HAEDAL ACADEMY, AM I RIGHT?
YES . . .
I STILL DON'T RECALL.
THAT'S RIGHT.
DO YOU REMEMBER US?
I HEARD YOU WON.
CONGR . . . CONGRATS.
ARE YOU GUYS COMPETING IN THE TOURNAMENT? I DIDN'T SEE YOU IN THE PRELIMS.
WE'RE NOT HERE TO COMPETE. WE JUST CAME TO WATCH. FOR FUN . . .

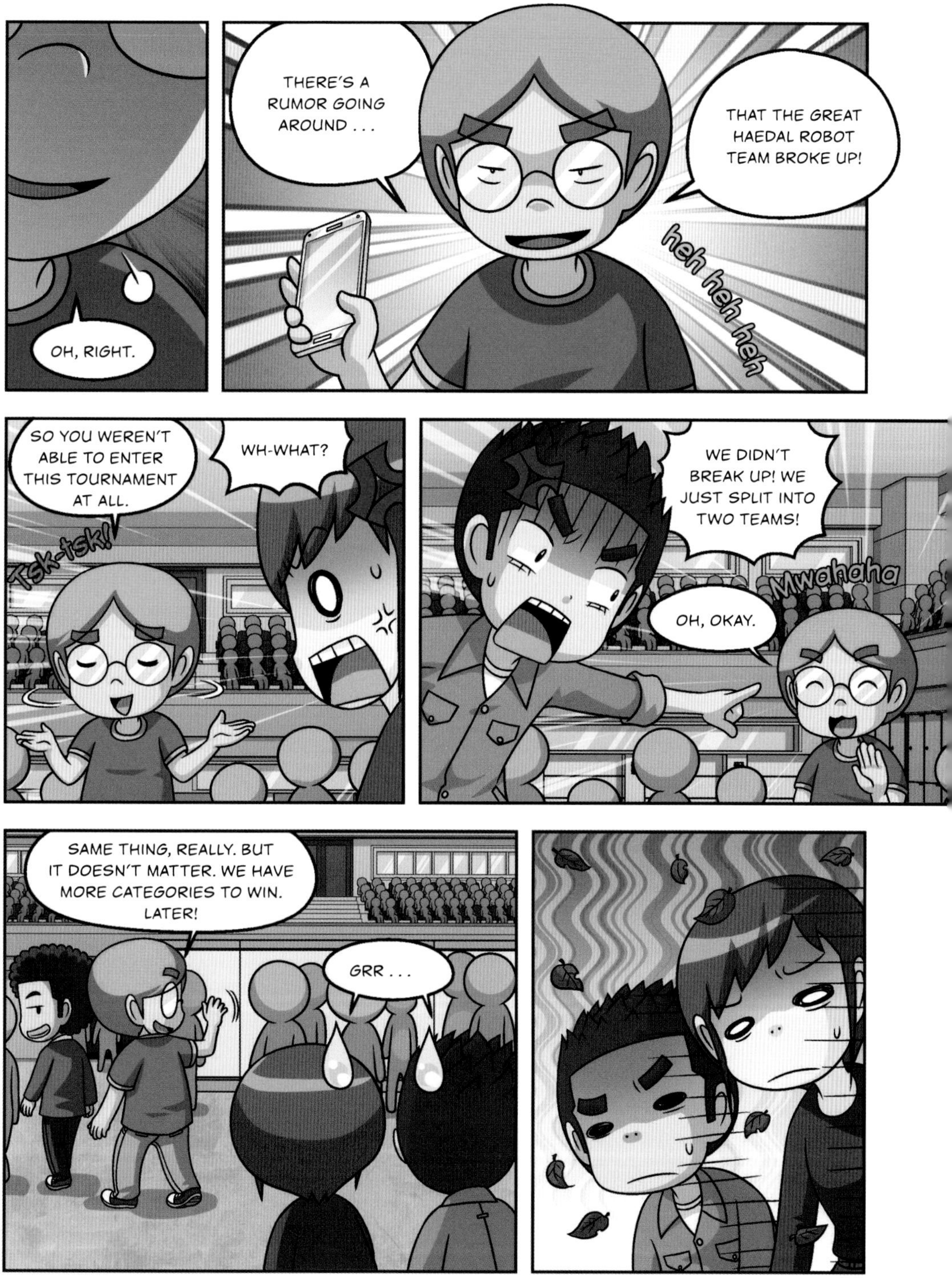

OH, RIGHT.
THERE'S A RUMOR GOING AROUND . . .
THAT THE GREAT HAEDAL ROBOT TEAM BROKE UP!
heh heh heh
SO YOU WEREN'T ABLE TO ENTER THIS TOURNAMENT AT ALL.
Tsk-tsk!
WH-WHAT?
WE DIDN'T BREAK UP! WE JUST SPLIT INTO TWO TEAMS!
Mwahaha
OH, OKAY.
SAME THING, REALLY. BUT IT DOESN'T MATTER. WE HAVE MORE CATEGORIES TO WIN. LATER!
GRR . . .

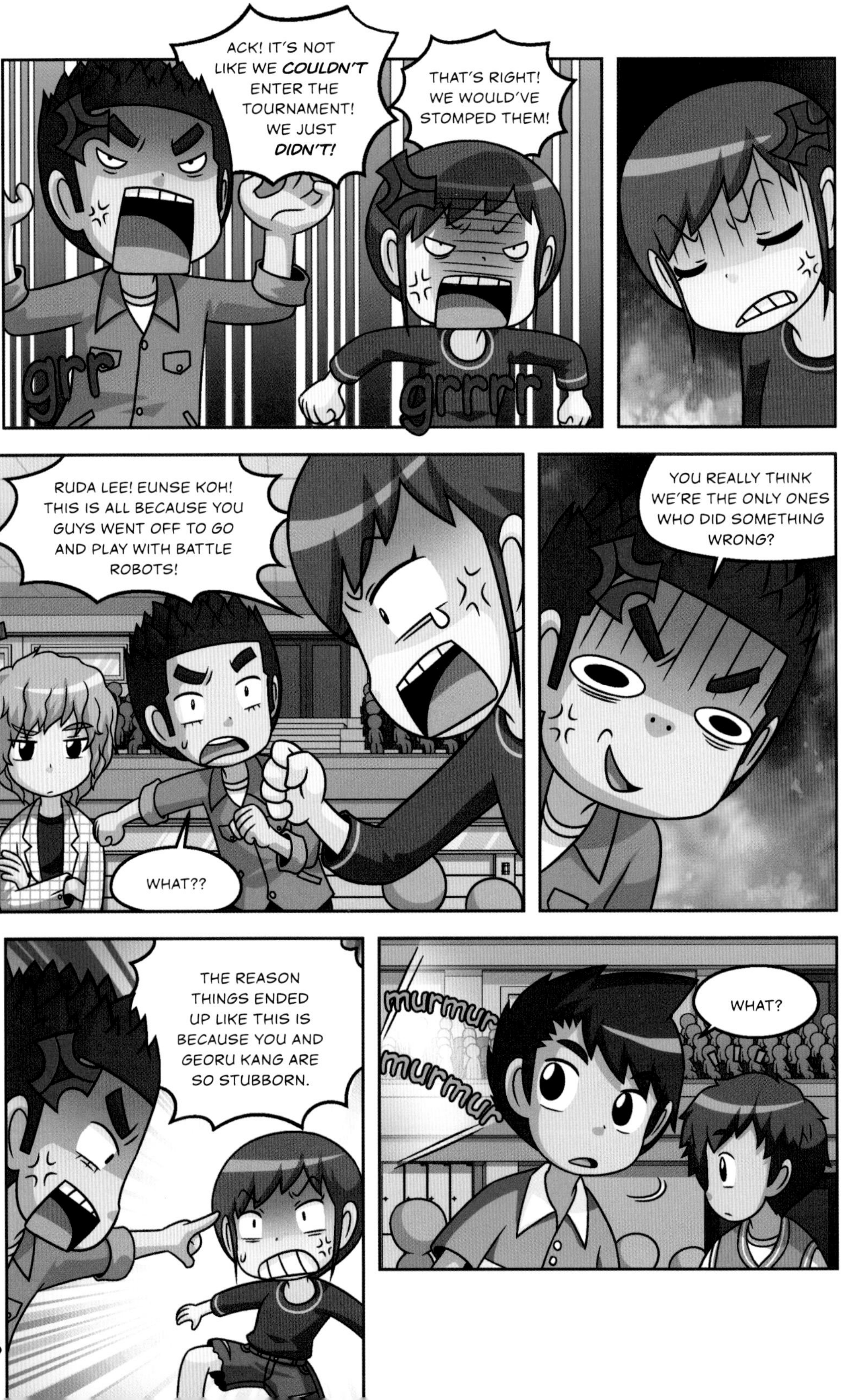

grr
ACK! IT'S NOT LIKE WE COULDN'T ENTER THE TOURNAMENT! WE JUST DIDN'T!
THAT'S RIGHT! WE WOULD'VE STOMPED THEM!
grrrr
RUDA LEE! EUNSE KOH! THIS IS ALL BECAUSE YOU GUYS WENT OFF TO GO AND PLAY WITH BATTLE ROBOTS!
WHAT??
YOU REALLY THINK WE'RE THE ONLY ONES WHO DID SOMETHING WRONG?
THE REASON THINGS ENDED UP LIKE THIS IS BECAUSE YOU AND GEORU KANG ARE SO STUBBORN.
murmur
murmur
WHAT?

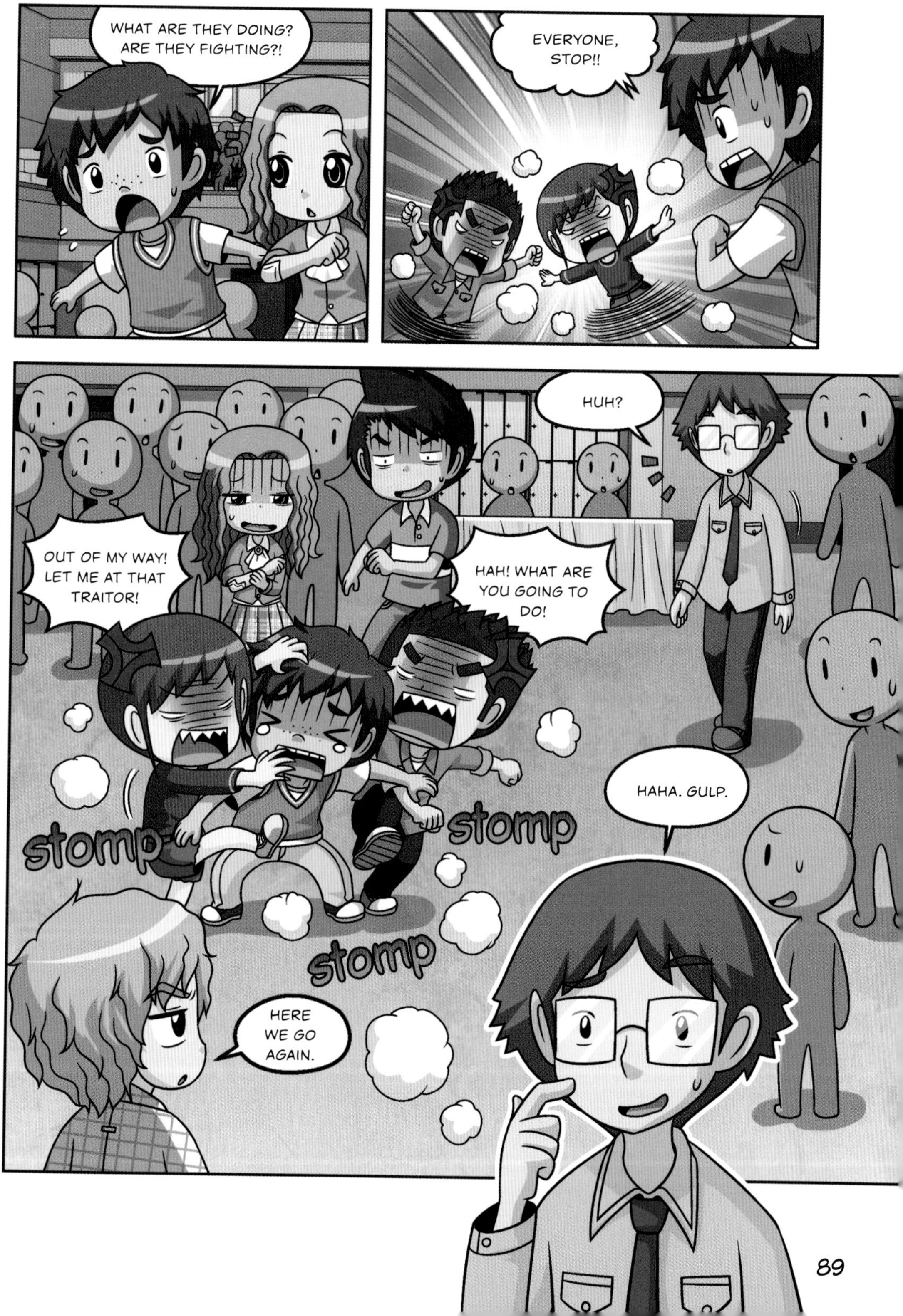
WHAT ARE THEY DOING? ARE THEY FIGHTING?!
EVERYONE, STOP!!
HUH?
OUT OF MY WAY! LET ME AT THAT TRAITOR!
HAH! WHAT ARE YOU GOING TO DO!
HAHA. GULP.
stomp
stomp
stomp
HERE WE GO AGAIN.

SENSORS IN ROBOTS

A robot moves according to its program, and it needs needs to be aware of its surroundings and react autonomously based on the circumstances. Just as humans use the five senses of vision, hearing, touch, smell, and taste, robots need a variety of sensors to perceive their surroundings.

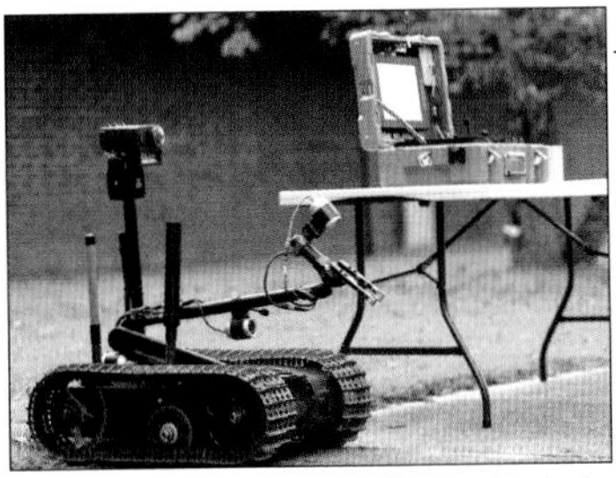
Wikipedia
An explosive ordnance disposal robot, equipped with a camera

Visual Sensor

A digital camera is widely used as a visual sensor. It plays the same role as the human eye. It can look around, take images or video, and send them to a remote operator. With a visual sensor, a robot is able to recognize the shape and size of obstacles in order to avoid them. It can also copy movements or chase moving objects. Robots equipped with visual sensor devices include household robots, military robots, and disaster robots. These machines need to monitor their surroundings and respond in real time.

Hearing Sensor

Researchers are working on artificial intelligence robots that can communicate with people and understand their emotions. This involves research on auditory sensors such as microphones and speakers. Historically, robots have struggled to understand a human's emotions by listening to the human's voice. This is because the expression of an emotion varies depending on a speaker's gender, age, dialect, and word choice. Robotics engineers are developing programs to help robots determine human emotions based on the context of a conversation and changes in vocal pitch.

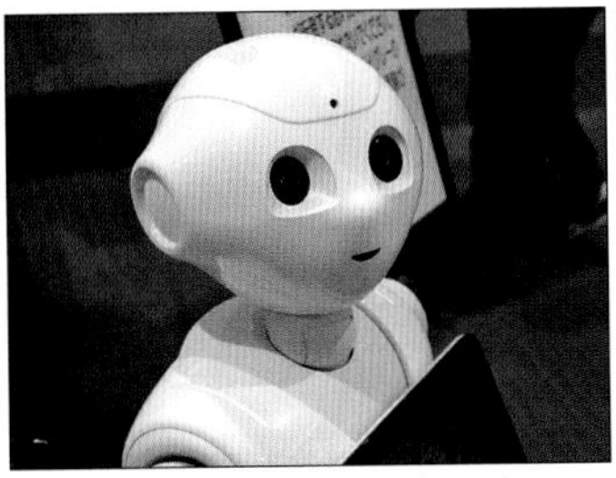
Max Pixel
Pepper the AI robot can listen to a human speaker and reply.

Touch Sensors and Collision Sensors

Touch sensors on a robot play the same role as a human's sense of touch. The information they give a robot when it is touched or touches another object sets off pre-programmed actions. A robot equipped with touch sensors on specific body parts may move differently in different situations, such as when being touched gently or roughly. Many home robots have sensitive touch sensors and will attempt to sense a person's mood depending on that type of touch. The collision sensors in a robot vacuum are similar to touch sensors. Collision sensors help a vacuum change directions after hitting a wall, a step, or another obstacle.

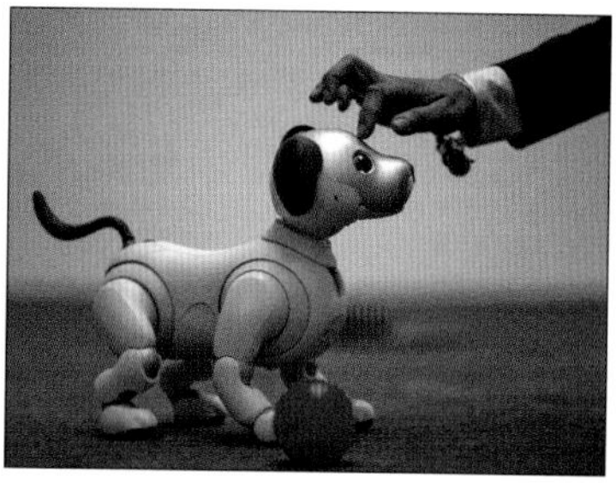

Wikipedia

The home robot aibo is programmed to determine a human's attitude toward it through its touch sensors.

Distance Sensors

Robots must recognize the locations of obstacles in advance to avoid collisions while moving. To do this, they are equipped with ultrasonic sensors and laser sensors, which help them determine their distance from an object. An ultrasonic sensor sends ultrasonic waves toward an object, calculating distance and direction from the reflected object. However, it is difficult to avoid objects safely and quickly with this method, because noise can interfere with ultrasonic waves. Laser sensors use wireless beams, which are faster and more accurate than radio waves. Laser sensors are widely used in robots as well as self-driving vehicles, which need to monitor their surroundings at all times.

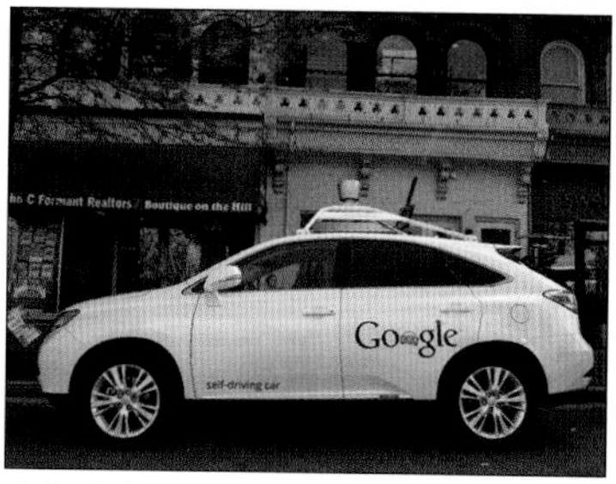
Google

Wikipedia

A 360-degree laser sensor is mounted on Google's self-driving car.

Chapter
5

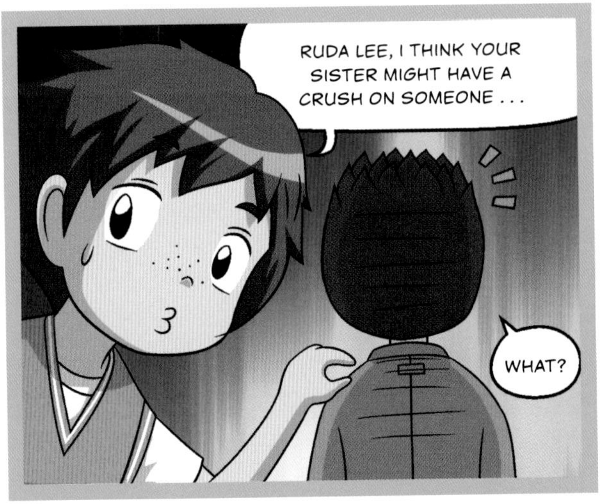
RUDA LEE, I THINK YOUR SISTER MIGHT HAVE A CRUSH ON SOMEONE . . .
WHAT?

Get Ready for the Robot Dance Tournament

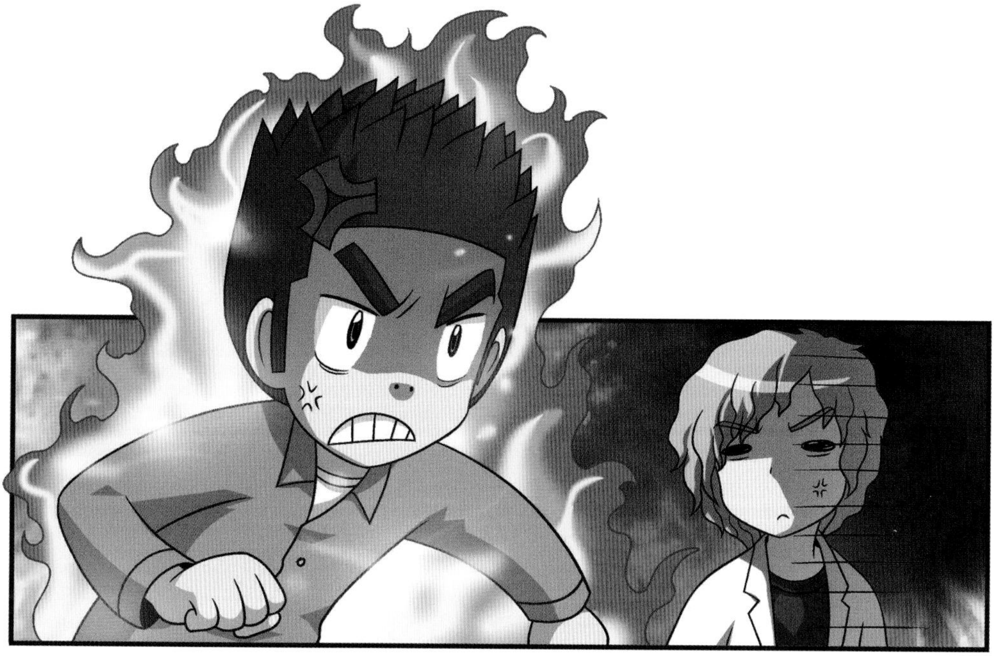

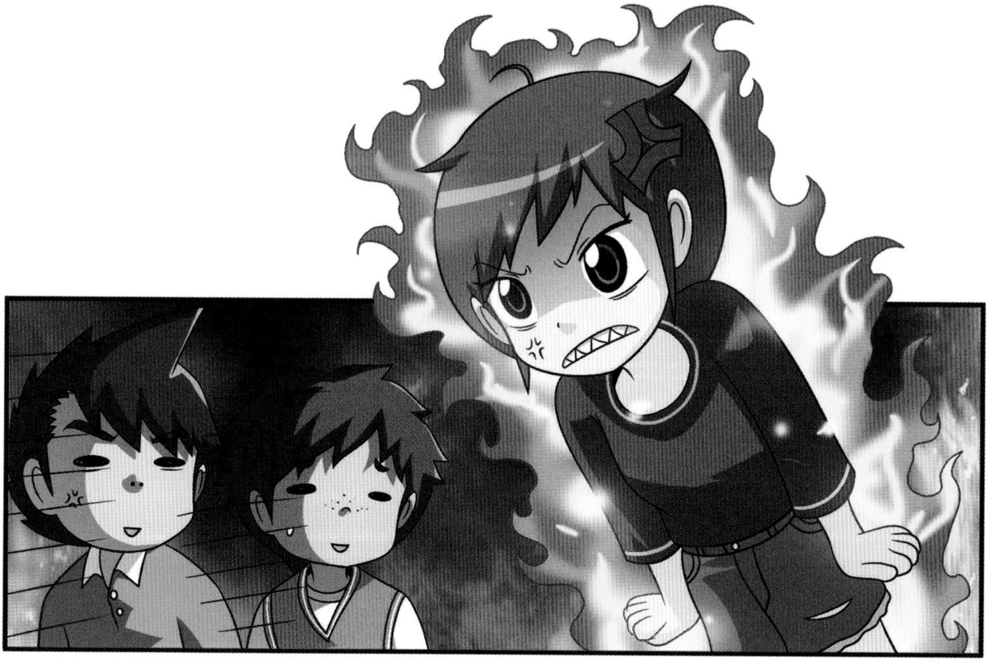

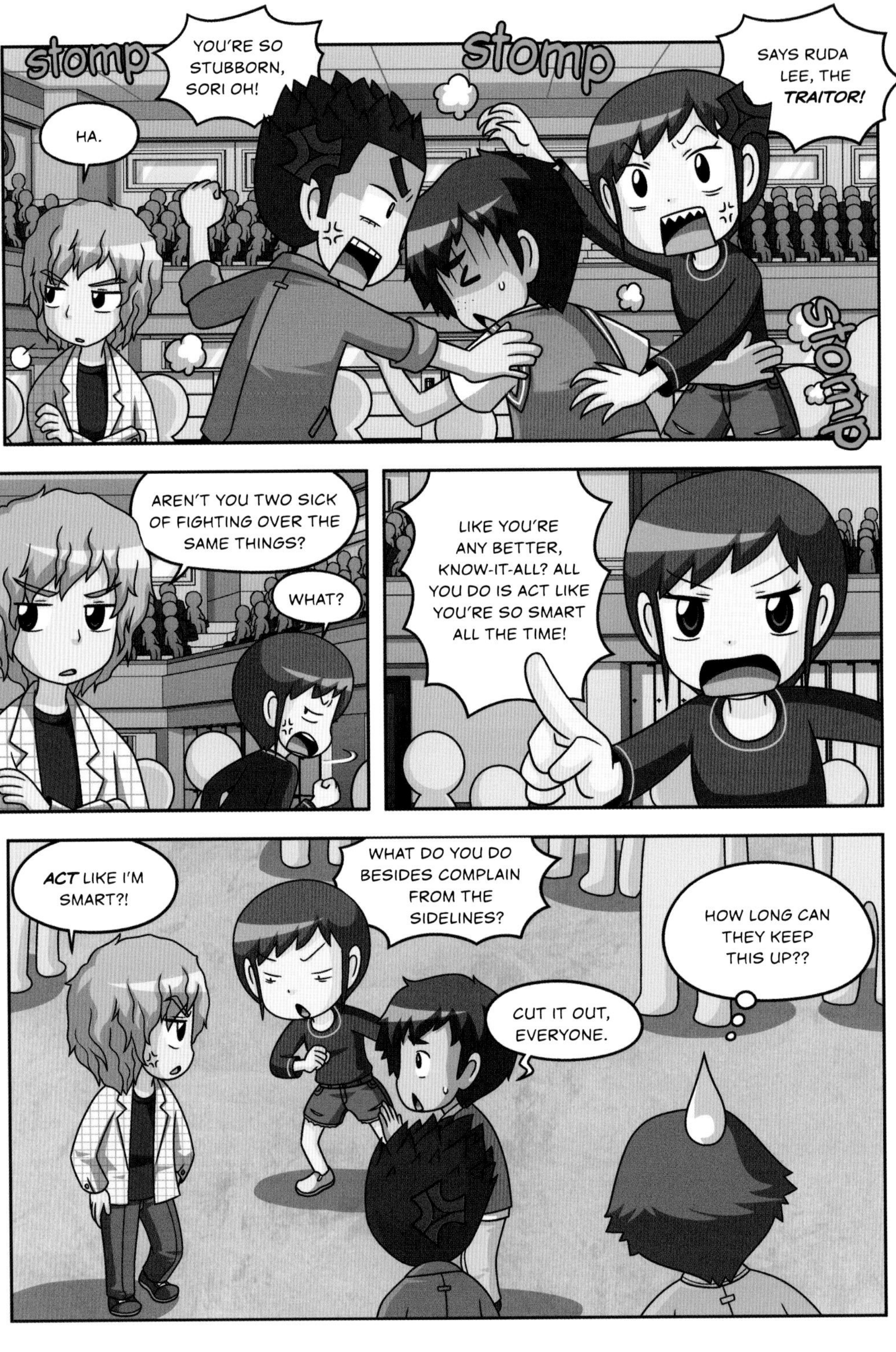
stomp
YOU'RE SO STUBBORN, SORI OH!
HA.
stomp
SAYS RUDA LEE, THE *TRAITOR!*
stomp
AREN'T YOU TWO SICK OF FIGHTING OVER THE SAME THINGS?
WHAT?
LIKE YOU'RE ANY BETTER, KNOW-IT-ALL? ALL YOU DO IS ACT LIKE YOU'RE SO SMART ALL THE TIME!
ACT LIKE I'M SMART?!
WHAT DO YOU DO BESIDES COMPLAIN FROM THE SIDELINES?
CUT IT OUT, EVERYONE.
HOW LONG CAN THEY KEEP THIS UP??

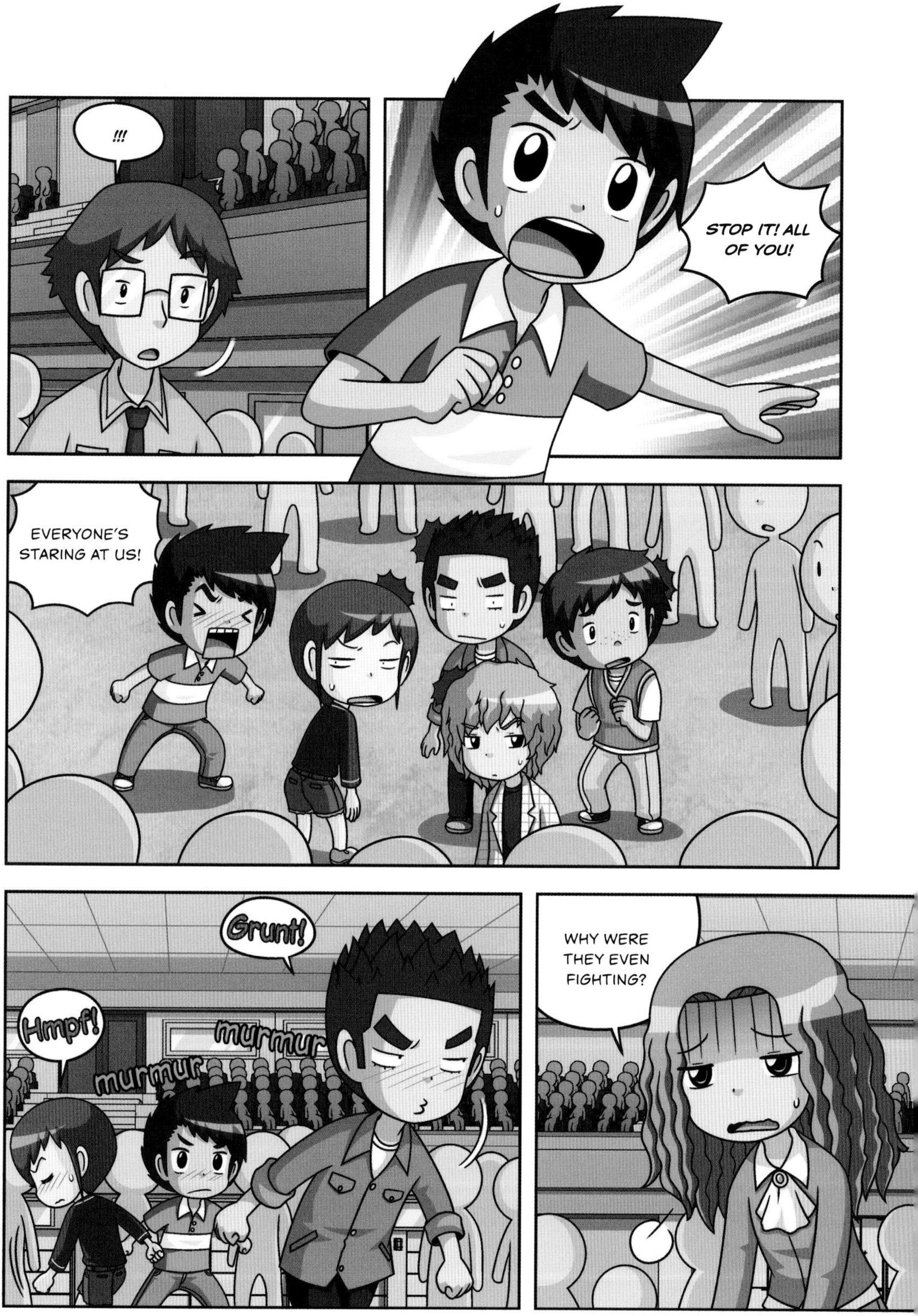
!!!
STOP IT! ALL OF YOU!
EVERYONE'S STARING AT US!
Grunt!
Hmpf!
murmur
murmur
WHY WERE THEY EVEN FIGHTING?

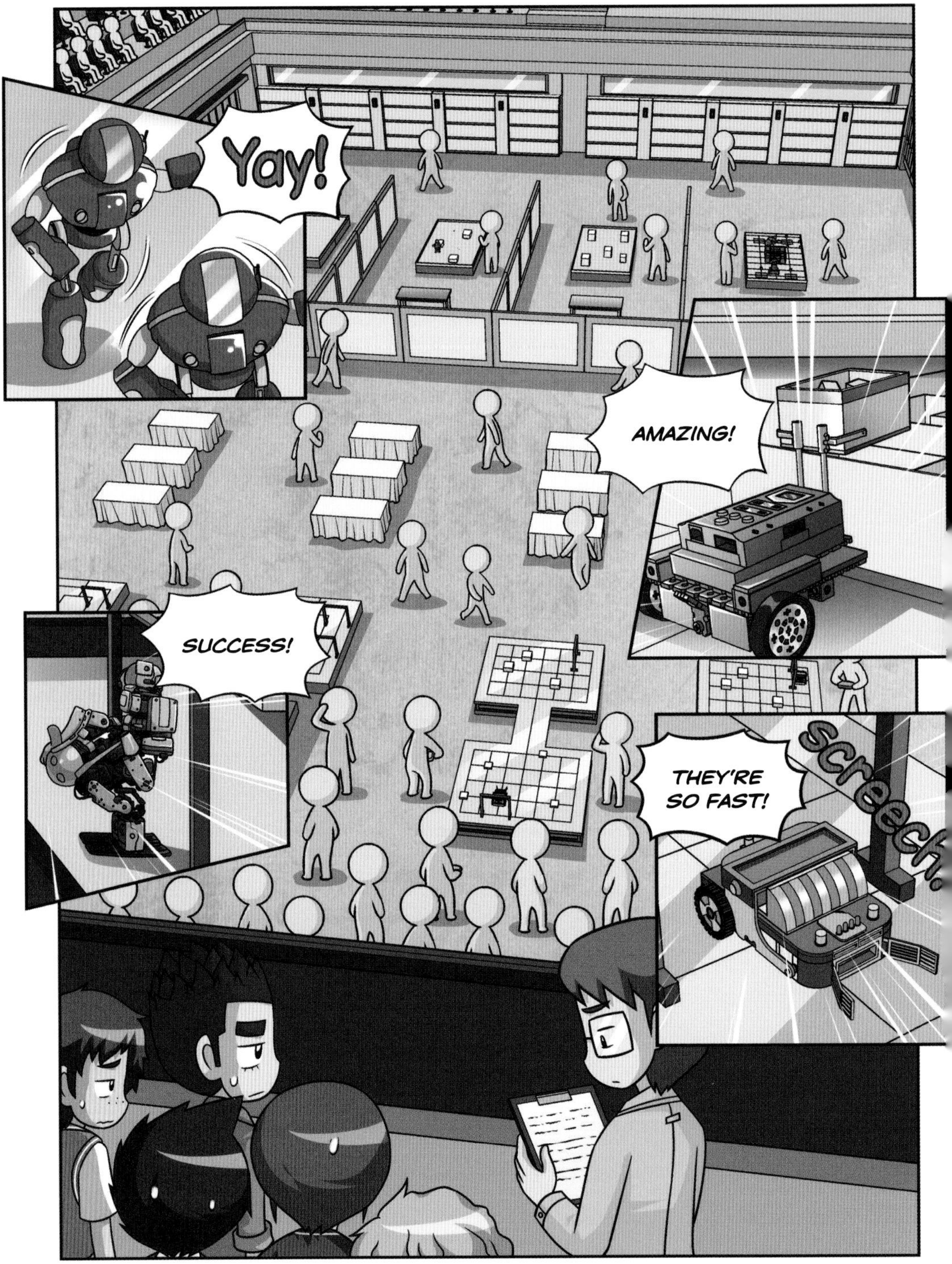
AMAZING!
Yay!
THEY'RE SO FAST!
screech!
SUCCESS!

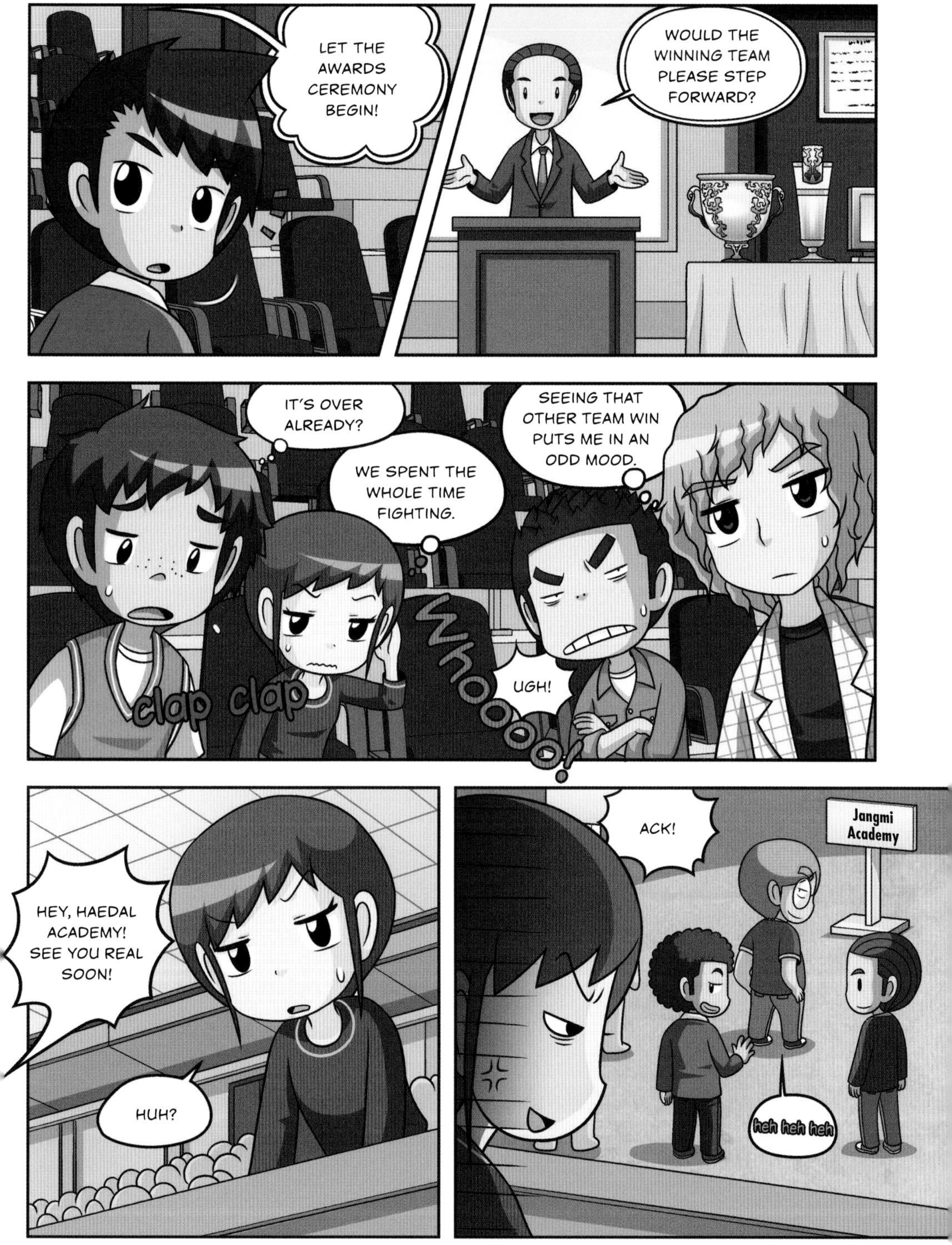
LET THE AWARDS CEREMONY BEGIN!
WOULD THE WINNING TEAM PLEASE STEP FORWARD?
IT'S OVER ALREADY?
WE SPENT THE WHOLE TIME FIGHTING.
clap clap
SEEING THAT OTHER TEAM WIN PUTS ME IN AN ODD MOOD.
Whoooo!
UGH!
HEY, HAEDAL ACADEMY! SEE YOU REAL SOON!
HUH?
ACK!
Jangmi Academy
heh heh heh

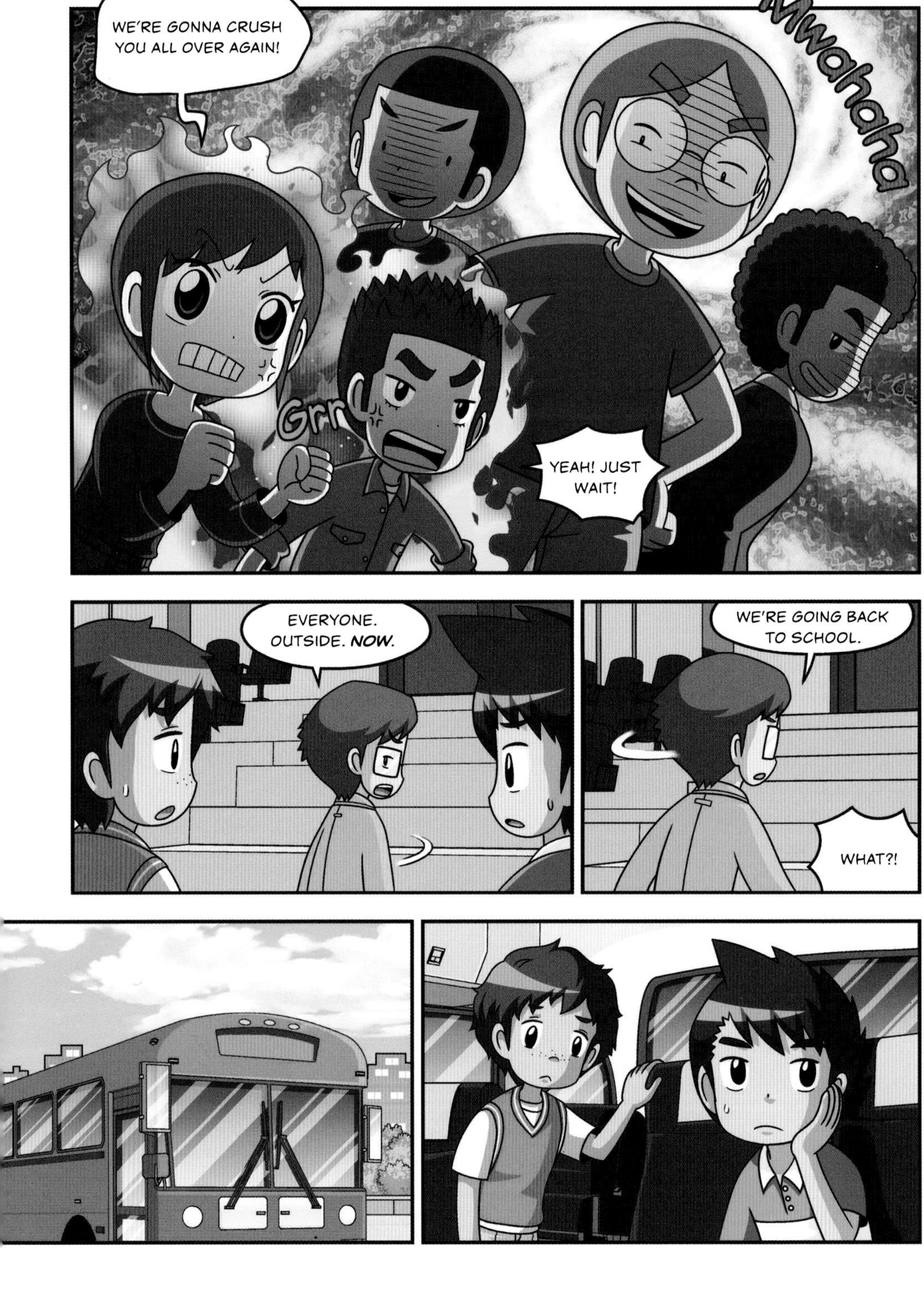
WE'RE GONNA CRUSH YOU ALL OVER AGAIN!
Mwahaha
Grr
YEAH! JUST WAIT!
EVERYONE. OUTSIDE. **NOW**.
WE'RE GOING BACK TO SCHOOL.
WHAT?!

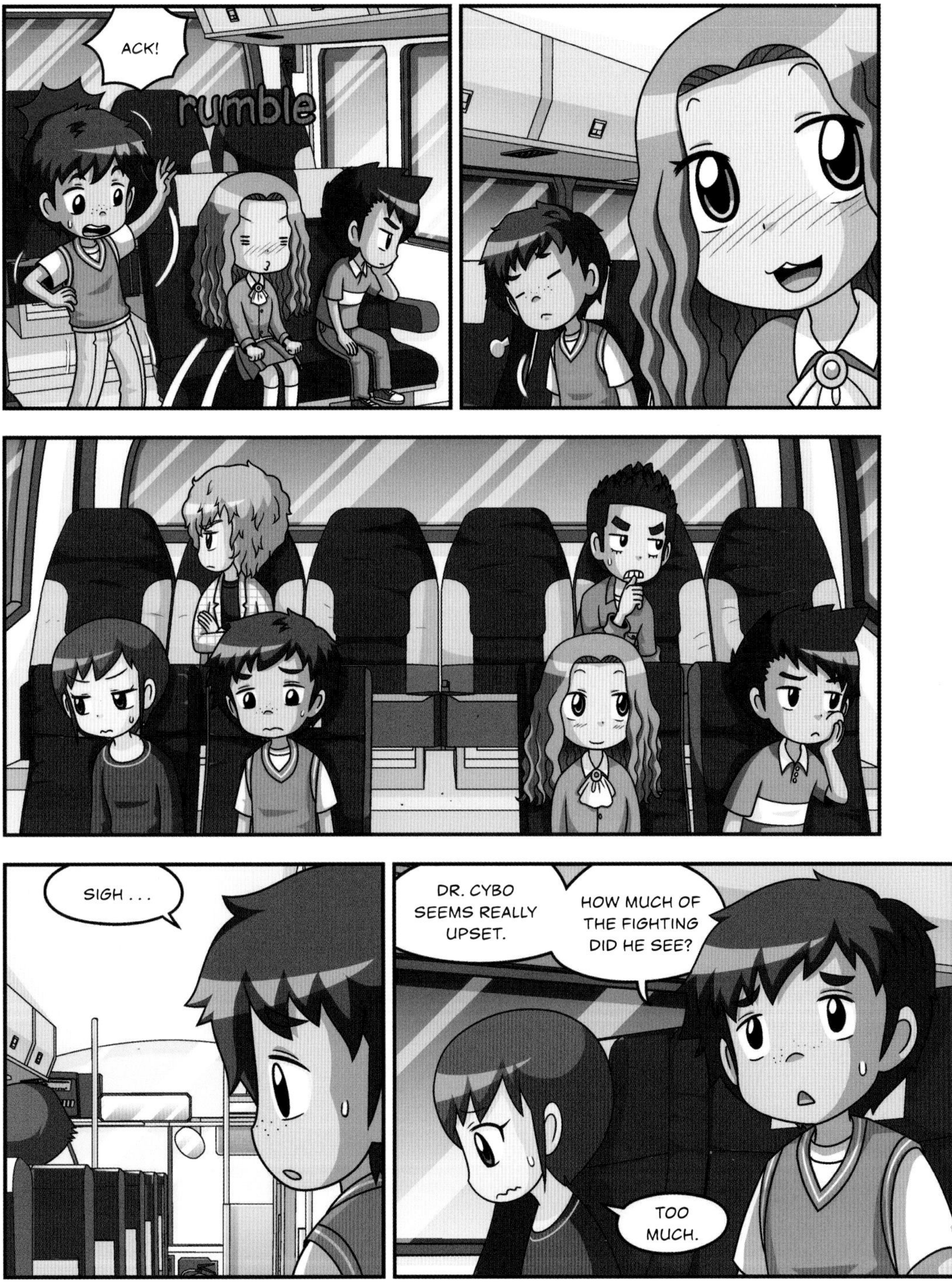
ACK!
rumble
SIGH . . .
DR. CYBO SEEMS REALLY UPSET.
HOW MUCH OF THE FIGHTING DID HE SEE?
TOO MUCH.

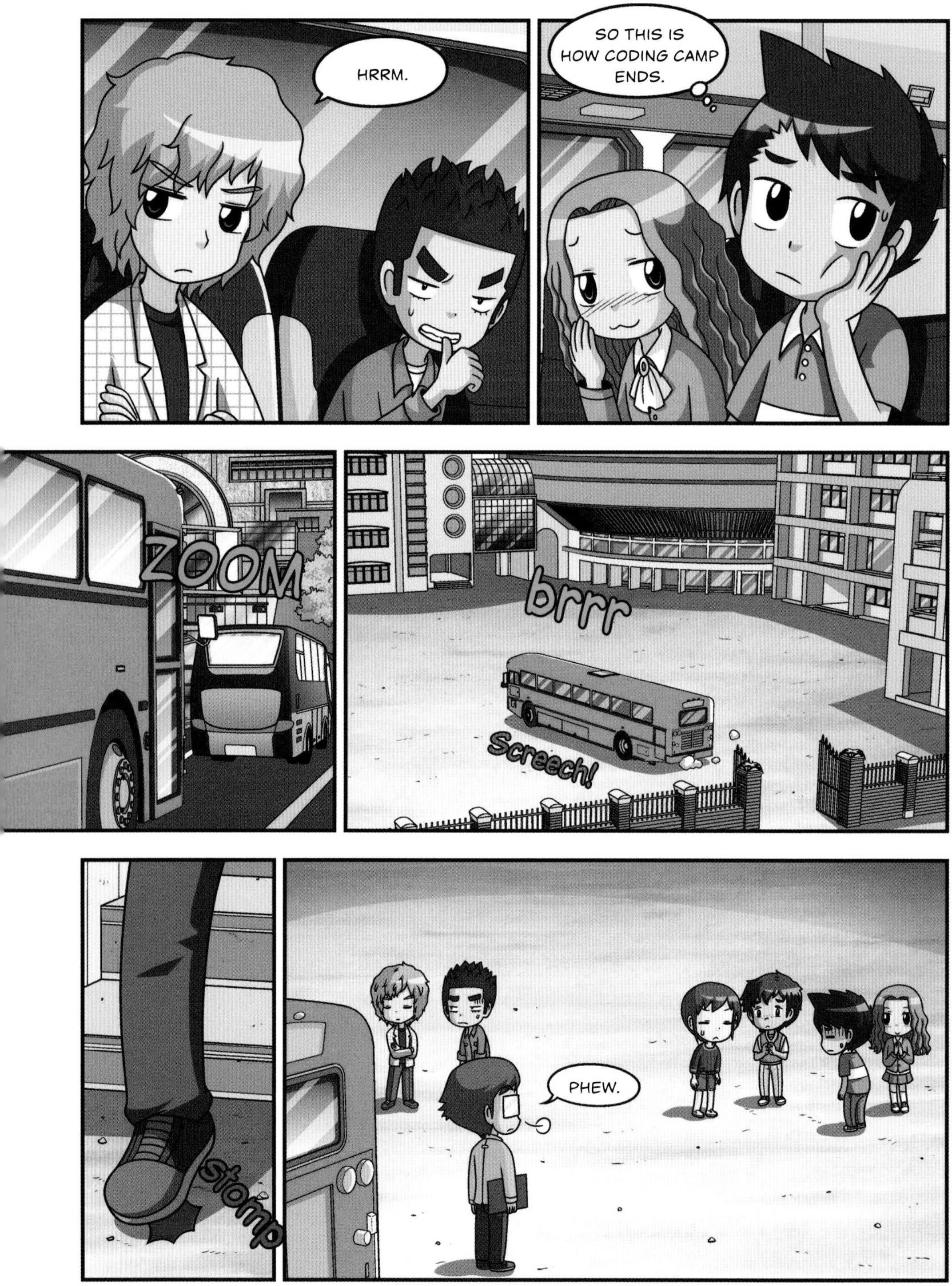
HRRM.
SO THIS IS HOW CODING CAMP ENDS.
ZOOM
brrr
Screech!
stomp
PHEW.

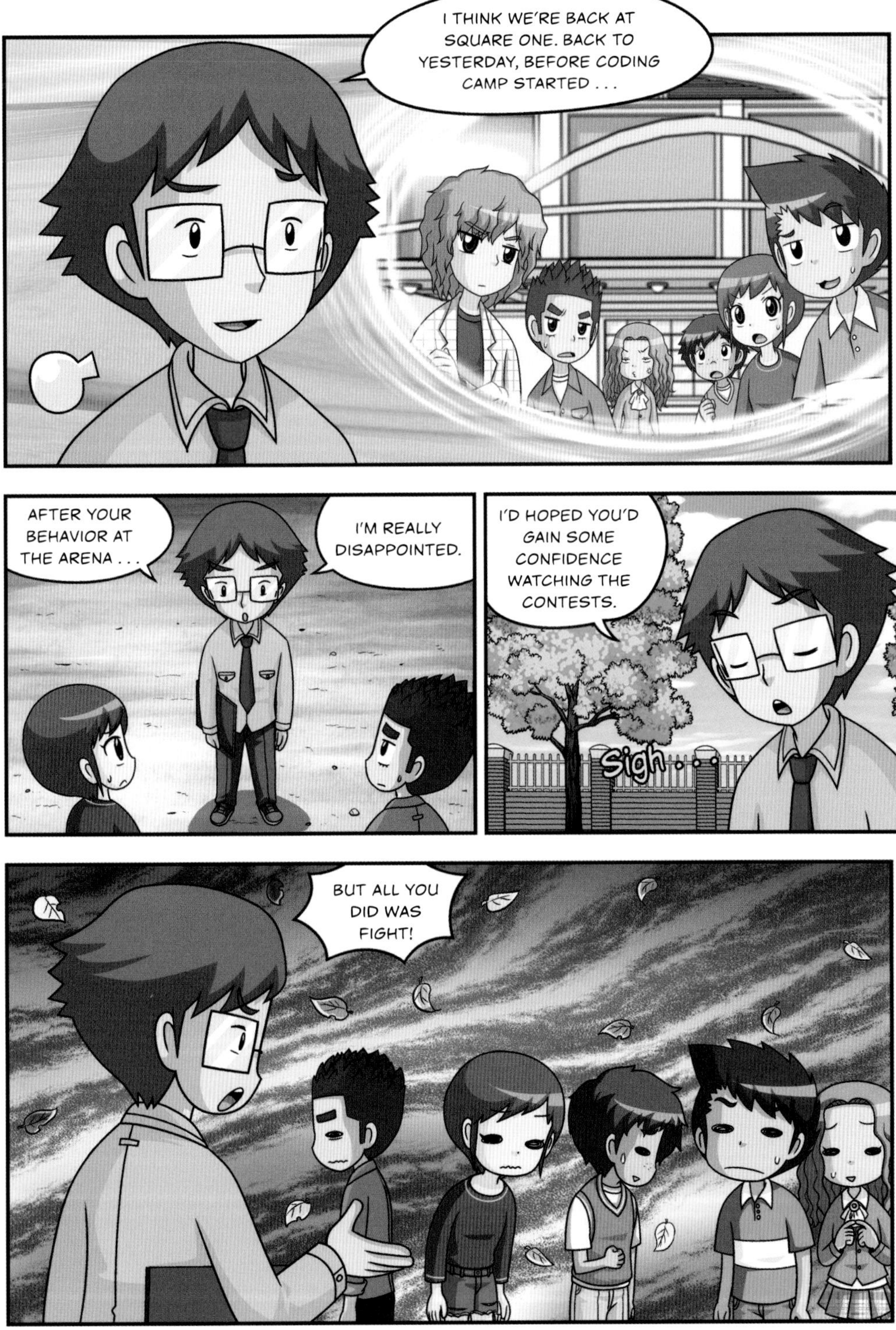
I THINK WE'RE BACK AT SQUARE ONE. BACK TO YESTERDAY, BEFORE CODING CAMP STARTED . . .
AFTER YOUR BEHAVIOR AT THE ARENA . . .
I'M REALLY DISAPPOINTED.
I'D HOPED YOU'D GAIN SOME CONFIDENCE WATCHING THE CONTESTS.
Sigh . . .
BUT ALL YOU DID WAS FIGHT!

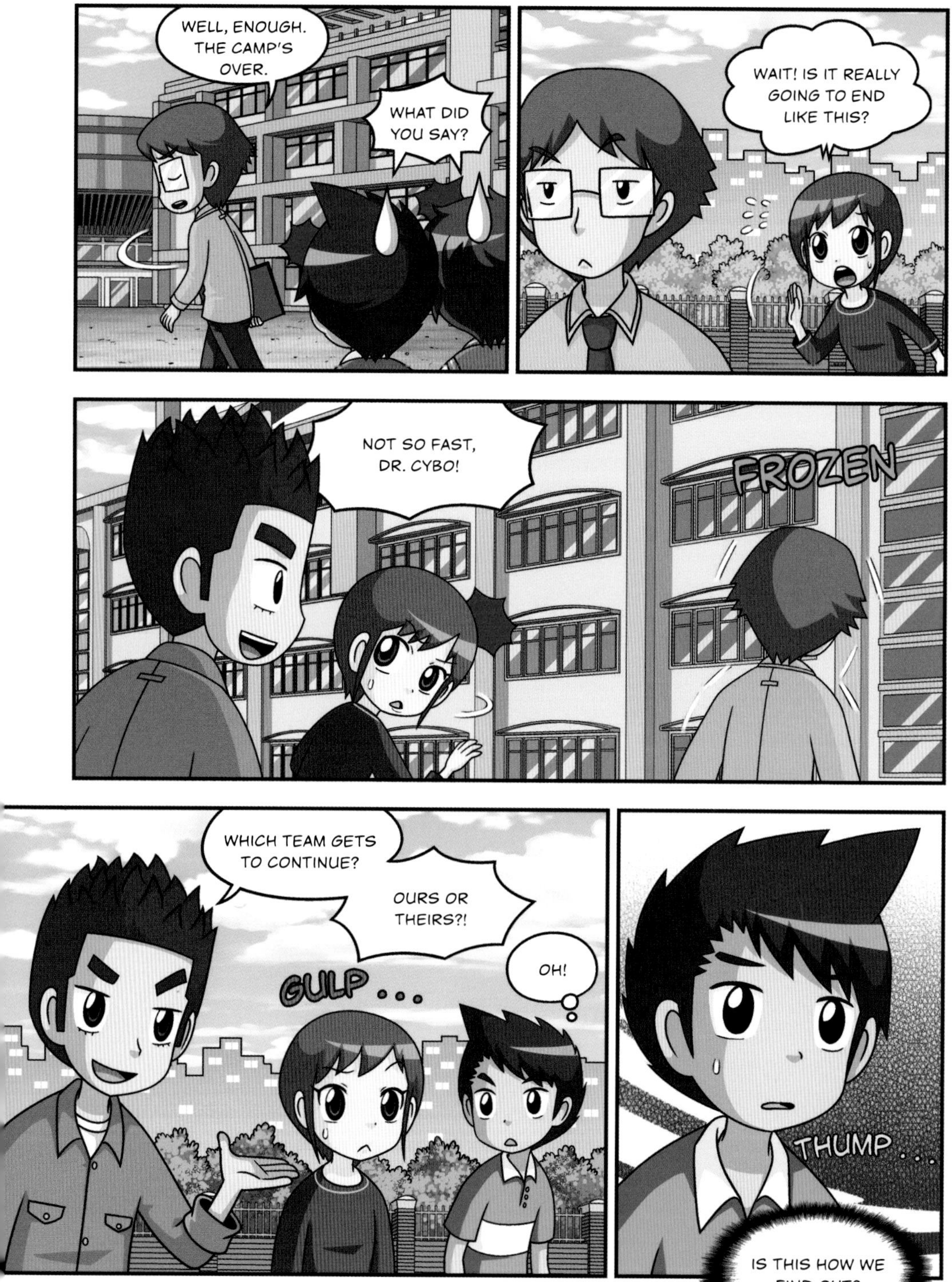
WELL, ENOUGH. THE CAMP'S OVER.
WHAT DID YOU SAY?
WAIT! IS IT REALLY GOING TO END LIKE THIS?
NOT SO FAST, DR. CYBO!
FROZEN
WHICH TEAM GETS TO CONTINUE?
OURS OR THEIRS?!
GULP . . .
OH!
THUMP . . .
IS THIS HOW WE FIND OUT?

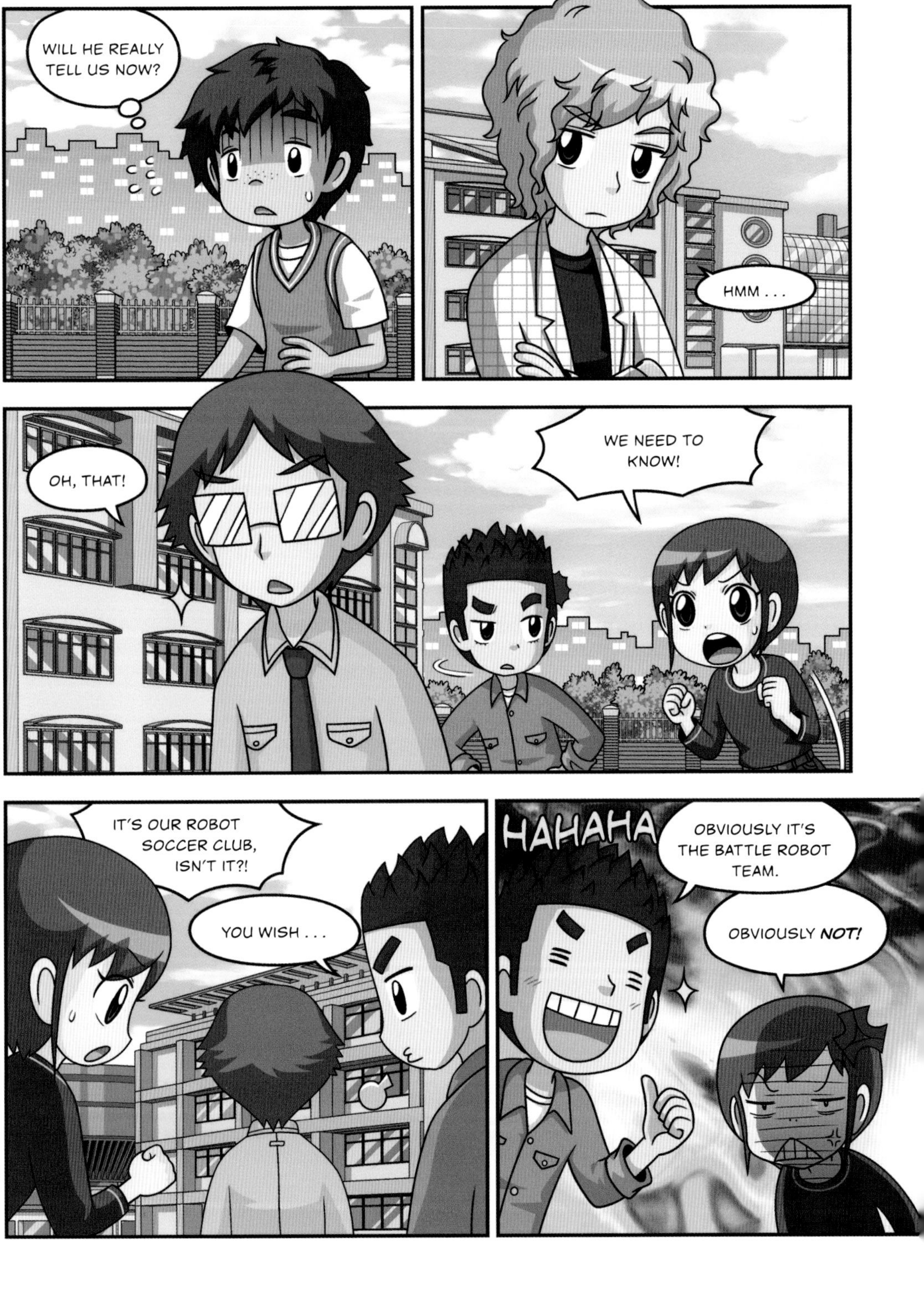
WILL HE REALLY TELL US NOW?
HMM . . .
OH, THAT!
WE NEED TO KNOW!
IT'S OUR ROBOT SOCCER CLUB, ISN'T IT?!
YOU WISH . . .
HAHAHA
OBVIOUSLY IT'S THE BATTLE ROBOT TEAM.
OBVIOUSLY NOT!

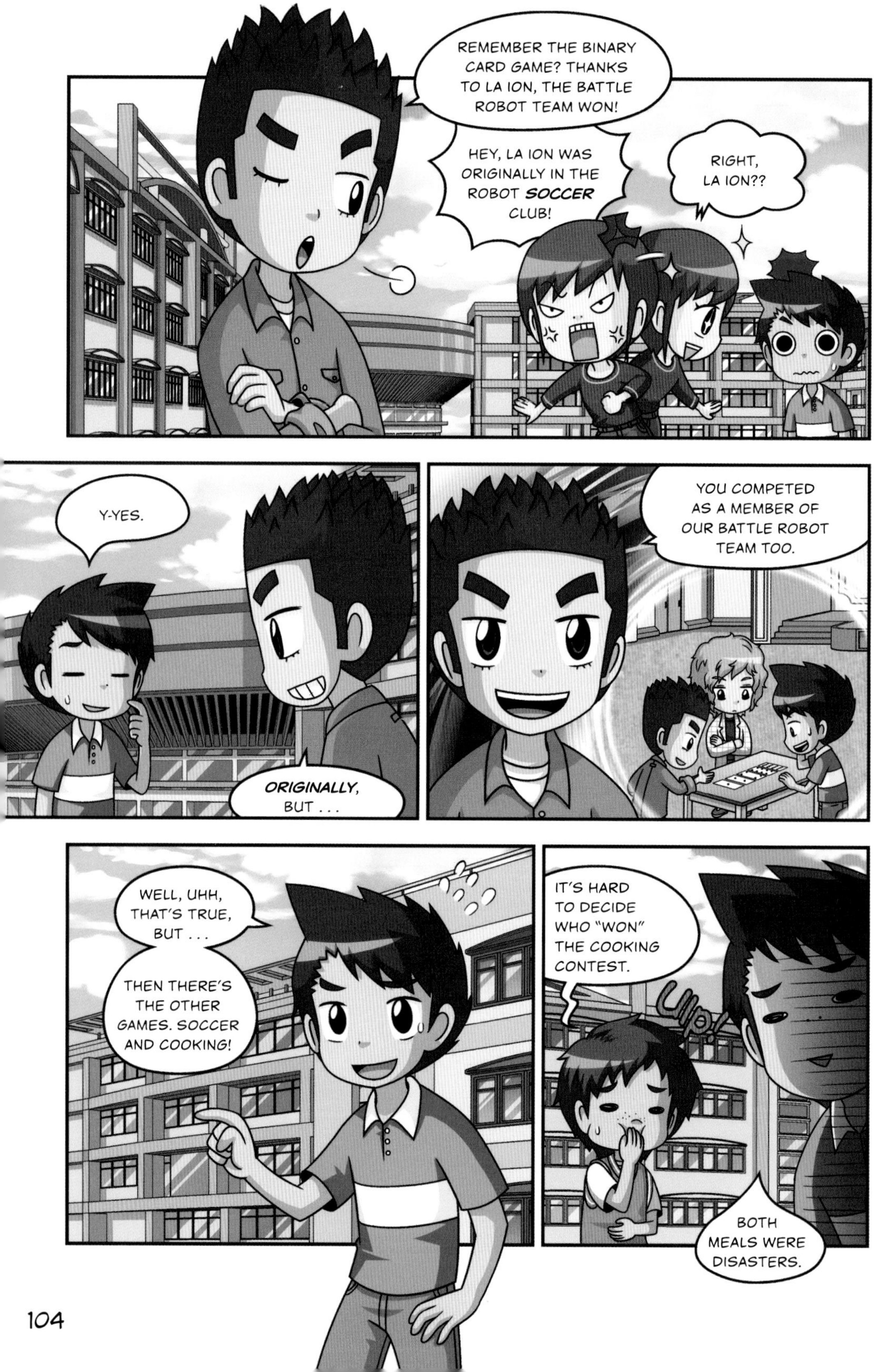
REMEMBER THE BINARY CARD GAME? THANKS TO LA ION, THE BATTLE ROBOT TEAM WON!
HEY, LA ION WAS ORIGINALLY IN THE ROBOT ***SOCCER*** CLUB!
RIGHT, LA ION??
Y-YES.
ORIGINALLY, BUT . . .
YOU COMPETED AS A MEMBER OF OUR BATTLE ROBOT TEAM TOO.
WELL, UHH, THAT'S TRUE, BUT . . .
THEN THERE'S THE OTHER GAMES. SOCCER AND COOKING!
IT'S HARD TO DECIDE WHO "WON" THE COOKING CONTEST.
BOTH MEALS WERE DISASTERS.

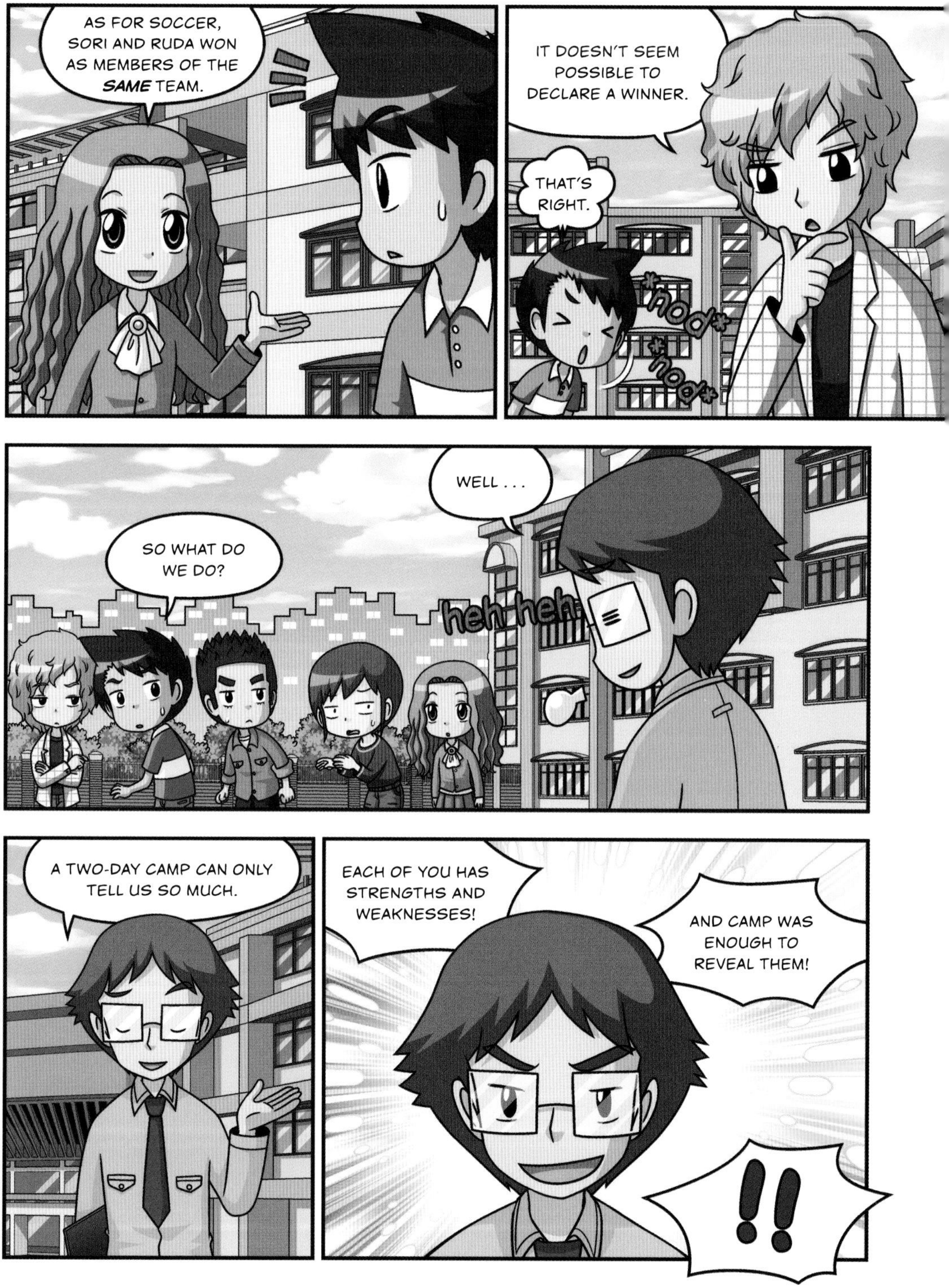
AS FOR SOCCER, SORI AND RUDA WON AS MEMBERS OF THE *SAME* TEAM.
IT DOESN'T SEEM POSSIBLE TO DECLARE A WINNER.
THAT'S RIGHT.
nod *nod*
WELL . . .
SO WHAT DO WE DO?
heh heh
A TWO-DAY CAMP CAN ONLY TELL US SO MUCH.
EACH OF YOU HAS STRENGTHS AND WEAKNESSES!
AND CAMP WAS ENOUGH TO REVEAL THEM!
!!

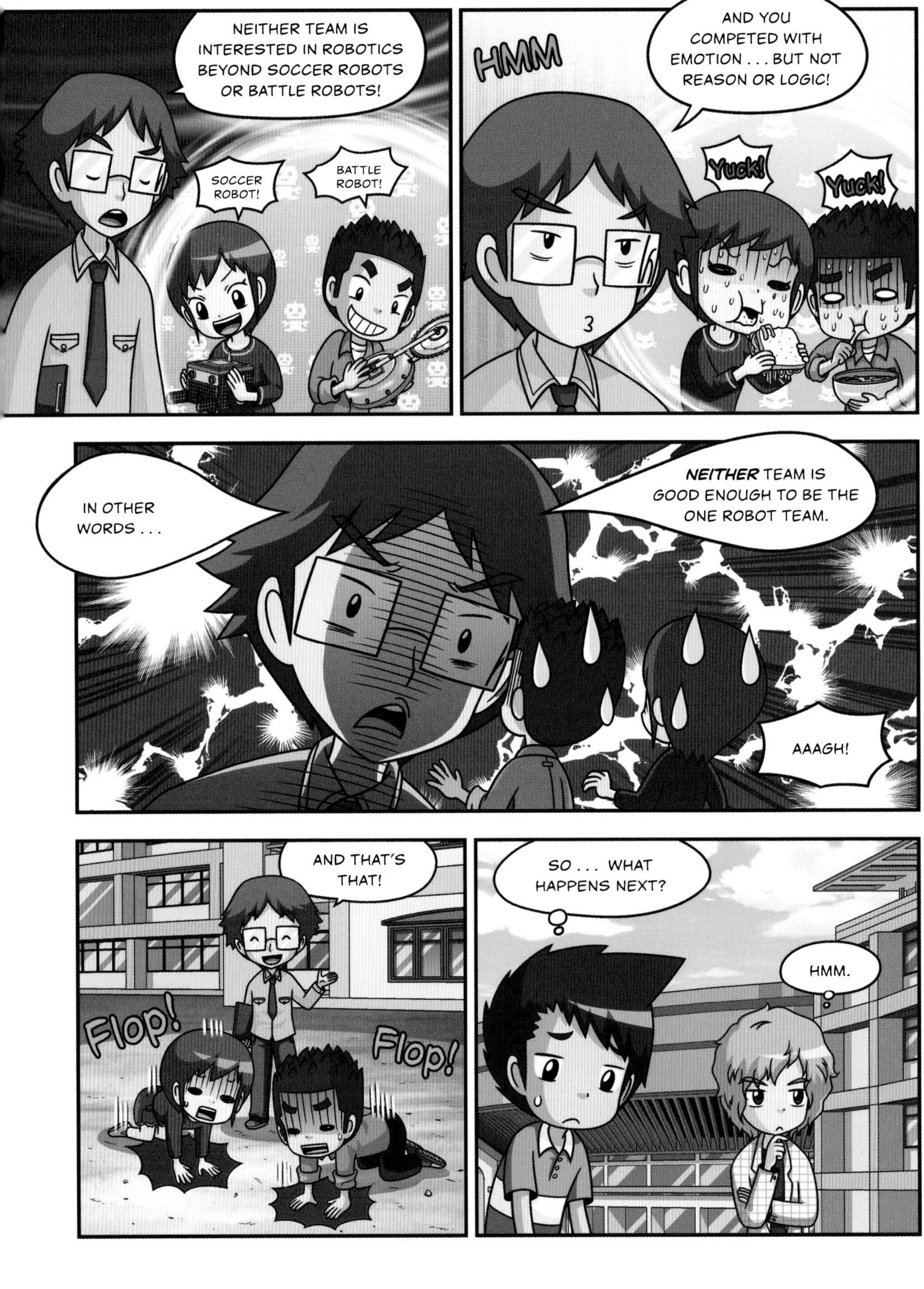
NEITHER TEAM IS INTERESTED IN ROBOTICS BEYOND SOCCER ROBOTS OR BATTLE ROBOTS!
SOCCER ROBOT!
BATTLE ROBOT!
HMM
AND YOU COMPETED WITH EMOTION . . . BUT NOT REASON OR LOGIC!
Yuck!
Yuck!
IN OTHER WORDS . . .
NEITHER TEAM IS GOOD ENOUGH TO BE THE ONE ROBOT TEAM.
AAAGH!
AND THAT'S THAT!
Flop!
Flop!
SO . . . WHAT HAPPENS NEXT?
HMM.

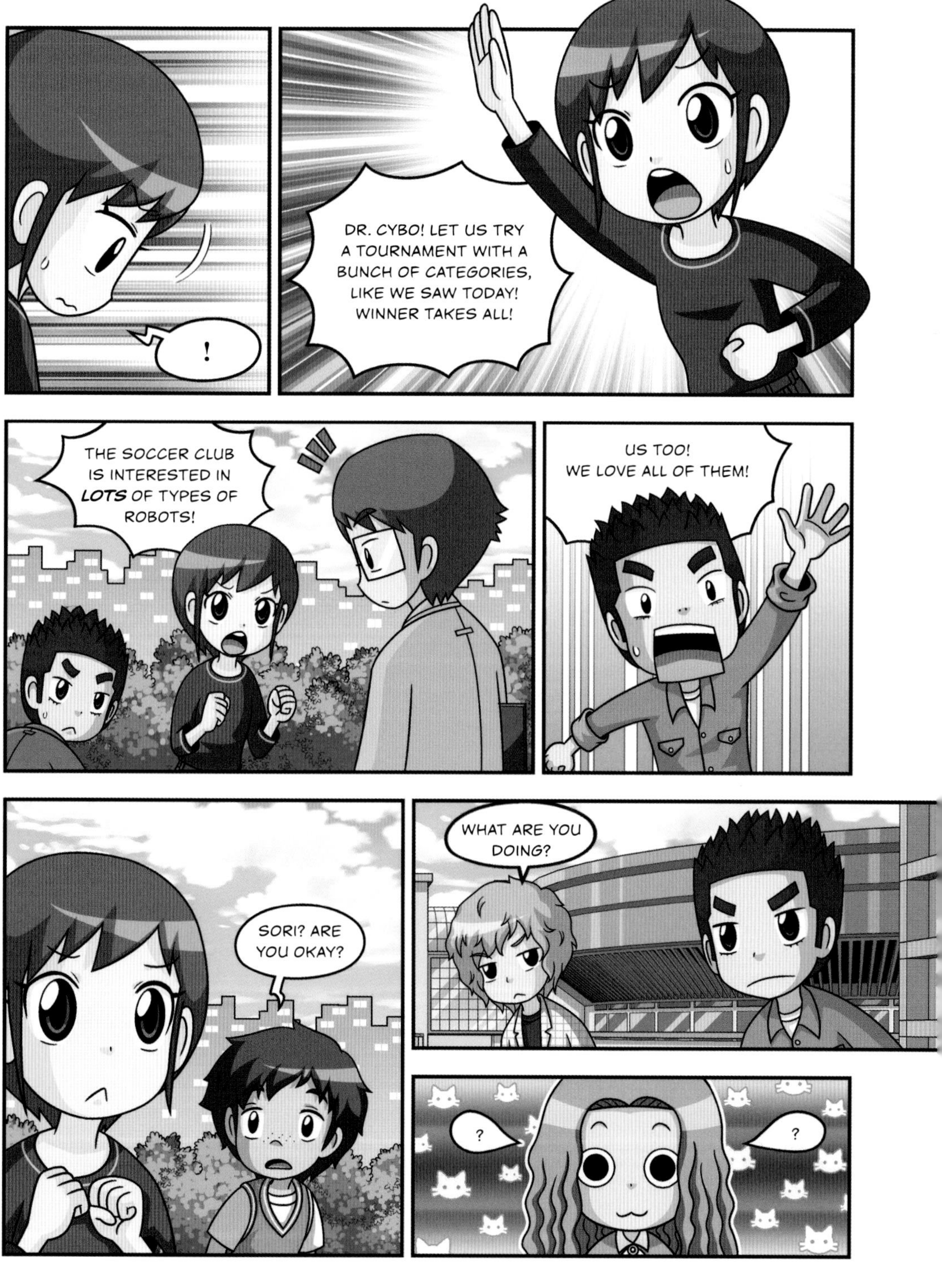
!
DR. CYBO! LET US TRY A TOURNAMENT WITH A BUNCH OF CATEGORIES, LIKE WE SAW TODAY! WINNER TAKES ALL!
THE SOCCER CLUB IS INTERESTED IN LOTS OF TYPES OF ROBOTS!
US TOO! WE LOVE ALL OF THEM!
SORI? ARE YOU OKAY?
WHAT ARE YOU DOING?
?
?

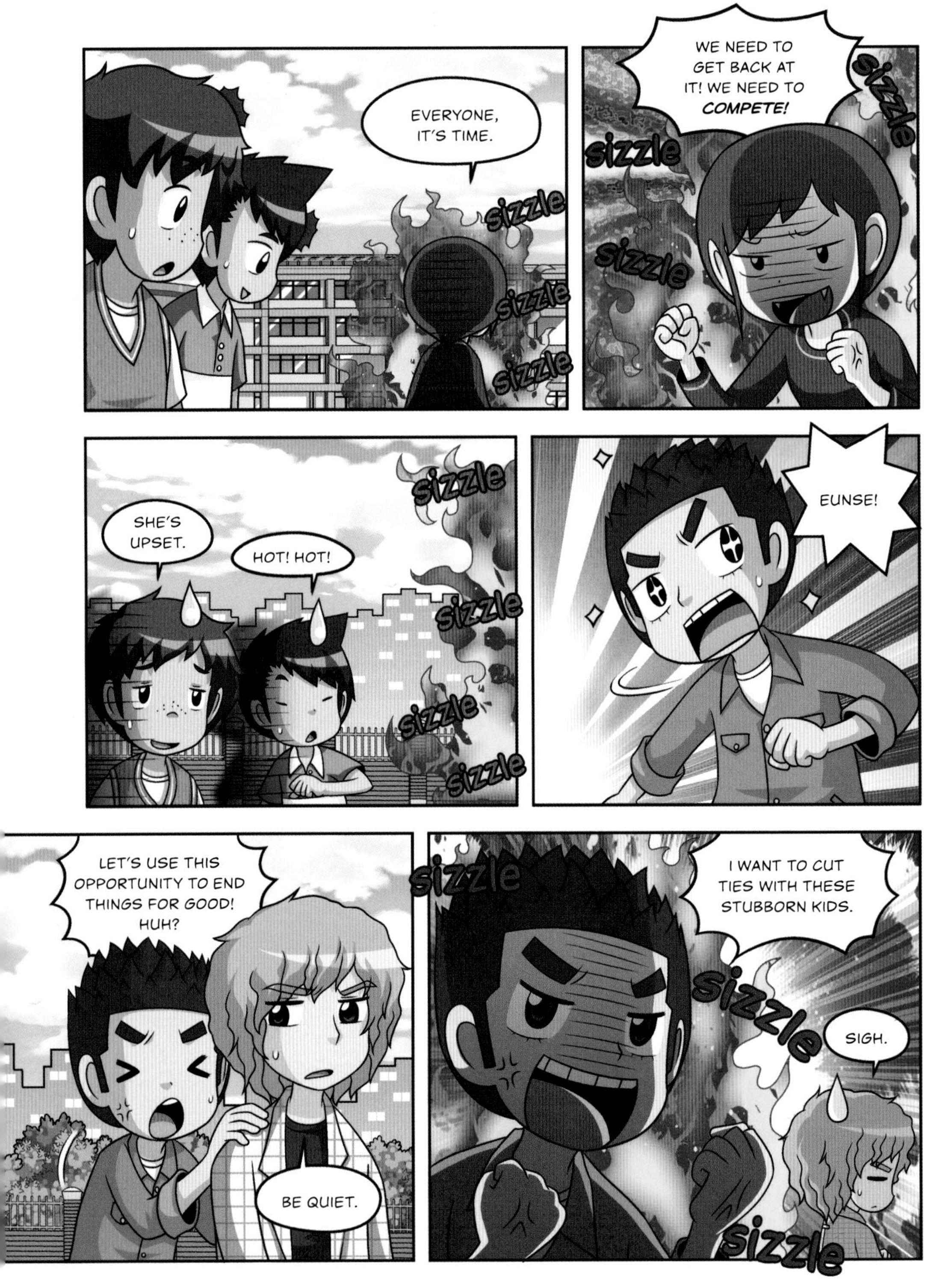
EVERYONE, IT'S TIME.
sizzle
sizzle
sizzle
WE NEED TO GET BACK AT IT! WE NEED TO *COMPETE!*
sizzle
sizzle
sizzle
sizzle
SHE'S UPSET.
HOT! HOT!
sizzle
sizzle
sizzle
sizzle
EUNSE!
LET'S USE THIS OPPORTUNITY TO END THINGS FOR GOOD! HUH?
BE QUIET.
sizzle
I WANT TO CUT TIES WITH THESE STUBBORN KIDS.
sizzle
SIGH.
sizzle

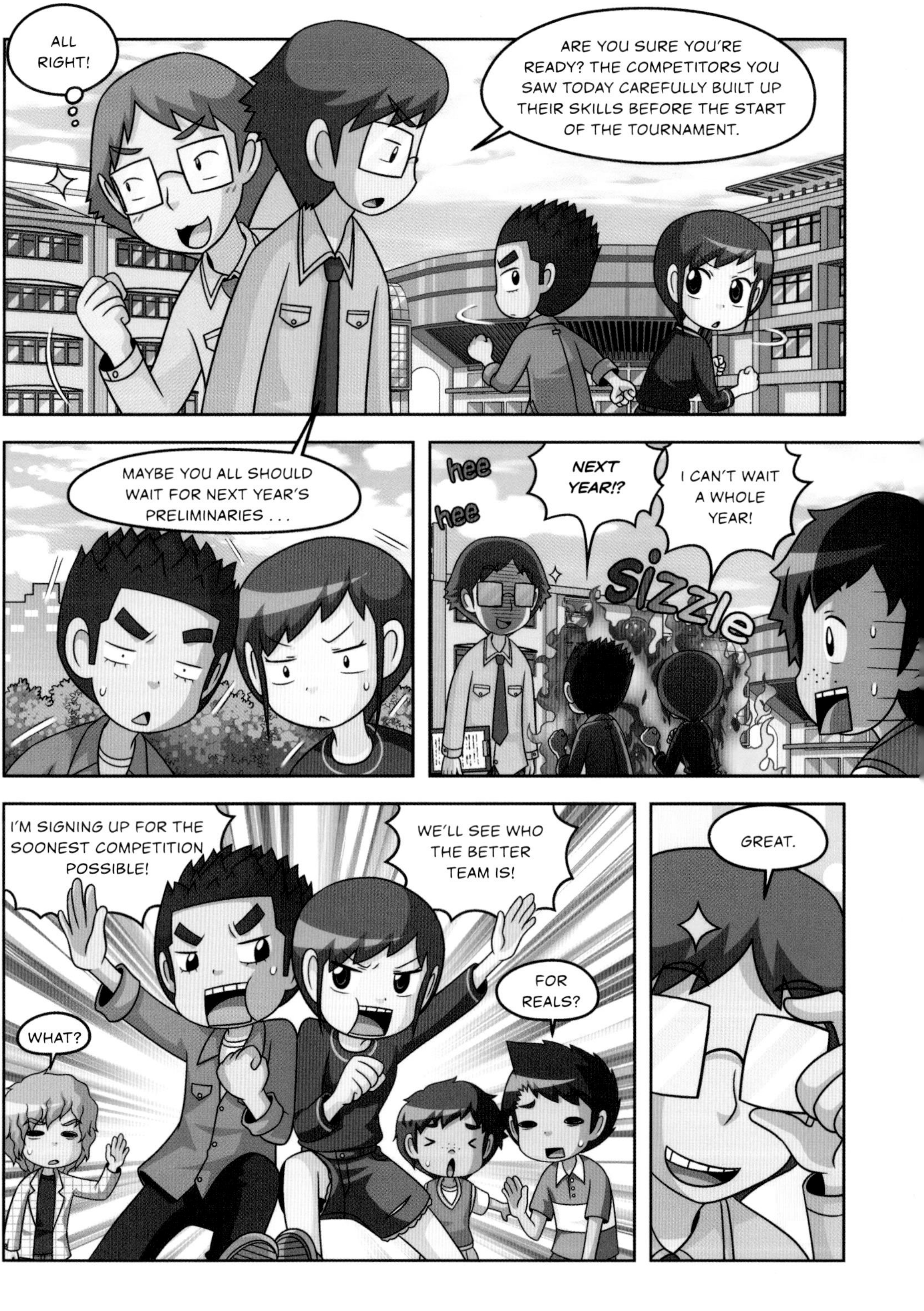
ALL RIGHT!
ARE YOU SURE YOU'RE READY? THE COMPETITORS YOU SAW TODAY CAREFULLY BUILT UP THEIR SKILLS BEFORE THE START OF THE TOURNAMENT.
MAYBE YOU ALL SHOULD WAIT FOR NEXT YEAR'S PRELIMINARIES . . .
hee
hee
NEXT YEAR!?
I CAN'T WAIT A WHOLE YEAR!
sizzle
I'M SIGNING UP FOR THE SOONEST COMPETITION POSSIBLE!
WE'LL SEE WHO THE BETTER TEAM IS!
WHAT?
FOR REALS?
GREAT.

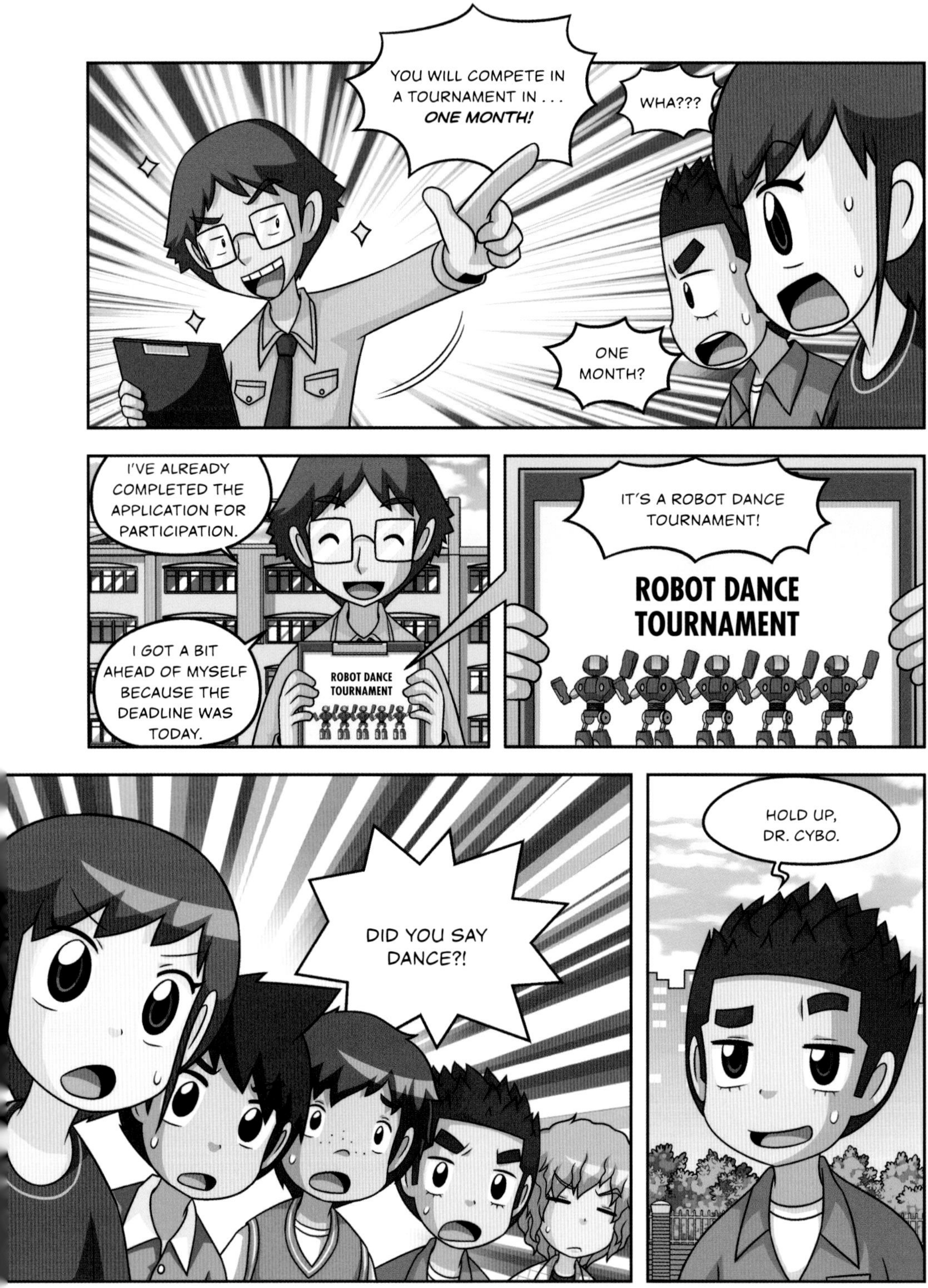
YOU WILL COMPETE IN A TOURNAMENT IN . . . ONE MONTH!
WHA???
ONE MONTH?
I'VE ALREADY COMPLETED THE APPLICATION FOR PARTICIPATION.
I GOT A BIT AHEAD OF MYSELF BECAUSE THE DEADLINE WAS TODAY.
ROBOT DANCE TOURNAMENT
IT'S A ROBOT DANCE TOURNAMENT!
ROBOT DANCE TOURNAMENT
DID YOU SAY DANCE?!
HOLD UP, DR. CYBO.

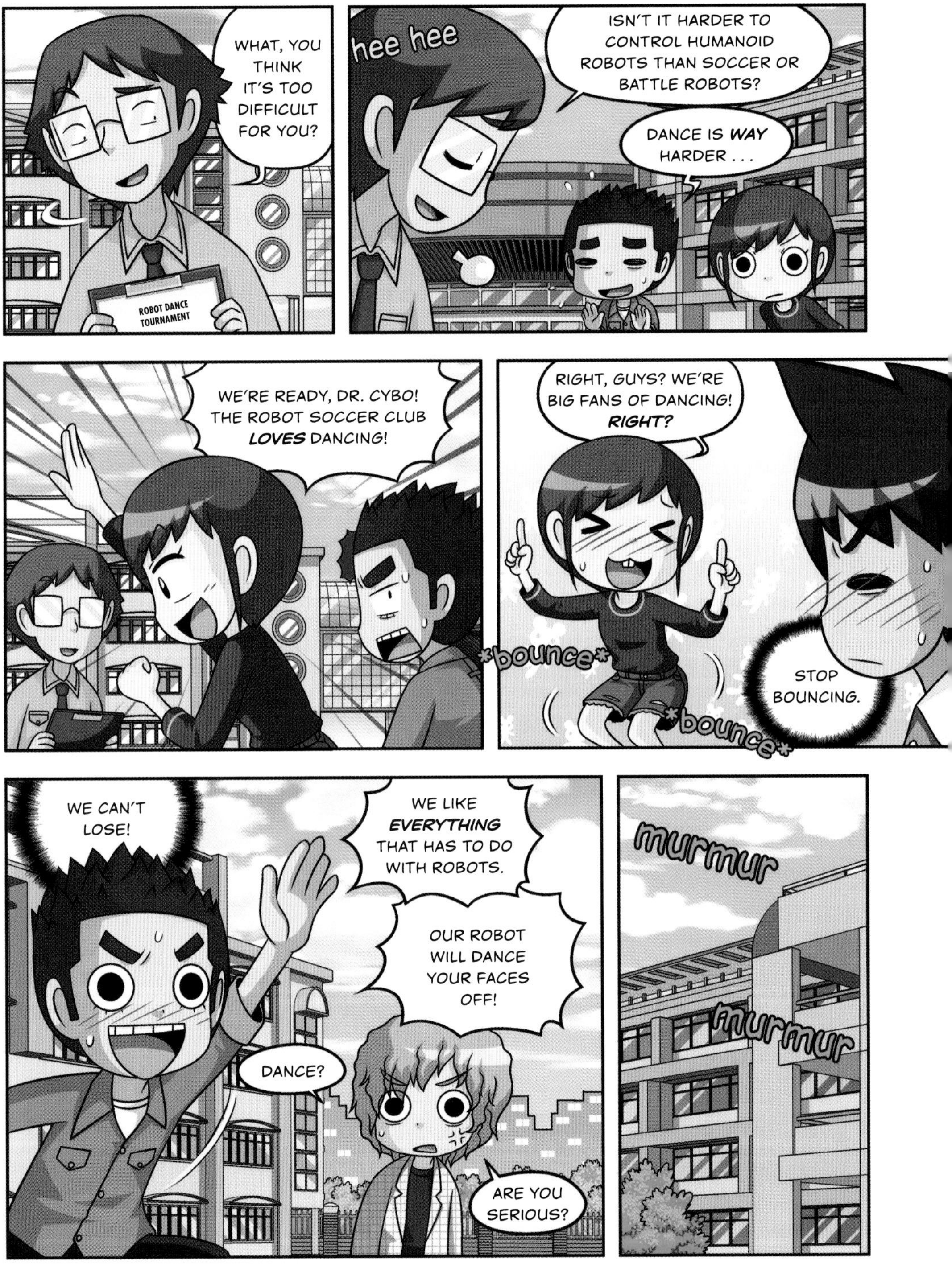

WHAT, YOU THINK IT'S TOO DIFFICULT FOR YOU?
ROBOT DANCE TOURNAMENT
hee hee
ISN'T IT HARDER TO CONTROL HUMANOID ROBOTS THAN SOCCER OR BATTLE ROBOTS?
DANCE IS WAY HARDER . . .
WE'RE READY, DR. CYBO! THE ROBOT SOCCER CLUB LOVES DANCING!
bounce
RIGHT, GUYS? WE'RE BIG FANS OF DANCING! RIGHT?
STOP BOUNCING.
bounce
WE CAN'T LOSE!
WE LIKE EVERYTHING THAT HAS TO DO WITH ROBOTS.
OUR ROBOT WILL DANCE YOUR FACES OFF!
DANCE?
ARE YOU SERIOUS?
murmur
murmur

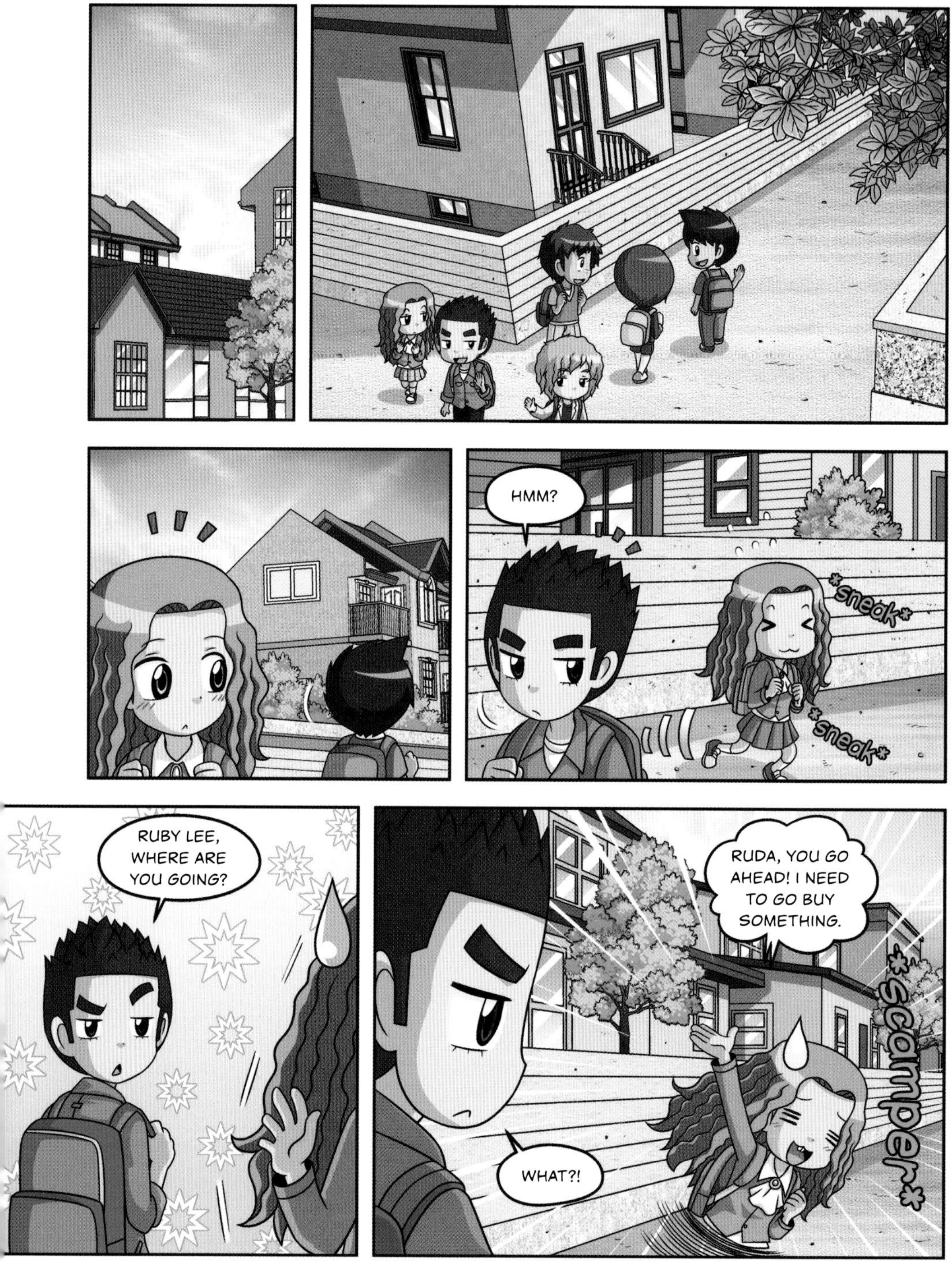
HMM?
sneak
sneak
RUBY LEE, WHERE ARE YOU GOING?
RUDA, YOU GO AHEAD! I NEED TO GO BUY SOMETHING.
scamper
WHAT?!

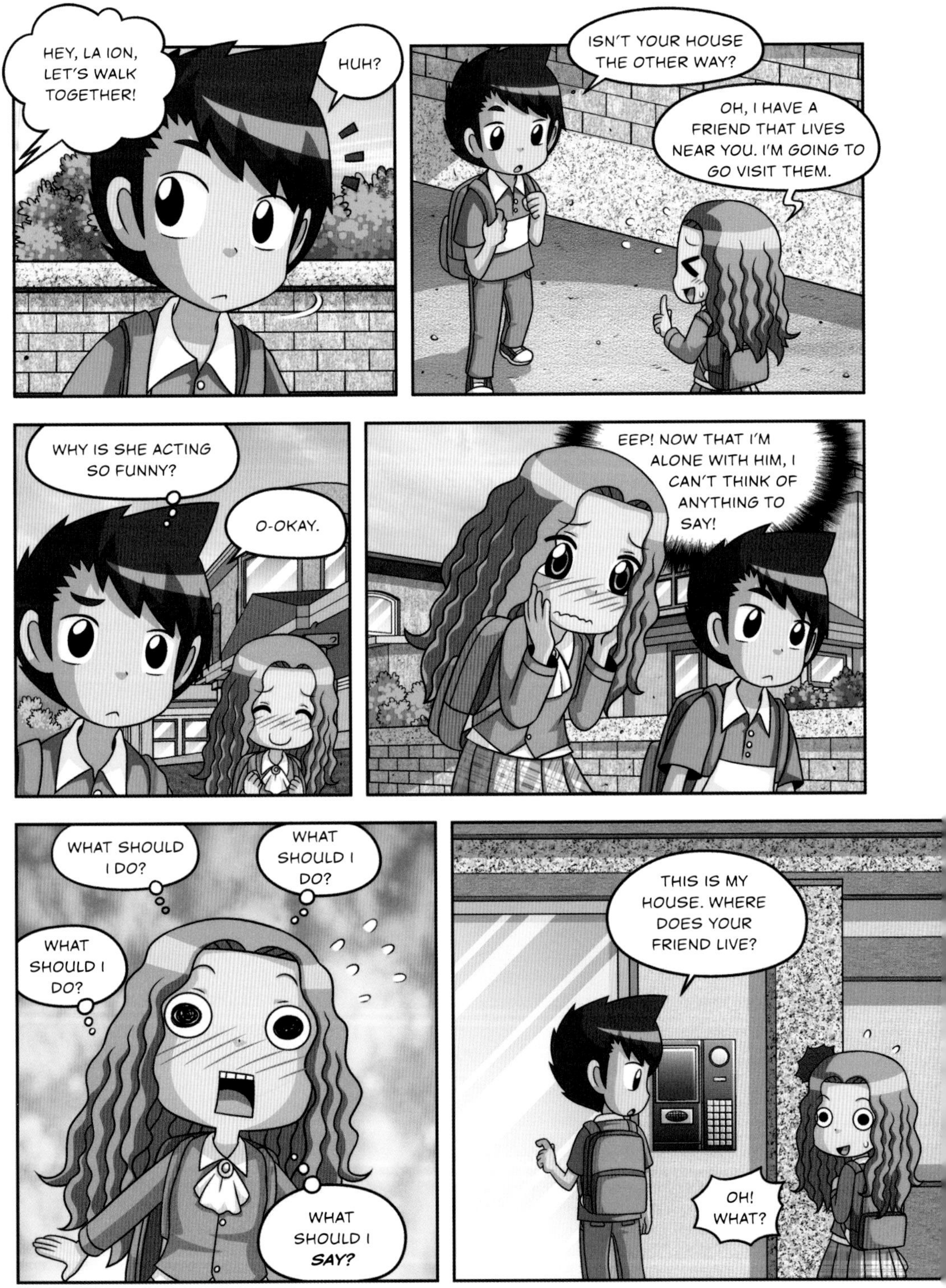
HEY, LA ION, LET'S WALK TOGETHER!
HUH?
ISN'T YOUR HOUSE THE OTHER WAY?
OH, I HAVE A FRIEND THAT LIVES NEAR YOU. I'M GOING TO GO VISIT THEM.
WHY IS SHE ACTING SO FUNNY?
O-OKAY.
EEP! NOW THAT I'M ALONE WITH HIM, I CAN'T THINK OF ANYTHING TO SAY!
WHAT SHOULD I DO?
WHAT SHOULD I DO?
WHAT SHOULD I DO?
WHAT SHOULD I *SAY?*
THIS IS MY HOUSE. WHERE DOES YOUR FRIEND LIVE?
OH! WHAT?

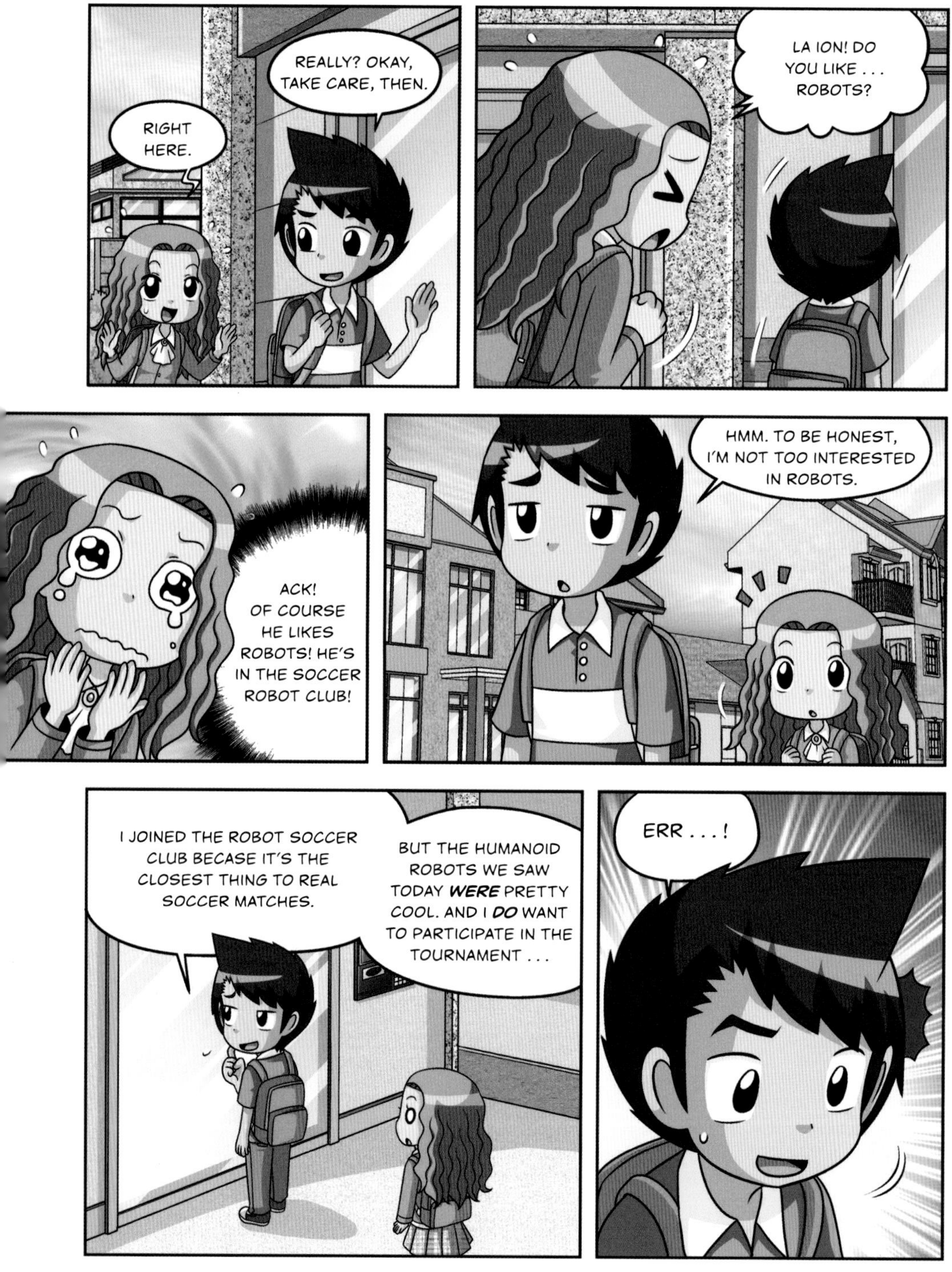
RIGHT HERE.
REALLY? OKAY, TAKE CARE, THEN.
LA ION! DO YOU LIKE . . . ROBOTS?
ACK! OF COURSE HE LIKES ROBOTS! HE'S IN THE SOCCER ROBOT CLUB!
HMM. TO BE HONEST, I'M NOT TOO INTERESTED IN ROBOTS.
I JOINED THE ROBOT SOCCER CLUB BECASE IT'S THE CLOSEST THING TO REAL SOCCER MATCHES.
BUT THE HUMANOID ROBOTS WE SAW TODAY *WERE* PRETTY COOL. AND I *DO* WANT TO PARTICIPATE IN THE TOURNAMENT . . .
ERR . . . !

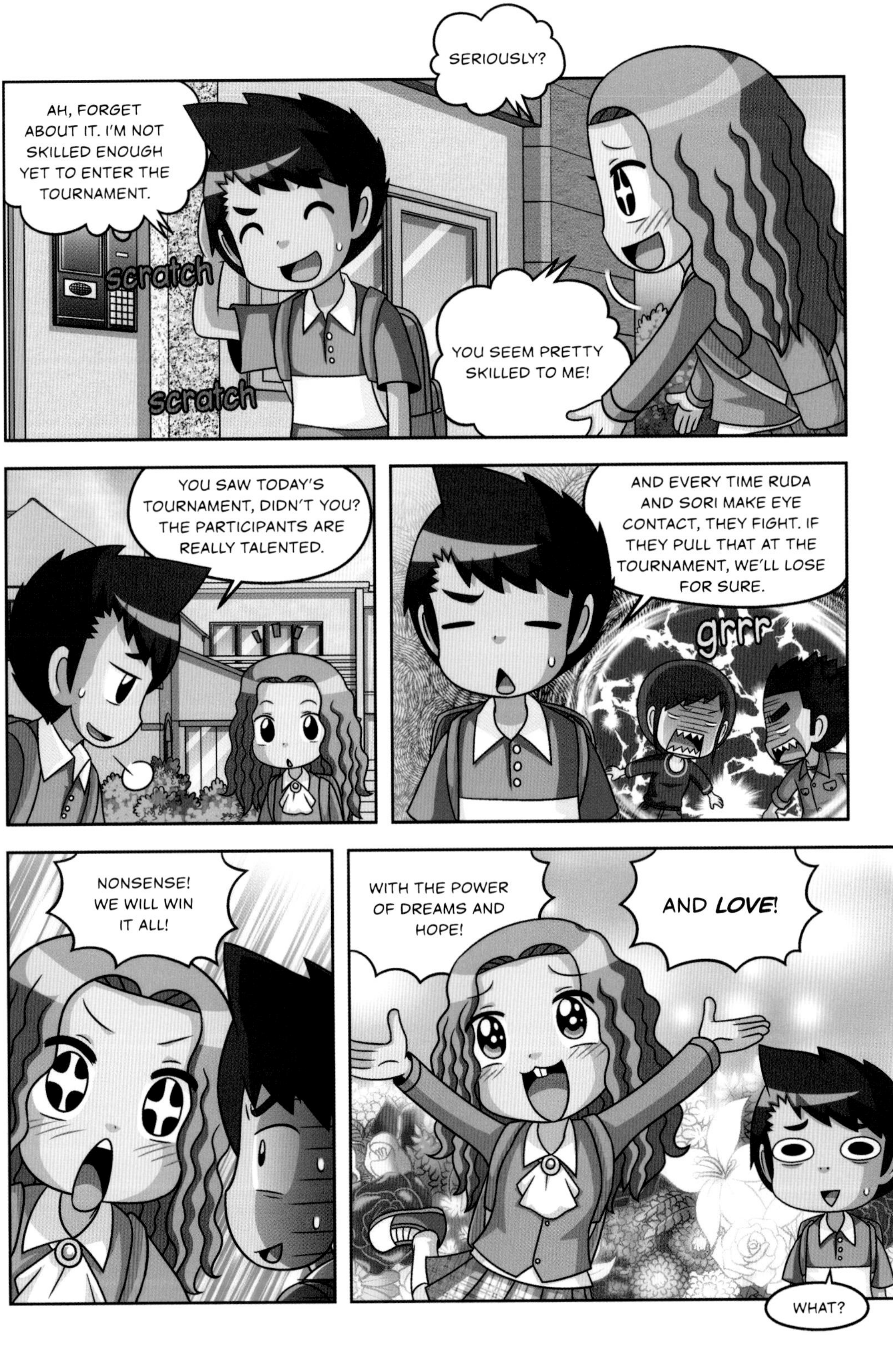
AH, FORGET ABOUT IT. I'M NOT SKILLED ENOUGH YET TO ENTER THE TOURNAMENT.
SERIOUSLY?
scratch
scratch
YOU SEEM PRETTY SKILLED TO ME!
YOU SAW TODAY'S TOURNAMENT, DIDN'T YOU? THE PARTICIPANTS ARE REALLY TALENTED.
AND EVERY TIME RUDA AND SORI MAKE EYE CONTACT, THEY FIGHT. IF THEY PULL THAT AT THE TOURNAMENT, WE'LL LOSE FOR SURE.
grrr
NONSENSE! WE WILL WIN IT ALL!
WITH THE POWER OF DREAMS AND HOPE!
AND *LOVE*!
WHAT?

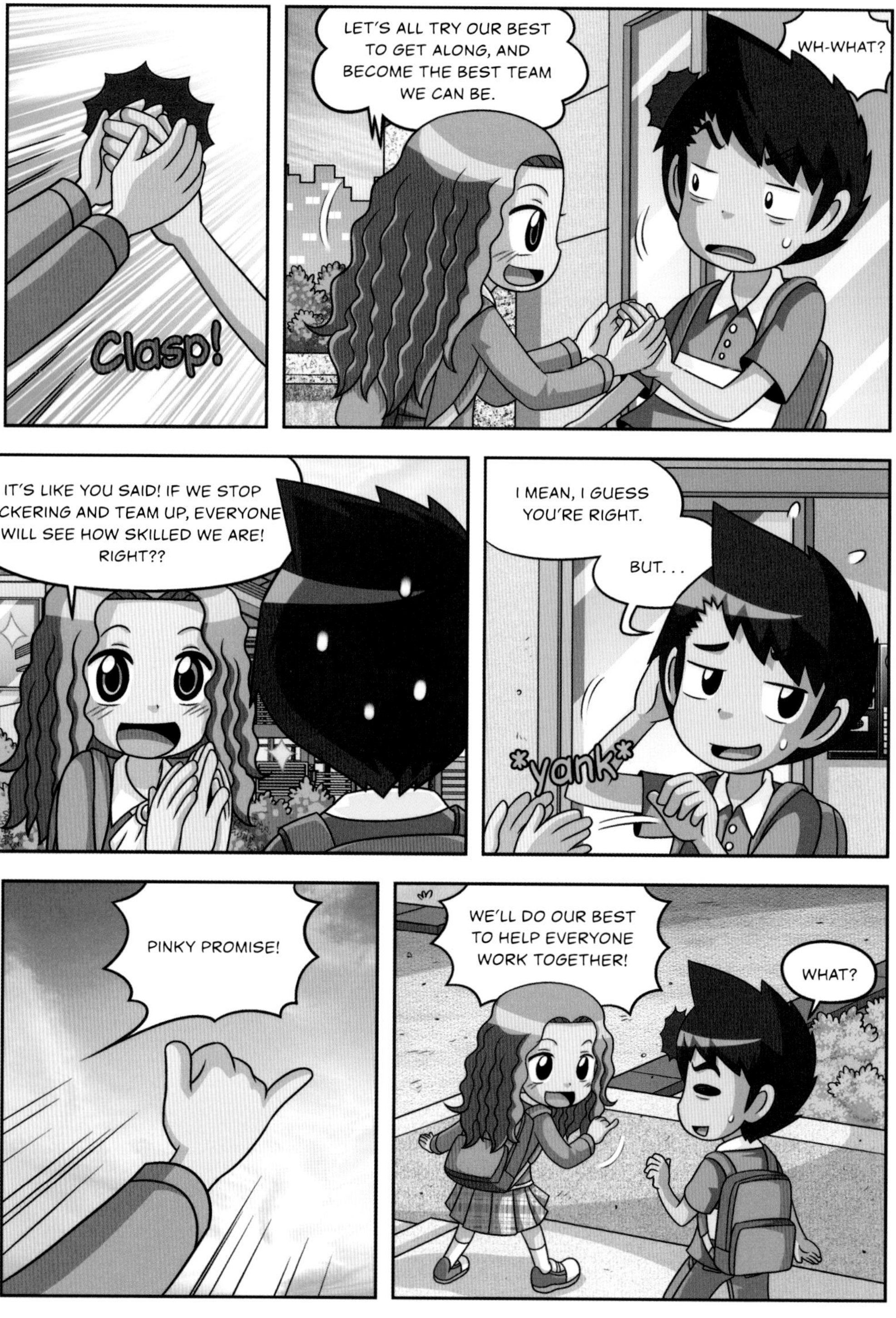
Clasp!
LET'S ALL TRY OUR BEST TO GET ALONG, AND BECOME THE BEST TEAM WE CAN BE.
WH-WHAT?
IT'S LIKE YOU SAID! IF WE STOP BICKERING AND TEAM UP, EVERYONE WILL SEE HOW SKILLED WE ARE! RIGHT??
I MEAN, I GUESS YOU'RE RIGHT.
BUT. . .
yank
PINKY PROMISE!
WE'LL DO OUR BEST TO HELP EVERYONE WORK TOGETHER!
WHAT?

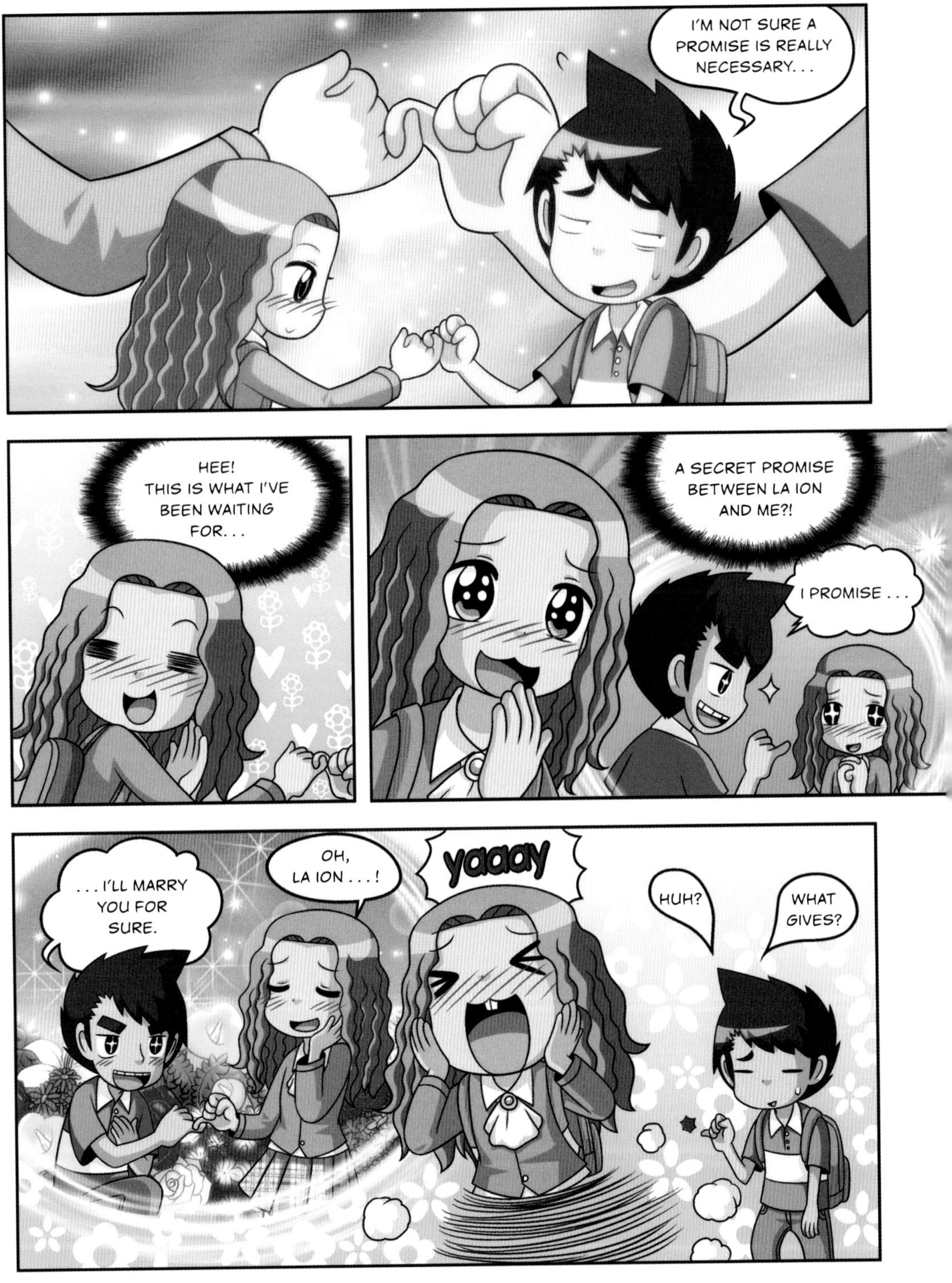
I'M NOT SURE A PROMISE IS REALLY NECESSARY. . .
HEE! THIS IS WHAT I'VE BEEN WAITING FOR. . .
A SECRET PROMISE BETWEEN LA ION AND ME?!
I PROMISE . . .
. . . I'LL MARRY YOU FOR SURE.
OH, LA ION . . . !
yaaay
HUH?
WHAT GIVES?

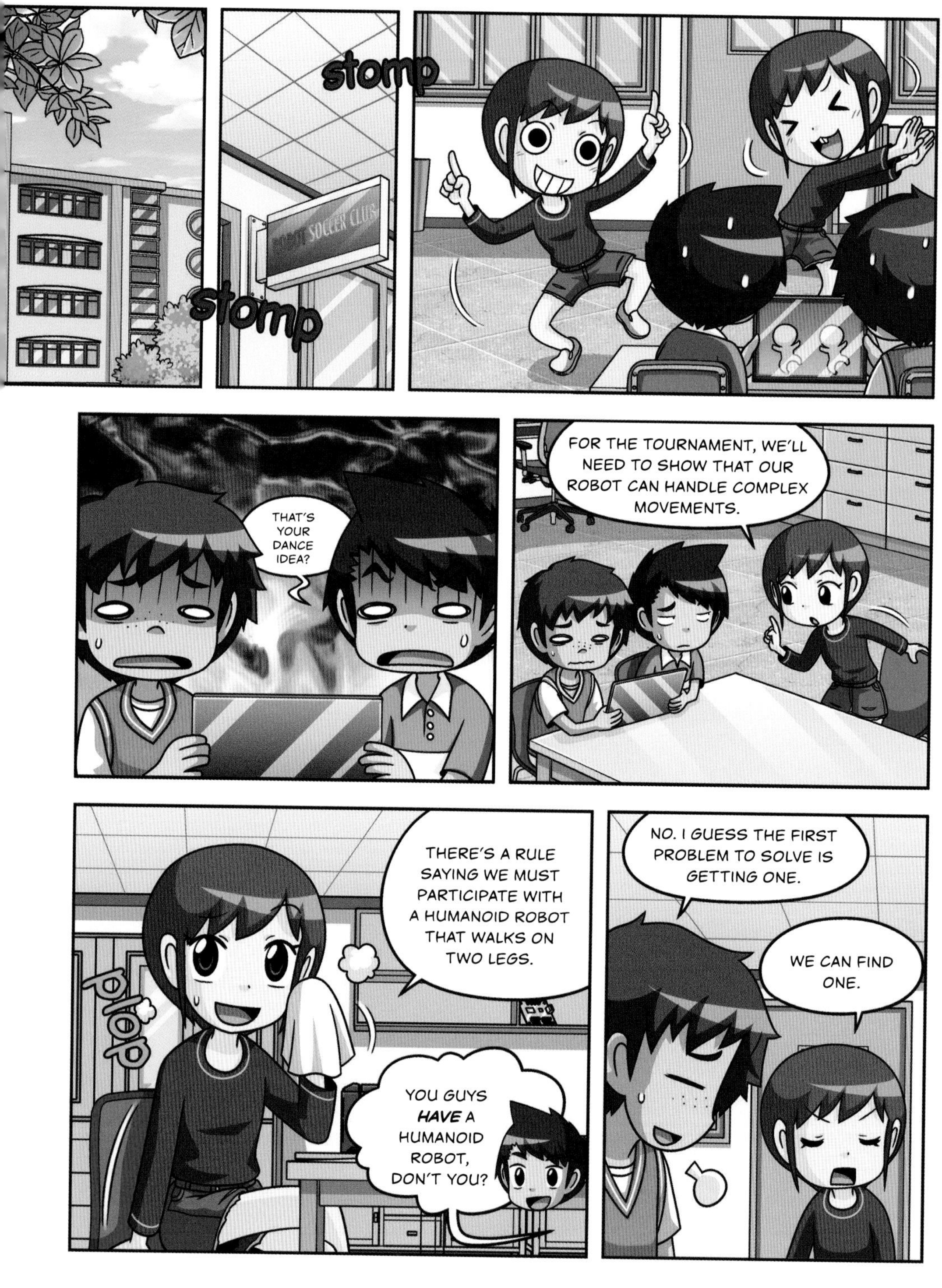
stomp
SOCCER CLUB
stomp
THAT'S YOUR DANCE IDEA?
FOR THE TOURNAMENT, WE'LL NEED TO SHOW THAT OUR ROBOT CAN HANDLE COMPLEX MOVEMENTS.
THERE'S A RULE SAYING WE MUST PARTICIPATE WITH A HUMANOID ROBOT THAT WALKS ON TWO LEGS.
plop
YOU GUYS **HAVE** A HUMANOID ROBOT, DON'T YOU?
NO. I GUESS THE FIRST PROBLEM TO SOLVE IS GETTING ONE.
WE CAN FIND ONE.

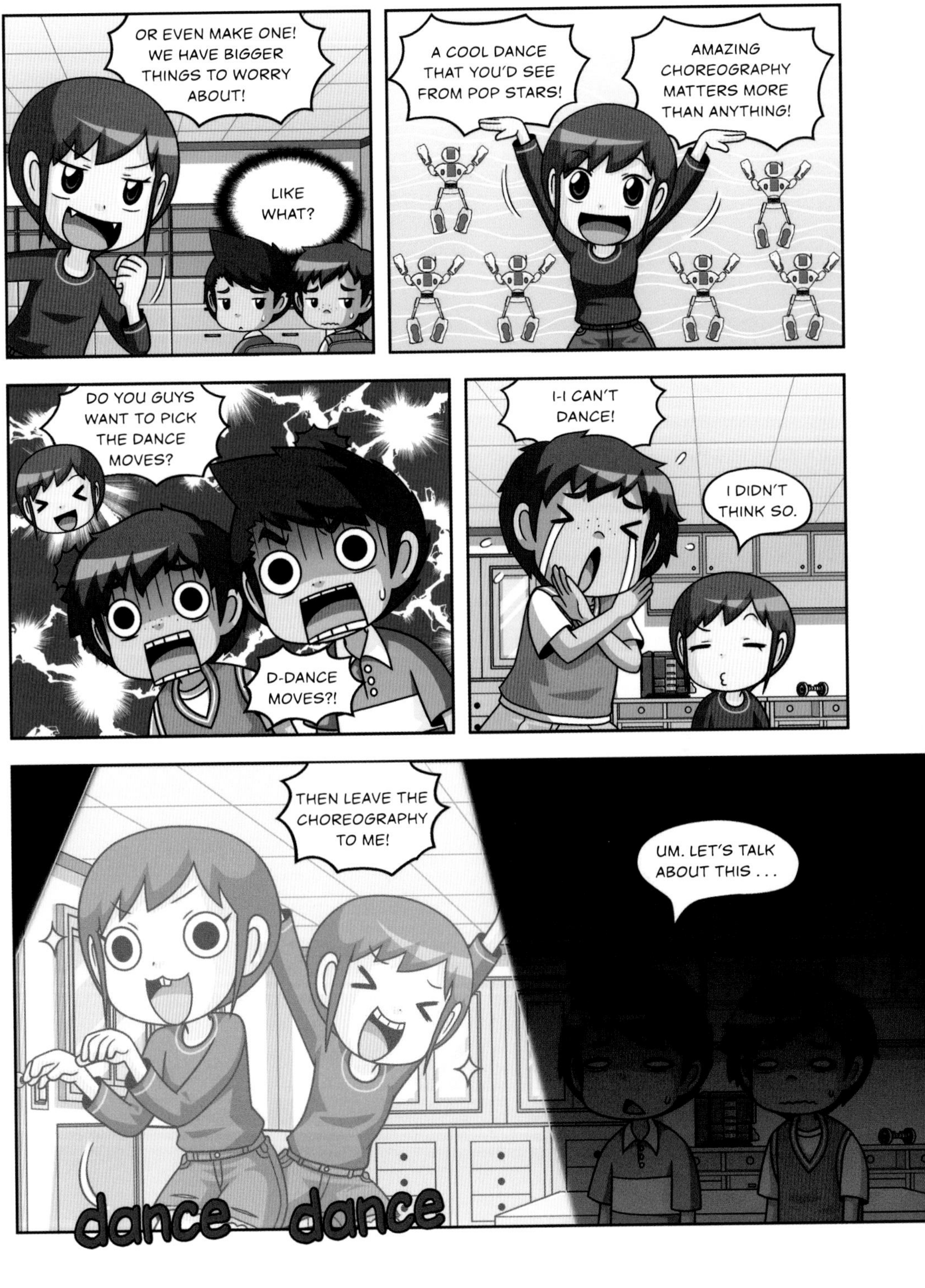
OR EVEN MAKE ONE! WE HAVE BIGGER THINGS TO WORRY ABOUT!
LIKE WHAT?
A COOL DANCE THAT YOU'D SEE FROM POP STARS!
AMAZING CHOREOGRAPHY MATTERS MORE THAN ANYTHING!
DO YOU GUYS WANT TO PICK THE DANCE MOVES?
D-DANCE MOVES?!
I-I CAN'T DANCE!
I DIDN'T THINK SO.
THEN LEAVE THE CHOREOGRAPHY TO ME!
UM. LET'S TALK ABOUT THIS . . .
dance dance

LA ION'S JOURNAL

Transporter and Robot Gathering

WOW, IT GOES FAST WITHOUT DRIFTING OUT OF THE LANE!

When I visited that robotics competition, a bunch of games were going on. The ones I liked most were called transporter and robot gathering. In transporter, robots use their sensors to recognize a lane. They have to stay in the lane while moving a particular object to a particular spot. Competitors are ranked by the speed and accuracy of their missions.

A robot in transporter must drive autonomously according to a program. Players can't perform additional operations on a robot after the game begins. Once the robots left the starting line, I saw participants watching their robots anxiously, which made me nervous too. Robot gathering is another game with line-tracing robots. After moving an object to its destination, a robot must cross a finish line. The robots I saw had hands or grippers of different shapes, for grabbing, lifting, and pushing different targets.

The game field covers two zones connected by a bridge. If a robot goes in the wrong direction, it can fall off the field. Whenever a robot was about to cross the bridge, everyone held their breath. After completing a mission, a robot must reach the finish line and stay there for more than three seconds to end the race. It was nerve-wracking to watch the referee and the competitors count to three out loud. I can't wait to make my own robot and enter different competitions.

©IROC

A range of games takes place at Robot Olympiad, including robot gathering, transporter, battle cubes, and emergency response.

Battle Cubes

For some reason, but probably because of the word *battle*, Ruda Lee was most interested in a game called battle cubes. This game's field includes 12 small cubes, and robots need to put the cubes in a basket located in the middle. The game looked kind of like basketball. A robot's not supposed to be in the opposing team's area, and only a limited number of cubes can be moved at once. Players can get penalties for violating game rules, but the participants (and the robots) seemed focused throughout the game. It was sad to see the winning team's robot get a penalty because it had moved in the wrong direction, entering the opposing team's zone.

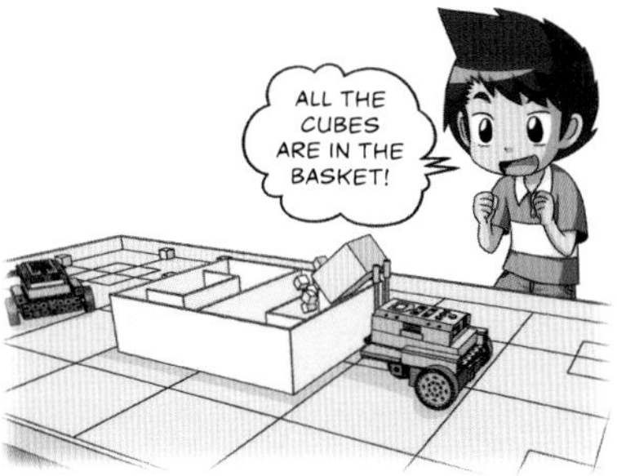
ALL THE CUBES ARE IN THE BASKET!

Eunse Koh stayed by himself, watching games in the creative-mission category. It was a perfect fit for the origami genius Eunse, because competitors need to creatively solve missions depending on a given situation. Equipped with various motors and sensors, robots in this category were interesting because they looked different than robots in other competitions. Often devices were decorated with everyday materials like paper and hard foam, which aren't commonly used in making robots. Participants were ranked on how accurately they completed their missions.

With the combination of Eunse's origami skills, Sori's incredible imagination, and Ruda's robot-making skills, they could make the best bot ever! I hope they all make up and participate in the competition together.

©IROC

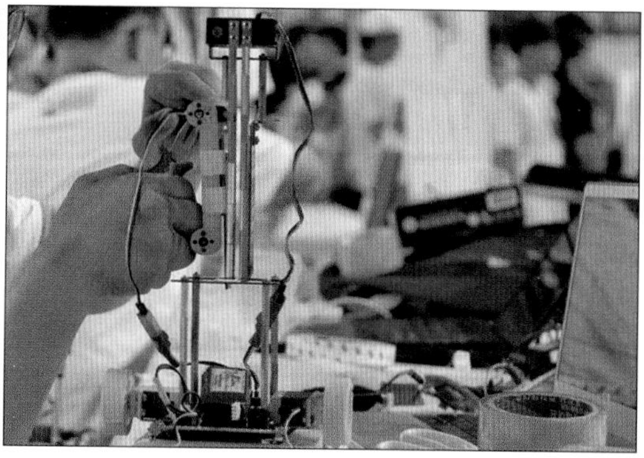

Participants in the creative-mission category compete in scientific knowledge, robot production skills, and problem-solving.

Chapter 6

WHO'S TRYING TO FLIRT WITH MY SISTER? ***WHO'S FLIRTING WITH RUBY!!***
UM.
I THINK YOU'RE THE ONLY ONE WHO DOESN'T KNOW.

Ruby Lee: Dance Genius

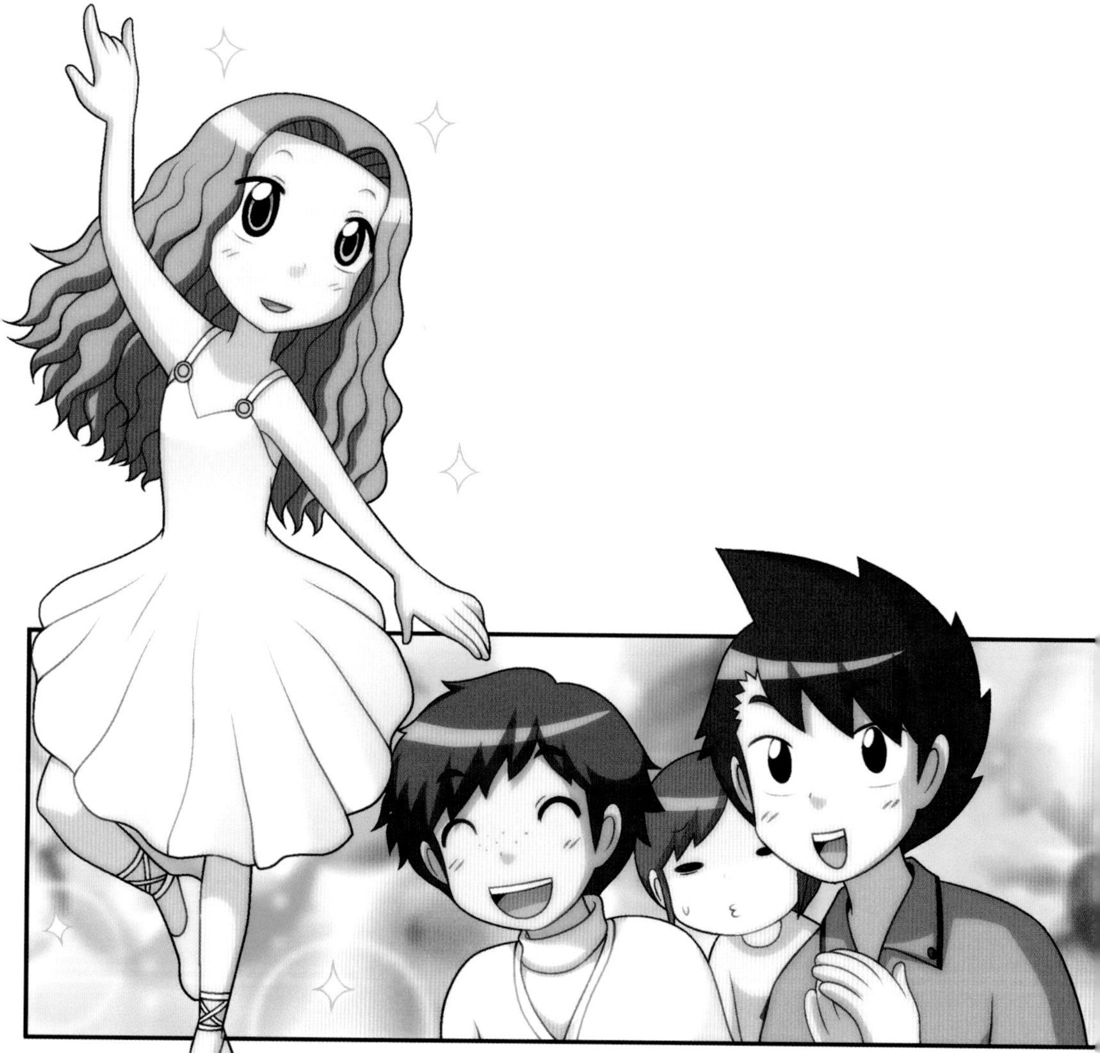

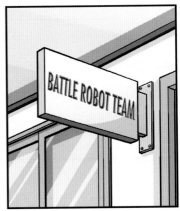

BATTLE ROBOT TEAM

OKAY, HERE'S WHAT I CAME UP WITH.

I SEARCHED ALL NIGHT FOR IT.

heh heh

SO WHAT ARE ITS *FUNCTIONS?*

THE VERY BEST! A HUMANOID ROBOT THAT CAN PERFECT ANY MOVEMENT. IT'S WHAT WE NEED TO WIN THE TOURNAMENT.

HMM

IT HAS A LONG-LASTING BATTERY, SEVERAL SENSORS, AND DOZENS OF SERVOMOTORS!

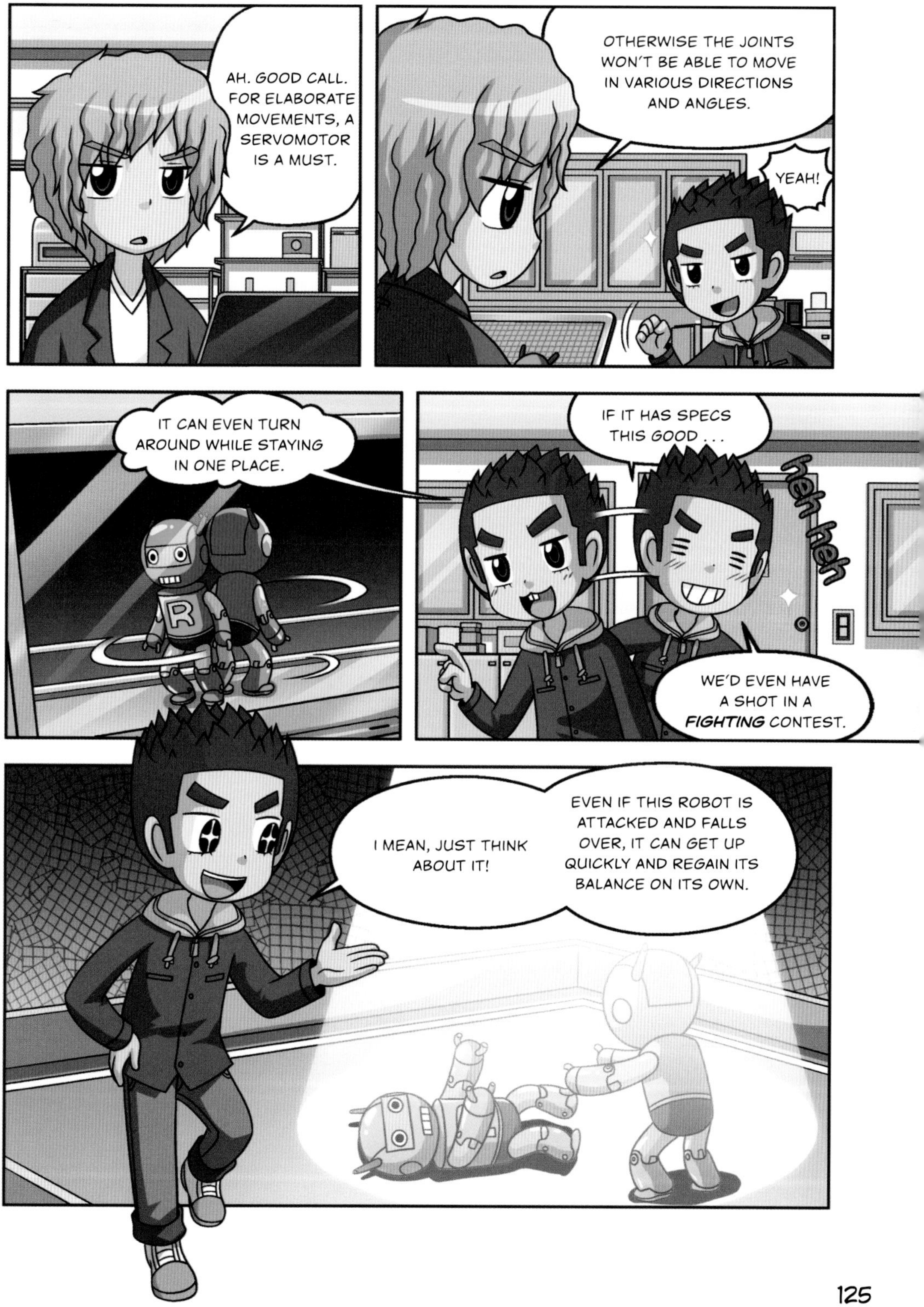
AH. GOOD CALL. FOR ELABORATE MOVEMENTS, A SERVOMOTOR IS A MUST.
OTHERWISE THE JOINTS WON'T BE ABLE TO MOVE IN VARIOUS DIRECTIONS AND ANGLES.
YEAH!
IT CAN EVEN TURN AROUND WHILE STAYING IN ONE PLACE.
IF IT HAS SPECS THIS GOOD . . .
heh heh
WE'D EVEN HAVE A SHOT IN A ***FIGHTING*** CONTEST.
I MEAN, JUST THINK ABOUT IT!
EVEN IF THIS ROBOT IS ATTACKED AND FALLS OVER, IT CAN GET UP QUICKLY AND REGAIN ITS BALANCE ON ITS OWN.

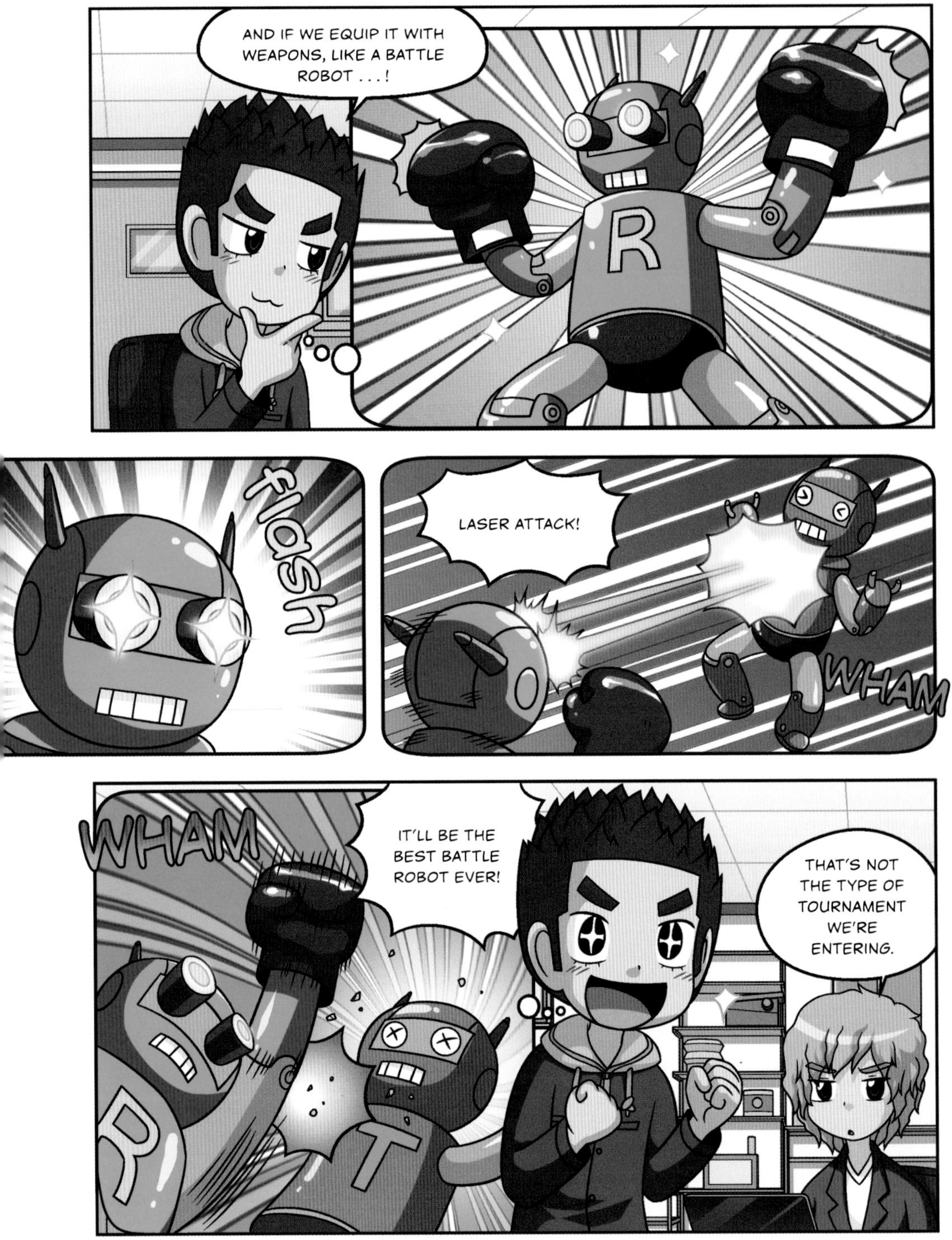
AND IF WE EQUIP IT WITH WEAPONS, LIKE A BATTLE ROBOT . . . !
R
flash
LASER ATTACK!
WHAM
WHAM
IT'LL BE THE BEST BATTLE ROBOT EVER!
THAT'S NOT THE TYPE OF TOURNAMENT WE'RE ENTERING.
R
T

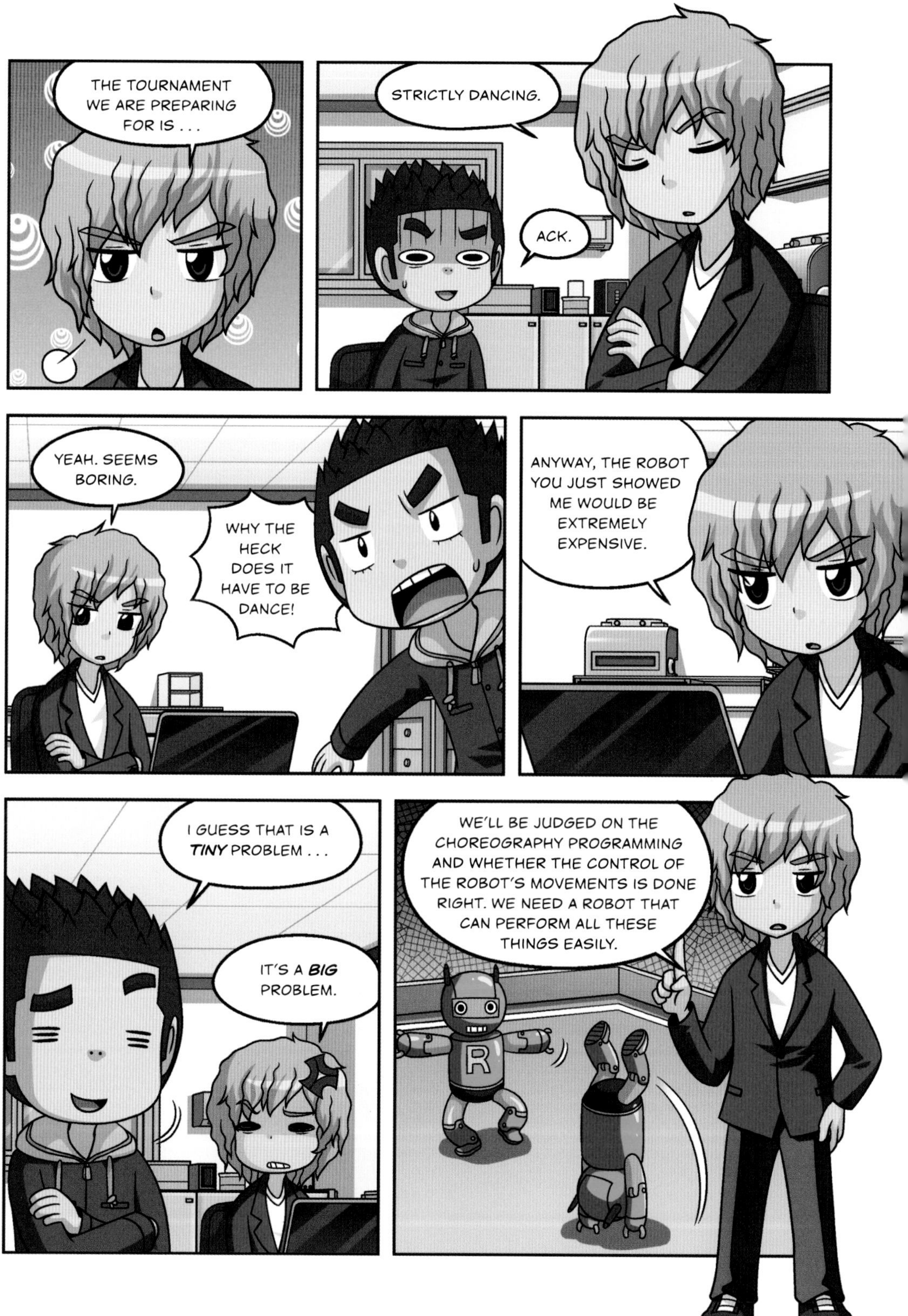
THE TOURNAMENT WE ARE PREPARING FOR IS . . .
STRICTLY DANCING.
ACK.
YEAH. SEEMS BORING.
WHY THE HECK DOES IT HAVE TO BE DANCE!
ANYWAY, THE ROBOT YOU JUST SHOWED ME WOULD BE EXTREMELY EXPENSIVE.
I GUESS THAT IS A *TINY* PROBLEM . . .
IT'S A *BIG* PROBLEM.
WE'LL BE JUDGED ON THE CHOREOGRAPHY PROGRAMMING AND WHETHER THE CONTROL OF THE ROBOT'S MOVEMENTS IS DONE RIGHT. WE NEED A ROBOT THAT CAN PERFORM ALL THESE THINGS EASILY.
R

MAYBE WE'LL FIND AN AFFORDABLE VERSION!

BUT WE PROBABLY WON'T.

WE COULD SELL ALL *THESE* ROBOTS.

WHAT ARE YOU TALKING ABOUT?!

WE'VE FIXED THEM AND UPGRADED THEM OVER AND OVER! HEY'RE LIKE MY PRECIOUS CHILDREN!!

MY BELOVED ROBOTS!

WE **CAN'T!**

THEY'RE JUST ROBOTS.

YOU WANT TO WIN, RIGHT?

YEAH, OF COURSE!

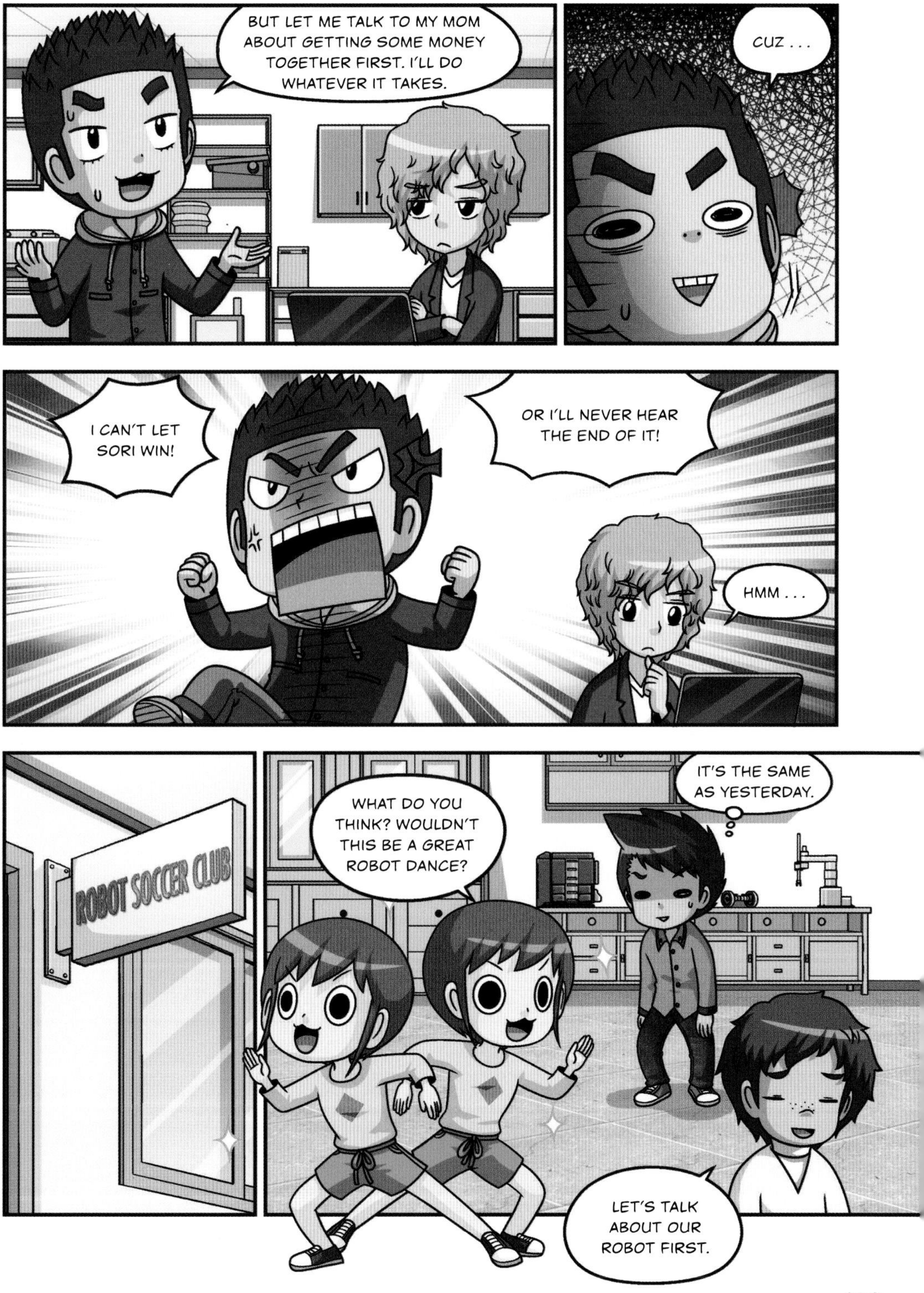
BUT LET ME TALK TO MY MOM ABOUT GETTING SOME MONEY TOGETHER FIRST. I'LL DO WHATEVER IT TAKES.
CUZ . . .
I CAN'T LET SORI WIN!
OR I'LL NEVER HEAR THE END OF IT!
HMM . . .
ROBOT SOCCER CLUB
WHAT DO YOU THINK? WOULDN'T THIS BE A GREAT ROBOT DANCE?
IT'S THE SAME AS YESTERDAY.
LET'S TALK ABOUT OUR ROBOT FIRST.

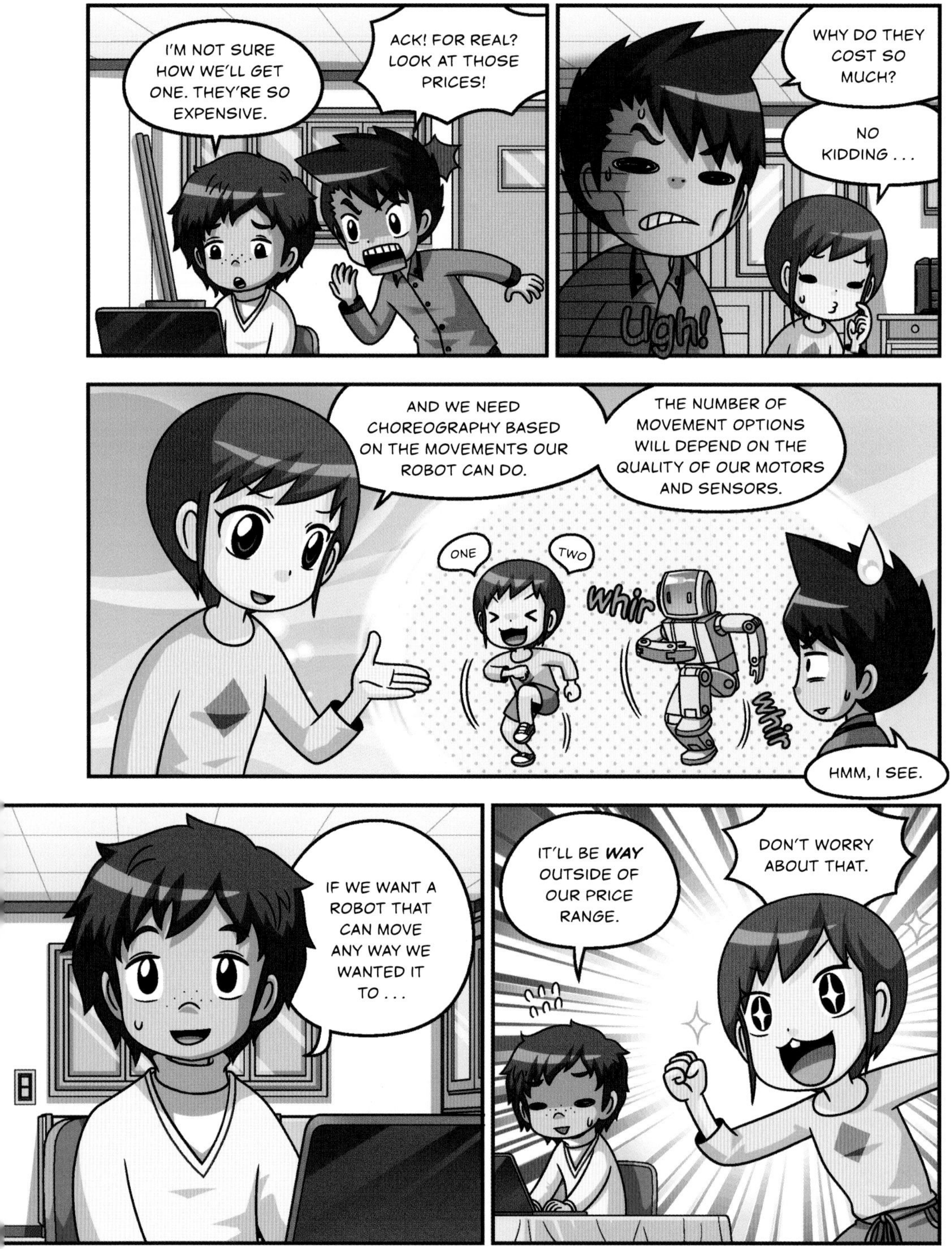

I'M NOT SURE HOW WE'LL GET ONE. THEY'RE SO EXPENSIVE.
ACK! FOR REAL? LOOK AT THOSE PRICES!
WHY DO THEY COST SO MUCH?
NO KIDDING . . .
Ugh!
AND WE NEED CHOREOGRAPHY BASED ON THE MOVEMENTS OUR ROBOT CAN DO.
THE NUMBER OF MOVEMENT OPTIONS WILL DEPEND ON THE QUALITY OF OUR MOTORS AND SENSORS.
ONE
TWO
whir
whir
HMM, I SEE.
IF WE WANT A ROBOT THAT CAN MOVE ANY WAY WE WANTED IT TO . . .
IT'LL BE **WAY** OUTSIDE OF OUR PRICE RANGE.
DON'T WORRY ABOUT THAT.

IF WE PERFECT OUR PLAN, AND SHOW PRINCIPAL PARK, I'M SURE HE'LL HELP US OUT!

FOR REALS?

WELL, MAYBE. THERE **ARE** SOME SUPPORT FUNDS FOR CLUBS.

BUT THE **MOST** IMPORTANT THING IS THE CHOREOGRAPHY!

HUH?

ARE YOU GOING TO DANCE SOME MORE?

Clap!

I SHOULD, RIGHT?

UH. RIGHT.

THAT'S RIGHT! SO, LET'S DO OUR BEST!

THE MORE SHE TRIES, THE WEIRDER IT GETS.

EVERYONE! LEAVE THE DANCING TO ME.

HUH?

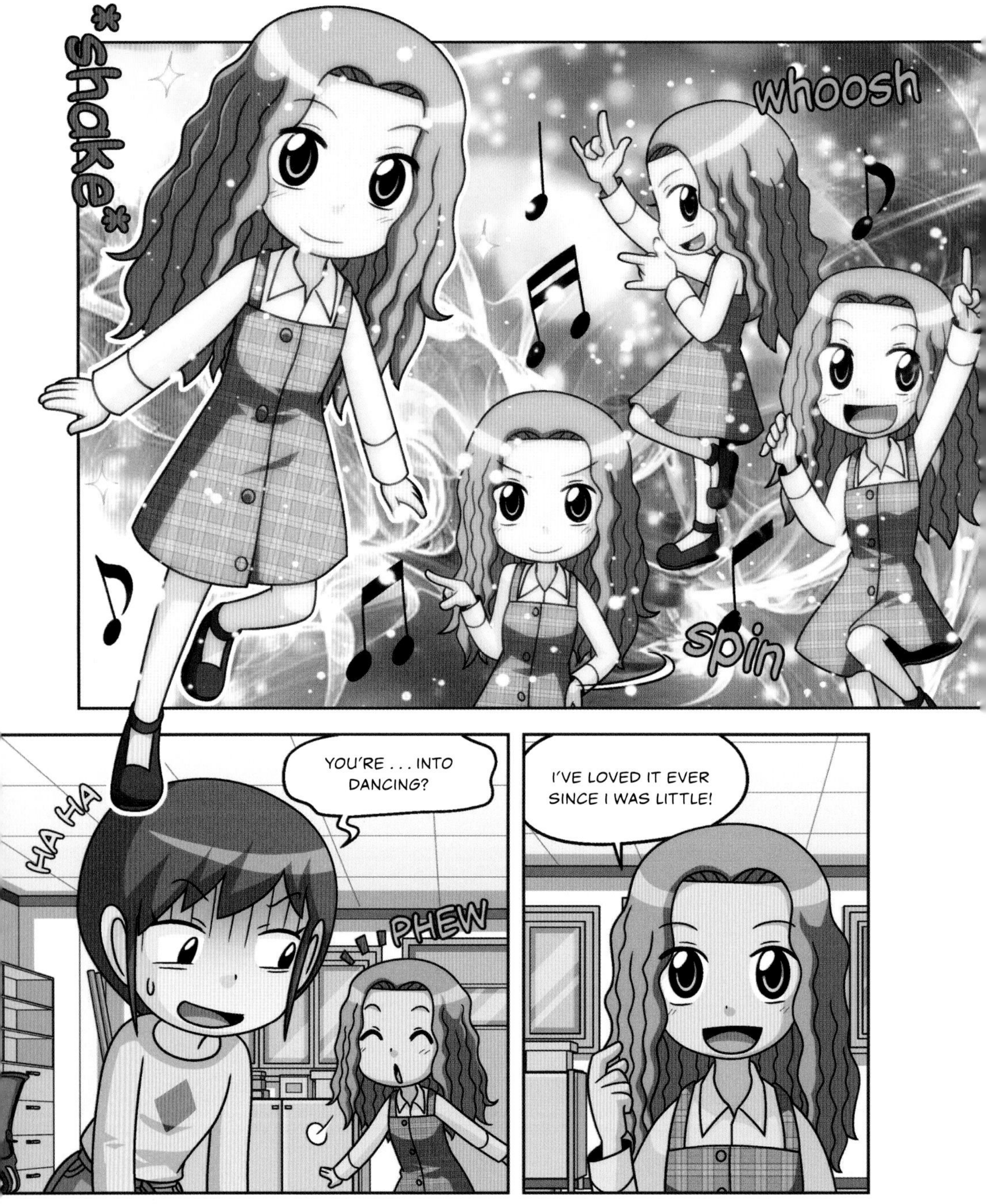
shake
whoosh
spin
HA HA
YOU'RE . . . INTO DANCING?
PHEW
I'VE LOVED IT EVER SINCE I WAS LITTLE!

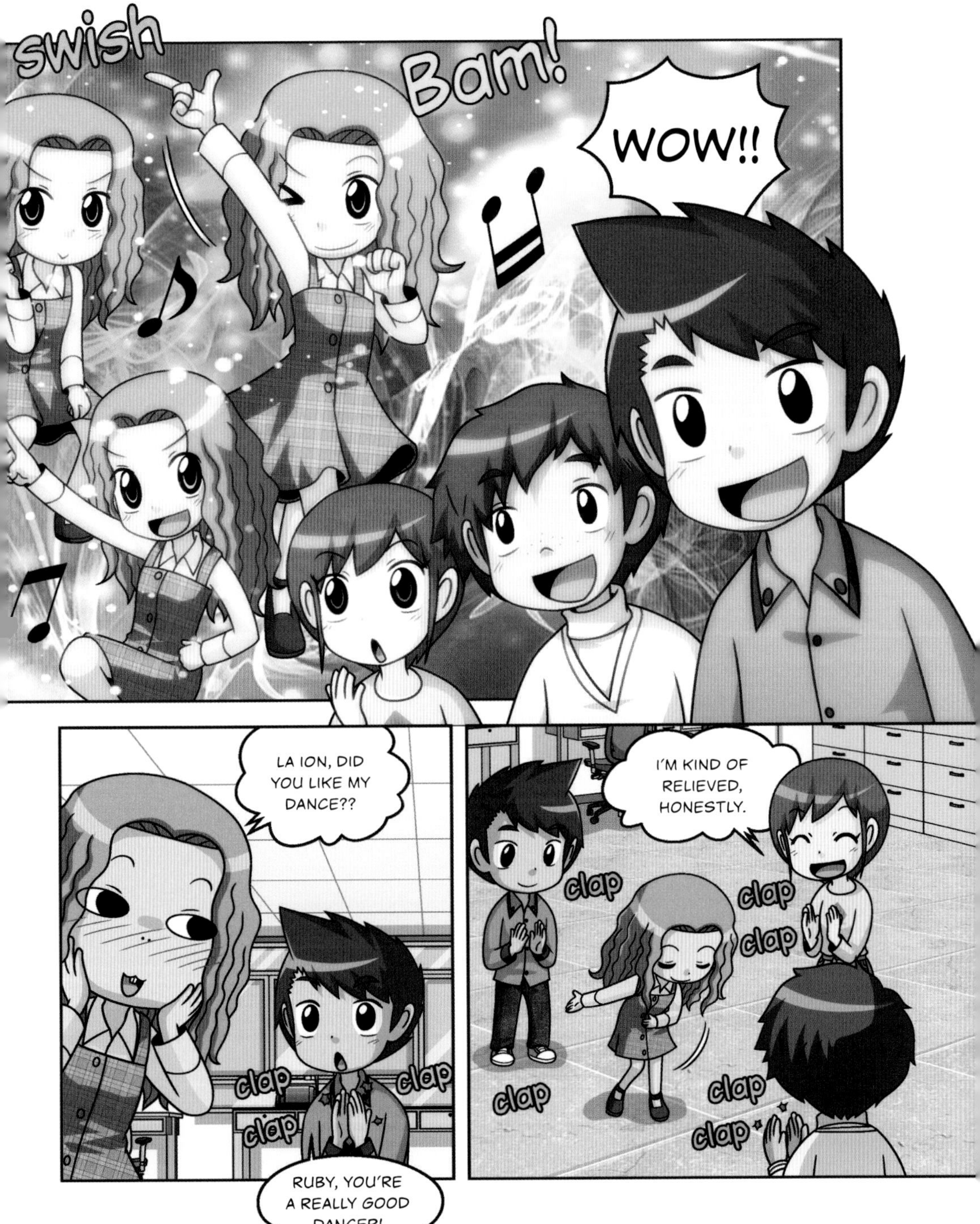
swish
Bam!
WOW!!
LA ION, DID YOU LIKE MY DANCE??
clap
clap
clap
RUBY, YOU'RE A REALLY GOOD DANCER!
I'M KIND OF RELIEVED, HONESTLY.
clap
clap
clap
clap
clap
clap

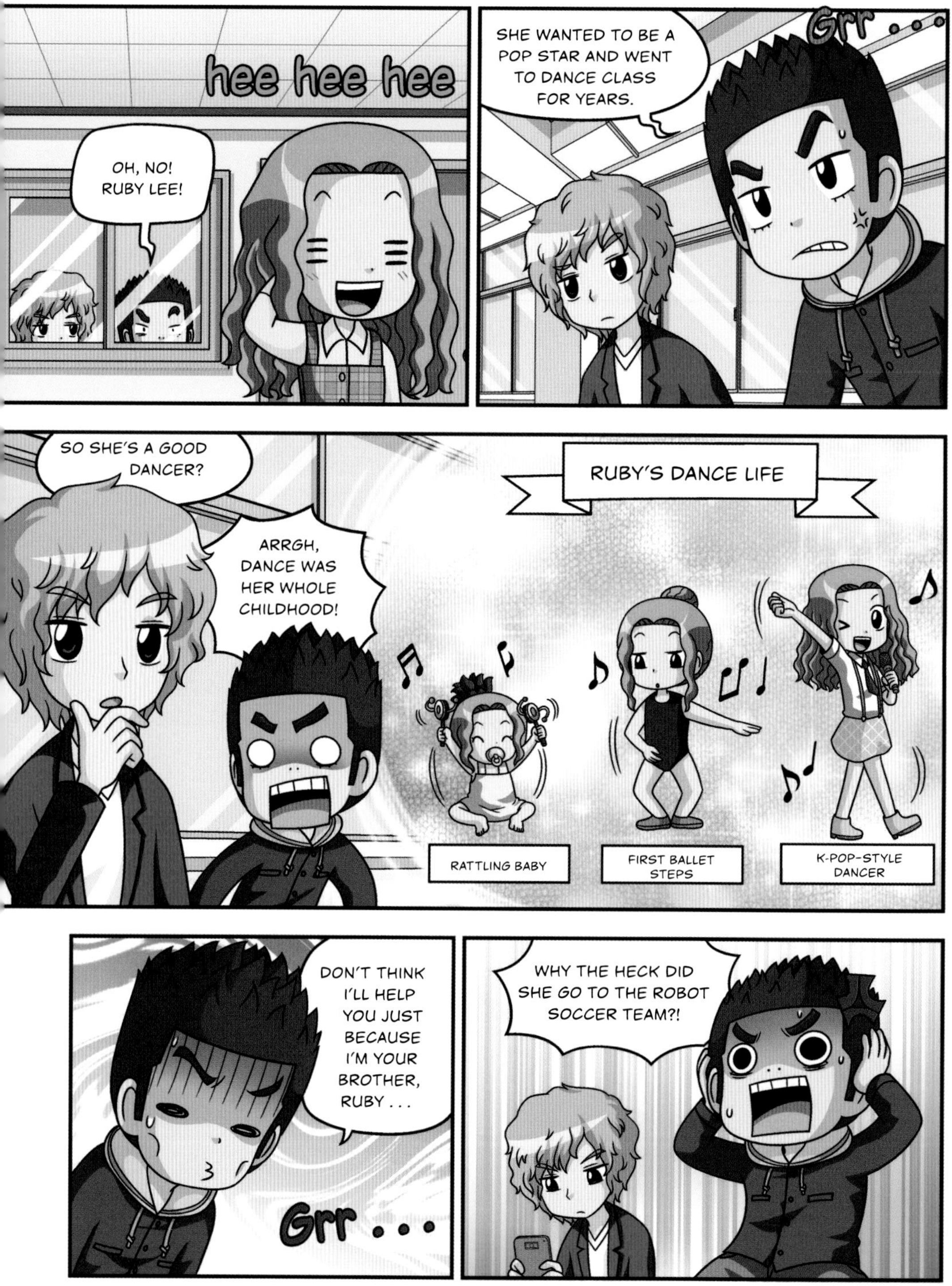
hee hee hee
OH, NO! RUBY LEE!
SHE WANTED TO BE A POP STAR AND WENT TO DANCE CLASS FOR YEARS.
Grr . . .
SO SHE'S A GOOD DANCER?
ARRGH, DANCE WAS HER WHOLE CHILDHOOD!
RUBY'S DANCE LIFE
RATTLING BABY
FIRST BALLET STEPS
K-POP-STYLE DANCER
DON'T THINK I'LL HELP YOU JUST BECAUSE I'M YOUR BROTHER, RUBY . . .
Grr . . .
WHY THE HECK DID SHE GO TO THE ROBOT SOCCER TEAM?!

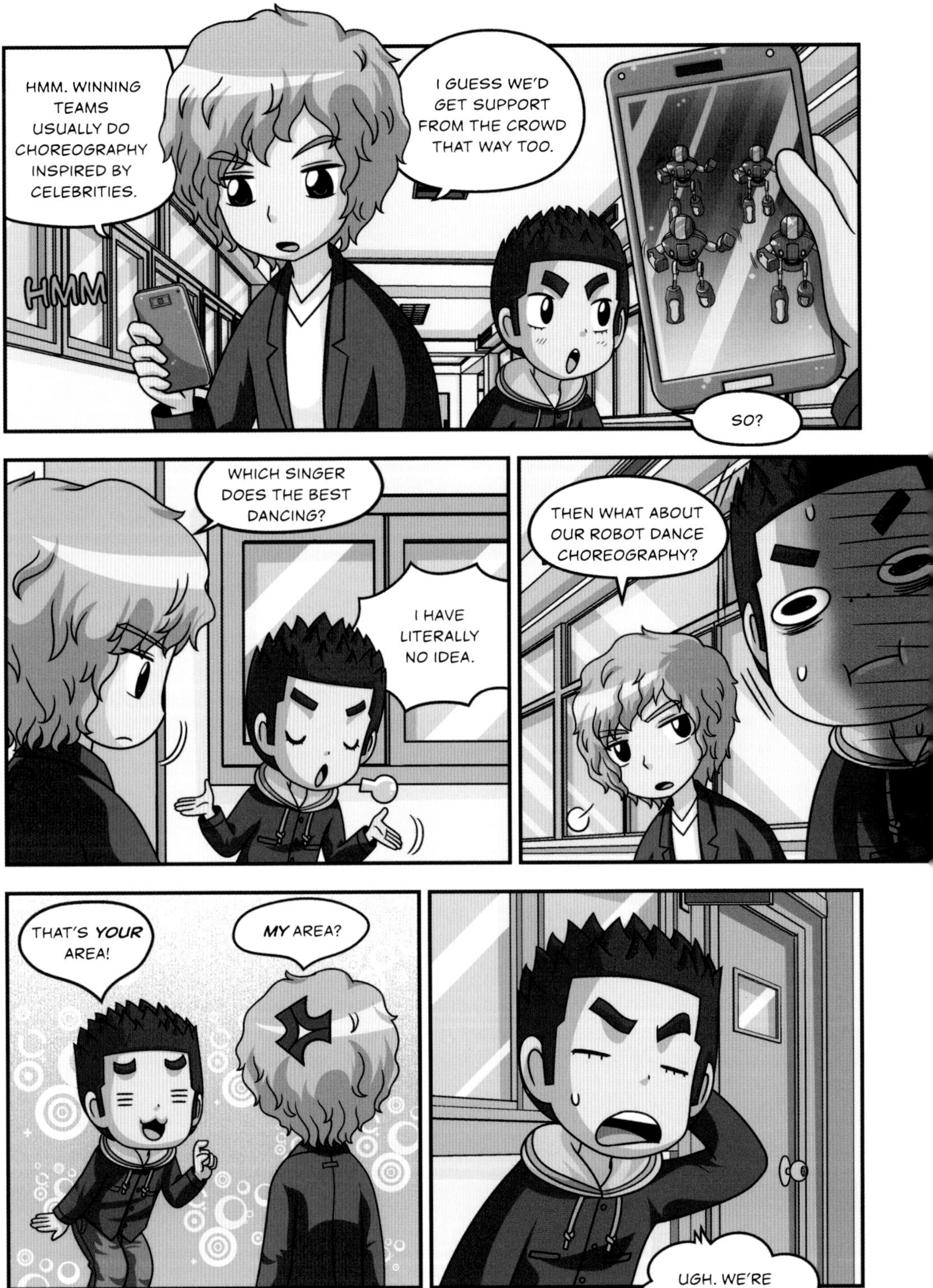
HMM. WINNING TEAMS USUALLY DO CHOREOGRAPHY INSPIRED BY CELEBRITIES.
HMM
I GUESS WE'D GET SUPPORT FROM THE CROWD THAT WAY TOO.
SO?
WHICH SINGER DOES THE BEST DANCING?
I HAVE LITERALLY NO IDEA.
THEN WHAT ABOUT OUR ROBOT DANCE CHOREOGRAPHY?
THAT'S ***YOUR*** AREA!
MY AREA?
UGH. WE'RE DOOMED.

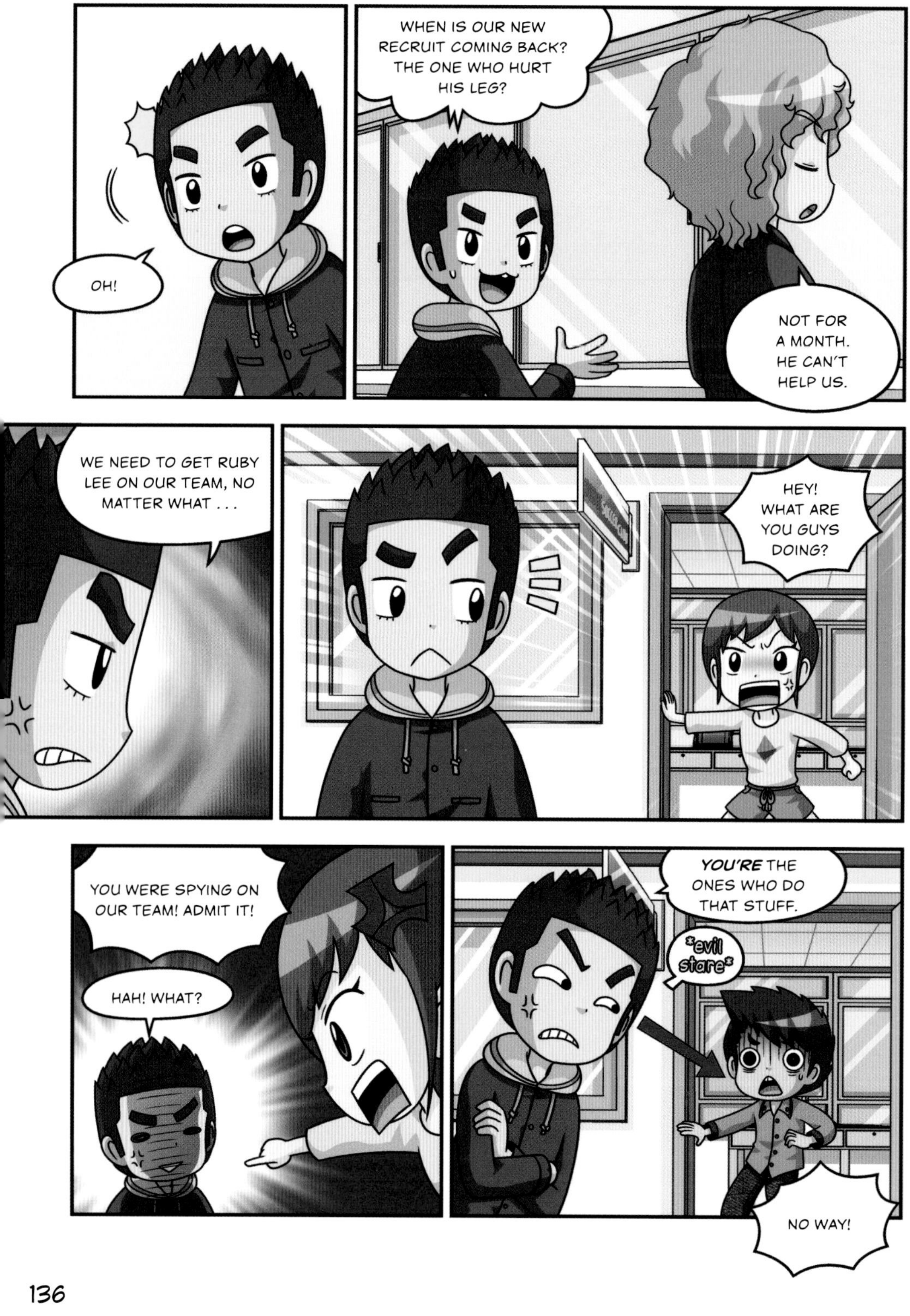

OH!
WHEN IS OUR NEW RECRUIT COMING BACK? THE ONE WHO HURT HIS LEG?
NOT FOR A MONTH. HE CAN'T HELP US.
WE NEED TO GET RUBY LEE ON OUR TEAM, NO MATTER WHAT . . .
HEY! WHAT ARE YOU GUYS DOING?
YOU WERE SPYING ON OUR TEAM! ADMIT IT!
HAH! WHAT?
YOU'RE THE ONES WHO DO THAT STUFF.
evil stare
NO WAY!

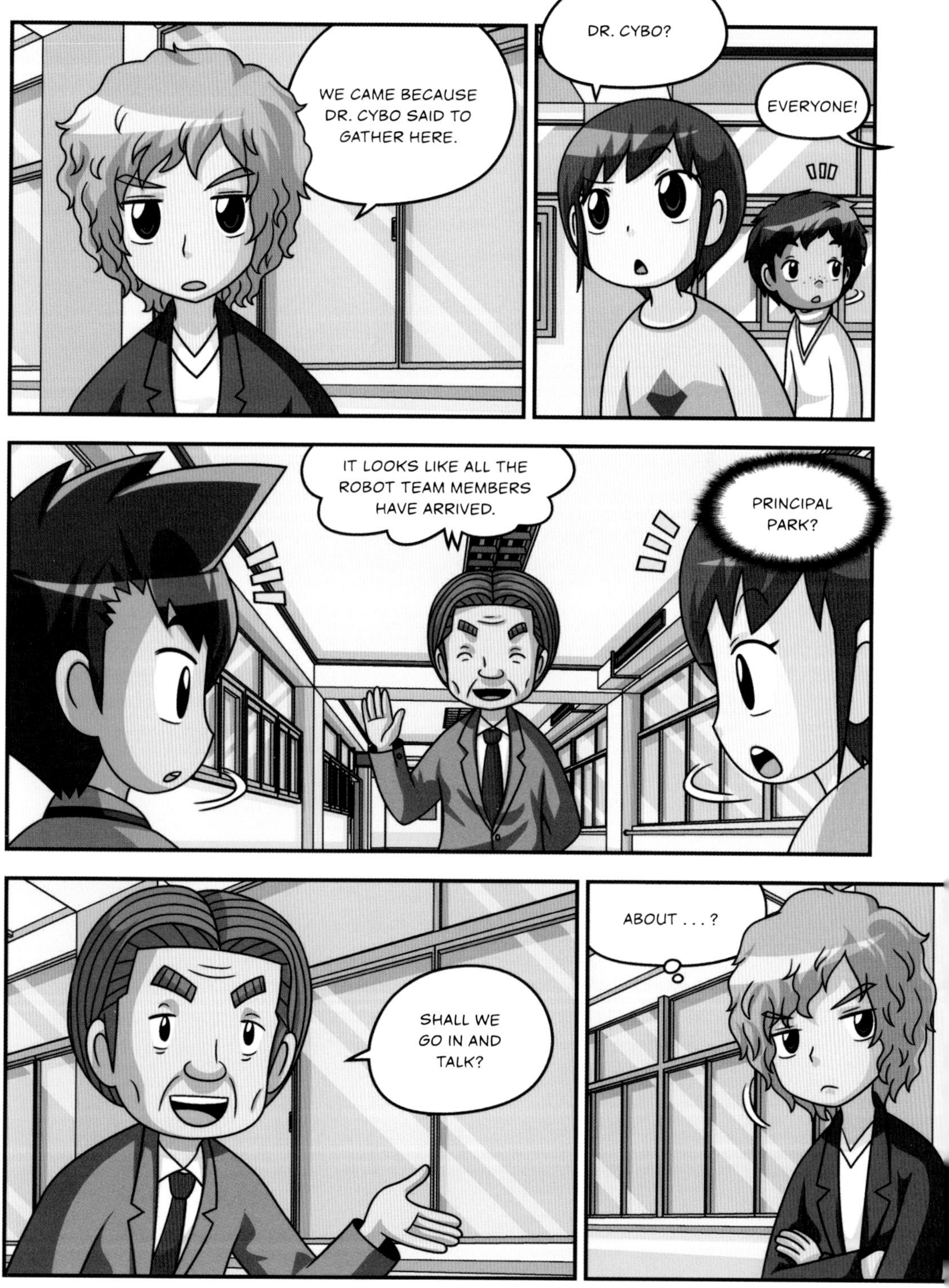
WE CAME BECAUSE DR. CYBO SAID TO GATHER HERE.
DR. CYBO?
EVERYONE!
IT LOOKS LIKE ALL THE ROBOT TEAM MEMBERS HAVE ARRIVED.
PRINCIPAL PARK?
SHALL WE GO IN AND TALK?
ABOUT . . . ?

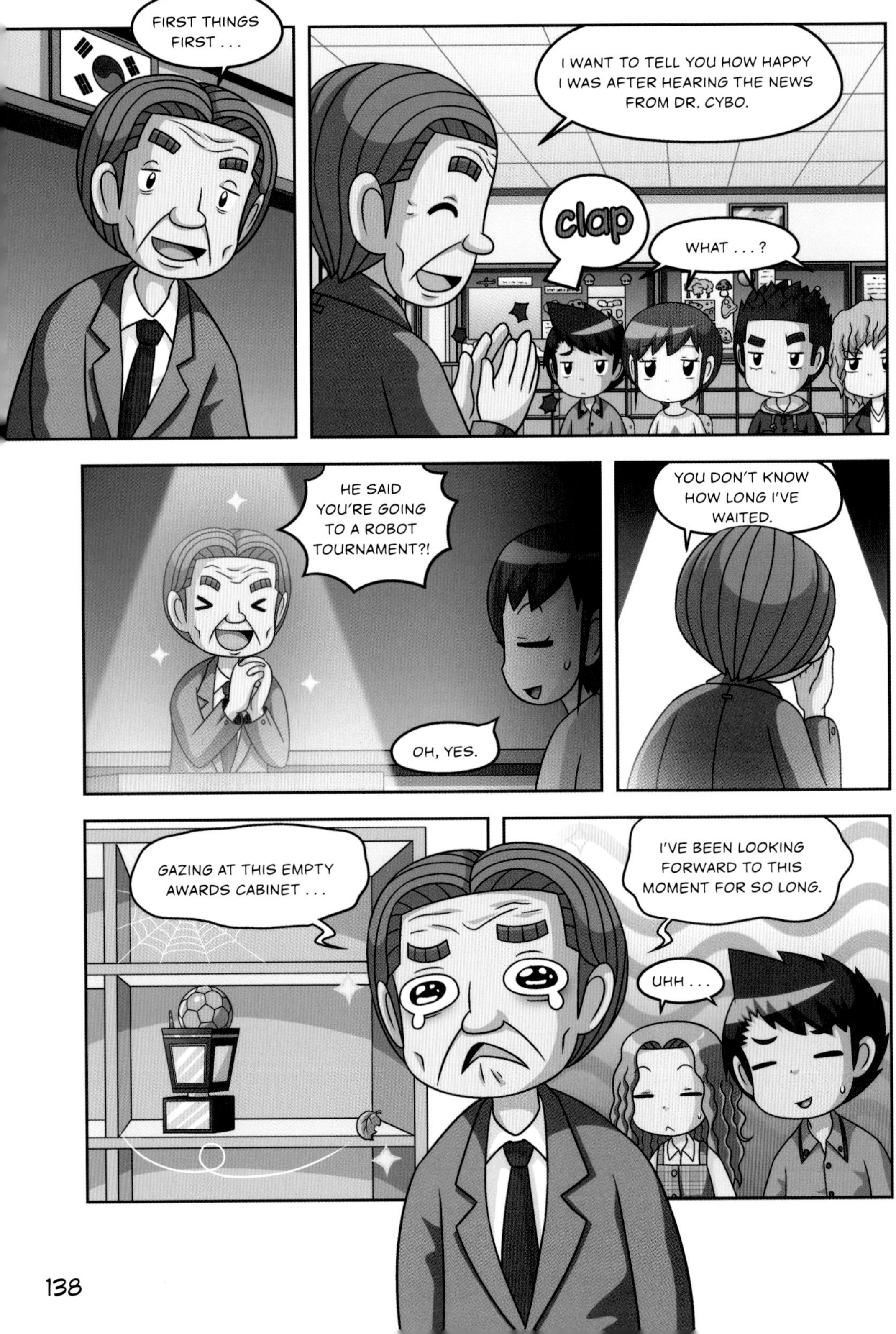
FIRST THINGS FIRST . . .
I WANT TO TELL YOU HOW HAPPY I WAS AFTER HEARING THE NEWS FROM DR. CYBO.
clap
WHAT . . . ?
HE SAID YOU'RE GOING TO A ROBOT TOURNAMENT?!
OH, YES.
YOU DON'T KNOW HOW LONG I'VE WAITED.
GAZING AT THIS EMPTY AWARDS CABINET . . .
I'VE BEEN LOOKING FORWARD TO THIS MOMENT FOR SO LONG.
UHH . . .

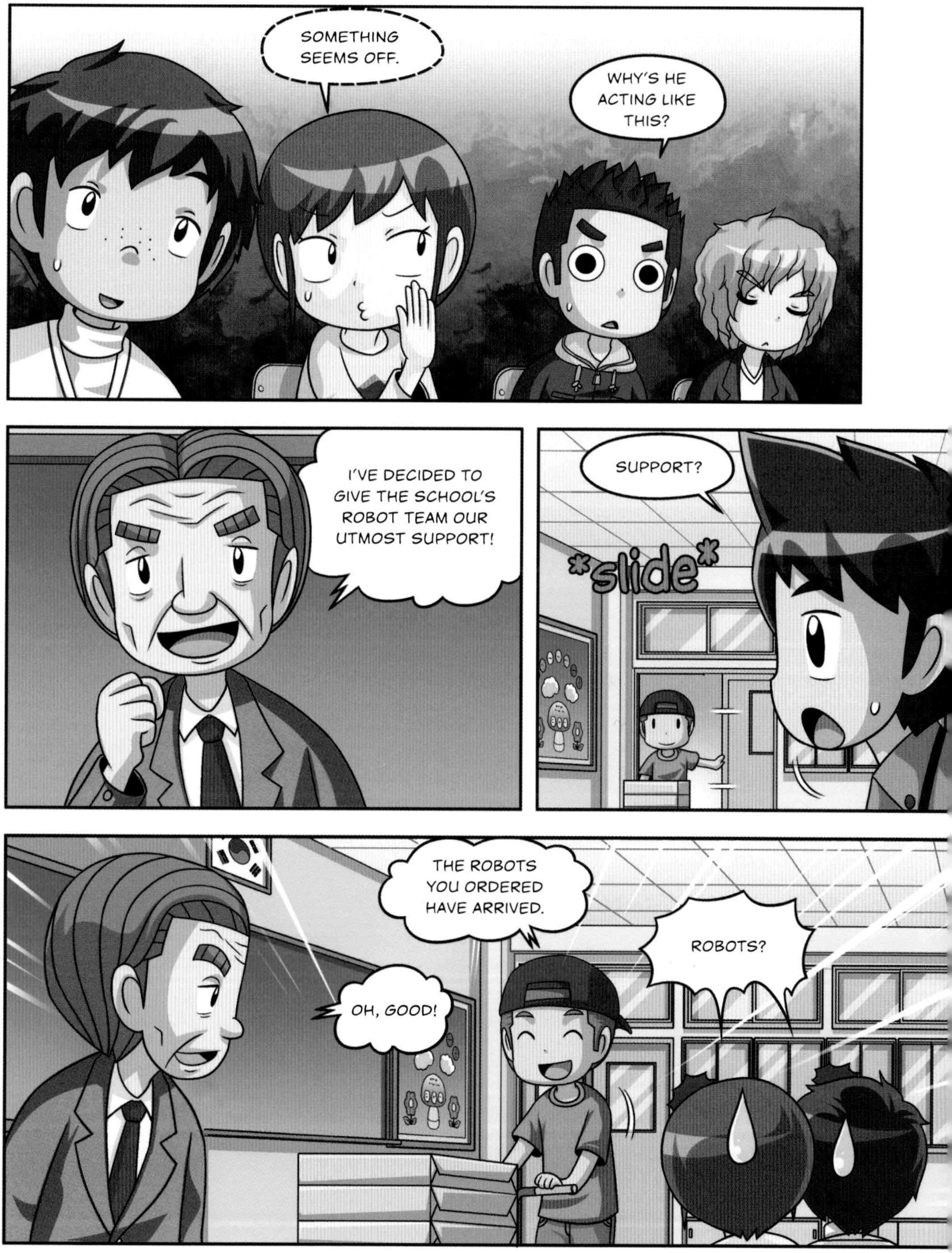
SOMETHING SEEMS OFF.
WHY'S HE ACTING LIKE THIS?
I'VE DECIDED TO GIVE THE SCHOOL'S ROBOT TEAM OUR UTMOST SUPPORT!
SUPPORT?
slide
THE ROBOTS YOU ORDERED HAVE ARRIVED.
ROBOTS?
OH, GOOD!

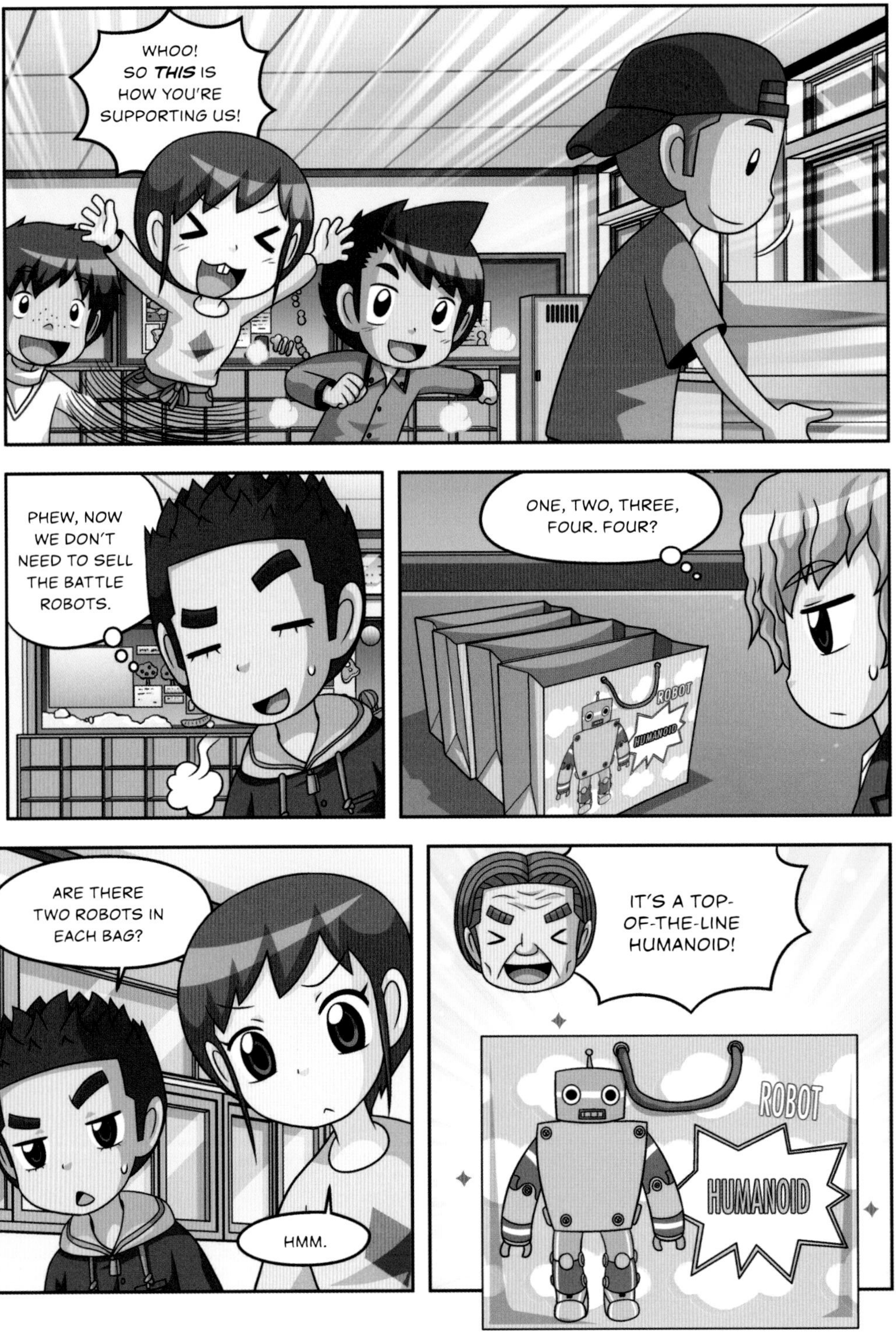
WHOO! SO *THIS* IS HOW YOU'RE SUPPORTING US!
PHEW, NOW WE DON'T NEED TO SELL THE BATTLE ROBOTS.
ONE, TWO, THREE, FOUR. FOUR?
ROBOT
HUMANOID
ARE THERE TWO ROBOTS IN EACH BAG?
HMM.
IT'S A TOP-OF-THE-LINE HUMANOID!
ROBOT
HUMANOID

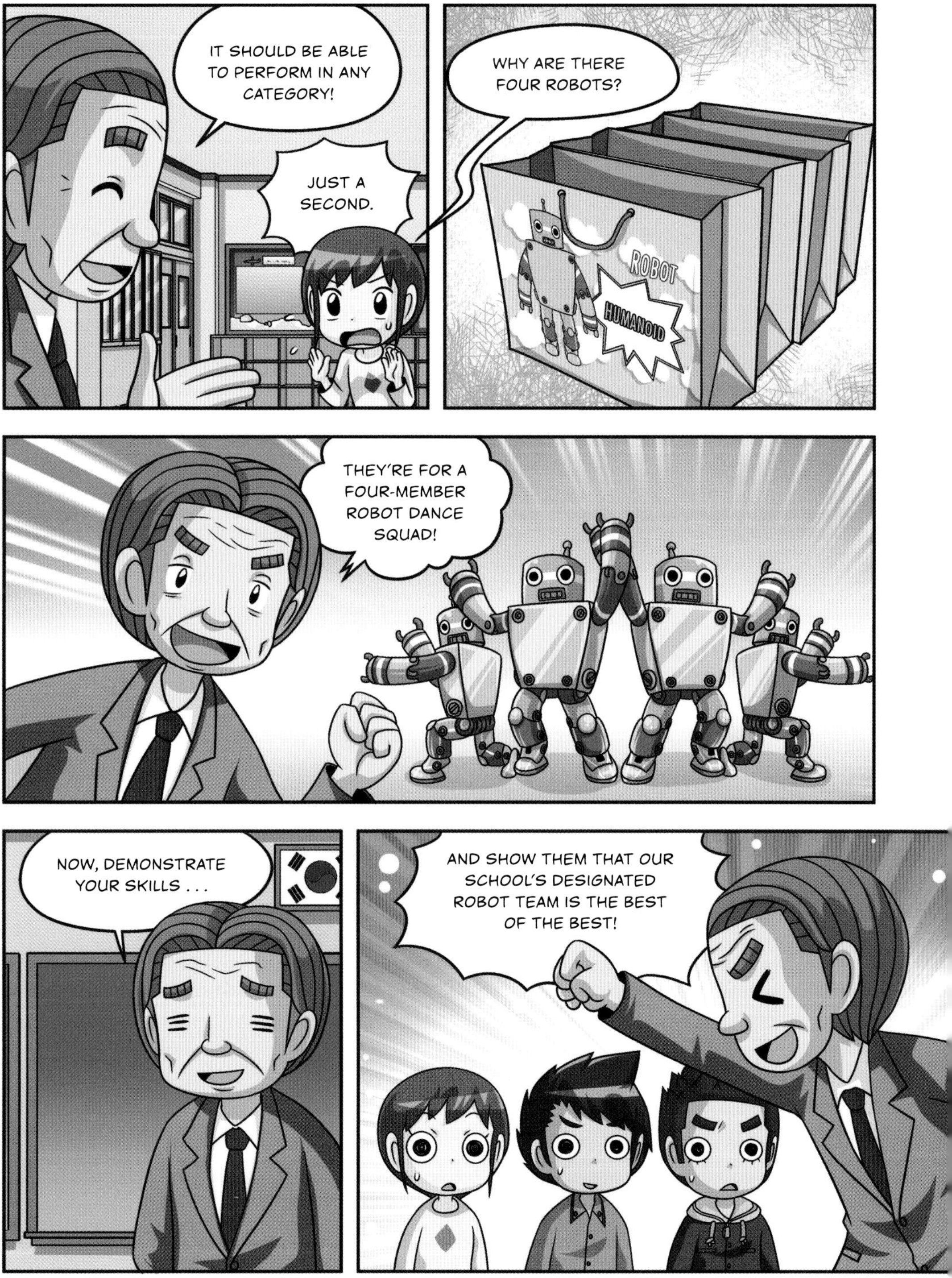
IT SHOULD BE ABLE TO PERFORM IN ANY CATEGORY!
JUST A SECOND.
WHY ARE THERE FOUR ROBOTS?
ROBOT
HUMANOID
THEY'RE FOR A FOUR-MEMBER ROBOT DANCE SQUAD!
NOW, DEMONSTRATE YOUR SKILLS . . .
AND SHOW THEM THAT OUR SCHOOL'S DESIGNATED ROBOT TEAM IS THE BEST OF THE BEST!

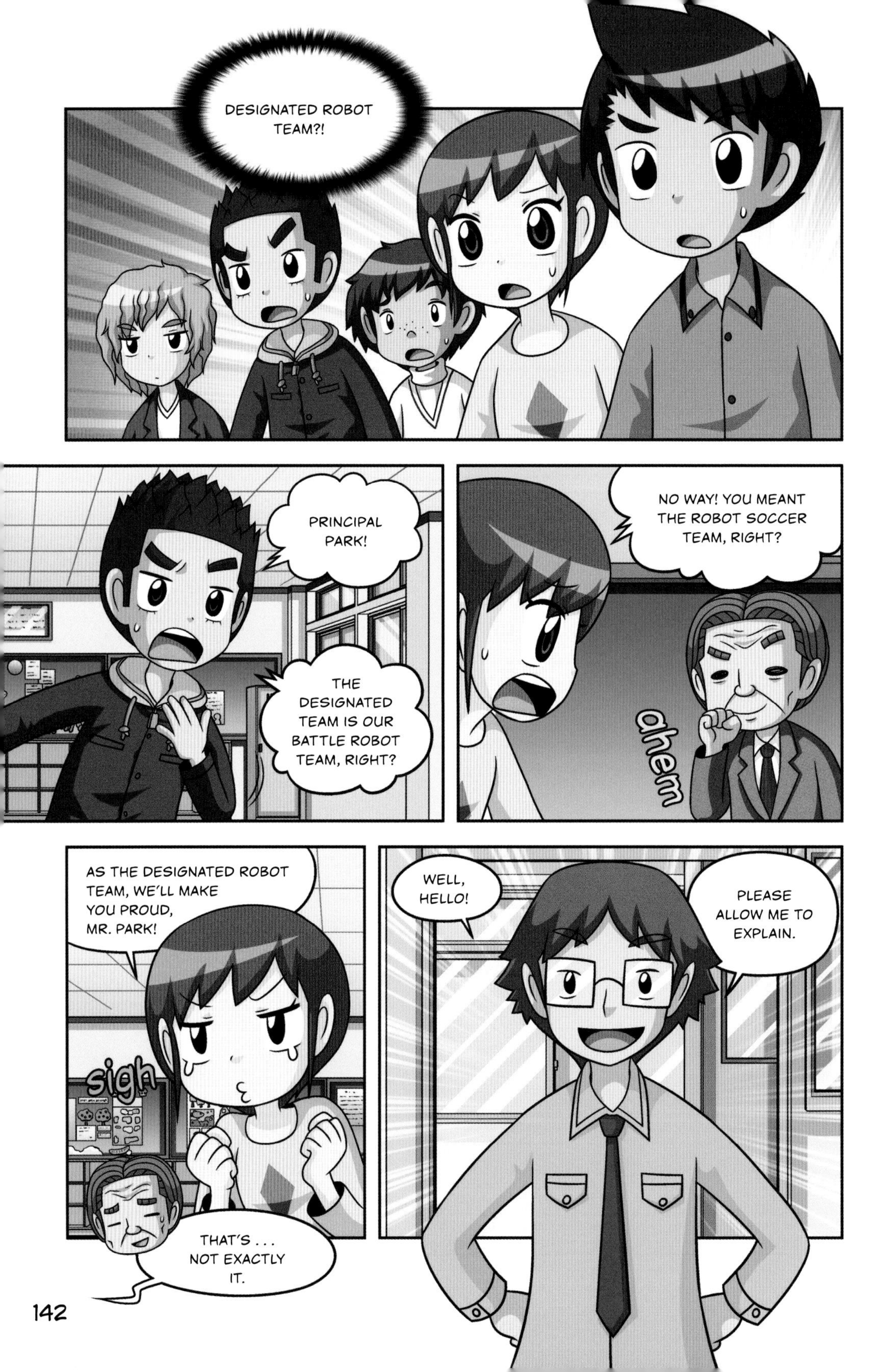
DESIGNATED ROBOT TEAM?!
PRINCIPAL PARK!
THE DESIGNATED TEAM IS OUR BATTLE ROBOT TEAM, RIGHT?
NO WAY! YOU MEANT THE ROBOT SOCCER TEAM, RIGHT?
ahem
AS THE DESIGNATED ROBOT TEAM, WE'LL MAKE YOU PROUD, MR. PARK!
sigh
THAT'S . . . NOT EXACTLY IT.
WELL, HELLO!
PLEASE ALLOW ME TO EXPLAIN.

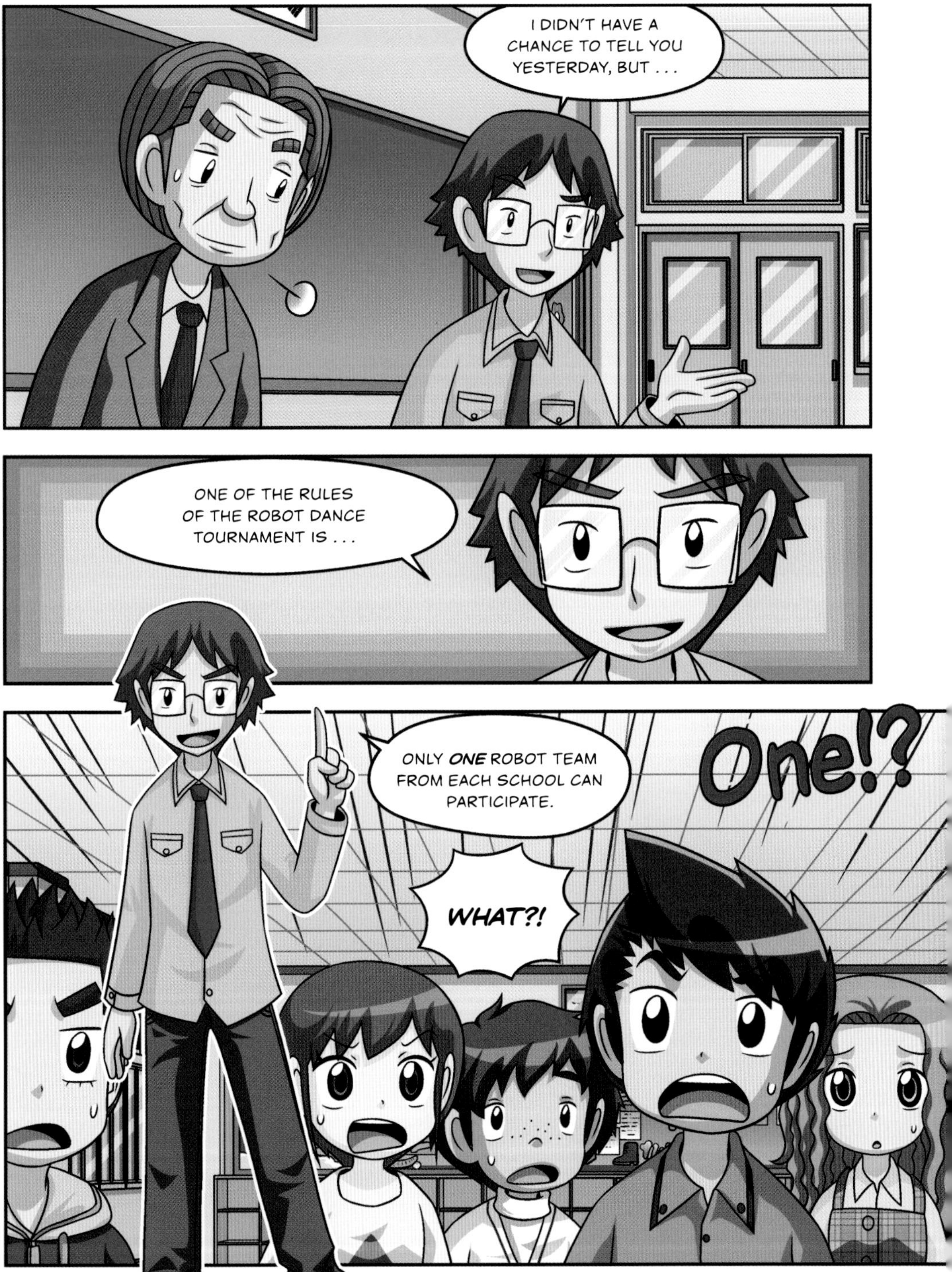
I DIDN'T HAVE A CHANCE TO TELL YOU YESTERDAY, BUT . . .
ONE OF THE RULES OF THE ROBOT DANCE TOURNAMENT IS . . .
ONLY *ONE* ROBOT TEAM FROM EACH SCHOOL CAN PARTICIPATE.
One!?
WHAT?!

HOW ROBOTS MOVE

Depending on the purpose of a robot, it can move on wheels or treads or walk on two legs like a human. Let's learn about different movement methods.

Wheels

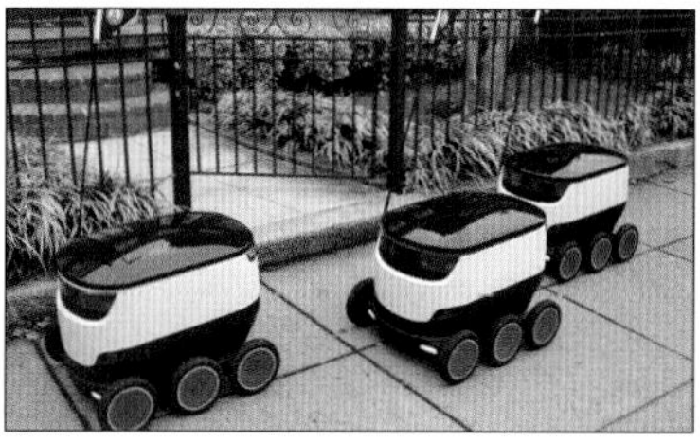

Wikipedia

The six-wheeled robot Starship is designed for package delivery. It can move autonomously at 3.7 miles (6 km) per hour.

Early robots were designed mainly for industrial use. They were fixed in one spot. Later, demand increased for robots that could move from one place to another, performing multiple steps of a task. This led to the invention of robots that moved on wheels. Wheels are still the most common method of robot movement. They enable free movement back and forth, or left and right, for a long time. Wheels also require less energy than other forms of movement.

Bipedal Walking

A humanoid robot is able to move on two legs. In order to walk on two legs, it must be able to fully support its entire body with one leg while lifting the other. Because a robot can't easily control its center of mass the way humans do, it must be programmed to *change* its center of mass. Commands are required for each action that is a part of this process.

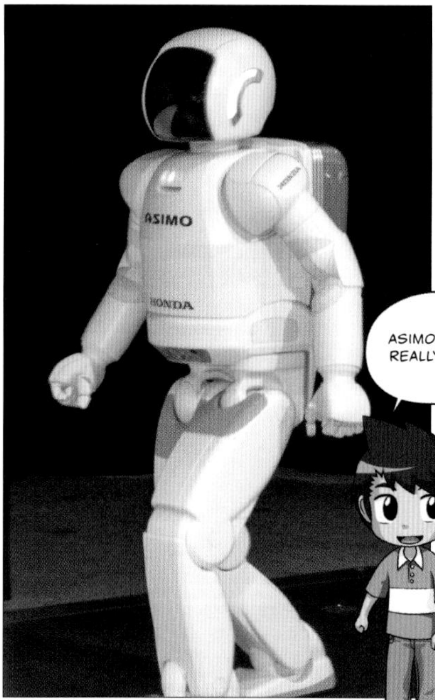
ASIMO
HONDA

Wikipedia

ASIMO can walk, run, and go up and down stairs using both legs. Its top speed is 5.6 miles (9 km) per hour.

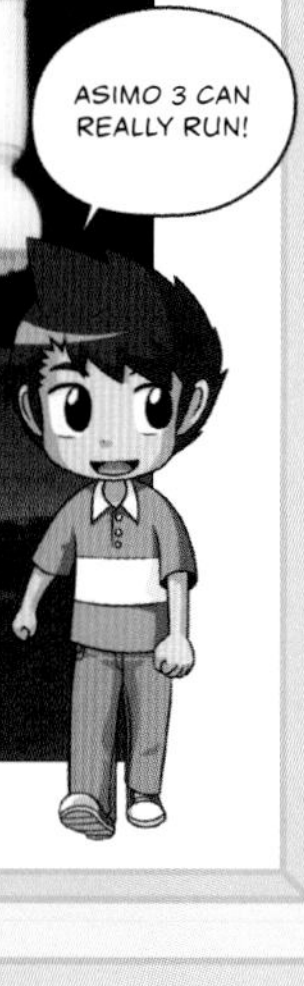
ASIMO 3 CAN REALLY RUN!

Multipedal Walking

Some robots have three or more legs. Multilegged robots are often modeled after insects or other animals. Since they can maintain their centers of mass and move stably on multiple legs, they have uses in military activity and disaster response.

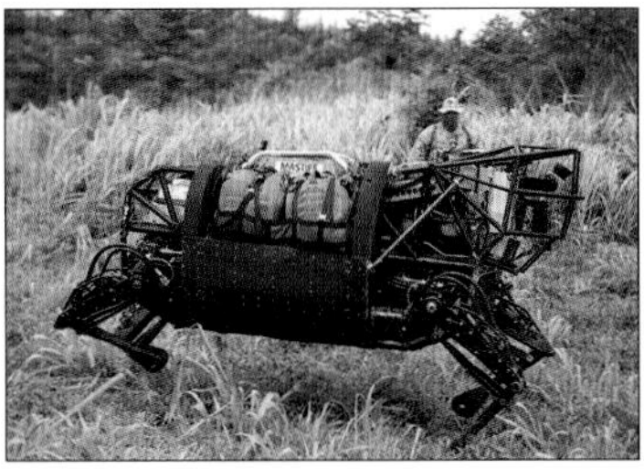

Wikipedia

The dog-shaped BigDog, a quadruped military robot, can use its four legs to move on rough roads, although the process can be noisy.

Tracks

It's hard for robots that roll on wheels to get over obstacles. Treads are one method for overcoming this flaw. They are made by connecting pieces of steel plate to form a belt and then hooking the belt to a set of wheels. With this setup, a robot can move over obstacles more easily. Treads are used on robots that go where humans can't, like burning or other dangerous area.

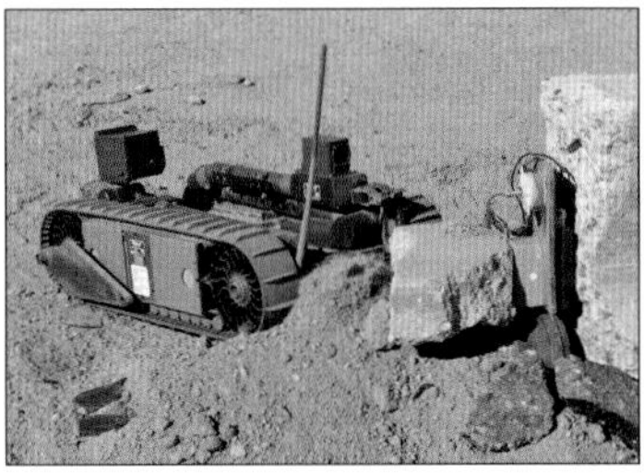

Wikipedia

The bomb disposal device PackBot uses tracks to climb stairs and other impediments.

Flying

Professor Ilhan Bae of South Korea has developed Robot Drone Man by adding flying capabilities to a robot that moves on the ground. Robot Drone Man flies to its destination and then runs on wheels after reaching the ground there. Because this new creation has the strengths of both robots and drones, it is expected to be particularly useful in the field of delivery services.

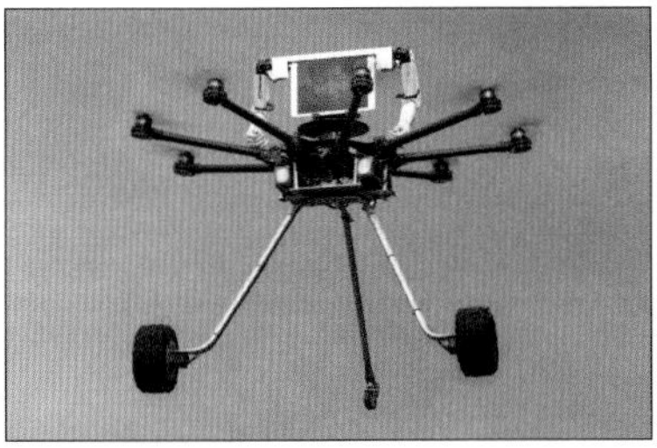

Wikipedia

This remote-controlled drone can operate both on the ground and in the air.

THE ROBOT MAKERS

INTRODUCES READERS TO THE CONCEPTS THAT MAKE ROBOTICS POSSIBLE—THROUGH A SERIES OF EXCITING COMPETITIONS

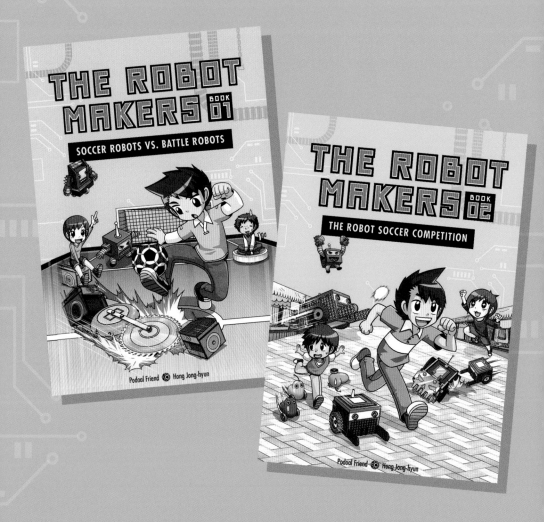

THE ROBOT MAKERS
BOOK 03
CODING CAMP CHAOS
01001
10111
10110
Hong Jong-hyun
Podoal Friend

THE ROBOT MAKERS
BOOK 04
NEXT-LEVEL COMPETITION
Podoal Friend
Hong Jong-hyun

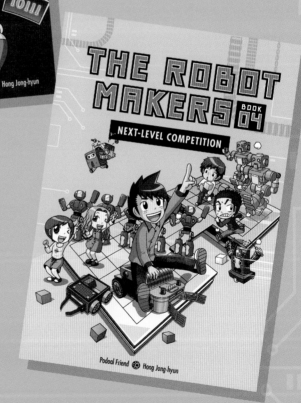

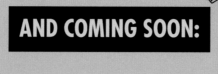

AND COMING SOON:

THE ROBOT MAKERS BOOK 05

ROBOTS CAN DANCE?

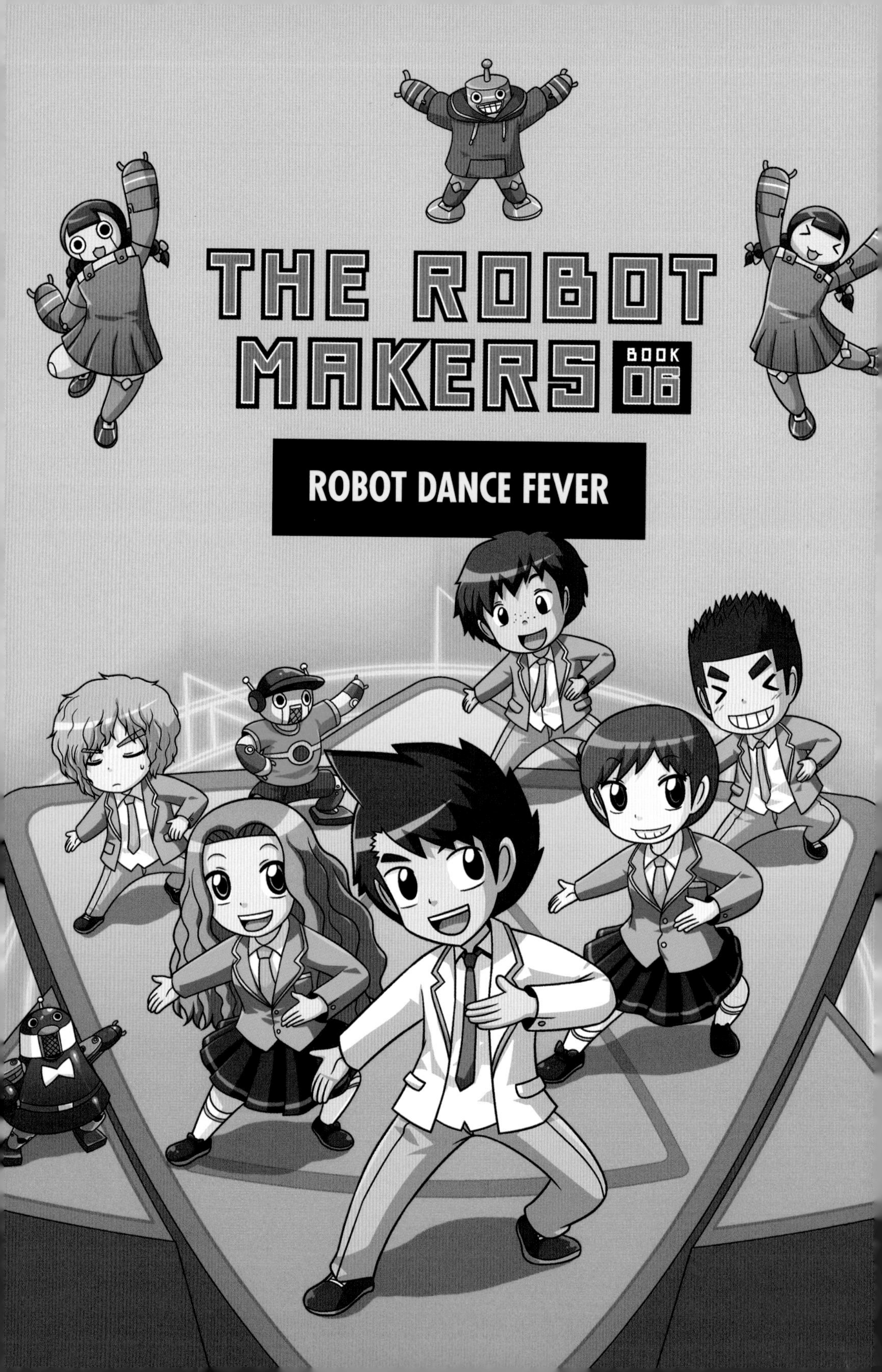
THE ROBOT MAKERS
BOOK 06
ROBOT DANCE FEVER

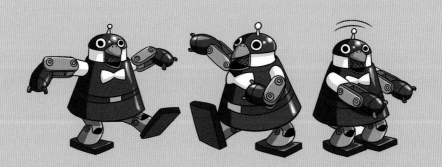